ALSO BY JAMES MCBRIDE

The Color of Water

Miracle at St. Anna

Song Yet Sung

The Good Lord Bird

Kill 'Em and Leave

Five-Carat Soul

Deacon King Kong

Praise for
THE HEAVEN & EARTH GROCERY STORE

AN INSTANT *NEW YORK TIMES* BESTSELLER

A *NEW YORK TIMES* NOTABLE BOOK

NAMED A BEST BOOK OF THE YEAR BY NPR/*FRESH AIR*,
THE WASHINGTON POST, *THE NEW YORKER*, AND *TIME*

ONE OF BARACK OBAMA'S FAVORITE BOOKS OF 2023

"With this story, McBride brilliantly captures a rapidly changing country, as seen through the eyes of the recently arrived and the formerly enslaved. . . . And through this evocation, McBride offers us a thorough reminder: Against seemingly impossible odds, even in the midst of humanity's most wicked designs, love, community, and action can save us." —*The New York Times Book Review*

"We all need—we all deserve—this vibrant, love-affirming novel that bounds over any difference that claims to separate us." —*The Washington Post*

"[A] tour de force . . . [a] mesmerizing, moving, almost magical tale . . . [McBride] writes sentences and paragraphs that swing like jazz melodies." —Associated Press

"As he's done throughout his spectacular writing career, McBride looks squarely at savage truths about race and prejudice, but he also insists on humor and hope. *The Heaven & Earth Grocery Store* is one of the best novels I've read this year. It pulls off the singular magic trick of being simultaneously flattening and uplifting." —NPR

"Classic McBride: He doesn't shy away from bold statements about the national catastrophes of race and xenophobia, and he always gives us a spoonful of sugar to help the medicine go down. The sugar is McBride's spitfire dialogue and murder-mystery-worthy plot machinations; his characters' big personalities and bigger storylines; his wisecracking, fast-talking humor; and prose so agile and exuberant that reading him is like being at a jazz jam session. . . . Reading McBride just feels good—we are comforted and entertained, and braced for the hard lessons he also delivers." —*The Atlantic*

"I keep thinking every time I read one of his books, 'That's his best book.' No. THIS is his best book." —Ann Patchett

"This is one of those novels that becomes a part of you. It's a great book. Every character is rich; every detail is rich. I can't recommend this one highly enough. He's a great author and I think this is his best work." —Harlan Coben

"Heartwarming and heartbreaking, a feat of language, life, and imagination."
—*Oprah Daily*

"A compassionate and ultimately heartwarming story." —*People*

"A stunning page turner . . . and an utterly captivating, compassionate story."
—*Real Simple*

"Powerful." —*Town & Country*

"Sharp and nimble and warm as a wool hat, James McBride's prose seems to transcend all earthly concerns, allowing him to write with compassion, humor, and authority." —*The Philadelphia Inquirer*

"A story of community, care, and the lengths to which we'll go for justice, McBride's tale is a wondrous ode to the strength of humanity in a small town." —*Time*

"Enchanting . . . [a] rich, carefully drawn portrait of a Depression-era community of African Americans and Jewish immigrants as they live, love, fight, and, of course, work." —*The Boston Globe*

"McBride . . . would never advance any of his books as candidates for the Great American Novel. . . . I'd like to make a case, though, for *Deacon King Kong* and, now, *The Heaven & Earth Grocery Store* as better contenders for the twenty-first-century GAN than many other, more vaunted specimens. . . . In the words of Walt Whitman (an American writer McBride often brings to mind), they contain multitudes." —*Slate*

"An entertaining, meaningful story about the community formed when people take advantage of America's opportunities for cross-cultural connection."
—*Star Tribune*

"When it comes to James McBride, you can always be sure that you're in for a wild and rewarding read. . . . Like *The Good Lord Bird* and *Deacon King Kong*, McBride brings a wealth of wit and charm to every page of this novel, as well as a refreshing sense of humanity and optimism for this makeshift community."
—*Chicago Review of Books*

"Frank and affectionate, this latest triumph from James McBride stresses the challenges of accessing America's promises." —*The Christian Science Monitor*

"McBride portrays his characters vividly; they possess the warts and faults of ordinary people, which is why, I believe, the story is so enthralling. . . . McBride also includes beauty, compassion, and healing as well. Where there is hate in his story, love and compassion also can be found." —*The Mercury*

"*The Heaven & Earth Grocery Store* is a full course of a literary meal. . . . McBride has a talent for finding the humor in something that we normally wouldn't laugh at, and we don't feel bad for enjoying it." —*Bookreporter*

"McBride's pages burst with life. . . . This endlessly rich saga highlights the different ways in which people look out for one another."
—★*Publishers Weekly*, STARRED REVIEW★

"McBride is a lyricist and musician, and there's a rhythmic quality to this unique novel, which began as an ode to a beloved figure in McBride's life, Sy Friend, the director of a camp for disabled children where the author worked for four years in his youth . . .[a] heart-rending and hopeful tale of cross-cultural solidarity, love, and redemption." —★*BookPage*, STARRED REVIEW★

"A compelling novel, compellingly written, and not to be missed."
—★*Library Journal*, STARRED REVIEW★

"The interlocking destinies of [McBride's] characters make for tense, absorbing drama and, at times, warm, humane comedy. . . . If it's possible for America to have a poet laureate, why can't James McBride be its storyteller-in-chief?"
—★*Kirkus Reviews*, STARRED REVIEW★

"Funny, tender, knockabout, gritty, and suspenseful, McBride's microcosmic, socially critiquing, and empathic novel dynamically celebrates difference, kindness, ingenuity, and the force that compels us to move heaven and earth to help each other." —★*Booklist*, STARRED REVIEW★

THE
Heaven
& Earth
GROCERY STORE

James McBride

RIVERHEAD BOOKS
New York

RIVERHEAD BOOKS
An imprint of Penguin Random House LLC
penguinrandomhouse.com

Copyright © 2023 by James McBride
Penguin Random House supports copyright. Copyright fuels creativity, encourages diverse voices, promotes free speech, and creates a vibrant culture. Thank you for buying an authorized edition of this book and for complying with copyright laws by not reproducing, scanning, or distributing any part of it in any form without permission. You are supporting writers and allowing Penguin Random House to continue to publish books for every reader.

Riverhead and the R colophon are registered
trademarks of Penguin Random House LLC.

The Library of Congress has catalogued the Riverhead
hardcover edition as follows:

Names: McBride, James, 1957– author.
Title: The Heaven & Earth Grocery Store / James McBride.
Other titles: The Heaven and Earth Grocery Store
Description: New York : Riverhead Books, [2023]
Identifiers: LCCN 2023009854 (print) | LCCN 2023009855 (ebook) |
ISBN 9780593422946 (hardcover) | ISBN 9780593422960 (ebook)
Subjects: LCGFT: Novels.
Classification: LCC PS3613.C28 H43 2023 (print) |
LCC PS3613.C28 (ebook) | DDC 813/.6—dc23/eng/20230301
LC record available at https://lccn.loc.gov/2023009854
LC ebook record available at https://lccn.loc.gov/2023009855

First Riverhead hardcover edition: August 2023
International trade paperback edition (August 2023) ISBN: 9780593714669
International trade paperback edition (July 2024) ISBN: 9780593854051

Printed in the United States of America
1st Printing

Book design by Nicole LaRoche

This is a work of fiction. Names, characters, places, and incidents either are the product of the author's imagination or are used fictitiously, and any resemblance to actual persons, living or dead, businesses, companies, events, or locales is entirely coincidental.

To Sy Friend, who taught all of us

the meaning of Tikkun Olam

Contents

PART I: Gone

1. The Hurricane — 3
2. A Bad Sign — 7
3. Twelve — 18
4. Dodo — 36
5. The Stranger — 49
6. Challah — 59
7. A New Problem — 72
8. Paper — 81
9. The Robin and the Sparrow — 93
10. The Skrup Shoe — 112
11. Gone — 129

PART II: Gotten

12. Monkey Pants — 143
13. Cowboy — 154
14. Differing Weights and Measures — 166
15. The Worm — 182

16. The Visit	*197*
17. The Bullfrog	*206*
18. The Hot Dog	*218*

PART III: The Last Love

19. The Lowgods	*229*
20. The Antes House	*248*
21. The Marble	*262*
22. Without a Song	*273*
23. Bernice's Bible	*284*
24. Duck Boy	*294*
25. The Deal	*311*
26. The Job	*319*
27. The Finger	*331*
28. The Last Love	*341*
29. Waiting for the Future	*356*
Epilogue: The Call Out	*377*
Acknowledgments	*383*

PART I
Gone

1

The Hurricane

There was an old Jew who lived at the site of the old synagogue up on Chicken Hill in the town of Pottstown, Pa., and when Pennsylvania State Troopers found the skeleton at the bottom of an old well off Hayes Street, the old Jew's house was the first place they went to. This was in June 1972, the day after a developer tore up the Hayes Street lot to make way for a new townhouse development.

We found a belt buckle and a pendant in the well, the cops said, and some old threads—from a red costume or jacket, that's what the lab shows.

They produced a piece of jewelry, handed it to him, and asked what it was.

A mezuzah, the old man said.

It matches the one on the door, the cops said. Don't these things belong on doors?

The old man shrugged. Jewish life is portable, he said.

The inscription on the back says "Home of the Greatest Dancer in the World." It's in Hebrew. You speak Hebrew?

Do I look like I speak Swahili?

Answer the question. You speak Hebrew or not?

I bang my head against it sometimes.

And you're Malachi the dancer, right? That's what they say around here. They say you're a great dancer.

Used to be. I gave that up forty years ago.

What about the mezuzah? It matches the one here. Wasn't this the Jewish temple?

It was.

Who owns it now?

Who owns everything around here? the old man said. He nodded at the immense gleaming private school seen through the dim window. The Tucker School. It sat proudly atop the hill behind wrought-iron gates, with smooth lawns, tennis courts, and shiny classroom buildings, a monstrous bastion of arrogant elegance, glowing like a phoenix above the ramshackle neighborhood of Chicken Hill.

They been trying to buy me out for thirty years, the old man said.

He grinned at the cops, but he was practically toothless, save for a single yellow tooth that hung like a clump of butter from his top gum, which made him look like an aardvark.

You're a suspect, they said.

Suspect shuspect, he said with a shrug. He was well north of eighty, wearing an old gray vest, a rumpled white shirt holding several old pens in the vest pocket, a wrinkled tallit around his shoulders, and equally rumpled old pants, but when he reached inside his pants pocket, his gnarled hands moved with such deftness and speed that the state troopers, who spent most days ticketing tractor-trailers on nearby Interstate 76 and impressing pretty housewives during traffic stops with their bubble-gum lights and stern lectures about public safety, panicked and stepped back, their hands on their weapons. But the old man produced nothing more than several pens. He offered the cops one.

No thanks, they said.

They milled around for a while longer and eventually left, promising to return after they pulled the skeleton out of the well and studied the potential murder scene some more. They never did, though, because the next day God wrapped His hands around Chicken Hill and wrung His last bit of justice out of that wretched place. Hurricane Agnes came along and knocked the power out of four counties. The nearby Schuylkill River rose to a height of seven feet. To hear the old black women of Chicken Hill tell it, white folks was jumping off their rooftops in Pottstown like they was on the Titanic. All those fancy homes down there were swept away like dust. That storm killed everything it touched. Drowned every man, woman, and child that come near it; wrecked bridges, knocked down factories, tore up farms; that thing caused millions in damages—millions and millions—that's whitefolks language, millions and millions. Well, for us colored folks on the Hill, it was just another day of dodging the white man's evil. As for the old Jew and his kind that was on this hill, they got all their time back from them that stole everything from 'em. And the Jew lady they wronged, Miss Chona, she got her justice, too, for the King of Kings fixed her up for all the good things she done, lifted her up and filled up her dreams in an instant in only the way He can. That evil fool who called hisself Son of Man, he's long gone from this country. And that boy Dodo, the deaf one, he's yet living. They put that whole camp up there in Montgomery County now on account of him, the Jews did. Theater owners they was, God bless 'em. And them cops and big-time muckity mucks that was running behind them Jews for the body they found in that old well, they can't find a spec against 'em now, for God took the whole business—the water well, the reservoir, the dairy, the skeleton, and every itty bitty thing they could'a used against them Jews—and washed it clear into the Manatawny Creek. And from there, every single bit of that who-shot-John nonsense got throwed into the Schuylkill, and from there, it flowed into the Chesapeake Bay down in Maryland, and from there, out to the Atlantic. And that's where the bones of that rotten scoundrel whose name is not worthy to be called by my lips is floating to this day. At the bottom of the ocean, with the fish picking his bones and the devil keeping score.

As for old Malachi, the cops never did find him. They come back for him after the hurricane business died away, but he was long gone. Left a sunflower or two in the yard and that's it. Old Mr. Malachi got off clean. He was the last of 'em. The last of the Jews round here. That fella was a wizard. He was something. He could dance, too . . . Lord . . . That man was magic . . .

Mazel tov, honey.

2

A Bad Sign

Forty-seven years before construction workers discovered the skeleton in the old farmer's well on Chicken Hill, a Jewish theater manager in Pottstown, Pennsylvania, named Moshe Ludlow had a vision about Moses.

Moshe had this vision on a Monday morning in February as he was cleaning out the remnants of a Chick Webb one-night stand at his tiny All-American Dance Hall and Theater on Main Street. Webb and his roaring twelve-piece band was the greatest musical event Moshe had ever witnessed in his life, except for the weekend he managed to lure Mickey Katz, the brilliant but temperamental Yiddish genius of klezmer music, out of Cleveland to play a full weekend of family fun and Yiddish frolic at Moshe's All-American Dance Hall and Theater two months before. Now *that* was something. Katz, the kid wizard of clarinet, and his newly formed seven-piece ensemble braved a furious December snowstorm that dropped fourteen inches in the eastern Pennsylvania mountains to make it to the gig, and thanks to blessed G-d, they had, because Moshe counted 249 Jewish shoe salesmen, shop owners, tailors, blacksmiths, railroad painters, deli owners, and their wives from five different states, including Upstate New York and Maine, who came to the event. There were even four couples from Tennessee who drove through the Blue Ridge Mountains for three days, eating cheese and eggs, unable to keep kosher on the Sabbath, just to be with their fellow Yids—and right before Hanukkah, for which they all should be at home lighting candles for eight days. Not to mention one of the husbands was a fanatic and believed that the fast of Tisha B'Av, normally celebrated in July or August, should be celebrated twice a year instead of once, which meant staying home every December and starving and peppering the walls with pictures of flowers for three weeks straight as a show of thanks to the Creator for His generosity in helping the Jewish people of Eastern Europe escape the pogroms for the relative peace and prosperity of America's Promised Land. Thanks to him and the weather, all four couples were in a foul mood once they arrived, having squeezed into two ancient Packards—one of which had no heat—and driven through the savage snowstorm. They announced plans to leave immediately when they heard talk of more snow, but Moshe talked them out of it. That was his gift. Moshe could talk the horns off the devil's head. "How many times in life does one get to hear a young genius?" he said to them. "It will be the greatest event of your life." He led them to his pocket-sized room in a boardinghouse on Chicken Hill, a tiny area of ramshackle houses and dirt roads where the town's blacks, Jews, and immigrant whites who couldn't afford any better lived, set them before his warm woodstove, filled them with warm iced tea and gefilte fish, and amused them with the story of his Romanian grandmother who jumped out a window to avoid marrying a Haskalah Jew, only to land atop a Hasidic rabbi from Austria.

"She knocked him to the mud," he exclaimed. "When he looked up, she was reading his palm. So they got married."

That brought smirks and chuckles to their faces, because everyone knew the Romanians were crazy. With their laughter ringing in his ears, he rushed back to the crowd who waited anxiously in the snow for the theater doors to open.

As Moshe made his way down the muddy roads of Chicken Hill to his theater on Main Street, his heart sank. The makeshift line that had formed an hour before had exploded into a mob of close to three hundred. Moreover, he was informed that the temperamental genius Katz had arrived but was inside the theater in a foul mood, having braved the terrible storm, and was now threatening to leave. Moshe raced inside and found to his relief that his always-dependable helper, an old colored man named Nate Timblin, had settled Katz and his band backstage before the warm woodstove, serving them hot tea in water glasses, fresh kosher eggs, gefilte fish, and challah bread, all neatly laid out buffet-style. The young Katz seemed pleased and announced that he and his band would set up as soon as they finished eating. From there, Moshe went back outside to stall the waiting crowd.

When he saw that more people were coming—stragglers rushing from the train station carrying satchels and suitcases—he grabbed a stepladder and climbed atop it to address them all. He had never seen so many Jews in one place in America in his life. The reform snobs from Philadelphia were there in button-down shirts, standing next to ironworkers from Pittsburgh, who crowded against socialist railroad men from Reading wearing caps bearing the Pennsylvania Railroad logo, who stood shoulder to shoulder with coal miners with darkened faces from Uniontown and Spring City. Some were with wives. Others were with women who, given their fur coats, leather boots, and dazzling hairdos, were not wives at all. One fellow was accompanied by a blonde goy six inches taller than him, clad in gay Irish green, complete with a hat that looked like a cross between a clover leaf and the spikes on the Statue of Liberty's crown. Some yammered in German, others chatted in Yiddish. Some yelled in a Bavarian dialect, others spoke Polish. When Moshe announced there would be a short delay, the crowd grew more restless.

A handsome young Hasid in a caftan and fur hat, bearing a gunny sack, his curly hair jammed into the hat he wore cocked to the side as if it were a fedora, announced he had come all the way from Pittsburgh and would not dance with a woman at all, which caused laughter and a few harsh words, some of them in German, about Polish morons dressing like greenhorns.

Moshe was flummoxed. "Why come to a dance if you're not going to dance with a woman?" he asked the man.

"I'm not looking for a dancer," the handsome Hasid said tersely. "I'm looking for a wife."

The crowd laughed again. Later, under the spell of Katz's gorgeous musical wizardry, Moshe watched in wonder as the man danced like a demon all night. He frolicked through every dance step that Moshe had ever seen, and Moshe, who had spent his childhood as a fusgeyer—a wandering Jew—in Romania, had seen a few: horas, bulgars, khosidls, freylekhs, Russian marches, Cossack high-steps. The Hasid was a wonder of twisted elbows, a rhythmic gyroscope of elastic grace and wild dexterity. He danced with any woman who came close, and there were plenty. Moshe later decided the guy must be some kind of wizard.

The next four nights were the most extraordinary gathering of joyful Jewish celebration that Moshe had ever seen. He considered it a miracle, in part because the whole business had nearly fallen apart before it even got off the ground, thanks to a series of flyer notices he'd sent out weeks before to drum up advance ticket sales. Using a Jewish cross directory that listed synagogues and private homes where traveling Jews could stay, Moshe sent flyers to every country Jewish synagogue, boardinghouse, and hostel between North Carolina and Maine. The flyers, proudly proclaiming that the great Mickey Katz Road Show of Winter Yiddish Fun and Family Memories from the Old Country was coming to the All-American Dance Hall and Theater in Pottstown, Pa., on December 15, were printed in four languages: German, Yiddish, Hebrew, and English. But Moshe had badly overestimated the organizational power of country Jewish rabbis, and most of the notices were lost in the ongoing rush of death notices, bar mitzvah commitments, once-in-a-lifetime sales, kosher cow-slaughtering requests, tallit-making services, business-dispute refereeing, mohel (circumcision) mix-ups, and marriage-arrangement snafus that were the daily bread and butter of a country rabbi's life. The few souls who had the presence of mind to open Moshe's letters containing the flyers only added to the confusion, for many were fresh immigrants from Eastern Europe who didn't speak English. They considered any letter that bore a typed address some kind of government notice that meant immediate shipment of you, your family, your dog, and your green stamps back to the old country, where the Russian soldiers awaited with a special gift for your part in the murder of the czar's son, who, of course, the Russians had killed themselves and poked his eyes out to boot, but who's asking? So the flyers were tossed.

Moreover, Moshe sent the wrong flyers to the wrong congregations. The Yiddish flyers went to German-speaking congregations. The German flyers were sent to Yiddish shuls who despised the German-loving snobs. The Hebrew ads went to Hungarians who everybody knew pretended they couldn't read English unless it referred to Jews as "American Israelites"—in Hebrew. Two English ads went to a Polish congregation in Maine that had vanished, the greenhorns up there likely having frozen their tuchuses off and dropped into the ice somewhere. One Baltimore merchant even accidentally forwarded his Yiddish flyer to the advertising department of the *Baltimore Sun*, which caused a ruckus, the advertising executive being under the impression that the Jewish clothing-store merchant from East Baltimore's Jewtown who regularly advertised in the *Sun* intended it for Yiddish-speaking customers only. In actuality, the kind merchant was translating the flyer from Yiddish to English in the back of his store when an argument between two customers broke out in the front of the store. When he stepped out to quell the fuss, his Yiddish-speaking wife wandered into the back storeroom, recognized the words "*Baltimore Sun*" among the papers on her husband's crowded desk, stuffed the half-translated flyer into an envelope along with their weekly advertising check, and mailed it to the paper. The ad executive who received it was too dumb to know the difference between advertising and editorial, and forwarded it to the city desk with a note saying, "Run this tomorrow because the Jew always pays," whereupon the night city editor, a devout well-meaning Catholic, handed it to a new nineteen-year-old Hungarian copy clerk—hired, in part, because he claimed he could speak Yiddish. The kid sent the whole badly translated mess back to advertising with a note saying, "This is an ad." The advertising department placed it in a large font on page B-4 on a Saturday on the last day of Sukkot, the Jewish holiday that celebrates the gathering of the harvest and the miraculous protection the Lord provided for the children of Israel. The result was a disaster. Moshe's original flyer read, in Yiddish:

"*Come see the great Mickey Katz. Once-in-a-lifetime event. Family fun and Jewish memories. Red-hot klezmer like you've never heard before.*"

The translated ad read, in English:

"Mickey Katz is coming. Once a life, always a life. Watch the Jews burn and dance and have fun."

The ad caused panic and fury in East Baltimore's Jewtown, as many of its residents still remembered how the town's first rabbi, David Einhorn, spoke out against slavery during the Civil War and was run out of town, his house burned to the ground. They demanded that the merchant close his store and quit the city.

Moshe nearly fainted when he got word of the disaster. He sped to Baltimore and spent four hundred dollars straightening out matters with the good-natured merchant, who kindly helped him write a second, better ad. But it was too late. The first ad was too much for Baltimore's Jews. It was simply too good to be true. A klezmer dance? With the great Mickey Katz? Why would a star like Katz play for poor salesmen and tailors in the freezing hills of eastern Pennsylvania? In an American theater? Owned by a fusgeyer, a Romanian? Fusgeyers don't own theaters! They wander around and sing songs and get the crap beat out of them by the czar's soldiers. Where is Pottstown anyway? Were there any Jews there at all? Impossible! It was a trap!

The result was that only four Jewish couples from Baltimore bought advance tickets to see the great Katz, and Moshe had been counting on Baltimore's Jewish community in big numbers.

Five weeks before the concert, $1,700 in the hole to his cousin Isaac in Philadelphia, from whom he borrowed the theater rental and deposit money, and feeling lower than he felt when his father died, Moshe dropped to his knees, prayed to G-d for spiritual renewal, felt none, and found himself moping around the back storeroom of the Heaven & Earth Grocery Store, the sole Jewish grocery in Chicken Hill. The owner, a rabbi named Yakov Flohr, felt sorry for the young Romanian and offered to let Moshe study Hebrew from his Talmud, which he kept in the same storeroom where his youngest daughter

Chona toiled. She was crippled from polio, with one leg shorter than the other, requiring her to wear a boot with a sole four inches thick. Chona spent her days sorting vegetables and making butter by stirring yellow dye into creamed milk stored in barrels.

Knowing he was up to his balls in hock and needing G-d, Moshe took the rabbi up on the offer and spent several afternoons glumly poring through the text, thinking of his late father and peeking at Chona, whom he dimly remembered as a quiet, mousey young thing as a child but who now, at age seventeen, had developed into quite a package. Despite her foot and limp, she was a quiet beauty, with a gorgeous nose and sweet lips, ample breasts, a sizable derriere that poked against the drab, loose-fitting woolen skirt, and eyes that shone with gaiety and mirth. Moshe, at twenty-one, in full bloom himself, found himself looking up several times from his Hebrew studies to gawk at Chona's rear end as she stirred the butter on those cold Pennsylvania nights, the swish of her hips moving with the promise of the coal stove in the far corner that heated only half the room. She turned out to be a spirited soul, full of wry humor and glad to have company, and after a few days of easy conversation, regaling him with warm jokes and smiling with her bright gay eyes, young Moshe finally confessed his problem: the upcoming concert, the massive debts, the money already spent, the wrong ads, the demands of a difficult star. "I'm going to lose everything," he said.

It was there, in the back of the rabbi's store, standing over the butter barrel, a churn in her hand, that Chona reminded him of the story of Moses and the burning coals.

She put down her churn, glanced at the door to make sure no one was watching, went to the desk where he sat, lifted her father's dusty, weathered Talmud—which they both knew she was forbidden to touch—grasped the Midrash Rabbah beneath it, and placed the

Talmud back down. Then she opened the Midrash Rabbah, which contained the five books of Moses, and flipped to the story of Moses and the burning coals. She was a student of religion, she confided, and the story of Moses always brought her solace.

It was there—the collapse of his theater imminent, peering at the holy Midrash Rabbah with one eye and the lovely hand of the beauty Chona with the other, his heart throbbing from the first flush of love—that Moshe first came upon the story of Moses and the burning coals, which Chona read to him in Hebrew, of which he understood every fourth word.

Pharaoh placed a plate of burning coals on one side of the infant Moses and a plate of sparkling coins and jewelry on the other. If the infant was intelligent, he would be attracted to the sparkling gold and jewelry, and would be killed as a threat to the pharaoh's heir. If he touched the black coals, he would be perceived as too stupid to be a threat and allowed to live. Moses started to reach for the coins, but as he did, an angel appeared and deftly moved his hand to the hot coals, burning his fingers. The child put his fingers in his mouth, stinging his tongue and giving him a life-long speech impediment. Moses spoke with a defect for the rest of his life, but the life of the leader and most important teacher of the Jewish people was saved.

Moshe listened in rapturous silence, and when she was done, he found himself bathed in the light of love only heaven can deliver. He returned to the storeroom for several days, filling himself with words of the Midrash Rabbah, about which he had been previously ambivalent, and the young flower who led him to words of holy purpose. At the end of the third week of Midrash Rabbah lessons, Moshe asked Chona to marry him, and to his amazement, she agreed.

The next week Moshe deposited $140 in Yakov's bank account as a gift, then approached Yakov and his wife with his marriage proposal for their daughter. The parents, both Bulgarian, were so overjoyed that someone other than a cyclops was willing to marry their disabled daughter—so what if he was Romanian?—they readily agreed. "Why not next week?" Moshe asked. "Why not?" they said. The modest wedding was held at Ahavat Achim, the tiny shul that serviced Pottstown's seventeen Jewish families. It was attended by Moshe's cousin Isaac from Philadelphia, Chona's deliriously happy parents, and a few local Yids Yakov had drummed up to create the necessary minyan of ten Jews to say the seven wedding blessings. Two of them were Polish workers from the Pennsylvania Railroad train yard who had hustled up to Chicken Hill to grab a kosher bite. The two agreed to attend the wedding but demanded four dollars apiece for cab fare to Reading, where they were expected to report to work the next morning. Yakov refused, but Moshe was happy to pay. It was a small price for marrying the woman who brought him more happiness than he ever dreamed possible.

So inspired was he by his new love that he forgot all about the $1,700 he'd spent. He sold his car for $350, borrowed another $1,200 from Isaac, and spent the money on ads, this time properly placed, then watched in amazement as ticket sales zoomed. More than four hundred tickets were sold.

For four nights Mickey Katz and his magical musicians poured forth the most rousing, glorious klezmer music that eastern Pennsylvania had ever heard. Four nights of wild, low-down, dance-till-you-can't Jewish revelry. Moshe sold out of everything—drinks, food, eggs, fish. He even put up twenty exhausted New Yorkers in his theater's second-floor balcony, normally reserved for Negroes. The four couples from Tennessee who had threatened to leave stayed the entire weekend, as did the Hasid dancer who swore he would dance with no woman. It was a rousing success.

The morning after the festivities ended, Moshe was sweeping the sidewalk in front of his theater when he saw the dancing Hasid hurrying toward the train station.

Gone was the fur hat. In its place was a fedora. The caftan had been cut into a sportcoat-length jacket. Moshe barely recognized him. As the young man approached, Moshe spoke out. "Where are you from?" he asked. But the man was fast and silent and already moving down the sidewalk past him. Moshe called to his back, "Wherever you live, it's home to the greatest dancer in the world, that's for sure."

That did it. The Hasid stopped, reached into his gunny sack, and without a word, walked several steps back to Moshe, handed him a bottle of slivovitz (plum brandy), then turned and continued down the sidewalk moving fast.

Moshe called out cheerfully to his back, "Did you find a wife?"

"I don't need a wife," he said, waving a hand without looking back. "I'm a twart of love."

"A what?"

"A sponge cake," he said. "Don't you Romanians know anything?" Before Moshe could reply, a distinct pop was heard—a tiny explosion like the sound of a cork popping but louder. Both men froze. They looked up at the tiny tangle of houses on Chicken Hill behind Moshe's theater. A small puff of black smoke wafted into the air, apparently from one of the scruffy homes, the smoke vanishing into the sky.

"That's a bad sign," the Hasid said, then rushed off.

Moshe called out, "What's your name?"

But the Hasid was gone.

3

Twelve

The day after the Hasid left, Moshe walked to his theater to find Nate hard at work out front, manning a long-handled grabber, carefully pulling the letters off the theater facade.

"Did you hear that pop yesterday?" Moshe asked. "It sounded like something blew up on the Hill."

Nate shrugged, looking up at the facade. "Ain't nothing blowing up there except hard times. Plenty of that."

Moshe laughed. He was still in a glorious mood from the wonderful windfall Katz had brought him and his recent wedding, so he reached in his pocket, counted off fifteen dollars. "For you," he said.

Nate, looking up at the facade, glanced down at the money, then shook his head.

"You don't like my money?" Moshe asked.

Nate leaned on the long pole. He was a tall, light-skinned man with smooth skin and sinewed, muscled arms from some kind of outdoor work, Moshe guessed.

"I likes it fine," Nate said. "But I like my job more. How I'm gonna keep a job if you keep giving away your last dime, Mr. Moshe? I ain't seen a dance like that since Erskine Hawkins come through Anna Morse's place in Linfield. I used to make good coin over there."

Moshe faintly recalled Anna Morse, a well-dressed Negro woman who drove a Packard. He also knew her building, a tiny brick structure on a back road outside Linfield, a farming community about seven miles away. "Isn't that a funeral home?" he said.

"It *was* a colored dance hall," Nate said. "But Anna's making more money now from dead bodies than live ones. Shame, too. Coloreds got to go all the way to Chambersburg to find a place to dance. Unless you wanna go to a jook joint and get all shot up."

Moshe nodded, but his mind began to churn. Later that night, he took the matter to Chona. "What if I open my theater to the colored?"

"So?"

"The goyim won't like that."

Chona was standing at the stove cooking dinner, her back to him. She laughed and raised her spoon in the air, spinning it in a circle. That was her gift. Not an ounce of bitterness or shred of shame. Unlike Moshe, Chona was an American. She had been born in Pottstown. She was a familiar sight in Chicken Hill in her worn woolen dress, old sweater, and wearing her special-soled boot that cost a fortune, laughing and joking with neighbors. She seemed to know every family. When Moshe came home for lunch and even late at night, he often found his wife standing in front of the store laughing with one of the local Negroes. "That woman," his cousin Isaac once grumbled, "is a real Bulgarian. Whenever they feel like working, they sit and wait till the feeling passes. They can't pour a glass of water without making a party of it." But Isaac was a sourpuss whom Moshe had long ago learned to ignore on certain matters.

Standing at her stove, Chona said in Yiddish, "Me ken dem yam mit a kendel nit ois' shepen." (You can't ride in all directions at once.) "What does it matter what they think? The coloreds' money spends just like ours."

Four weeks later, Moshe booked Chick Webb, the colored entertainer.

The night of Webb's show, Pottstown's Negroes slipped into Moshe's All-American Dance Hall and Theater like ghosts. They entered silent and somber; the men in sober suits and ties, the pretty women in flowered dresses and large handsome hats. Some were clearly nervous. Others seemed agitated. A few looked outright terrified. Downtown Pottstown was off-limits to Negroes unless they came to work as janitors, maids, or to use a public faucet when the tap water on Chicken Hill mysteriously vanished, which was frequently.

But once Chick Webb's band struck up, the silent, reticent Negroes of Pottstown transformed: they became a leaping mass of wild, dancing humanity. They frolicked and laughed, dancing as if they were birds enjoying flight for the first time. Webb's band played like wizards, four sets of gorgeous, stomping, low-down, rip-roaring, heart-racing jazz. The result was an outrageously joyous event, matched in intensity only by the great Mickey Katz affairs.

Moshe watched spellbound from the wings as Webb, a tiny man with a curved spine clad in a white suit, roared with laughter and enthusiasm as he played, egging his band on from the rear with his masterful drumming, the thunderous band shaking the floor with rip-roaring waves of gorgeous sound. That man, Moshe decided, was a joymaker. And Moshe could not help but notice that Webb, like his lovely Chona, had a physical disability. Though he was a hunchback of some kind, he moved with a certain feeling of joy, a lightness, as if every moment were precious.

Cripples, Moshe thought, *have brought me fortune: Moses, Chona, and Chick.*

It was then that Moshe began to have dreams about Moses. They came in twelves. Twelve different visions. Twelve different nights. Moses walking through twelve different gates. Twelve different cities. Moses on Mount Sinai, staring at twelve different peaks below. He began to see everything about him as a function of twelve. Twelve bands in twelve months. Twelve hundred dollars invested in twelve different stocks, bringing fantastic returns. Even the home he purchased, a tiny brick affair in Chicken Hill, was located in a neighborhood that comprised twelve blocks in one square mile.

Moshe told no one about his dreams, not even his wife. Instead, he followed the visions, investing first a few pennies in twelve different stocks, then more as the stocks grew, and in his theater, bringing in twelve different Negro bands in twelve months, including Webb again, who came back four times. The dances drew Negroes from far and wide, and over the next twelve months, his fortunes grew.

As they did, the response of the town's rival theater owners evolved from grumbles to murmured complaints to roaring outrage. Negroes were crawling all over downtown, they howled, to a Jewish theater! Everybody knows the Jews bake their matzahs with Christian blood!

The response was swift. First, the city building inspector arrived at the theater and told Moshe his pipes were bad and that his plaster was peeling, and fined him. The owner of the theater building complained about the litter. The fire commissioner cited him for creaky doorways and missing emergency exits. Even his own synagogue fined him five dollars.

Moshe fought back. He paid off the building inspector. He presented the fire chief, a drunk, with four bottles of scotch and a new fishing rod. He had the ever-faithful Nate and a crew of Negroes sweep the front of every single store on the block, then he approached the landlord and promised to pay him $150 for every Negro act he booked, offering to buy the building at a substantial price in a year's time if the landlord kept quiet about the Negroes. The landlord agreed.

To address the synagogue, Isaac traveled up from Philadelphia and met with the chevry, the men's group that had fined Moshe. Isaac was a grim, forbidding soul, four years older, who'd been Moshe's protector since their shared childhood in Europe. Isaac walked into the meeting, laid a silver dollar on the table, and said, "I'll give ten of those to any man in this room who can prove he was at the Mickey Katz dance with his wife." Not a soul moved. That ended the conversation about Moshe's fine.

With the profits from the Negro dances, Moshe bought his theater outright within two years, and then later a second theater two blocks off. Over the next five years, he expanded and made real money—enough to buy his mother a warm house in Romania and provide Chona with a comfortable apartment above the Heaven & Earth Grocery Store, which he bought from Yakov after Chona's mother passed and Yakov moved on to run a bigger temple in Reading. Moshe planned on demolishing the store but Chona wouldn't allow it.

"How can you sell Heaven and Earth?" She laughed.

Moshe did not see the humor. "You don't have to spend your life selling kosher cow meat and onions to coloreds. Let's close the store. The Jews are leaving the Hill. Let's follow them."

"Where?"

"Down the hill to town. Where the Americans are."

"Which Americans?"

"Chona, don't be difficult."

"I'll run the store."

"How will that look? My wife selling cheese and biscuits while I run one of the best theaters in town? We have plenty now."

Chona's exuberant smile molded into a smirk. "So I'm to sit home all day while you have fun at your theater full of music?"

Moshe gave in.

It gave the Jewish housewives of Pottstown much to talk about. What kind of husband would let his wife run his business? Why didn't they move off the Hill like the other Jews? Her father had moved to Reading after her mother passed; why hadn't Chona made her husband move there to help her father? What's more important than family?

But Chona's years of stirring butter, sorting vegetables, and reading in the back room of the Heaven & Earth Grocery Store had given her time to consider. She read everything as a child: comics, detective books, dime novels; and by the time she became a young wife, she'd evolved into reading about socialism and unions. She subscribed to Jewish newspapers, publications in Hebrew, and books on Jewish life, some from Europe. The readings gave her wild ideas about art, music, and worldly matters. She knew more Hebrew than any Jewish woman in town, many of whom had little more than a rudimentary knowledge of the language. She could recite the Talmud better than most of the men in shul. Instead of sitting with the women in the balcony, she insisted on davening downstairs with the men, claiming her bad foot prevented her from climbing stairs. Someone in the temple had the bright idea to at least construct a curtain to separate her from the men in the congregation. Like most ideas in the Ahavat Achim congregation of Pottstown, that, too, proved to be a disaster, for after Chona's father departed, he was replaced by a fumbling but well-meaning bumbler named Karl Feldman, who spoke with a lisp and whom the congregation called Fertzel—fart—behind his back. Many a morning the hapless Feldman would find his garbled interpretations of Jewish law amended by the pretty housewife whose sharp Talmudic corrections from behind the curtain fluttered into the air like butterflies as she piped out, "Karl, what are you talking about? There are four different versions of how Cain died!" Moreover, her lovely singing voice would occasionally break in to help Feldman's faltering cantoring that mangled the glorious Talmudic melodies. Everyone knew women weren't supposed to be cantors, yet Chona's lovely voice brought smiles of relief to even the crankiest congregants. Chona's misbehavior was tolerated by the Ahavat Achim congregation. Her father had been the town's first rabbi. He'd built the shul. Most congregants had grown accustomed to her craziness. Even Irv and Marvin Skrupskelis, the grim identical twins from Lithuania who ran Pottstown's shoe store and fought about everything, loved Chona. She was one of the few things the two agreed about—and everybody knew those two were the most disagreeable Jews in town. Besides, Irv pointed out, "Cantoring is the cry of Zion, and with Fertzel, that's what you get. Crying." The two were outspoken in their belief that America was a land where Jews of all types should be of one voice. Why not let the prettiest voice be heard?

Still, Moshe pleaded with his wife. "Chona, do you have to carry on in shul all the time? Cantoring is Fertzel's—Karl's—job."

She waved him off. "There are hobos in Chicken Hill who know more Hebrew than Fertzel. Read the Book of Moses!"

Moshe was afraid to tell his wife of his twelve dreams of Moses. He assumed his dreams were somehow unholy, a superstition from his Romanian past, and felt his American-born wife would not approve.

She would correct him, and he felt no need to be corrected. He had money now. He was an American. He was paying for her store, which was, financially, a bona fide loser.

As the months passed and the Jews continued their flight from Chicken Hill, Moshe kept pressing his wife about moving. There're better homes downtown, he argued, better lighting, richer customers. We can open a profitable store downtown, he insisted. Chona, lighthearted as always, refused. "We have wonderful neighbors," she said.

Finally, Moshe confessed to her about seeing the black cloud. "There was an explosion on the Hill somewhere behind the theater after the Mickey Katz dance. The amazing dancer, he saw it, too. He said it was a bad omen. I'm afraid he might be right."

"Superstition," Chona scoffed with a firmness that ended the discussion.

Moshe let the matter drop. He forgot about the Hasid's prediction, gave up the idea of closing Chona's store, and pushed forward. Besides, life was good. Profits were made. He kept his two theaters filled with lively Yiddish bands, Jewish theater troupes, and romping, stomping black jazz bands. He worked hard to keep up appearances and to keep from getting thrown out of town, for his wife wrote letters every month to the Pottstown *Mercury* about Jewish causes and union meetings. She even wrote an angry letter protesting the annual parade of the Ku Klux Klan in which she announced she knew *exactly* who one of the head marchers was. She could tell, she wrote, by the way he walked. That was a dangerous letter, Moshe declared, and the two argued about it, for the telltale limp belonged to the town's physician, Doc Roberts, who was well-connected with the town's power brokers. To make peace with the town powers, every month or so Moshe booked a bevy of terrible bands that Pottstown's high-class, pasty-faced Presbyterians enjoyed, just to keep the peace: the Colonial Dames of America, the Pennsylvania Potting Club, the Nineteen Mountain People Whose Fourteenth Cousin Arrived on the *Mayflower*. The bands were horrible outfits that sounded like owls hooting. Moshe watched in puzzlement as these Americans danced with clumsy satisfaction at the moans and groans of these boneless, noise-producing junk mongers, their boring humpty-dumpty sounds landing on the dance floor with all the power of empty peanut shells tossed in the air. The couples moved in sad circles holding hands like children, dancing in silence, the women clomping about in wooden clogs no self-respecting Jewish woman would wear, the businessmen swaying in top hats and bow ties from years of yore. Each event was interrupted by heartfelt speeches about the town's founder, the great John Potts, whose portrait loomed in every town building, the old man's face peering over every citizen's shoulder like a ghost taking attendance.

Thoughts like this made Moshe feel ashamed of himself. He was a successful American. The country had been good to him. Yet he still believed in sorcery and witchery and the stupid business of twelves. *This is old thinking in a new time*, he told himself, *and I must change*.

By 1935, eleven years after his initial Mickey Katz success, when his cousin Isaac wrote to him saying he'd bought a brand-new Packard, Moshe had had enough. After dinner one night at the kitchen table, he drilled the matter home.

"We don't need to live above a grocery store anymore. We can have our own house. We are moving."

"Where?" Chona asked.

"Downtown. To a new house. We'll put a new grocery store near it. I've already made a deposit."

"Go get your money back."

"I will not."

"Then enjoy yourself there," Chona said. "I will visit you from time to time." She sat at the table calmly, her fine features determined. And once again, his love for her was too strong. The idea of parking his big Packard in front of an empty house without his Chona terrified him, and his resolve broke.

"Chona, please."

"I do not want a house downtown. I do not want a store downtown. Living up here and going downstairs to work is easier. There's not a lot of walking."

"But the Jews are leaving Chicken Hill."

"Ten blocks from here is leaving?"

"You know what I mean. Let's go where they are. They're our people."

"Moshe, I like it here. I grew up in this house. The postman knows where I live."

Exasperated, Moshe pointed out the kitchen window toward Pottstown below. "Down the hill is America!"

But Chona was adamant. "America is here."

"This area is poor. Which we are not. It is Negro. Which we are not. We are doing *well*!"

"Because we *serve*, you see? That is what we do. The Talmud says it. We must serve."

"But the Negro is our only customer here."

"Hasn't their money always spent?"

"That's not the issue."

His hands were on the table cradling a cup of tea. She gently placed one of her hands over his. "Don't you see what they have, Moshe? Don't you see the well they draw from?"

"What well? What are you talking about?"

She remained silent for a moment, then said calmly, softly, "I remember Mickey Katz. He had a mandolin player who was missing two fingers. I remember watching him play. He played so wonderfully. Don't you remember?"

"There were so many acts between then and now...," he mumbled.

"What about Chick Webb?" she said. "He made you a fortune."

"Webb was expensive, for a cripple," Moshe said.

He meant it as a joke, but he felt a hammer of cold silence drop into the room.

"Is that how you see me?" she said softly.

She rose from the table and limped off, and did not speak to him for several days. She forgave him only after he presented her with a volume of the *Shulchan Aruch*, which spelled out the seven requirements of Jewish life: wisdom, meekness, fear of God, love of truth, love of people, possession of a good name, and dislike of money. He apologized, and she became the Chona of old, marching about the house, proclaiming merrily, "Charity of mind! Without charity of mind, what is life? I was in town and heard a woman say, 'That poor crippled woman.' I thought to myself, *Who is the cripple? The one who worships a thing? Or the one who worships something higher?*"

This kind of talk chafed against his growing belief that more money made for an easier life. But he tolerated it because he knew her heart, and it was a priceless heart indeed. So he remained silent and they stayed in Chicken Hill.

ON A GRAY morning in 1936, the twelfth year of their marriage, Chona woke with a cough and pain in her stomach.

She avoided doctors, so Moshe waited a day, but then she worsened. Thus began a series of long pilgrimages, going from one doctor to the next, with none having answers. The illness was puzzling. She was fine one day, walking about, laughing, reading her crazy Jewish books; the next day, ill and bedridden, barely able to move. Back and forth it went. As her condition worsened, Moshe hired Nate's wife, Addie, to help at the grocery store and for Sabbath chores. Chona hated help of any kind, but as her illness worsened, she was forced to give in.

Moshe took her to doctors in Philadelphia, Baltimore, even New York City, with no results. Her strange illness, pain in the stomach and sudden fainting spells, continued. Doctors were bewildered.

Moshe's old fears and superstitions began to take hold. Could it be that his secret dream of Moses and the twelves, and his ridiculous belief in the bad luck prediction of the Hasid he had seen but once, had pushed his fortunes to turn? The couple had no children, a fact that Chona bore without complaint, though at times she would stare out the window at the colored children of the neighborhood and fall silent, only to recover and become the Chona of old, laughing and vibrant, chatting about some radio soap opera she'd heard lately. Theirs had been a happy marriage. Twelve wonderful years, just like his dream of Moses and twelves had strangely preordained. He wanted to tell his wife about his dreams, but as her illness worsened, he didn't want to bother her with such triviality. When Rabbi Feldman came by the house one night to sing and pray as Chona lay restless and swooning with fever, Moshe wanted to confess it to the rabbi, but it didn't seem the proper time. So when the rabbi announced, "I feel Chona will improve," Moshe was relieved.

But Chona did not improve. She began to black out for no reason and the closest doctor that she would see was in Reading, a good eighteen miles away. Chona despised the local doctor, Doc Roberts, and would not allow him to treat her. "I grew up with him," she said. "If I must see a goy doctor, I will see one. But not him."

This made matters more difficult; for Doc Roberts, a stout man who still traveled by horse and cart despite the fact that his shiny new Chevrolet sat in the driveway of his ivy-clad home next to the town cemetery, was Pottstown's sole physician. He had a limp similar to Chona's, and yet he marched every year at the head of the local Ku Klux Klan parade. Despite the sheet covering him, everyone knew it was Doc. His girth and limp gave him away. No one complained. It was just one of those things. Once a year, on Klan parade day, the Negroes in town disappeared, the Jewish stores closed, the Klan marched, and that was it. But Chona found the whole business distasteful, and to Moshe's horror, she refused to shutter her store like the other Jewish merchants. "Why should I close because of them?" she fumed. "Even the post office isn't closed." As for Doc Roberts, she told Moshe, "He's so fat the back of his neck looks like a pack of hot dogs." She couldn't stand him.

But now Moshe needed Doc, and because Chona refused to see him, every doctor visit meant trooping to Reading to see the kind Jewish doctor there. Yet nothing he did was helping, and Chona's blackouts were getting dangerous.

She recovered a bit in the spring, then backtracked into deep illness and walking became nearly impossible. By summer, she was completely bedridden. It was not her bad foot that seemed to be pulling her toward death but rather her stomach, which began to bulge peculiarly, as if mocking her infertility.

Moshe frantically sought help from one doctor after another, with increasing urgency, even taking Chona to a nationally known specialist in Boston. But that doctor was as confounded as the rest had been. So Moshe took her home.

He put her bed in the front room of the apartment near a window, so she could see the sunrise and read the Talmud as the day broke, for while it was forbidden, it didn't seem to matter now. The room was just above the store, allowing Chona to yell instructions downstairs to Addie, for she insisted on keeping the store open. "My work keeps me alive," she said. Chona took to writing letters to the newspaper reminding readers of Jewish holidays and reading joke books to amuse her husband, whose long, exhausted face appeared at her bedside each night after work. She'd offer a slew of jokes and light chatter before falling off to sleep, whereupon he'd dutifully rub her feet and ankles, which had swelled to a disturbing size. He read the Talmud aloud to her even as she slept because he knew she loved it so much.

Still, by winter, she worsened. Her fainting spells increased and fever crept in and lingered.

It was then, as Chona arced toward death, that the Negroes of Chicken Hill began a steady trek to the Heaven & Earth Grocery Store. They filed in day and night, bringing soup, fresh garden vegetables, pies, and country remedies, as well as warm laughter and jokes for the kind, crazy Jewish lady who forced her husband to open his theater to the colored and who extended so much credit to the colored families of Chicken Hill that neither she nor they had any idea of who owed what. The Negroes of Chicken Hill loved Chona. They saw her not as a neighbor but as an artery to freedom, for the recollection of Chona's telltale limp as she and her childhood friend, a tall, gorgeous, silent soul named Bernice Davis, walked down the pitted mud roads of the Hill to school each morning was stamped in their collective memory. It was proof of the American possibility of equality: *we all can get along no matter what, look at those two.* Chona, for her part, saw them not as Negroes but as neighbors with infinitely interesting lives: Darlene, whose daughter had the longest case of hiccups Chona had ever seen. Larnell, the twelve-year-old who could not read but could do complex math in his head. And of course Bernice, who had been her next-door neighbor and best friend when they were children but who now rarely spoke and had so many children that the Negroes on the Hill laughingly referred to Bernice's brood as "forty mules on an acre," because nobody knew exactly *how many* children Bernice had and they were afraid to ask.

The Negroes filled Chona's bedroom with life. They told jokes, recounting tales of spooks and haints, telling humorous stories about fleeing America's South that made Chona laugh and forget the pain. Addie and her sister Cleota took shifts running the store, keeping kosher on the Sabbath, turning light switches on and off and lighting the stove, keeping the plates and silverware properly separate, both aware at Chona's insistence that no matter what, they should allow Moshe to wake her when he got home from work. Some nights Moshe would arrive to find Addie seated by Chona's bed and Chona asleep, the Talmud on her nightstand, her hand on the open page that she had selected for him to read. He'd nudge her awake and read aloud. She'd compliment his Hebrew, saying how beautiful it sounded, though they both knew it was horrible. Then she'd fall back asleep as he read, whereupon he'd stare at her dark, beautiful face, mesmerized, and weep. Sorrow charged his mind at those moments, electrified his memory. The quaint symbols of holy suppliance in Hebrew signage, which had seemed meaningless to him when he was a child, now gave him impetus during those cold nights, twelve years after they first fell in love. After weeping a bit, he would charge ahead and continue reading as she slept. He read the Word now to keep her alive, and in doing so, a part of him came alive as well.

But as the winter turned to spring, Chona began the long fade.

One night in late spring, she fell unconscious and was rushed to the hospital in nearby Spring City. She regained consciousness and was released the next day, but not before the doctors told Moshe that if her fever returned, she'd have to come back to the hospital because the end was near.

The next day Moshe stayed at her bedside all day, though she didn't seem to know he was there. She talked feverishly until medicine and fatigue finally took effect, and she spent a good part of the afternoon sleeping. She slept into evening, at which point Addie pushed Moshe out of the house, telling him to get some air. He walked down the Hill to his theater to check up on things. He found the ever-loyal Nate and a small crew of Negroes cleaning up after a rousing three-night appearance by the Negro bandleader Louis Jordan. He grabbed a broom and was about to join them to keep himself from losing his mind when he noticed a figure coming through the backstage door. It was his cousin Isaac from Philadelphia.

"Let's take a walk," Isaac said.

Moshe declined. Instead, he nodded at an empty table and chairs in front of the stage.

Isaac, tall and long, wedged himself into a chair. He wore his frock coat and fedora, neither of which he removed. Apparently, he was not planning to stay long. He motioned for Moshe to sit, but Moshe again declined, standing across from his cousin.

At thirty-seven, Isaac was an imposing man, nothing like the skinny fourteen-year-old who led his meek young cousin on foot for more than a thousand miles through the foot of the Carpathian Mountains and across Eastern Europe—from Bârlad, Romania, to Hamburg Germany—the two boys dodging police and soldiers, ducking into alleys and hiding behind garbage bins, fusgeyers, stealing a little here, borrowing a little there, until a kind old woman in Hamburg let them live in her basement where they rolled cigars for her sick husband who did piecework for a local cigar factory, the old man dying upstairs in bits and pieces while the boys worked downstairs for three years to earn boat passage to America. He was a big American now, big in every way, a man of arrogant raw power, with a broad chest and wide shoulders, the owner of nine successful show houses in Philadelphia. He was proudly dressed in a dark suit, crisp white shirt, bow tie, and shiny shoes, a far cry from their days in Romania where they walked about in ragged pants and beaten shoes, shoving stolen bread into their mouths as they fled from angry storekeepers and Russian soldiers.

"I came to ask you about how to book colored bands," Isaac said.

Moshe immediately smelled a rat. Isaac was Philadelphia's biggest theater owner. The smallest of Isaac's nine theaters was bigger than Moshe's two theaters combined. Isaac booked everything from Yiddish shows to vaudeville acts to moving pictures. He could book a traveling circus of trained fleas if he wanted. He needed no help booking Negro bands.

Yet Moshe played along, offering a few pointers, with Isaac asking a few surface questions. Then, as Moshe expected, Isaac gently curved the conversation to Chona. He suggested a Jewish home for the sick in Philadelphia.

"I know people there," he said. "They're good people. Your wife can live out the rest of her time there. She'll be in a warm, safe place, among friends."

Moshe nodded his head, working hard to stifle his outrage. He said softly, "You are rarely wrong about things, cousin. But you are wrong now."

"Be sensible. She's very ill."

"I have thought this through," Moshe said.

"And what have you thought?"

Moshe felt the blood rush to his face. "Are you mocking me?"

Isaac found himself startled. "I am not."

"You better not! Because if you do, I'll give you such a chamalyah (wallop) in the kishkes (guts) you won't forget it!"

Isaac—survivor of a thousand street fights from Romania to South Philadelphia—was stunned. The punishing hardships of his childhood had changed him from a fast-moving boy of keen wit into a man of resilience and strength. He was a hard man now. He knew it. His wife knew it. His children knew it. He lived a bleak, empty life. But he also knew that the one bright spot in his clean, rich, loveless American life was that the only person in the world who had experienced every bit of the hatred and evil that he had never uttered a harsh or angry word toward anyone ever—until that moment.

Seeing the rage on Moshe's face shook Isaac badly. He felt as if the earth were shifting beneath his feet. "I'm only looking out for your interests, cousin," he mumbled.

"I know what my interests are," Moshe said. "Why is it that you come to me and speak this way?"

"How is the best way to speak of it?"

"Why is it that our people can't speak about illness aloud?"

"Our people don't know about such things," Isaac said. "I'm just telling you what I know."

"Then you don't know enough," Moshe said. *"She will live!"*

4

Dodo

Four houses from where Chona lay dying, a slender elderly black woman named Addie Timblin stood at the front door of her tiny brown house and peered through its cracks into the cold darkness. Her eyes scanned the muddy road, looking for a lantern, which would mean her husband, Nate, was making his way up the Hill. Behind her, at the kitchen table in the front room, the monthly meeting of the Pottstown Association of Negro Men was going full blast, with the usual shouting and nonsense.

The association met every third Saturday night around her kitchen table, ostensibly to talk about ways for the Negro in Chicken Hill to get more jobs and opportunity, and maybe even one day running water and a sewer line, as opposed to the outhouses, cesspools, and wells that dotted the neighborhood like blisters. It was run by Pottstown's concerned Negro men leaders—each one, Addie thought wryly, worse than the other. Mostly the men met to play cards, gossip, tell jokes, brag about cars they would never own, and figure out ways to slither around the white man's rules without pissing off the white folks downtown.

There were three men at the table: Rusty, a wide-shouldered, brown-complexioned twenty-two-year-old in work overalls and a straw hat; Rusty's uncle Bags; and Reverend Ed Spriggs, whom everyone on the Hill called Snooks. Next to Snooks sat his wife, Holly, who busied herself knitting. At the moment, the conversation focused around Miss Chona, whom every person in the room knew was dying, and to whom every person in the room, except Addie, owed money for groceries, favors, phone use, extra clothing, and all sorts of life bric-a-brac.

Addie stared out into the night as she heard cards being shuffled. She glanced behind her to see Rusty, a pack of cigarettes peeking out from the front pouch of his overalls, slide the deck over to Snooks and ask, "Snooks, do Jews cover the clocks in the house when one of 'em dies?"

Snooks, a heavyset man in a rumpled suit and bow tie, pulled the cards closer and winked at Bags as he shuffled. "Sho nuff, Rusty. They chew with their teeth, too. Plus, their women wear fur coats in winter. And the men pee standing up."

Bags laughed, but Snooks glanced at his wife, Holly, who frowned.

Snooks shot a glance at Addie in the doorway. "Addie, make sure you dress Miss Chona in her finest. Don't pleat her hair, nor comb it out in any way. Just leave it free. And put a dish of salt on her chest. It keeps the body from surging up."

"She ain't gonna pass," Addie said as she stared into the night.

Snooks waved a fat hand in the air dismissively and turned back to the table, shuffling cards, then said, "If you growed up down home, you'd know about the old ways. Those are good ways. A dish of salt keeps the devil out."

"Do Jews believe in the devil?" Rusty asked.

"I hope so," Snooks said.

"Then why'd they murder Jesus Christ?" Rusty asked.

Snooks, momentarily flummoxed, turned to his wife for an answer, but Holly pretended to be too busy knitting.

"I didn't say they murdered Jesus Christ," Snooks said.

"Yes, you did. You said it in church. Many times."

Snooks ignored him. "There's sixty-six books in the Bible, Rusty. I can't recollect all of 'em. Addie, if Miss Chona passes, put a bit of molasses at her feet and a piece of cornpone on her hair. And put quarters on her eyes."

"For what?" Rusty asked.

"It keeps their eyes from popping open," Snooks said. "Addie, do it before her kin shows. They might not cotton to that."

"Ain't no kin to speak of," Addie said. "The father's over in Reading. The mother died years back, before you come up to this country."

"I don't recollect the mother," Snooks said.

"You wouldn't want her around no how, Snooks. She was a rough shuffle for anybody who talked ignorant." She wished Nate would hurry up. She spoke into the crack of the door again, but the bitter words were loud enough for the room to hear.

"If Miss Chona dies, every one of these sorry, half what-I-might-say men in this town is gonna roll up their pouting lips. They'll cry their eyes out, pretending to be sad. Truth is, they'll be glad to see her go."

The words and a cold wind blew into the room together. An embarrassed silence descended.

"Addie's wore out," Snooks said cheerfully. "Holly, stand by the door and look for Nate. Addie, come set down here and feel some of the Lord's quiet."

Addie turned to him. "Spell it out, Snooks."

"Huh?"

"Spell out how I'm gonna feel the Lord's quiet while you busy setting here fending and proving 'bout nothing. Talking about devil in one breath and putting quarters on Miss Chona's eyes the next. Spell it out. Where's the Lord's quiet in all that?"

"Take it easy, Addie," Bags said. He was a stonemason, a stout, large-chested man. "Reverend don't mean nothing."

"He means just what he says, talking about the Lord while holding a deck of cards. Over on Hemlock Row, they runned a man out of town for doing that very thing. Called hisself Son of Man. They say he was a walking devil."

"Ain't no such thing as Son of Man on Hemlock Row," Snooks said. "That's just some boogie joogie them country Negroes cooked up. They need a real preacher over there."

"Go on over and preach at 'em then."

"The Row's three miles from here, Addie, and I got gout in my feet."

"Whyn't you leave off him, Addie," Bags said. "God ain't against a man playing cards."

"It's all right, Bags," Snooks said. "We is all different. Women got their own understanding about things."

"There's men's understanding and there's women's understanding and there's wisdom," Addie said. "You wasn't singing them songs about the Jew when your son was sick and Miss Chona made Doc Roberts come see about him. And she can't stand him no more than you and I can."

"Doc Roberts ain't come to Chicken Hill on Miss Chona's account," Snooks said. "He come to forget his amnesia. I paid him in advance and he forgot I was colored and thanked me."

The men laughed.

Addie had had enough. She slipped out into the cold air, closing the door behind her.

She was a thin, pretty woman, with dark eyes that shone brightly, giving her face the innocence of a child—eyes full of surprise, glowing, expectant. They topped a wide nose and the high, gaunt jaws of a Native American. Her family had emigrated from the South to Chicken Hill when she was a tiny child. Unlike most blacks on the Hill, she had no memories of "back home," the world of the South, chinaberry and pecan trees or dewberries or hearing laughter from the field truck that drove the Negroes out to pick cotton. Sometimes she wished she could remember the South just to have something pleasant to dream about, like the others in Chicken Hill who referred to North Carolina or Alabama or Georgia as "home." Home for Addie was Chicken Hill, Pottstown, Pa.

She took a few tentative steps, peering down the dark road, her eyes scanning the darkness, looking for the familiar Irish schoolboy cap and short-sleeve white cotton shirt Nate favored even on the coldest days. The wind bit into her skin, but she stayed where she was, her eyes searching the road.

Nothing.

Just as she was about to head inside, a tall, thin shadow crossed under the lone streetlight that illuminated the far corner. She saw it was him, the long strides stopping as he carefully stepped over the narrow ditches that carried sewage and rainwater. As he approached, she walked up to him and placed a warm hand on his face. "Whyn't you bring your lantern?" she asked.

Nate ignored that. He didn't need a lantern. He'd been walking the same route from the theater for years. He stood for a moment as she held her hand to his face, and only after he brought his long hand up to touch hers did she move toward the house, Nate behind her.

The laughing and chatting ceased when Nate walked in. He looked about the room, then nodded toward the door of Chona's Heaven & Earth Grocery Store and addressed Addie. "Is she passed?"

"No. How's Mr. Moshe?"

Nate shook his head. "His cousin come all the way up from Philadelphia. Talking about putting her in a home of some kind."

"What for? She got her right mind."

Nate sighed. He pulled a chair out from the table and sat, draping his long frame across it. "Don't matter what they decide. The Lord's got His own plan for her."

"That's right," Snooks said quickly.

A plume of embarrassment drifted into the room. On paper, Snooks was the "community leader" of Chicken Hill. When the city fathers wanted to make a donation or announce plans to do anything on the Hill, they approached Snooks, whom they referred to as "Reverend Spriggs." But on the Hill, it was Nate Timblin's opinion that counted.

Nate smiled at Snooks. "You still reading out the Book of Revelation, Snooks?"

Snooks nodded. "I am."

"Tell me one then."

Snooks shifted uncomfortably. Like most colored on the Hill, Snooks was a little afraid of Nate. There was a silent pool in Nate Timblin, a stirring that did not invite foolishness, a quiet that covered a kind of tempest. Like most on the Hill, Nate claimed the South as his home, but unlike his fellow Hill residents, he never spoke of his past. That was a dark hole. He was a light turned off. But to the colored of the Hill, a light switched off did not mean it could not be switched back on. Anything could happen in this world, especially on the Hill, where the occasional peace of chickens and goats squawking and bleating happily could disintegrate into a wild scramble of booze, bullets, spilled guts, and chaos. Nate was easygoing, quiet, deft, slow-moving, with a wide smile and hands that gripped hammers tightly and eyes that gazed at you dead-on, but he was, even at sixty, what the old folks called "much of a man." Even Fatty Davis, the muscled, gregarious, gold-toothed force who ran the Hill's only speakeasy and who fist fought the cops and wrestled with the Irish firefighters at Empire Fire Company in town, made it a point to steer clear of crossing Nate. "I'd rather die in a storm," he said.

Snooks, seated at the kitchen table, was angry at himself for noodling with Addie, for she was, everyone knew, a serious woman and also Nate's wife. He managed to spurt out, "'We shall not all sleep, but we'll be changed at the last trumpet in a moment.'"

Nate nodded. He removed his cap and tossed it on the table. Addie, standing at the stove behind Holly, decided to drop the bomb quickly.

"Dodo's missing," she said.

Nate's dark eyes locked on Addie's face. "He's what?"

"Gone missing."

"When?"

"Today. They say he's gone fifty miles. All the way to Philadelphia."

"How you know he's gone that far?"

"That's what they say."

"Who's they?"

"Yula's boys—CJ and Callie. They was out fishing in the Manatawny Creek this morning, behind that new tire factory. They seen him riding on the freight shuttle to Berwyn, hanging on the ladder. The road from that yard there runs straight to Philly, 'bout ten or twelve miles. He can walk it. Or ride another freight train. He's tried that before."

The three men at the table stared in alarm at Addie. "Why didn't you say something?" Rusty said.

"Which one of y'all got a car?" she asked. None did.

Nate was incredulous. "The boy's deaf as a pole. Them boys didn't think enough to snatch him?"

"They jumped up to get him, but a white man from the tire factory came out and runned them off. They had to circle all the way round the other side of the Manatawny and cut through the Hill School to get here. It was dark by then."

"Ain't none of 'em had a nickel to call?"

"What phone they gonna use?" Addie asked. "Miss Chona's got the only pay phone here on the Hill that the coloreds free to use. Them children ain't going into no white folks' place asking about nobody's phone."

Nate pursed his lips as frustration and irritation moved across his smooth face. He stood up and reached for his hat.

"Who's up that got a car at this hour?"

"Fatty."

"Lloyd's busy selling sip sauce at this time of night," Nate said. The room noted that Nate called Fatty, owner of the local jook joint, by his real name. He turned for the door.

"Where you going?" Addie said.

"Fabicelli's bakery. Mr. Fabi got a truck."

"He's gone," Addie said.

"Since when?"

"Two weeks ago. He sold his store."

"To who?"

"Jewish fella."

Nate searched his memory. "I know every Jew in this town. Ain't heard of nobody buying no new business."

"New man. Mr. Malachi. Rusty helped him put up a sign just yesterday," Addie said.

Nate's hard stare turned to Rusty. "What's he like, Rusty?"

"He's all right," Rusty said carefully.

"All right then. I seen Mr. Fabi's truck parked outside the bakery on the way up here. I reckon the new man must'a bought it."

"I'll go with you," Snooks said.

"No, you won't," Nate said. "One colored knocking at night is enough." To Addie, he asked, "Where's my long coat?"

"I washed it yesterday. It's drying in the shed out back. I don't know that it's dry yet."

But Nate had already grabbed a gas lamp from the stove, stepped out the back door, and was gone.

NATE MOVED SILENTLY down the dark garden rows behind his house. There was no moon, and the lamp shone eerily on the rows of okra and collard greens. He moved past them with the swift ease of familiarity. He'd dug that garden with his own hands. He and his wife had planted every vegetable there.

A tiny creek flowed at the far end of the yard behind the shed, which was also used as a curing house for tobacco and ham. He unlatched the shed door, stepped inside, pulled his long coat off a meat hook hanging from the ceiling, closed the door, and thrust one hand up the sleeve of his coat.

As he did, he heard a splash in the creek just a few yards behind him. He froze, suspecting it might be a beaver. He listened but heard nothing else, so he stepped away from the door, then heard another splash.

He extinguished the lamp, slipped his coat all the way on, and moved around the side of the shed toward the creek.

He peered into the darkness, seeing nothing at first. The water was illuminated from the light seeping out of the houses on the top side of the Hill, the reflections creating short shadows in the trees on his side of the bank. From where he stood, he could see the bank for a few yards. But nothing farther.

Then twenty-five yards out, less than twenty steps away, he saw the boy.

Nate Timblin was a man who, on paper, had very little. Like most Negroes in America, he lived in a nation with statutes and decrees that consigned him as an equal but not equal, his life bound by a set of rules and regulations in matters of equality that largely did not apply to him. His world, his wants, his needs were of little value to anyone but himself. He had no children, no car, no insurance policy, no bank account, no dining room set, no jewelry, no business, no set of keys to anything he owned, and no land. He was a man without a country living in a world of ghosts, for having no country meant no involvement and not caring for a thing beyond your own heart and head, and ghosts and spirits were the only thing certain in a world where your existence was invisible. The truth was, the only country Nate knew or cared about, besides Addie, was the thin, deaf twelve-year-old boy who at the moment either was riding a freight train to Philadelphia or was a full-blown ghost wearing a schoolboy cap, old boots, and a ragged shirt and vest, standing ten feet from him and tossing small boulders into the Manatawny Creek before his eyes. Which one was it?

"Dodo."

It was surprise that caused him to utter the boy's name, for he knew he might as well have been talking to himself. The boy couldn't hear. Even so, the child was busy, moving with the swiftness of an athlete, sorting through stones at the riverbank, stacking large ones to make some kind of embankment along the creek's edge, tossing smaller rocks into the water.

Nate knelt, relit the lamp, and held it high, waving it to get the deaf boy's attention. With Dodo, everything was sight, feel, and vibration, not sound. The light cast an eerie glow on the water. Yet the boy was so involved in what he was doing that Nate had to wave the light several times.

The boy saw the lamp's reflection in the water first, then dropped the rock he was holding, turned to the source of the light, and stood up straight, a thin arm raised in a shy hello as Nate approached.

Nate pointed at the rock formation. "What you doing, boy?"

Dodo smiled. He motioned Nate closer. He drew a wide circle with his arms, demonstrating a circle of rocks, then aped holding a cradle like he was rocking a baby.

"Say what now?"

The boy rubbed his hands together, as if creating magic or heat, then cupped his hands to his ear, as if he could hear sound.

Nate shook his head, not understanding. He stepped inside the embankment of rocks, which formed a wall about two feet high. They were shaped like a kind of five-by-five box.

"What kind of foolishness you workin' on here?"

Dodo looked at him blankly, then rubbed his hands on his pants, drying them.

"You got a hole in your head, son? Was you riding the train this morning? Was that you?"

Dodo blinked, standing patiently, still rubbing his hands on his pants. Nate gently touched one of the boy's hands. They were freezing. He placed the lamp high, holding it so that his lips could be seen. The boy had not been born deaf. An accident killed his hearing. A stove blew up in his mother's kitchen when he was nine. Killed his eyes and ears. His eyes came back. His ears did not. But he could read lips. Nate held the lamp next to his face so Dodo could see them.

"What you doing?"

The boy's eyes danced away, then he said, "Making a garden."

"For what?"

"To grow sunflowers."

"CJ and them said you was on a train this morning."

Dodo looked away. It was his way of ignoring conversation.

Nate calmly reached out and slowly turned the boy's head so that the boy faced him. "Was you on that train or not?"

Dodo nodded.

"All right then." Nate looked about, then pointed to a dogwood tree nearby. "Tear me off a branch from that tree yonder and make a switch. Then come on in the house. Your auntie'll even you out."

Nate turned to move back toward the house. He took several steps, then noticed that he was alone. Dodo remained where he was, amid his rock embankment.

Nate waved him on, irritated. "C'mon, son. It's cold out here. Your auntie'll warm your little toasters and it'll be over."

Dodo's breath quickened, but he stood where he was.

Nate took several quick steps to close the distance between them, knelt, and placed a big hand on the boy's shoulder. "Taking a lickin' is to your benefit, son. The truth never hurt nobody. That was you on that train, right?"

"Yes."

"You picked a poor time to go jollying. You know that, don't ya?"

Dodo nodded.

"Well then. When you hauls trouble to circumstance, you got to pay. Your auntie'll heat up your little cookers for a minute. The lesson behind it will last, and that'll do it, I reckon."

He reached for the boy's hand, but instead of reaching out, the boy drew from his pocket a folded and wrinkled white piece of paper.

Nate gently removed it from the boy's hand and, unfolding it, held it up to the lantern. He read the words slowly, running his eyes closely across the paper. When he was done, he lowered the paper and his gaze settled on the boy. "I can't read fancy words, Dodo. But Reverend Spriggs inside reads good. We'll ask him to figure them out."

Dodo spoke. "I know what it says," he said.

"What's that?"

"My ma's dead."

Nate was silent a moment. He peered up the slight embankment, toward the shed and the house, thinking to himself of all that was wrong in the world. So many of God's dangers, he thought, are not the gifts they appear to be.

"You don't need no paper to tell you your ma's got wings, son."

"Then why I got to leave?"

"Who says you leaving?"

"This paper says it."

Nate gently took the paper from the boy, crumpled it, and tossed it in the creek. The tall man leaned down and tapped the boy's chest gently. "God opened up your heart when He closed your ears, boy. You got a whole country in there. Don't fret about no paper. That paper don't mean nothing."

He took the boy's hand, and led him up the slight embankment, around the shed, and toward the house.

5

The Stranger

Two days later, Moshe was fast asleep in a chair next to Chona's bed when knocking at the door downstairs awakened him. He watched through heavy eyelids as Addie, sleeping in a chair on the other side of the bed, woke up, staggered sleepily to the doorway, and clomped down the stairs to the darkened grocery store below.

Moshe looked at his watch. It was 4:30 a.m. He gazed at his wife. She lay with her eyes closed. He leaned forward and checked her pulse, then placed his hand on her chest. She was, he noted with relief, breathing, still very much alive.

Addie marched back upstairs and stood in the doorway, looking irritated. "There's a man down there wanting to see you."

"Tell him to go away."

"He won't."

"Who is it?"

"He's the feller who bought Mr. Fabicelli's bakery."

"He's a baker?"

"I don't know what he is."

"What's he want?"

"He said something about"—she paused—"giving away hollers."

"What?"

"Something about helping Miss Chona and hollers."

"Hollers?"

"I reckon it's Jewish words, Mr. Moshe."

"How do you know it's Jewish words?"

Addie frowned. "I don't know what it is. I'm guessing. Whyn't you ask him yourself? He came by yesterday, and the day before that. He came here three times already."

"Send him away."

Addie stood in the doorway, wavering, then with decided movement, stepped into the room, pulled her chair close to Chona's head, and sat hunched over, her forearms resting on her knees, and stared at the floor. She glanced at the sleeping Chona through misty eyes, coughed, then wiped her tearing eyes with the back of her hand.

"I ain't going back down there."

Moshe hesitated, confused. Between Addie and Chona, he felt like a Ping-Pong ball. The two women had taken turns babying him over the years. He never had to cook. Nor clean. Nor do any of the chores that he'd had to do as a child back in the old country. But they conspired against him. Chona gave Addie a voice, let her run the store, make decisions, run the place while she read her socialism books and crazy-women nonsense. Now look at this mess! His own help in his own house was telling him to answer his own door in the middle of the night. If Chona left this world, he'd be stuck with Addie nagging him to death. He wanted to stand up and yell, but instead found himself staring at his wife. He leaned over, gently rubbing his wife's forehead. "Suppose she wakes while I'm downstairs? Or doesn't wake at all?"

Addie, seated on the other side of the bed, had gathered herself. She reached over and fluffed the edges of Chona's pillow, then wiped her face gently with a soft cloth. "She wakes every day, Mr. Moshe," she said. "She wakes like a clock. She's all right."

Moshe took one last worried glance at his sleeping wife, then made for the door. At the bottom of the stairs, he turned on the light, walked past the rows of home goods, boxes, and jars of candies in the darkened store. Dawn was coming. As he approached the glass-paned outer door, he could see the sunlight peering over the edge of a small figure whose silhouette was framed in the doorway. He opened the door a crack and found himself peering at a small, stout Jewish man, in his thirties, with sparkling eyes, a thin mustache, and wide corners at his mouth, giving him an impish look. The man looked vaguely familiar. He was also smiling, which made Moshe hate him immediately.

"Good morning," he said in Yiddish.

"What do you want?" Moshe replied in English. He was in no mood for favors.

"Don't you remember me?" the man asked. He spoke again in Yiddish, which irritated Moshe even more. It meant he definitely wanted something.

Moshe snapped off a quick response—"Ver fahblondjet! Trog zich op!" (Get lost!)— and pushed the door to close it. But the man jammed a mangled old boot in the doorway, which was struck by the closing door.

"Ow!" he cried. "Could you let my foot out?"

"Will you put your foot in the road if I do?"

"I will."

Moshe pulled the door slightly ajar to release the foot, but instead of pulling his foot out, the stranger placed his forearm on the door and tried to push it open farther. Moshe, surprised, held it firm, leaning against it. "What are you doing?"

"I just need flour!" he said.

"We're closed!"

"I need kosher. For challah bread."

Moshe frowned and sucked his teeth. "Challah," not "holla." That's what Addie heard. He pushed against the door to close it, but the man on the other side of the glass-paneled door held firm. "Is that what you told my maid?" Moshe asked.

The man chuckled. "Another American Jew with a maid. She's rude," he said.

"Go to Reading. They got plenty kosher there! And rude maids, too, if you want one," Moshe said. He pushed against the door, but the man held firm.

"That's twelve miles away!"

"What am I, a taxi? Get a horse and buggy then!" Moshe pushed against the door harder. To his surprise, the man, whom he could see through the door, was much smaller than he was and yet still firmly held his side quite easily.

I have to eat better and sleep more, Moshe thought. He pushed harder, and to his disbelief, the door remained cracked. The man held it partway open without straining.

"What's wrong with you?" Moshe snapped. Frustrated, he threw his shoulder into the door. The little man did the same, and the door remained cracked a precious few inches, wide enough for Moshe to see the outline of his adversary's face, which, much to his consternation, was not straining at all. "What kind of devil are you!" he cried.

"I just need flour! To make challah."

"Get it someplace else!" Moshe pushed with all his might now. Sweat broke out on his forehead. His teeth clenched tightly, the side of his face pressed against the edge of the door. He glanced at his adversary through the glass panel; his face was just inches away. The small man, still not working hard, held his side. He appeared to be amused. Was he some kind of demon? *The angel of death*, Moshe thought. *Come for my wife!* He suddenly felt helpless. He wished Nate were here. Nate was strong enough to slam the door with one arm and push this monkey to the street. Or his cousin Isaac. One glare from Isaac would send this mule fleeing. But he was alone. He almost called out for Addie, then decided against it; he was too embarrassed. Instead, he pushed now with everything he had, every muscle straining. Still, the stranger, who seemed to have the might of three men, held firm.

Moshe felt his strength ebbing. He was exhausted. Between running the theater and all-night vigils at Chona's side and not eating, he hadn't much energy anyway. He felt his spirit leaving his body through his feet. *Ridiculous*, he thought.

"Please go," he gasped.

"I want to tell you something," the man said.

"You're a devil!" Moshe grunted in Yiddish through gritted teeth, then said to himself, *Why am I speaking Yiddish? I hate Yiddish.*

From the other side of the door, the little man said evenly, "Do not call me a devil. I am a dancer."

"Dance down the road then, or I'll yell for the police. You're breaking into my property!"

"I'm not breaking in."

"Get away! My wife is sick."

"That's why I'm here," the stranger said. With one great shove, he pushed the door wide, sending Moshe tumbling backward. Moshe landed on his rear end on the cold wooden floor next to the glass-counter butcher case with a heavy *thunk* that shook the bottles and goods on the shelves.

From the floor, he heard Addie yell from upstairs. "What's going on down there! Y'all be quiet!"

Moshe looked up, expecting the stranger to stomp into the store, lean over, and clobber him.

Instead, the little man stood in the doorway several feet off, peering down, his hands on his hips, his stout body filling the doorway. A tallit hung out from his waistband. His fedora was worn and his suit was ratty, as if mice had chewed on the edges. His shirt was white, and a clipped string tie hung down to his waist. He puffed his cheeks and looked about the darkened store. "Don't worry about your freethinking Jewish wife, friend. She won't swallow her birth certificate anytime soon. Her type of Jew does well in this country. I've seen it."

"May onions grow in your navel, to talk about my wife that way!"

"That's a Spanish saying, friend. Do you speak Spanish?"

"No. Do you?"

"As a matter of fact, I do. I've even been to Spain."

"Then do me a favor, you nut. Go back there!"

"Not till I get my flour!"

Moshe instinctively fell back to one of the many wily tricks he'd learned as a child in Romania, when the leaders of the traveling Jewish theater troupe of which he was a part would stand at the edge of town, facing hordes of Russian peasants armed with rifles and clubs demanding last-minute payment for some infringement, usually imaginary, on the part of the troupe, for it was always easier to refuse to pay for entertainment already provided, especially since the lovely Jewish maidens whose dancing inspired the peasantry to enjoy the troupe in the first place weren't putting out. Moreover, since then, Moshe had picked up a few tricks of his own in twelve years of negotiating with hard-boiled band managers at his theater.

Seated on his duff, with one hand leaning on a glass cabinet holding candies, sewing needles, and other store supplies, he looked up and said gently, "I will leave it to you, friend, to decide what is best for you to do; for while you are a stranger to me, it is my duty to welcome you, for I am no stranger to hardship, having come from a land where a horse's hoof is more valuable than a piece of bread. A horse's hoof, you see, can help plow a field and feed an entire village. But bread? What does bread do? You eat it and then you must bake another. Myself, I have neither. I am but a poor merchant who sells candy and dry goods. Come in. Take all the flour you want. And I will leave it to you to decide what to pay."

The stranger chuckled and said in Yiddish, "Be careful, you Romanian rascal."

"Are you Hungarian?"

"Polish."

"They've got schmeichlers (fast-talkers) in Poland, too."

"Look who's talking. The only thing you'd earn in Poland with your fast-talk is an empty feeling." He glanced around the store. "Poor you are not, friend. The important thing is, I have good news. I come to tell you I found a wife."

"You found a what?"

"A wife."

Moshe, seated on the floor, stared up at him, stunned. "Why should I care that you found a wife? I have my own wife to worry about."

For the first time, the man in the doorway, his face brimming with confidence, seemed to wither. He looked genuinely hurt. "But you said I should get one!"

"What am I, mashed potatoes? What do I care if you have a wife? My own wife is sick at this very moment. Pox on you that you should bother me at this time. Yellow and green, you should become! Take all the flour you want and go flap your tongue someplace else, you dumb Pole! Get away from me!"

"But I did what you said!"

"Peddle your fish elsewhere, sir!"

"You said without a wife, why should I come to a dance. But you did not make me leave. You let me stay. And I danced. That's why I'm here now. You invited me."

"I did no such thing."

"You said it. You said wherever I live is home of the greatest dancer in the world."

"What are you talking about? Get out of my house!"

"You don't remember the dance?"

"What dance?"

The man drew his head back in disbelief. He spread his hands in disappointment.

"What dance?" he said merrily. "What dance? The only dance. The *greatest* dance. The greatest dance of family fun and frolic that this country has ever seen. The greatest dance ever!"

Moshe, from his place on the floor, stared at the figure as slices of his memory fluttered back like pages in a book. In the dawn's early light, as the sun glimmered its first peek over the eastern slopes and shone down on the shacks and shanties of Chicken Hill, inside the very building where, in the warm basement twelve years before, love flew into his heart with the grace of a butterfly, and a beautiful young girl, now his wife, churned yellow into butter, pointing out the magic words of the Torah to him, a book she was forbidden to touch, her hand running across the page, revealing the promise held by words of sanctity, love, and history—the shutters of memory flickered again and he saw amid the crowd outside his theater the impish face, the hat, the tallit, the dimples of a young man standing among Jews of all types; then, as if a distant bell were ringing, like a train whistle in the distance, he heard, in distant memory, the wonderful wailing clarinet of Mickey Katz.

And he remembered in full that wonderful cold December afternoon when freshly married and in the full flush of love, he turned the corner of High Street and looked up to see more Jews in one place in America than he had ever seen in his life, the hordes rising into focus like the great temples of Egypt rising in the sunlight of the Arab dawn, hundreds and hundreds of Jews, assembled in front of his theater, eager to flood the door, to make him rich, to clamber inside so they could howl, yelp, dance, and have a joyful moment like the times of old.

And among them a young Hasid who announced that he would not dance with any woman. Because he was looking for a wife.

Staring at the man, Moshe felt the same lightness he felt when he first turned the corner of High Street and saw all those people; it was as if a great weight had been lifted off his chest and placed on his back where it belonged, seated and solid. Twelve years fell away and he was a young man again, standing in the wings of his theater watching Mickey Katz's merry band peeling off the wallpaper with sound as hundreds of happy American Jews danced. And among them was the gyrating, twisting body of the crazy Hasidic dancer. The young man who announced he did not want to dance with any woman. The young man who proclaimed he was not looking for a dancer but rather a wife, yet who danced with every woman on the floor. And what a dancer he was.

"I remember you!" Moshe said excitedly. "You were the greatest dancer I ever saw. What's your name?"

Instead of answering, the young Hasid proudly removed his hat, scratched at his forehead, and gazed down his nose at Moshe, still on the floor next to the butcher's case. He spoke slowly, as if he were a wise old man: "Our rabbinical sages tell us we have three names: One given by our friends. One given by our family. And one we give ourselves."

"So I should call you peas, tomatoes, or onions?"

"Malachi," he said.

He started to say something else, but Moshe, in full flush of memory, was bursting with excitement, for a question had gnawed at him for years and he couldn't believe his luck. "I saw you the next day!" he said. "After Katz left. Outside the theater. You gave me a bottle of plum brandy. We heard something pop on the Hill. We saw black smoke. You said it was a bad sign."

"That was a bad time," Malachi said, stepping into the store and reaching out a hand to help Moshe to his feet. "Those times have ended."

6

Challah

Chona's fever broke two days later. Her feverish rants ceased a day after that. The following day she sat up, then peacefulness seemed to descend on her small frame, and wellness began a long, slow return. But alas, she could not stand for long periods or walk unassisted. A visit from a special doctor from Philadelphia that Moshe's cousin Isaac had arranged confirmed that some kind of blood problem had produced a brain attack that, given her bad foot, may make walking unassisted difficult. Moshe didn't care. Even if she needed a wheelchair for the rest of her life, as long as she could be the Chona of old, he was happy.

After a week, he saw the light return to her eyes. A week later, she began to talk in long sentences, albeit slowly. By the third week, she was standing with the support of Addie and giving orders, demanding to go downstairs and open the store.

Moshe happily complied. He attributed her improvement to the arrival of Malachi, who insisted on dropping by the theater every day to deliver a loaf of his challah for Moshe to carry home to his wife. "This will be part of your wife's healing," he said proudly.

He delivered his very first challah to Moshe at the theater, still wearing his ragged costume of sportcoat, hat, tallit, and homburg. He held the loaf proudly, like he was carrying a child. "You will be my first customer," he said.

Moshe took the loaf with the same dainty care it was offered. Although he never liked challah, he was charmed. He preferred regular white sliced bread and American sandwiches of ham and cheese, which were like everything in America—neat and quick, not fluffy and thick and soupy like old European food. But Malachi's bread was new and something about him lifted Moshe's heart, so Moshe readily tore off a piece, shoved it in his mouth, and nearly gagged. He managed to gurgle a thank-you but only to keep from vomiting onto the floor the turgid mess of what tasted like onions, sand, and grease.

"Wonderful," he said.

"It will bring healing wherever it goes," Malachi said proudly. "It will be like your wonderful theater. It will bring people together."

To a hospital maybe, Moshe thought, nodding. But he smiled and said nothing. He hated to offend his new friend. He promised to bring the bread home to his wife that very evening, but instead he offered it to Nate as they walked home together after the theater closed, the two climbing the tight dirt roads of Chicken Hill in the wee hours. He did it with a disclaimer, saying, "The new baker is just learning."

Nate took a chaw out of the bread, uttered no comment, and tossed the whole mess to a brown spotted mutt who emerged from one of the claptrap houses that lined the roads up onto the Hill. The dog was a nuisance who regularly terrorized them on their night walks home, and when Moshe walked home alone, he took a roundabout route to avoid the creature altogether.

The mutt swallowed the challah in one gulp, and thus, when Malachi asked Moshe the next day if his challah was "bringing healing" to his home, Moshe was happy to inform him, "Yes indeed. And peace as well," for the mongrel, to his surprise, left him alone for the first time ever.

Indeed, as horrible as the challah was, it was proof of the magic that seemed to accompany everything Malachi touched, for the dog never bothered Moshe again. Calamity and disorganization seemed to follow Moshe's new friend everywhere, yet it never touched or stirred him. Malachi was not a neat man. His suit was forever rumpled, his hat furrowed, his tallit frayed, his clear blue eyes always somewhat distant. His head was constantly bowed, his attention deep in the pages of his prayer book, sometimes for hours, even when he baked, allowing his pies and bread to burn. It was clear to Moshe that his new friend was not a born baker. He noted that Malachi's apartment above the bakery was full of junk, items he had gathered, sold, bought, and somehow assembled from here and there, for Malachi confessed he'd been a traveling salesman of one kind or another since his arrival in the new land from the old country. His travels had clearly broadened him, as he was an endless fount of knowledge about everything from automobiles to the iron-making factories of Pottstown. For all his horrible baking and utter disorganization, Malachi had a lightness and boundless enthusiasm about worldly matters. He seemed to bring light and air and goodness to everything he touched. He marveled at the simplest items—an apple peeler, a barrel, a menorah, a paper cup, a marble—with enthusiasm and humor, often holding the item up and saying, "Marvelous! Imagine. Who thought of this?"

MOSHE HAD FEW friends. Most of Pottstown's Jews had left Chicken Hill by then. Nate was a friend, but he was a Negro, so there was that space between them. But with Malachi, there was no space. They were fellow escapees who, having endured the landing at Ellis Island and escaped the grinding sweatshops and vicious crime of the vermin-infested Lower East Side, had arrived by hook or crook in the land of opportunity that was Pennsylvania, home to Quakers, Mormons, and Presbyterians. Who cared that life was lonely, that jobs were thankless drudgery, that the romance of the proud American state was myth, that the rules of life were laid carefully in neat books and laws written by stern Europeans who stalked the town and state like the grim reaper, with their righteous churches spouting that Jews murdered their precious Jesus Christ? Their fellow Pennsylvanians knew nothing about the shattered shtetls and destroyed synagogues of the old country; they had not set eyes on the stunned elderly immigrants starving in tenements in New York, the old ones who came alone, who spoke Yiddish only, whose children died or left them to live in charity homes, the women frightened until the end, the men consigned to a life of selling vegetables and fruits on horse-drawn carts. They were a lost nation spread across the American countryside, bewildered, their yeshiva education useless, their proud history ignored, as the clankety-clank of American industry churned around them, their proud past as watchmakers and tailors, scholars and historians, musicians and artists, gone, wasted. Americans cared about money. And power. And government. Jews had none of those things; their job was to tread lightly in the land of milk and honey and be thankful that they were free to walk the land without getting their duffs kicked—or worse. Life in America was hard, but it was free, and if you worked hard, you might gain some opportunity, maybe even open a shop or business of some kind.

Moshe, the proud owner of two thriving theaters and a grocery store that lost money every year thanks to his American-born Jewish wife, felt proud to be American. He cherished American life. He tried hard to convince his new friend of the goodness of America's ways. He gave his new friend a mezuzah pendant—a mezuzah normally adorns the doorway of a Jewish home. But this pendant could be worn around the neck, and it bore a special inscription on the back that read "Home of the Greatest Dancer in the World." That way, Moshe explained, Malachi would feel at home and welcome everywhere he went.

But Malachi, normally amused by kind gestures and small gifts, returned the mezuzah and politely begged Moshe to give it to Chona, which he did, to her delight. Unlike most Jews, Malachi was proud of what he laughingly called his "clankety-clank" life in Europe that he'd left behind. He didn't mind being a greenhorn. He refused to dress like an American, preferring to wear his tallit under his shirt, the ends of which hung down his pants. He was kosher to the point of what Moshe considered to be useless. A fat worn prayer book, a machzor, bulged out of the back pocket of his oversized pants like a big-city cop's ticket book. It went with him everywhere. He was constantly snatching it out of his pocket, stopping whatever he was doing, flipping it open expertly to a well-read passage, sometimes so moved by what he read that he'd place the book to his chest and bow his head, humming a fervent prayer in Hebrew. One afternoon, as the two enjoyed tea, Malachi placed his prayer book on the table. Moshe tapped it and said carefully, "I'm shy about Jewish things in this country."

"Why?"

"It's not too good to waste time with old things."

Malachi smiled. "The prayers in that siddur volume," Malachi said, "are not old." He picked up the old machzor. "These are actually for high holidays like Pesach and Sukkot. They're not for everyday matters. But I use it for everyday matters anyway."

"Isn't that wrong?" Moshe asked.

Malachi chuckled. "The prophet Isaiah condemns routine, mechanical prayers anyway. So it doesn't matter."

"Are you a rebbe?" Moshe asked.

"Depends on who's asking."

"Doesn't a rebbe have to be educated at yeshiva?"

"Why are you worried if I'm a rebbe or not? So long as your words are uttered thoughtfully and with full intent, it doesn't matter. Our ways give comfort rather than cause sorrow. They bring joy rather than pain. I told you your wife would get well. And she did. What does it matter if a rebbe delivers those words or me? I'm not a rebbe, by the way. I just follow the Talmud, though my bread did make your wife well."

Moshe laughed. "My cousin Isaac said his doctor made her well."

Malachi smiled sternly. "Friend, the truth is neither made her well. Not my bread. Nor your cousin's fancy doctor. The fullness of the earth made her well. Psalm Twenty-four says mankind must enjoy the fullness of the earth. Is bread not part of the earth's fullness?"

Moshe shrugged and let the matter rest. He was so happy that Chona was improving that he was afraid to jinx matters. "Why not come to the house to eat," he said. "You haven't actually met my wife."

"In time," Malachi said.

It was just that kind of response that kept Moshe on edge and curious about his new friend—the series of odd behaviors that seemed to be part and parcel of him. He guessed that perhaps Malachi did not want to meet Chona because he was prohibited, at least in his mind, from touching her. But still, he visited the theater with bread nearly every afternoon after closing his shop and was always bright and cheerful, full of questions about the theater, Moshe's crew, his business, life in America. And while he always asked about Chona's continuing improvement, Malachi declined to talk of his own wife, of whom he'd bragged so freely when he first arrived. Moshe never asked. He understood that marriage for new Jews in America was complex. Some men had wives back in Europe and took new wives here. Others missed their wives so terribly that to mention them brought tears, ranting, and even cursing and fighting. Some worked for years to save enough to send for their wives, only to discover after the wife arrived that both had changed so much the marriage was no longer tenable. Moshe, aware of those matters and happy that his own marriage was intact, stayed quiet on the matter. Still, Malachi's reticence about his past and his wife was a strange divide between them, and it only made Moshe more curious. He wanted to cross it and would have but for Malachi's floundering bakery, which took precedence, for its failure began almost immediately.

Even if Malachi had been the best baker in the world, he'd arrived in Pottstown at a bad time. Fabicelli, the kind old Italian baker who set his week-old pastries out every Sunday evening on a wooden crate for whoever in the Hill wanted them, and from whom Malachi had purchased the bakery, was one of the last white merchants remaining in Chicken Hill. Only Herb Radomitz's Ice House, which delivered ice by horse and cart, and the irascible Lithuanian shoe-store owners, Irv and Marvin Skrupskelis, who scared the bejesus out of everybody, were left. The other white stores had descended to the greener pastures of High Street, just ten blocks away.

And while the kind, old Fabicelli was happy to sell his old delivery truck, bakery, and building that contained the upstairs apartment to the itinerant Jew, he obviously did not sell his recipes, for the rest of Malachi's baked goods were as bad, if not worse, than his challah. His cakes were catastrophes. They looked like finger paintings done by a six-year-old, with dripping icing and ragged edges. His buns tasted like chopped liver. The interior of his meat pies looked like moldy corned beef in need of a painter with a brush and a can of red paint. Even Chicken Hill's Negroes, long used to rotting food and old goods, avoided Malachi's shop. It was a testament to the seventeen Jewish families in Pottstown that the bakery survived the first few weeks at all.

Moshe watched this deterioration with concern, and one afternoon, when Malachi came by the theater to drop off his usual gift of flour and water disguised as challah, Moshe decided to bring up the matter of Malachi's baking. The two were standing near the front of the theater as they talked while Nate and a small crew were preparing the stage for an appearance that night by the mighty Count Basie Orchestra.

Before Moshe could even broach the subject, Malachi, in the mood to talk about his business, tossed a loaf of challah wrapped in brown paper on the edge of the stage and confessed, "I closed the bakery early."

"Why?"

"Business is slow. People don't like my bread. What's wrong with my bread? It's good bread." He leaned on the edge of the stage, glancing at Nate and the three other Negroes in the back who were wiping tables and sweeping up trash from the previous night's event.

Moshe asked carefully, "Have you owned a bakery before?"

"Of course not."

"Why buy a bakery then?"

"It was for sale."

"There are many other businesses."

"What's wrong with buying a bakery?"

"Nothing. But you need to be apprenticed in these matters."

"Why? I am a good cook."

"Baking is not cooking. Baking, from what I understand, requires precision. Did you bake in the old country?"

Malachi did not answer directly. Instead, he removed his hat, ran his fingers through his thick, curly hair, placed his hat back on his head, then fished through his coat jacket pockets, pulling out all manner of baking tools: shaker, sifter, pastry mat, scraper, dough scoop, spatula, and rolling pin. He carefully placed them on the stage edge, lining them up neatly.

"These are my tools. I practice all the time. I'm teaching myself."

"You cannot teach and sell at the same time, friend."

"Why not? Isn't this how they do it in America?"

"Maybe. But *before* you buy a business. Not after."

Malachi's normally bright eyes darkened a bit. "I'm confused. When I first came to America, I went to Pittsburgh. But nobody wanted to hire me because I went to yeshiva. They thought I was too intellectual. I went to a big department store. I said, 'I can be an interpreter because I speak many languages. I speak Yiddish, German, Polish, Russian, and Spanish. I can talk to customers in their language and suggest things.' Instead, they put me to work tagging dresses. So I worked on a vegetable cart. But the man who owned it wanted me to work on the Sabbath, so I left. Then I worked in a diner cleaning pickle barrels. My fingers were swollen from pickle juice. Then I sold wife supplies off a horse and wagon. I eventually bought the horse and wagon from the man who owned them. From there, I saved enough to buy a bakery. It took nine years."

"Was your wife there during that time?" Moshe asked.

Malachi's eyes misted and he ignored the question, pointing to the bakery tools on the stage.

"I practice all the time. Even at night. I make the prettiest cakes. Have you ever tried my pies?"

Given his experience with Malachi's challah, Moshe had no intention of doing that. Instead, he gently pointed to Nate at the back of the theater cleaning and setting up with his small crew. "My Nate can help you find some colored workers."

Malachi shook his head. "Does he keep kosher?" he asked.

"A kosher bakery doesn't need a kosher baker," Moshe said.

Malachi was silent a moment, then said, "It's not wise to mix things the way they do here in America."

Moshe was stunned by this admission, which he considered ignorant. "What difference does it make? You want your business to succeed or not?"

But Malachi wasn't listening. He was staring at Nate and his men, who were busy moving chairs and tables, putting white cloths on the tables, setting up candles. He pointed to the back of the hall. "Who is that boy?" he asked.

Moshe followed the direction of Malachi's finger that pointed to the lone Negro child among the men who were wiping tables near one of the exits. He was tall and thin for his age, not more than ten or twelve, Moshe guessed, athletic, with long arms and neck, and skin that looked as if he'd been dipped into a vat of chocolate. He had a dark oval face, wide nose, high cheekbones, and the longest eyelashes of any child Moshe had ever seen. Beautiful, expressive eyes. The child was sweeping popcorn and candy wrappers off chairs with a whisk broom. He noticed them, smiled shyly, then ducked his head, hurrying back to work as Nate directed, the boy moving quickly, as if he wanted to disappear into the tables and chairs.

Moshe watched, transfixed. He was accustomed to Negroes disappearing, vanishing, and slipping off. But as he watched the Negro boy work his way across the littered dance floor, corralling the garbage, moving tables and chairs with speed and desperate efficiency, he felt a sudden gust of memory, as if his past had suddenly swept into the room and blew into the back of his shirt collar, like a breeze from an open door that puffs into an office and ruffles all the loose papers, sending them to the floor. He saw himself back in Romania at age nine, hungry and exhausted, standing outside a bread shop in Constanța, one terrified eye on the road watching for soldiers, the other eye on the baker's door, as Isaac burst out holding a loaf of challah under his arm like it was an American football, an old woman on his heels, as Isaac hissed, "Hurry, before the soldiers come!" The two boys ran, gobbling the bread like wolves as they fled. No wonder he hated challah.

He looked away from the child to see Malachi staring at him.

"It's the strangest thing about challah," Moshe said. "Do you want to hear?"

"No."

"Why not?"

"Because I know it's not my baking that you dislike, friend," Malachi said. "It's what it stirs inside you. And for that I cannot help you. Only prayer can help that."

Moshe's eyes widened. How could he know? "What are you talking about?" he said. "You are making up things. It's just bread."

Malachi ignored that. Instead, he pulled himself up so he could sit on the edge of the stage, his legs dangling off it, watching the Negro boy work among the line of men moving fast across the dance hall. He glanced at his watch, then at the boy. "It's one o'clock. That child should be in school."

Moshe shrugged. The boy's schooling wasn't his business. "Nate brought him. Nate brings all my workers."

Malachi's eyes grew sallow. Despondency climbed into his face as he watched the Negroes work. "When I got off at Ellis Island, the first American I ever saw was a Negro. I thought all Americans were Negroes."

Moshe laughed nervously. Conversations about race always made him uneasy. He tried to change the subject. "I had never tasted a tomato until I came here," he said cheerily. "I had never eaten a banana. When I did eat one, I didn't like it."

But Malachi seemed distracted. He stared at the boy, watching him toss papers into a small can as he moved toward the back of the hall. "That's what's wrong with this country," he said. "The Negroes."

Moshe shrugged. "They've done nothing wrong. They're good friends . . . my Nate. His wife, Addie, the helpers they bring. They help me a great deal."

Malachi smirked. "Did you know that all the historical sources of Hanukkah are in Greek?"

"What's that got to do with my Negro workers?"

"Light is only possible through dialogue between cultures, not through rejection of one or the other."

Moshe chuckled and nodded at Nate, who had worked his way to the back of the hall, directing the kid. "My Nate doesn't speak Greek."

"*Your* Nate? Does he belong to you?"

Moshe looked flummoxed. "You know what I mean," he muttered.

Malachi frowned. "The American ways you've learned." He shook his head. "This country is too dirty for me."

"What's wrong with you? Nate is my friend."

"Is he now?"

"Of course."

"Because you pay him?"

"Of course. Is he supposed to work for free?" Moshe sputtered.

But Malachi wasn't listening. He stared at Nate, and at the boy working behind him, and at the other Negroes. He watched them for several long moments, then murmured, "I think the Negroes have the advantage in this country."

"How's that?"

"At least they know who they are."

He hopped down from the stage and began to gather his baker's tools, the rolling pin, the spatula, cramming them in the oversized pockets of his worn jacket, the tools clanking as he did so. When he next spoke, he spoke in Yiddish: "We are integrating into a burning house," he said.

"What are you talking about?" Moshe demanded. Malachi turned to look at the back of the hall, his blue eyes following the Negroes. Suddenly one of them began to sing softly, a church hymn; and the others joined in, moving in sync, working faster now, as they shifted tables and tossed garbage into barrels.

I'll go where You want me to go,
O'er mountain, plain, or sea.
I'll say what You want me to say.
Lord, I'll be what You want me to be.

The song wafted up and across the dank, dark dance hall.

Malachi listened a moment, then said in Yiddish: "I would like you to sell my bakery for me. I will drop the papers off in the morning. If there is a profit, please send it to me."

"Where are you going?"

But Malachi was already at a side door and was gone.

Moshe watched the door close, puzzled. He glanced at the stage. Malachi had left several tools behind, a pie pan, a shaker. He thought, *I'll give these things to him when I see him tomorrow.*

But he did not see Malachi the next day. Or the next. He didn't see him again for three years.

7

A New Problem

A month after Malachi left Pottstown, Moshe was inside the theater moving tables on the dance floor after cleaning up the remnants of last night's blues sock hop starring Jay McShann when Nate put down his broom and approached Moshe.

"Can I have a word?"

Moshe almost didn't hear him. He was still troubled by Malachi's sudden disappearance. He had sent Nate over to the bakery a few days later, and Nate reported that the bakery was shut and the apartment overhead was dark. A few days after that, Moshe received a letter, postmarked Chicago, then two days later, a second, postmarked Des Moines, Iowa, both in Malachi's beautiful cursive hand, giving instructions on the sale of the bakery, what should be done with all the tools and utensils, and where to send the money once the sale was complete. It was a headache Moshe was not anxious to get involved in.

Moshe waited a week, hoping somehow that Malachi might change his mind, then he finally moved on Malachi's request. After he made a few inquiries, his father-in-law in Reading produced two Jewish brothers from Lithuania who were happy to buy the bakery. They were greenies, freshly arrived and not cognizant of American ways. It meant Moshe had to go down to city hall and deal with the goyim and their snide questions and puzzling forms. Isaac offered to send a Jewish lawyer from Reading to assist, but Moshe declined. He knew all the town employees. He could get it done quickly. Besides, Malachi was a friend even if he believed in things that he, Moshe, now that he was an American, did not. Malachi, he decided, was part of the past. The old ways simply didn't fit in America. Still, what Malachi had said bothered him. "This country is too dirty for me," he'd said. How dare he! America was clean, clean, clean—far cleaner than Europe. What's wrong with him, that he should speak this way about this great country? Look what it had done for him!

It was what Malachi said about the Negro, however, that bothered Moshe most. "I think the Negroes have the advantage in this country. At least they know who they are."

"That's ridiculous," Moshe had said.

He looked up to find Nate staring at him. "What's that for?" Nate asked, staring down at Moshe's hand.

Moshe found that he was holding a ten-dollar bill. It was a tip he'd planned to give to Nate for his handling of the McShann band with his usual grace. He always tipped Nate. Nate was his man.

He blankly held the money out. "For you."

Nate stared at him. "You all right, Mr. Moshe?"

Moshe looked around the theater. At the back, two of Nate's workers, including the boy Malachi had noticed a month earlier, had returned. He nodded at the boy. "Who's that?" he asked.

Nate's soft eyes smoothed into concern. "That's who I come to talk to you about. That there's my nephew, Dodo."

"What kind of name is that for a child?"

"That's what we call him. He's a good boy. He's deaf and dumb . . . well, not dumb."

"Feebleminded?"

Nate shrugged. "No . . . He had an accident, well . . . Addie's sister's stove blew up one day and something got in his eye. He couldn't see out of it for a while and he still can't hear good. But he talks okay."

"Did you take him to Doc Roberts?"

Nate smiled. It was, Moshe noticed, a bitter smile. Doc Roberts marched every year in the local Klan parade. It was Chona who had called him out about it. Her letters to the newspaper protesting the men who marched down Main Street in white sheets, forcing the Jewish merchants to close, caused more trouble than they were worth as far as Moshe was concerned. Then following it up with a letter pointing out the exclusion of Jews from the Pottstown Tennis Club and the ice-skating rink, which the Pottstown *Mercury* was bold enough to print, didn't help. That caused a stir not just in the town but in the shul as well. Most of the seventeen original Jewish families on Chicken Hill were German and liked getting along. But the newer Jews from Eastern Europe were impatient and hard to control. The Hungarians were prone to panic, the Poles grew sullen, the Lithuanians were furious and unpredictable, and the Romanians, well, that would be Moshe—the sole Romanian—he did whatever his wife told him to do, even though they didn't agree on everything. But the relatively new Jewish newcomers were not afraid to fight back. They seemed to operate with the tacit understanding that while fights were bad for business, if the Jews of Pottstown quit their jobs and businesses, Pottstown would break down in about five minutes. Chona, an American-born Bulgarian, had clout, her American pedigree giving her status with the highbrow Jews at social service agencies who looked down their noses at their newer Jewish brethren who arrived in smelly clothes fresh off the boat speaking only Yiddish. Her father had started the shul. Her husband was the richest merchant in town even though he trafficked in Yiddish plays and nigger shows, and her husband's cousin was the biggest theater owner in Philadelphia with contacts all the way to Hollywood. Isaac's appearance at the chevry, where he defended Moshe's decision to open his theater to the colored, had gone a long way. So no one challenged her openly. Chona was a cripple anyway. Who could argue with a cripple? Let her rant, they seemed to say. But the town's older Jews observed her movements with fearful watchfulness.

Her illness complicated matters, because Chona refused to allow Doc Roberts to treat her. He was the town's pride, a hometown boy made good, and the story of her long trips to doctors in far-off places was an embarrassment. Doc Roberts had even sent word that he would come up to the Hill to see her and had been ignored. Moshe sought to avoid the confrontation by claiming that Chona's illness required specialists, which was to some degree true—if there had been a diagnosis. But there was none, really. Her turnaround came, she was happy to tell people, when Malachi showed up and prayed for her out of his thick machzor. And wouldn't you know it, she declared, the poor man didn't last five minutes in Pottstown. Because people did not support him. Now he's out somewhere healing the world. Pottstown be damned! And we are stuck with Doc Roberts marching in his silly white clown costume every year. Where did he learn to be a doctor anyway?

Moshe heard these things at his house and thanked his lucky stars that Chona's physical troubles made going downtown difficult. But that still did not solve the Doc Roberts problem. He was sorry every time the subject of Doc came up.

Nate, as if to affirm the trouble, immediately dismissed the Doc

Roberts suggestion. "Dodo don't need no doctor," he said. "He had an accident. He got sick. Then he got better. He's all right."

"So what's the problem?" Moshe asked.

Nate's hands slid nervously on the broom handle as he spoke. "I been meaning to ask you . . . if it's okay to bring him round to help out, cheer up the tide and all."

"You can bring whomever you want," Moshe said.

"Yes, but I wonder if I could, as they say . . . get your blessing on the matter."

Moshe looked at the youngster, who drifted closer, cleaning the floor. He was a beautiful boy. He had the smoothest, most glowing dark skin Moshe had ever seen. He shone like a light. Moshe smiled at him. The youngster glanced at him, then looked away, busying himself with picking up trash.

A thought struck Moshe and he recalled Malachi's words about the boy. He glanced at his watch. It was nearly 1 p.m. "How old is he?"

"Round 'bout ten."

"Isn't he supposed to be in school?"

Nate leaned on his broom. "Well, that's just it," Nate said. "Dodo's Addie's sister Thelma's boy. Remember Thelma?"

Moshe faintly remembered a quiet Negro woman Nate had called on from time to time to help in the theater. "I think so."

"Thelma got her wings last month."

"Got her wings?"

"Passed away."

"Oh."

Nate's brow furrowed and his old hands moved up and down the broom handle slowly. He said softly, "Me and my wife's got him."

Moshe looked down at the floor a moment, embarrassed. It rarely occurred to him that he and Nate shared one commonality. Neither of their wives could bear children. They had worked in the theater all day side by side for twelve years but rarely discussed their wives or matters of home. Why bother? Their wives did all the talking anyway. Chona's illness had shaken them all, and her recovery had given them something to be happy about. Or did it? He realized then that he'd always avoided asking Nate about his home life. It was better that way, a throwback to his own fusgeyer childhood, when he befriended children whose families joined the theater troupe, and then one day the friends suddenly departed, some were adopted, others carried off by sickness, disease, bad luck, death, or, in rare cases, opportunity. Food was scarce. Life was cheap. A Jew's life in the old country was worthless. Better to not make friends at all. How *dare* Malachi call this country dirty! It was so much better here.

"Well, I think that's fine," Moshe said. "You can run things as you like."

Nate's brow furrowed. "A man from the state come to the house last week. Says he's gonna carry Dodo off to a special school over in Spring City. Dodo don't wanna go to no special school. He's all right here with us."

Moshe's heart quickened. He felt a request coming, but Nate continued. "The man says he's coming back to fetch him next week. I'm wondering if you might let me slip Dodo into the theater here tonight, just for a few days till the man goes away. The boy's quiet. Can't hear nothing. Won't be scared or make no noise. He can work good, clean up and so forth."

"For how long?"

"Just a couple of days till the man's gone."

"But there's nowhere to sleep," Moshe protested. "It's too cold."

"He can sleep in the basement. We got a couch down there and the old brick fireplace. He'll be all right."

"What about the man from the state?"

"The government ain't gonna trouble theyself too much about a lil old colored boy, Mr. Moshe."

Moshe felt a flash of fear well up inside at the mention of the word "government." The USA. The law. Only the thought of Addie standing over his wife, Addie's tears falling from her face, tending to Chona long after Chona slept, waking up in his chair and still seeing Addie there in the morning, fighting off the sickness, fighting off the devil that was trying to deprive him of the love of the woman who had given him so much. Only that image gave him the courage to ignore the naked terror that surged in his throat and across his spine as he uttered, "I have to talk to my missus, Nate."

"All right then."

But Moshe already knew the answer even as he walked into his kitchen that night. He hadn't expected a different answer, really, for Chona had no fear of the government. When her father had moved to Reading and had insisted that Moshe sell his theater and move to be near him, Chona insisted they stay behind. "We are building our own future," she said. Unlike Moshe, who was terrified of the police, Chona was unafraid to challenge them. When the farmer whose well was closest to the synagogue refused to sell water to the shul for the women's monthly ritual bath, Chona called the police. When the police refused to act, claiming that their cars could not make it up the dirt roads of the Hill, she walked to the station and gave them a piece of her mind about the matter. Then, without asking anyone in the shul, she hired a colored man with a horse and cart, rode in the back as the man drove the cart to town, filled barrels from the town's water spigot herself, and had the colored man walk the barrels into the unoccupied mikvah and pour the water into the baths. The leaders of the shul were so outraged they threatened to drop Moshe and Chona from the rolls. The bad feelings lasted years, the upshot being that Moshe was certain that when he and Chona died, they would not be buried in the shul's cemetery next to her grandparents who had preceded them but on a slender slice of Jewish land owned by the shtetl near Hanover Street next to the cemetery used by the town's colored and poor.

Chona shrugged it off. "When I was dying, where were they?" She chuckled. "Busy trying to make a dollar change pockets is where they were. They call me the kolyekeh, the sick one. I'll outlast them all."

When he walked into the house that night, Moshe found her standing over the stove cooking gefilte fish and onions, and humming to herself. He told her the little deaf boy's mother had died, how Nate and his Addie had taken him in, and how he had allowed the boy to sleep in the basement of the All-American Dance Hall and Theater that night so the state government couldn't take him away from the only family he had.

Chona had her back to him, stirring the pot with one hand, with the other leaning on the countertop to keep her balance. She glanced at him over her shoulder, and one look at her bright, shining eyes clouded in irritation told him everything. Then she turned to her pot and spoke with her back to him.

"What's the matter with you?" she said.

"I said yes."

"You sent him to sleep in the cold theater basement? With the rats?"

"There's a stove down there. Nate and I fired it for him."

"So?"

"It's trouble, Chona. The government wants him."

"For what?"

"To put him in a special place."

"What kind of place?"

"A place for children like him."

He could see, and almost feel, the back of her neck redden. She was silent a moment, then said, "Children like him." She said it in Yiddish, which meant she was mad.

"But I allowed it," he said. "I even had Nate put some extra coals in the stove to keep it warm."

"You think because a child can't hear he's not cold at night? You think he's not afraid of the dark? You think he's happy to sleep in a cold theater? You think because his ears don't work he doesn't feel cold? Or lonely? Or that his heart doesn't break for his mother? You think that?"

"I run a theater," Moshe said. "What do I know about children?"

Chona tapped the spoon on the edge of the pot, placed it on the stove, and spoke over her shoulder.

"Go put that fire out and bring him home."

8

Paper

Chona's decision to hide Dodo from the state of Pennsylvania wasn't even the lead story when Patty Millison—known as Newspaper, Paper for short—held court inside Chona's Heaven & Earth Grocery Store that following Saturday.

Paper—whose smooth dark chocolate brown skin, perky breasts, slim buttocks, and wild cornrowed hair was appended by her running mouth that could keep neither secret nor food, for she ate like a horse but never gained an ounce—was a laundress who held court inside the Heaven & Earth Grocery Store every Saturday. Saturday was Miss Chona's Sabbath, which gave Paper free rein to trade quips, juicy gossip, and other vital local information out of Chona's hearing. The colored maids, housekeepers, saloon cleaners, factory workers, and bellhops of Chicken Hill who gathered near the vegetable bin each Saturday morning to hear Paper's news, however, loved her chatter. Paper knew more news than the local papers, which she actually never read. In fact, there was a rumor about that Paper couldn't read at all—she'd been seen at the Second Baptist church holding the hymnal book upside down more than once. That didn't matter. Her neat wooden frame house on Franklin Street was perched at one of the main roads leading up to Chicken Hill, giving her a view of the town in front and the Hill in the back. Still, it wasn't the location of her home that allowed Paper to serve as the source of the most intrepid reports on the Hill or her being as capable as the most able reporter from the nimble Pottstown *Mercury* or even the mighty *Philadelphia Bulletin*. Rather, it was her effect on the male species. Her beauty, her easy laughter, glimmering eyes, and instant smile for every stranger she met, made her a magnet for men. Men spilled their guts to her. Hardened thugs who gutted one another with knives in alleyways watched her sidle down the muddy roads of the Hill in the afternoon and felt a sudden urge to repent, recalling the innocence of their childhood, the glorious yellow sunlight that kissed their faces when they burst out of church after Sunday School in shirt and tie on Palm Sunday, whirling palm fronds in the air as their mothers laughed. Mild-mannered deacons who sat on their porches with grim faces after toiling all day as smiling waiters in white jackets at the Pottstown Social Club serving meals to the town's white fathers watched Paper's proud breasts swing freely beneath her dress as she floated past and suddenly heard the sound of a thousand drums pounding down the Amazon, accompanied by visions of drowning their bosses. Bricklayers paved her chimney just to watch her bend over the petunias in her gloriously full-flowered yard. Mule skinners hauled barrels of drinking water to her house just to hear the sound of her laughter. Pullman porter royalty from the nearby Reading Railroad floated by her porch regularly to drop off laundry and tell high stories about travels to far-off places like Iowa and Florida and even Los Angeles, dreaming of doing the bunga-bunga with Paper, whom they saw as the wild local. White men found her irresistible, which is why she held no lucrative maid's job. "I'm retired from days work," she told friends with a laugh. "Too much trouble. The men grope and the women mope." White housewives from town who wanted their husbands to climb the greasy pole of opportunity in Pottstown's thriving banking and manufacturing worlds made a steady trek to Paper's house bearing their husbands' laundry, for she washed with such thoroughness and ironed with such professional skill that even Willard Millstone Potts, the town's chief banker, grandson of Mr. John Potts himself, the old fart who lay in the graveyard gathering worms, thank God—parachuted over to hell even if the bridge was out, the old black folks prayed—sent *his* shirts to her house to have them cleaned and pressed. Paper, as the old folks said, had *turn*—talent. Women found her funny and interesting, for unlike most men, she was curious about their opinions, was *yet* to be married, and swore she had no plans to. "I can do better without a man," she declared, which made her high cotton and one up on the Chicken Hill's most respected stateswoman, Addie, Nate's wife, who was a Townsend, and everyone knew those Townsends were too bold to live long anyway. They'd been out of the South too long. Too black, too strong, too bold. They refused to step off the sidewalk when a white woman approached; they forgot to avoid looking a white person in the eye. They forgot all the behaviors that, back home, could have you seeing your life flashing before your eyes as a noose was lowered around your neck—or worse, staring at iron bars for twenty years with your hopes flatter than yesterday's beer, dreaming about old junk that you should've sold, or deer you should've shot but missed, or women you should have married and didn't, having wandered face-first into the five-fingered karate chop of the white man's laws. A colored person couldn't survive in the white man's world being ignorant. They had to know the news. That's why Paper was so important. She was a Pottstown special.

Thus, when she decided that the lead story in her Saturday morning announcements at Chona's Heaven & Earth Grocery Store had nothing to do with Miss Chona's decision to hide Dodo from the man from the state, not one of the group of housewives, bums, and factory janitors standing about questioned it. Everybody knew Dodo was doomed anyway. He was Addie's nephew, the child of her late sister, Thelma, who died three years after a stove in her house blew up and took the boy's ears away. The "special school," which everybody knew wasn't a school at all but rather the horrific Pennhurst sanatorium up the road in Spring City, was just another injustice in a world full of them, so why dwell on it? Plus, Paper's gossip that Saturday was too juicy to ignore. She rolled it out like this:

"Big Soap knocked Fatty's gold tooth out."

Big Soap was a relative newcomer and a Hill favorite, a huge Italian named Enzo Carissimi—six feet six, majestically built with wide shoulders, huge hands, alluring brown eyes, and a gentle nature—who was constantly bursting into laughter. He had emigrated from Sicily to America at twelve with his extended family, one of the few white families still on the Hill. Fatty Davis, a clever, stout, two-fisted, gregarious hustler who owned the Hill's only jook joint, was also twelve then, and the two became fast friends. Fatty happily served as Big Soap's translator and English tutor, the two sharing a love of building and hustling up dollars. After graduating from high school, they worked at several plants together, the most recent being Flagg Industries in nearby Stowe, which made steel nipples and fittings for steam pipes. They often walked home from work together.

Paper's announcement quickly drew a crowd. Rusty, standing at the edge of the group, received the news with disbelief.

"You telling what you seen, Paper? Or what somebody told you?"

Paper's huge brown eyes landed on Rusty, whose lean frame tensed as Paper's eyes took him in. "Rusty," she said patiently, "I *seen* Soap knock out Fatty's tooth, okay? With my own eyes. Yesterday."

"How come I ain't heard nothing from Fatty about it? I was over to his jook last night."

"Doing what?"

"That's my business."

"Did you see Fatty last night?"

"I wasn't looking for him. I was taking care of some business."

"Well, whatever that business was, Fatty wasn't in it. 'Cause he drove to Philly last night to get his lip fixed. His top lip had swolled up to the size of a hot dog."

The women standing in the circle laughed. Addie, working the far end of the counter near the back of the store, drifted over to listen. "Were they drinking?" she asked.

"I don't think so," Paper said.

Rusty smirked. "How do you know? You smell their breath?"

Paper tipped her head and gazed at him sedately. Rusty was handsome, she thought, but he looked terrible when he smirked. She wondered if he knew how good he looked when he remained calm as opposed to making those stupid faces. She decided he didn't. He was, after all, like most men: a moron.

"What you got against me, Rusty?" Paper asked coolly.

Rusty, standing with his hands in his overall pockets, reached for his cigarettes and suddenly couldn't remember which pocket they were in. He felt about his overalls, finding himself short of breath. He always felt like this when Paper was around. "All this who-shot-John nonsense don't mean nothing unless you seen the whole thing, Paper. You seen it all?"

"Only the end," she said.

"Which was . . . ?"

"I just said it. Soap popped him."

Still patting himself for his cigarettes, Rusty gave up and dropped his hands in his pockets, feeling as if something had slipped away. He heard himself plead, "C'mon, Paper . . . story it up like you know how. Put a little pop in it, a little scoop, y'know."

"Why should I?"

"'Cause if you tell it any other way, it'll sound like a lie."

For the first time, Paper softened a bit and smiled. Rusty, she had to confess, had some curve in him. He had an innocence about him, and despite the loose-fitting overalls, his muscled arms and firm chest gave her innards a kind of shove, one she hadn't felt in years, not since she was seventeen and took her first and last bus ride out of Vestavia, Alabama, north to points unknown.

"I hear your aunt Clemy's bringing her cheese cookies to the repast after church tomorrow."

"She calls 'em cheese straws."

"I don't care if she calls 'em George Washington. If she brings 'em, will you remember your friends?"

"I might."

Satisfied and now with a full audience, Paper launched in.

"I was weeding in my garden when I seen Fatty and Soap come up the Hill from work. They stopped a few feet from my yard and Fatty said, 'Go 'head, Soap, do it. I know you wanna. Go ahead. Do it. Get it over with.'"

Here she demonstrated, sticking out her lower jaw, her body curving with her back arched. This drew laughter from the crowd, which now included several new customers who wandered in, stranger coloreds from nearby Hemlock Row, Phoenixville, and Stowe, a few day laborers who lived at white farms outside town and came to Heaven & Earth on weekends to enjoy the sights and sounds.

Paper, glancing at her audience, had to work to keep the smile off her face as she continued. "You know how Soap is. He wouldn't hurt a fly. He said, 'I ain't gonna do it, Fatty.' But Fatty kept on him, saying, 'Go 'head, go 'head, get it over with.'"

And here her eyes sparkled and she stood up straight, her beautiful face shining in the sunlight that glowed into the store window, the light bouncing off the fruit and vegetables and cascading into the corners of the Heaven & Earth Grocery Store, illuminating the peppers and carrots, the Saltines and apple peelers, making life seem as full and new and fresh as the promise of Pennsylvania had once been for so many of those standing about who had come up from the South to the North, a land of supposed good, clean freedom, where a man could be a man and a woman could be a woman, instead of the reality where they now stood, a tight cluster of homes enclosed by the filth of factories that belched bitter smoke into a gray sky and tight yards filled with goats and chickens in a part of town no one wanted, in homes with no running water or bathrooms. Living like they were down home. Except they weren't down home. They were *up* home. And it was the same. But moments like this made life worthwhile, for Paper was a banging drum. And rolling out rumors and news chatter was her gospel song, always melodious and joyful.

She stood among them, her eyes glistening. "Soap didn't want to give in, but Fatty kept knocking at him, saying, 'Go 'head, Soap. I'm a man. Go 'head.' You could see the idea kind of hit Soap," she said. "It kind of growed on him. And with Fatty pushing him along, I reckon his mind told him it was okay."

And here she chuckled.

"So he balled up his fist . . . and I mean that white boy reached back and sent that big fist of his rambling through four or five states before it said hello to Fatty. It started in Mississippi, gone up through the Carolinas, stopped for coffee in Virginia, picked up steam coming outta Maryland . . . and boom! He liked to part Fatty from this world. It landed on Fatty's face something terrible. I can still hear the sound of it. Knocked Fatty clean off his feet and sent that gold tooth of his, the front one, sent that tooth rambling."

"Then?" Rusty asked.

"Weren't no *then*, Rusty," she said. "Soap turned and went on home. And Fatty set there on his poop hole. After he figured out his head was still on his shoulders, he got up and started crawling round on his hands and knees like a dog pooping a bone."

"And what'd you do the whole time?" Rusty asked.

"What you think? I went out there."

"You did not!"

"Sho nuff. I come out my yard and said, 'Fatty what's the matter?' He said, 'My gold tooth's gone!' It took us a good while searching round in the dirt, but we found it. That put a little dip in his stride, putting that thing in his pocket. He walked off with a hole in his teeth the size of Milwaukee."

Rusty and the others laughed, and when the cackling died down, Paper stuck a toothpick in her mouth. "Dick Clemens, who works over at Flaggs, he come by later and told me what happened. Turns out some big-shot inspector had come out there. He's a top dog. Shows up twice a year from Philly. They got to spic-and-span the whole place when he comes. Wash down everything: the machines, the windows, the trusses, the posts, all the gadgets. Got to give the beauty treatment to everything.

"Well, Fatty had just got a promotion over there, and Soap was under him. They were a team, but Fatty got too big for his britches. He got high siddity ordering that white boy around. He had Soap doing all the work while he sat around napping."

She paused, surveying the crowd, and out of instinct glanced at the empty chair at the far end of the counter where Miss Chona normally sat, lording over the sweets. The chair was empty.

"When the big inspector come to the room where Fatty and Soap was, he pointed to one of the fire hoses hanging on the wall and said, 'Has this fire hose been taken out and tested?' Fatty told him, 'Yes sir, it's been tested.' 'Who tested it?' 'Well, Soap here,' Fatty said.

"Soap didn't know any more about testing a fire hose than a hog knows a holiday. But being Italian and not speaking English too good, he saw Fatty nodding, so he said, 'Aye, aye, sì sì,' or however them Italians say yes.

"So the inspector pulled the hose off the rack and shook it. A peanut dropped out the nozzle. He said, 'I put that peanut in there six months ago when I was here before.'

Fatty said, 'But it's a clean peanut, sir.'

"Well, that big cheese got mad and fired 'em both on the spot. On the way home, I reckon Fatty wanted to clear things, since he knew Soap's momma will whip Soap bowlegged for losing his job. You know how Soap's momma is. That little lady'll put that giant into a condition! She'll clean his ass up!"

The crowd guffawed, and as they dispersed, several remarked that Fatty, rascal that he was, just had too many jobs, is what it was. He drove a cab. He had a laundry service. He worked at the plant. Plus ran his jook joint and hamburger stand. Others speculated that poor Big Soap felt he owed Fatty, since Fatty had taken him down to join the Empire Fire Company before they worked at Flagg and introduced him to the Irishmen down there who sat around drinking beer and playing cards all day while making Big Soap wash the company's new fire truck and pull the company's old horse-pulled fire wagon around the station just to prove to them he belonged, being that he was the first Italian in the fire company's history. Big Soap just had the wrong kind of friends, they all agreed.

As the crowd chatted, Paper drifted away to the back counter where Addie stood. She waited until the crowd drifted far enough away so that she could not be heard easily, then leaned over the counter.

"Gimme a packet of BC Powder," she said casually, pointing over Addie's shoulder.

Addie reached behind her, grabbed the item, and tossed it on the counter. Her eyes flitted left to the door near the vegetable stand, stopping on a tall Negro stranger in a white shirt and felt cap who stood over the vegetables pretending to regard the onions. Paper glanced at him, then draped her long pretty fingers around the headache powder.

"You got a headache, Paper?" Addie asked.

"Naw. But that nigger's gonna have one. It was all I could do to not tell Rusty about him. Rusty would beat the tar out of him."

"Maybe he's from Hemlock Row."

"No. The Hemlock Row colored are shorter, the heads are different, and they favors one another. He's from the state."

"The state ain't got no colored workers," Addie said. "Maybe he's a Pullman porter."

"If he's a Pullman porter, I'll eat him without salt. Look at them shoes. What kind of porter would be caught dead wearing them raggedy-ass shoes. Plus, I know every porter that comes through here. I'm thinking maybe he's a state man. Might be from the Pennhurst nuthouse. Sent to fetch Dodo."

"A colored? Colored don't do nothing but clean the floor and cheer up the tide out at Pennhurst, to my knowing. All the same. He could be. How we gonna know for sure?"

Paper thought a moment, then said, "Miggy Fludd, from Hemlock Row, she knows every colored up there. She might know who he is."

Addie watched the man, then glanced away, worried. "The state sent a white feller out here to fetch Dodo three times. Same man."

"You must'a really hit his button when you runned him off."

"I ain't run him off. Miss Chona run him off."

"Well, she set him off," Paper said.

The two watched as the man swiveled his head around quickly, looking through the crowded store and glancing around, then moved from the onions over to the okra, fingering one, then another. Paper smirked, "That's something. I never met a colored who worked for the state before. You want me to chat him up?"

"No," Addie said. "He got to pass your house when he leaves. If he's driving a car, write down the license number."

Paper chuckled. "I'm allergic to that. I can write a few wee old letters on a page here and there, but that's it. You want me to tell Fatty? Fatty can straighten him out."

"I thought you said Fatty went to Philly to see about his tooth."

"He'll be back."

"Leave him out of it."

"What about Miss Chona?" Paper asked.

"Keep her out of it, too, for God's sake. She ain't in as good a shape as she looks. If she finds out who he is, she might cuss him out. Or worse, fall ill on account of it, which'll stir up more trouble with the white folks. They about as fond of her round here as they are of peanut shells. Just keep it quiet."

Addie rubbed her jaw for a moment, then leaned on the counter, moving a bit closer to Paper. "One thing," she said, her voice lower. "Miss Chona told the man from the state *three* times the boy ain't in these parts no more. Why they still looking?"

"'Cause somebody on the hill is running their mouth," Paper said.

"How we gonna find the blabbermouth?"

Paper smiled, and her gorgeous eyes lit a shade of near green with anticipation. "Leave that to me," she said.

9

The Robin and the Sparrow

The home next door to Chona's Heaven & Earth Grocery Store was occupied by the lovely Bernice Davis, sister of Fatty Davis. Like Fatty, Bernice was related to just about every black person on the Hill. She was second cousin to Earl "Shug" Davis, driver for the vice president of Pottstown Bank; second cousin to Bobby Davis, who once worked as an all-around handyman for Buck Weaver, the great Pottstown baseball player who played for the Chicago White Sox; and also, by dint of a twisted, convoluted intermarriage between her grandfather and his son's stepdaughter, was great-aunt to Mrs. Traffina Davis, the wife of Reverend Sturgess, meaning Bernice was actually twelve years younger than her great-niece. She also served as stepsister to Rusty Davis, the handyman who fixed everything; fourth cousin to Hollis Davis, the Hill's only locksmith; and polished it off by being niece to Chulo Davis, the legendary jazz drummer who left Chicken Hill to play with the famous Harlem Hamfats in Chicago before he was shot dead over a bowl of butter beans.

Bernice was also the proud mother of, at last count, eight children, all of whom looked more or less like Bernice in varying degrees of skin color from light-skinned to dark.

That was not a bad thing. Nor was it a good thing. Everybody knew Bernice had the kind of face that would make a man wire home for money. The question was, who was the man and where was the money?

Chona, supporting herself with a cane, moved to the kitchen sink that afforded a view of the small clapboard house where Bernice lived. She stared out her window for a long time. The two homes had identical plots, shared a fence, and were twenty feet apart. Yet she hadn't seen Bernice face-to-face in years. She got her information about Bernice from Addie, one of the few on the Hill who talked to Bernice, whom Addie described as the "most disagreeable, mean-spirited, face-beating, strangle-mad soul" on the Hill next to Irv and Marv Skrupskelis—for whom Bernice, ironically, worked as a cook, which Chona thought seemed a right pairing, since if one had to choose the most evil, dispiriting, quarrelsome Jews on Chicken Hill, those two were the champions. She'd heard rumors that Bernice had been "tipping" with Irv for decades, then the rumor flipped that it was Bernice and Marv, then back to Irv until Irv got married and ended the rumors, or half of them anyway. No one, not even Nate, ever dared raise the subject of the father of Bernice's children with Bernice. Even Fatty, who loved to talk to anyone, when asked about his sister, said, "I don't ask her no questions. I like breathing."

Chona stared at the house and sighed. In the last fourteen years they had lived as neighbors, she and Bernice had not spoken more than five words to each other.

It hadn't always been that way. When Chona was a little girl, her father and Bernice's father, Shad, had been good friends. Chona's father, Yakov, arrived from Bulgaria in 1917, one of the first Jews in

Pottstown. He came as a peddler like many Jews did, with a rucksack full of kitchen utensils, used tools, and homemade devices he'd managed to procure from the Lower East Side, where he landed after being released from Ellis Island with six cents, a tiny mezuzah his mother gave him, and a grapefruit that was handed to him by a kind Negro fruit vendor who saw him crying on Delancey Street and felt sorry for him. Yakov had never seen a grapefruit before. The Negro had to show him how to peel it, and when he bit into it, it was so sour and tangy his eyes filled with even more tears and he realized he must give his life to spreading the Jewish Word lest he end up like this odd American, consigned to doling out fruit that caused weeping. He was a kind and generous chap, a hard worker; and after some months of working in a pants factory for $1.50 a week and studying the Torah at night, he had amassed a pile of junk, a bit of savings, and a desire to spread the Word. He headed west.

He arrived in Pottstown with a pile of good junk and limited English skills. He sold his junk cheaply but was quickly driven out of business by the town's hardware-store owner, who fetched the local police to run him off Main Street and up into Chicken Hill, where Reb, as he was called, got a job in a tannery with colored workers and then a second job working with livestock with more Negroes. Reb was a cheerful soul, a man of boundless enthusiasm, who believed the Talmud empowered him with the gift of making everyone around him happy and comfortable, including Negroes, whom he saw as fellow immigrants who, like him, were forced by poverty and lack of resources to learn many skills and continually adjust. After saving enough money to send to Europe for his wife, Reb bought an old sewing machine, and at night, the two sewed ready-made coats, pants, and jackets, which he sold to his Negro coworkers at the tannery who wanted nice, cheap clothing for Sunday church. On Sundays he delivered milk in the early morning hours, sold fresh fruit and vegetables in the afternoon, and at night manned the ticket booth of the local ice-skating rink, for while the Pottstown fathers prohibited Jews from skating in their wonderful ice-skating park, they had no issues with the race that murdered their beloved Jesus Christ roasting wonderful, tasty, excellent, marvelous chestnuts that were so popular they ended up on the table of nearly every Protestant household in town during the Christmas holidays, cooked by none other than Reb himself, as he was an excellent cook. "That Jew," one city councilman remarked, "is skilled."

Reb parlayed his skills into six hundred dollars, half of which he used to buy an old icehouse on Chicken Hill where he planned to build a grocery store with an apartment above it to house his family, and the other half to buy an old distillery atop a knob two blocks away for a shul he planned to call Ahavat Achim to service the town's Jewish population, which he prayed would come. In four years, they did. The Jewish population grew from two to ten to seventeen families, stopping at that number when the town's fathers decided through intimidation, clever laws, and outright thievery that seventeen Jewish families were enough. Even though Congress was beginning to pass immigration quotas into law, the seventeen Jewish families, German, Polish, and one Lithuanian, decided to stay. The groups did not get along. The Germans and Poles despised one another, and all feared the head of the sole Lithuanian family, Norman Skrupskelis, a thick, barrel-chested man of dangerous silences who rarely ventured outside his home, a modest brick house that sat between a pig pen on one side and a ramshackle house on the other. The rumor was that Norman's wife kept him in a cage and let him out only for Yom Kippur, the day of atonement, at which time he would emerge, walk to Reb's icehouse-turned-temporary-shul, pray for a few minutes, then disappear back into his basement, where he expertly crafted wonderful stylish shoes that his wife sold to a local shoe merchant for a fat fee. Norman Skrupskelis's shoes were extraordinary works of art, as comfortable as they were stylish. In later years, his sons Irv and Marv inherited his expert shoemaking ability and opened a store, though both had inherited his personality. Only Irv was temperate enough to manage sales in the store itself—so long as you didn't bring the merchandise back. Skrup Shoes, as they were called, were nonreturnable.

REB FLOHR'S FIRST job was to build his house. He liked to joke that the birth of the shul had as much to do with the birth of his house as it had to do with G-d's will, but the truth was, the actual construction of Reb's house required skills that he did not possess at the time. Muscle. Measurements. Bricks. Wood. And men. Men who could lift and haul things up the steep slopes of the Hill, muddy and unmanageable after every summer rain, cold and unforgiving after every snowstorm. He had no one to help him after he saved his six hundred dollars with plans to build his house and a shul, so Reb hired four Negroes and a fellow coworker from the tannery named Shad Davis, who owned a fat thousand-pound mule named Thunder. Shad lived in an old shack next door to the icehouse where Reb planned to build his store, and Reb noticed that the colored man had done a nice job transforming his old shack. Shad was a mild, neatly attired Negro who, unlike other Negroes on the Hill, avoided coveralls and farmers' clothing, preferring a gentleman's jacket, a tattered homburg, and leather shoes no matter what the job. How he managed to keep his battered coat and hat clean was, Reb thought, a tiny miracle, but then again, the soft-spoken Shad turned out to be the greatest stonemason Reb had ever seen. Shad could look at a plot of land and smell the cracks in the earth beneath it. He could hold a small boulder in his hand, balance it, measure its weight as he held it, and decide where the stone would sit, how much mortar it would need, and in what position it must lie in order to support hundreds of pounds of brick and mortar above it. He and his crew of Negroes built Reb's three-story house, complete with the Heaven & Earth Grocery Store on the first floor, in five weeks.

After the seventeen families arrived and decided to build the shul, Reb suggested that Shad be put in charge of directing the building of their first-ever temple. But the congregation, led by the Germans who always clambered for respectability among the town's white Christian natives, howled their disapproval. They insisted that a young, newly arrived architect be engaged for the design and build, since he was educated at one of America's great universities. Reb reluctantly agreed. After collecting $1,700, which represented the entirety of the congregation's building fund, the architect, a serious young man with a handlebar mustache, clad in fancy knee-high rubber boots, a handsome bowler, and a sheepskin coat, marched to the top of the muddy slopes of Chicken Hill and stood atop the appointed knob of land. He cast an arrogant gaze about the muddy slopes below, the churning yards filled with chickens, pigs, and goats, the open sewage ditches, the Negroes wandering about, then tromped back down the hill to town, whereupon he disappeared into his office, drew a few sketches, passed them on to a local construction crew along with three hundred dollars, pocketed the remaining balance of his fee, and departed Pottstown for points unknown. He was never seen again.

The construction crew started the project. and when the money ran out a month later, they quit. Three months later, the half-built structure collapsed.

Now, with their beloved shul a pile of rubble—some of which was marble, having come from a stone quarry in Carrara, Italy, and bought at a ridiculous price by Norman Skrupskelis, since it was to be used for the women's mikvah to be named in honor of his late mother, Yvette Hurlbutt Nezefky Skrupskelis, whom no one had ever seen since she died in Europe in a town whose name was so complex that the Germans called it Thumb-in-Your-Nose—the congregation faced its first real crisis. Their building fund was depleted. To raise another $1,700 among the seventeen families, who were shopkeepers, railroad workers, and laborers, was impossible. Even worse, Norman Skrupskelis had contributed nearly a third of the initial building fund in addition to contributing the wonderful Torah scroll, which he'd taken great pains to bring from Europe.

The thought of an angry Norman Skrupskelis having six hundred of his precious dollars wasted in a bungled construction project was more frightening than the idea of G-d raining his fury down on Moses and not allowing him to enter the land of Israel. "If I had a choice between being Moses or myself right now," the head of the chevry confessed to Reb Flohr, "I'd choose Moses." The congregation scrambled, calling friends and relatives in Reading, Philadelphia, Baltimore, and even Vermont, reminding their lundsmen of the wonderful part of the kaddish prayer that reads "Let His great name be blessed for ever and ever and to all eternity," and also pointing out that a crazy Lithuanian among them had sunk six hundred smackers into a deal that had melted away and was a cyclops who would clobber all within range if he should find out. With their help, the shul hastily plucked another $350 from its ass and offered it to Reb, saying, "You're the boss. Get moving."

It was then that Reb summoned Shad. The slim colored man climbed to the top of the knoll, leading Thunder and a wagon full of stone. He stood amid the splintered wood, shattered walls, and crushed stone, and peered silently about, removing his bowler hat to block the blaring sunlight and raising his hand over his face. Finally, he pointed to a corner of the splintered ruin. "The north is this way here. Your stone has got to come to the edge. All the way to the end. Run that stone along the edge, shorten it by ten feet on the south side this way, bring it farther along west by about six feet, and you'll have your wall and it'll hold. Then your windows will still face the east where the sun comes up, and you'll have your building."

Reb, with the congregation's relief money in his pocket, agreed, cut a quiet deal with Shad for the entire $350, and when the cornerstone of Ahavat Achim was laid again a month later, it was laid by Shad Davis.

It was an odd friendship, for Shad, as far as Reb could determine, was neither deeply religious nor overly friendly to anyone, including his own people. And while he built wonderful homes of solid brick and stone for others, he barely maintained his ramshackle house that stood next to Reb's Heaven & Earth Grocery Store. The home was built of neither brick nor stone. It was mostly wood and metal. It housed Shad, a wife named Lulu, who rarely spoke to anyone, and two silent, respectful children. Their two yards adjoined, the parcels matching exactly, stretching for nearly an acre all the way back to Manatawny Creek, but the similarities ended there. Reb's yard bore supplies, barrels, a cow, and several chickens for kosher purposes. Shad's yard remained bare, save for his mule, Thunder, and a few vegetables his wife grew. The men rarely talked outside of work, for Reb had learned that in America, what a man does to live often has nothing to do with how he lives. Besides, Shad's genius for building the shul attracted plenty of business from the town's Jewish residents, who applied Shad to the job of fixing up the ramshackle houses they purchased closer to town with brick, stone, and mortar as soon as they could afford to move off the Hill.

Reb believed the genius builder was likely a drinker or gambler until he learned from his wife, who chatted with Shad's wife, that Shad Davis had no long-term plans to stay on Chicken Hill. He was saving every penny to move to Philadelphia, to educate his young children there, then send them to Lincoln University, a Negro college in Oxford, Pa., or perhaps even to Oberlin College in Ohio, the first white university in America to open its doors to the Negro. Reb respected those aspirations. They lined up with Reb's belief that in America, anything was possible, and that Shad, a man of fullness, purpose, and talent, whose word was his bond, deserved the best of what the nation had to offer.

Alas, none of his dreams would come to pass.

Soon after he built the shul, Shad fell ill and died, devastating Shad's family. Reb assumed that Shad's savings would cover his family, at least for a little while, since Shad rarely spent money to fix his ramshackle home. But according to his wife, Shad was suspicious of banks and had placed his faith in a financial advisor who turned out to be as shady and fleet-footed as the shul's first architect. The man vanished right after Shad died, leaving the careful builder's family broke.

It was only because of the two men's friendship that Shad's family survived, for Reb grew accustomed to looking the other way as his wife slipped bread, milk, and butter from his store over to Shad's widow. And when the strangely odd Marv Skrupskelis, son of Norman Skrupskelis, appeared over at the Davis residence to do odd jobs for Shad's widow, and occasionally trailing Shad's daughter, Bernice, about the yard, Reb chose not to speculate, for children were children.

As it was, the families would have likely drifted apart altogether were it not for Chona, who, despite having contracted polio at age four, was an active child and a handful. Getting her to school was a challenge from the first, because Chona at age six refused to ride in any vehicle, wagon, or wheelchair, or in the bed of the ancient truck Reb had purchased for his grocery business. She preferred to walk to school like the other children of Chicken Hill, and since Pottstown's schools were integrated with whites and a scattering of Negroes, Shad's two children, Bernice and Fatty, would find themselves appended by the cute six-year-old Jewish girl in a dark skirt with curly hair that framed her oval face, limping along behind them as they descended the Hill toward the town's brick schoolhouse.

At age nine, Fatty couldn't be bothered with another girl pattering along behind him. He couldn't stand his sister as it was. But Bernice was dying for a little sister. The two girls started first grade together despite the fact that Bernice was a year older. On their first walk to school, Chona announced that Bernice was too tall to be in first grade. Bernice took the insult in silence, but the two cemented their friendship that afternoon when the teacher sat behind the piano and played "Polly Parrot Ate the Carrot," a popular children's ditty. She called each student to the front of the class and played the song, demanding that each child sing. If the child sang, she labeled them a robin. If they didn't, they were a sparrow.

Chona became a robin easily, hopping to the front of the class and singing in a clear, strong voice. But Bernice, the only black face in the class, when summoned, refused to sing.

"You're a sparrow," the teacher announced. "Sit."

Chona watched, stunned, as Bernice moved back to her seat. They were neighbors. They overheard each other's lives: the arguments, the chairs scraping across the kitchen floor, the creaking porch steps, the slamming doors. The one constant Chona loved was the sound of Bernice's voice. At home, Bernice sang like a bird. She had a gorgeous, soaring, beautiful soprano, a sorrowful sound full of sadness and longing. Bernice sang everywhere, in the yard as she weeded her mother's garden, on the porch as she swept, during the afternoons as she picked through the vegetables at the Heaven & Earth Grocery Store for her mother, her voice so clear and angelic that when Chona walked by the Second Baptist church on Sundays with her mother, they would pause just to hear Bernice's voice soaring out above the rest, stronger and more beautiful than ever.

When Bernice sat down, Chona piped up, "Bernie's not a sparrow. She's a robin."

The comment drew chortles from the class and a trip to the principal's office for both of them for speaking out of turn. That afternoon, as the two slowly made their walk home, Chona tried to raise the matter again. "You're not a sparrow, Bernice. You're a robin." But Bernice was sullen and silent.

Chona realized, for the first time, that Bernice was like the twins at shul, Irv and Marvin. Their father, Mr. Norman, who had made her special boot so carefully, was the same way. They were bottled up inside. There was something that was closed. She realized, looking at Bernice, that something inside her had turned off in some kind of way, like a water fixture closed tightly or a lamp that refused to light. But at age six, Chona couldn't express what it was. Instead, she grasped Bernice's hand and said, "I like flowers better than birds." She received a small smile in return.

Over time, the space between them lessened. Chona showed Bernice how to play pinochle, which she learned from watching her father play with the other Jewish men in the back of the store, how to crochet with her left hand or her right, and how to negotiate a flight of stairs quickly by sliding down the banister, her feet not touching the steps.

Bernice taught Chona how to make thick wool quilts that kept the cold out and how to grow parsley and greens and all manner of vegetables in her backyard. The two girls grew close.

Their relationship lasted all the way through high school as they shadowed each other, for neither joined any club or sport. They had to work at home. When both were assigned to make a dress for home economics, Chona dusted off her father's old sewing machine in the basement, a leftover from his days when he first arrived in Pottstown, and taught Bernice how to do French stitching, doing the first stitch on one side, turning it over, and doing the stitching again on the other. They worked on Chona's dress first, then Bernice's. "I'll do the first row on the machine," Chona announced, "you do the second."

They worked on each other's dresses and were delighted by the results. On the day of the exam, they brought them to school and proudly placed them on a table piled with dresses made by the other students. Chona had made a purple dress with azaleas; Bernice, a black dress with yellow daisies.

Their teacher, a gray-haired, pinch-faced soul who always wore black, held up each dress, examining each one and remarking about the handiwork.

When she reached Chona's dress, she was satisfied. But when she picked up Bernice's dress, which was clearly the most beautiful dress of the bunch, she summoned Bernice to the front of the class.

Bernice complied, her eyes blinking in embarrassment. The tall, lean girl glided to the front of the classroom and stood before the teacher at her desk. The teacher held up Bernice's dress and said, "This is not the stitch I told you to use," and ripped at the back stitching, tearing it apart.

As they walked home after school, Chona said, "I'll teach you another stitch. I have a better one." But Bernice said nothing. She glared at Chona in a way that Chona had never seen before.

"You made me do the wrong stitch," she said.

Before Chona could remind her that she had also used French stitching and that she didn't know why the teacher did not point that out, since both dresses were stitched identically, Bernice did something that she had never done in all the years they had known each other.

She picked up her pace and simply walked faster, leaving Chona behind.

The next day, when Chona emerged from her house to join the brood of black schoolkids trooping down the Hill to school, Bernice wasn't there.

Bernice did not return to school that day. Or the next. Or ever. She stayed inside, rarely appearing.

For Chona, the day Bernice Davis closed off the world was the beginning of her own adulthood, for the realization that lay before her had begun to clamp down on her and she could see Chicken Hill and the town for what they really were. She began to have opinions about what lay ahead, and to see the limitations of her own life, too. Her mother wanted her to marry a young Orthodox Jew from Reading she'd found. He was nice enough, a short, dour Pole who was in line to inherit his father's shoe store and was gentle in manner and seemed open to new ideas. But he had a habit of sucking his teeth that she found off-putting, and after having dinner with him once, decided he was horrible and avoided meeting him again. She saw the broken marriages of the town's Jewish community—the miserable housewives, the frustrated husbands; she noted the ragged disputes among the tiny Jewish populace dominated by the German-born Jews who strained their necks to peek over the shoulders of their Christian counterparts, holding their noses in their social service agencies and snobby organizations, looking down their noses at their Yiddish-speaking lundsmen from the European provinces, sending money, secondhand clothes, secondhand advice—in English, no Yiddish allowed. Sending everything but love. She had dreamed of leaving Chicken Hill after graduating from high school and even had a few tentative plans in that direction, but when Moshe wandered into her father's basement and walked love into her life, he changed everything. Here was a man who wanted her to be full, who never blocked the entrance to the doors of knowledge and growth and passion and life's reckoning, who brought her books and records and music. When she married him, she forgot about Bernice and the Davises who lived next door, for life took over. Her mother died two years after she married; her father departed for Reading and a bigger shul; and the challenges of propping up her mild husband so that he might not follow the rest of the Jews in town into obscurity took over, followed by her own illness, which swallowed the whole world. She had her own life and no children to show for it. Other than a hasty nod to Bernice, whose increasing brood of lovely children passed through her store and were quiet, beautiful shadows like their mother, and an occasional laugh with Bernice's brother, Fatty, who never changed, Chona had no room to see to Bernice's life. How Bernice procured her children, with whom, why she had so many, or the manner in which she led her life, Chona never inquired. Her own life was full, yet she felt incomplete. She had no children. Bernice, on the other hand, had plenty. Bernice was rich with children, yet she had blamed Chona for her French-stitched dress anyway, which was not true. The whole business was too complicated and too old, like the overgrown roots of an ancient tree.

But now she had a problem.

Chona had her own child now. He wasn't hers, but he was the closest thing to one. For the past four months, the deaf boy, Dodo, had been a dream. It didn't matter what the other congregants in the shul called him when she wasn't around. He'd come as a matter of conscience but now was a matter of love. He was smart. Sensitive. He saw things other people didn't. Even without his hearing, he understood everything. He was sharp. Bright. And necessary. For years she'd prayed for children, and when none came, she had accepted it as part of life. She'd spend hours reading about politics and socialism and change in places like New York, the wild world of Emma Goldman and progressive Jews, anarchists, troublemakers, union builders, and pacifists who shoved aside the constraints placed upon them to demand the same fullness of American life that others received—Jews who tried, in their own way, to bring light to the world. Isn't that what Judaism should do, bring light and reflection between cultures? All that high-handed talk of Judaism had seemed increasingly useless and distant as she grew older until it folded neatly into the sunshine reality that had arrived in the form of Dodo. The boy brought his own kind of light. She set him up in the back room of the store where she had frequently lain during her illnesses, and he brought light into the dark room in a way that vanquished pain from her memory. The silent, morose child who'd first arrived brought life anew. He was a spark, a whiz. He was there in the morning when she awoke. He wandered into her bedroom to say good night. He was twelve and learning his all-boy things out of sight of others; he drew pictures, played with balloons, and read comic books in his room. He fished in the creek at night. He cleaned the store after-hours. He was remarkably aware for someone who had no hearing. He read lips expertly. He collected bottle caps and marbles, loved jelly apples and roasted chestnuts, and found Chona's father's accordion and played it terribly in the basement. He littered her kitchen with peach pits. On Sabbaths, he was there in the morning when she awoke, having doused the lights the evening before and lit the stove the next morning. He couldn't sit still. As she and Moshe read quietly upstairs, the noise of banging and clattering emerged from the room behind the store where he slept that was equipped with a sink and wood stove. On other nights, Chona would wander down, turn on the light, and find the room a junkyard of joy, complete with mops used as broomsticks, old comic books, chalk, rocks, arrowheads, and wires. From the overhead fan, he hung flying contraptions that dangled on wires and spun in circles. In four months, he had become a living embodiment of l'chaim, a toast to life. A boy. A boy living a life. Something she'd wanted and prayed for ever since she was a girl. Who cared that he was Negro. He was hers!

And he responded. She had no idea how easy it would be. She never had to tell him to do anything twice. Brush teeth. Comb hair. Wash face. Hang laundry. Stack shelves. He loved chocolate. She had to force herself not to give him too much. Each day he would sweep and clean and work with such force and focus that she'd have to slow him down, and then, at the end of the week, he'd appear at the back of the store after closing and hold forth his hand containing a marble, indicating that he'd like to use that to pay for his piece of chocolate. It was a game she played with several neighborhood children. They would come into the store hungry, eyeing a can of pea soup, and ask, "How much does that cost?" at which point Chona would say, "How much do you have?"

"I only have a red marble."

"Do you have any green marbles?"

"I might have one at home."

"Okay. Take the soup and go home and bring me the green marble tomorrow, and I'll decide if that's the one I want."

The next day the child would bring in a red marble. And she would say, "No, that's not the one. I don't like the color. I want a blue marble." So the child would disappear and return the next day with a blue marble. Then a green one. Until the week passed and the marble was forgotten and the kid would come in the next week asking for a certain vegetable or a box of crackers and pay with the wrong color marble, and the game would begin again.

Back and forth it went, sometimes for weeks. There were several marble kids, and Dodo became one of them, joining her Marble Choir. She never gave in, never gave him too much chocolate. But she gave him enough. A red marble for a piece of chocolate here. A blue marble for a piece of chocolate there. The marbles she accumulated from the neighborhood kids she kept in a jar. The pile of marbles in the jar would diminish mysteriously, and a week later, the same marble would appear in a child's hand. She never minded. She understood. She loved Dodo's generosity. He was a simple child of love, easy to satisfy, easy to give.

She knew, even from the beginning, that the dream was not meant to last. She had not meant to love him so much. It was only shelter they were providing, a respite for the ever-loyal Nate and Addie and Addie's late sister, Thelma, who at times had helped nurse Chona during her many sick periods. But now, four months into keeping Dodo safe, the man from the state had discovered the boy's whereabouts. She knew the man faintly—Carl Boydkins. They were close in age. They'd attended the local high school at the same time. She recalled he'd been an athlete of some kind—football maybe. And that he, like most of her classmates, was not particularly fond of Jews. He was from one of the farming families that lost out by not selling when the big steel companies bought several thousand acres near the Manatawny. It had not worked out for those families that stayed.

So when Carl Boydkins came into the store asking questions, she'd tried to be pleasant. But he was in no mood for it. He made a few remarks about breaking the law and harboring fugitives. She was thankful that Moshe had not been there when the man appeared, because Moshe would've turned Dodo over instantly. Moshe was afraid of the authorities. But Moshe didn't know. Not yet. He would, though. The news about the two men that the state, first Carl Boydkins and now the Negro man, had sent to the store to find Dodo would pass quickly from Addie to Nate, and from Nate, it would pass to Moshe.

That's why she needed Bernice. Bernice had all those children—eight at last count. They looked like the colors of the rainbow, from light to dark, tall to short. How she got them, and who their fathers were, was not Chona's business. But none of Bernice's kids looked alike—they were all Negro-looking, and that was good enough.

Chona turned away from the window, cane in hand, and walked slowly to the front door of the store. Addie was behind the counter. Dodo was standing on a milk crate, stacking boxes of crackers onto shelves. She raised her walking stick in the air at him to get his attention. When he looked over, she said, "Come with me."

He complied. They left the store and walked the ten steps to Bernice's front door. Chona knocked. Bernice opened it.

There was no light in Bernice's eyes now. She looked worn and tired. Her face, thin and drawn, looked as if she'd been staring at the sun too long. But she was, Chona thought, still beautiful, made more beautiful by the lamp inside her, the lamp that always stayed dark. Behind her, several children peered curiously at Chona.

"What's the matter?" she said. She spoke calmly, nonchalantly, as if they had just finished talking last week, as opposed to not having spoken more than five words in fourteen years.

Chona felt her face flush. She found herself stammering, stuck for words. "I wanted you to meet . . . I have Thelma's boy."

"I know Dodo," Bernice said.

"He's staying with me now."

"And?"

"I was wondering if"—Chona halted—"there's a man from the state—"

But Bernice didn't let her finish. She nodded at the back of the house, over her shoulder, at the adjoining yards. "Cut a hole in the fence where nobody can see it," she said. "When the man from the state comes, put him in my yard while my kids are playing. One colored looks just like the other."

Chona smiled and turned to Dodo to explain that he had Bernice's permission to slip into her yard, that, in fact, she and the dear woman at the door had been friends at one time. But she was overwhelmed with confused emotion, for she'd also wanted to thank Bernice, to shake her hand, to hold her hand as she'd done when they were children and say, "You're not a sparrow. You're a robin," and ask why she had not heard the sound of her singing for years, a voice that had opened up a world of understanding for her when she was a child.

But before Chona could turn back to her, Bernice had closed the door and was gone.

10

The Skrup Shoe

Earl Roberts, known in Pottstown as Doc, had long heard the rumors of the Jewess in Chicken Hill hiding the Negro child from the state illegally. He had learned about it from his distant cousin Carl Boydkins. Carl worked for the state welfare office. The two men were not close. They had grown up on neighboring farms as boys. Both families were said to go back ten generations to the Blessington family, said to have arrived on the *Mayflower* all the way back in 1620. It was a point of pride for both families, although, as it turned out, neither was tied to the *Mayflower* at all. The family was actually tied to an Irish sailor named Ed Bole, a distant relative who worked as a manservant for Chinese emperor Chaing Kai Wu in Monashu Province in 1774. Bole, an English seaman and a drunk, had been tossed from the English freighter *Maiden* that year after the captain grew tired of his drunken shenanigans and left him at the port of Shanghai. He was picked up by Chinese authorities and dragged before the emperor, who found the idea of a white man serving him tea and Chinese crumpets, known as mantou, wonderfully satisfying. After three years,

Bole escaped and made his way back to England, announced himself as Lord Earl Blessington of Sussex, and with his newfound knowledge of the Chinese language and China teas talked his way into a job at a British shipping company, where he eventually made a fortune in salt and Chinese medicine, marrying the daughter of an English trader in London. In 1784, when a distant cousin of Bole's in Ireland showed up in London and started asking questions, Bole hastily packed his wife and four young children onto a ship called the *Peanut* and sent them off to America, a land where nobody asked questions about white people's pasts. Three days after the *Peanut* sailed, Bole choked to death on a char siu bao pork bun, for which he'd developed an affinity while living in the Land of Wonder. Luckily, he'd sent his wife and children abroad with a tidy sum of four thousand dollars, a fortune in those days, plus a nanny to help them, with the idea that it would be some months before he would join them—an idea that ended, unfortunately, when that char siu bao pork bun slid down his windpipe.

When news of the death of Lord Blessington, née Bole, reached his widow in America, it prompted the usual hand-wringing, howling, and hairpulling, after which she collapsed in tears and into the arms of her faithful nanny. The nanny hugged her tightly. Sparks flew. The two women promptly fell in love, decided to live together, pulled out a map, saw a creek near Pottstown, Pa., far from the prying eyes of New York society—which regarded the widow with suspicion anyway, since she seemed to eye the male species with neither contempt nor scorn but with total disinterest instead—and moved to Pottstown as the Blessington sisters, buying a huge tract of land off Manatawny Creek. They raised the children, with the help of local servants and farmers, and split the tracts among the four children after the women died.

Neither Doc nor Carl had interest in questioning their family lineage, for their childhoods were as full of as much happiness as any descendant of the *Mayflower* might enjoy. They were white Christian men born in an America seemingly ready-made for them. The two families, now splintered off and bearing different last names, were happily ensconced on neighboring farms at Pine Forge on wonderful acreage bordering Manatawny Creek, full of sunflowers and pastures and rich soil. The two families lived across the creek from one another: Doc's family, the Robertses, on one side; Carl's family, the Boydkinses, on the other. The two families often traveled to church together on Sundays by carriage—Presbyterian, of course. The civilized services filled the sanctuary to the brim with good white people. Those were wonderful days, Doc's childhood, full of strong men whose handshake was their bond and women who knew how to cook and raise children. Nice, clean families. This was before the "new people"—the Jews, the Negroes, the Greeks, the Mennonites, the Russian Orthodox—arrived.

The two families lived peacefully until just before the Great Crash, when Doc's father saw the future and sold out, thank God. But the Boydkins family stayed, and they suffered, for the new owner of the Roberts tract was a good Christian man who forged iron bits and steel parts, which produced smelly garbage and black runoff from dyes even though he promised the Boydkinses he would bury his garbage rather than pour the muck from his forge into the beautiful creek. They were pleased when he made that promise and believed him. He was, after all, a good Christian.

Shortly after, he was joined by a second man, another good Christian, who also kept his word. Then a third partner came, another good Christian . . . who, well, he was said to *want* to be a good Christian, which counted for something, though he left his wife for a fifteen-year-old girl named Uma who had boobs the size of cantaloupes and was said to have spent time in the Muncy penitentiary. The fellow eventually moved to New Orleans with his new wife and was replaced by a new man, an Irishman named Fitz-Hugh who was said to have made his fortune in opium. Fitz-Hugh bought out the original owners and thereupon the small one-man mill became two mills with four workers apiece. Then three mills, then four tiny mills. The Boydkins clan soon found themselves waking up and peering out their kitchen window to see eight workers slogging back and forth to the bank of the Manatawny, dumping buckets of sludge into the creek all day long. In six months the eight workers became nine, then twelve, then nineteen. The four mills became seven, then eight, splitting like amoebas, dotting the hillside above until the mills were replaced by small factories that made pipe nipples and tiny bolts and iron pieces, belching smoke from small chimneys into the clear Pennsylvania sky. The small factories then split into bigger factories that crafted iron pipes, steel fittings, and glass bottles for whiskey distilleries, followed by bigger factories that crafted eight-foot iron beams, joists, barrels, pipe fittings, castings, signs, entire window frames, and steel girders. In eight short years, the tiny mill was gone and in its place was a rambling, rumbling, half-mile-long gray factory-fortress that thrust a hundred-foot smokestack into the sky that belched gray fumes twenty-four hours a day. The crews of workers who tossed black muck to the Manatawny were gone, replaced by three six-inch pipes that vomited churning, filthy sludge into the once beautiful streams that fed the Boydkinses' cows and watered the crops. By the time the Boydkinses cried foul, three one-hundred-foot chimneys churned black smoke into the sky; 225 cursing, laughing workers speaking every language under God's sun trooped in and out of the buildings in three different shifts; and the work whistle shrieked three times a day including Sundays—all within 150 feet of their kitchen window.

The Boydkins family protested, saying that the unholy cursing of the workers within earshot of their kitchen table and children was outrageous and the sludge was ruining their land and making their cows sick. But it was 1932, and by then, Flagg, Bethlehem Steel, and Jacobs Aircraft Engine Company had arrived—along with their smooth lawyers in starched collars and shiny Packards. And the lawyers were firm: We have to make engines for the mighty American airplanes that will carry freedom across the world, they said. We have to make the great steel girders for the Golden Gate Bridge that will allow wonderful automobiles to cross. We need gunpowder and shell casings and steel for the war that is coming. In desperation, the Boydkinses approached the city fathers of Pottstown, who laid down the law: The war is coming. You have to move. So the Boydkins family was forced to sell their 147 acres bordering the creek for pennies on the dollar to keep America free. It had to be done.

It was a bad decision to remain on the Manatawny back in 1929, and Doc was grateful for his father's foresight.

He and Carl were not especially close in high school, in part because Carl was tall and a good athlete and all the girls loved him, whereas Doc was a bookworm who'd had polio, which affected his left foot. The foot curled oddly and bore a cleft in the middle where toes two and three should have been. It ached from the time he was aware of it. When he was a child, his mother instructed him to always keep it covered, but it ached so much and no shoe fit well so he ignored her orders as much as possible. He secretly felt his left foot didn't look that different from his right, but he learned a painful lesson in first grade when he slipped his sock off in gym class. The boys saw his foot and howled, calling him Hoof. From then on, he never bared his foot in public again.

But that didn't prevent Doc from enjoying high school. He loved biology, was voted president of the school debating team, and despite having what girls called a walnut nose—it protruded from his face like a bumpy walnut—he discovered that girls liked guys who were clever. He read books on comedy, love, biology, and sex, the latter revealing all kinds of secrets about what girls liked, including special go-to secret places where wiggly fingers doing feathery work could make girls do anything a guy wanted. He memorized a few of these tricks and tried them out junior year on Della Burnheimer, a bouncy blonde cheerleader who felt sorry for him, agreeing to picnic with him at the creek in nearby Saratoga Park. As they lay on a blanket after lunch, Doc confessed to her that he'd never kissed a girl and would like to try. Della, a generous soul, glanced at Doc's funny shoe, felt even more sorry for him, and agreed. Doc proved to be an enthusiastic kisser, leaping in and giving her full-on mouth-to-mouth resuscitation as his hands slid into her underwear, where he made good use of the wiggly-fingered techniques he'd read about. To his surprise and hers, Della moaned her approval. But in a burst of self-control, she suddenly sat up and suggested they wade into the nearby creek and hold hands like a real couple instead of doing things that would get them in trouble in the church they both attended. Doc agreed, a decision he would later regret, for when he removed his sock and Della's blue eyes took in his cleft foot, she declared that she wanted to go home. No more action for you, buddy.

Doc was not a particularly sensitive soul, but his mother was, and when he confessed to her what had happened with Della Burnheimer—leaving out the steamier details of the wiggly-fingered, warmy-swarmy, kissy-kissy part—she marched him up to Chicken Hill, where the town's best shoemaker, Norman Skrupskelis, lived. Everyone in town dreaded Norman, a grim, cigar-chomping Jew who rarely spoke and was rumored to wander Chicken Hill's muddy roads at night like a hunchback, terrorizing the town's Negroes and taking their money.

But he was a shoe-crafting genius, for his glistening shoes adorned the windows of all three shoe shops in Pottstown.

When they knocked, Norman led them to a dark basement workshop—no cage in sight, Doc's mother noticed. He sat at a stool before a cluttered worktable and didn't look at Doc's face once. Instead, he glanced at Doc's disabled foot clad in a shoe made by a shoemaker in Philadelphia—a shoe his parents had paid dearly for—and pointed to a chair next to his worktable and barked in a thick accent, "Shoe off." Doc sat and complied, handing him the shoe.

The old man tossed Doc's old shoe aside like it was an empty bottle and clasped Doc's aching, throbbing foot in his rough hand. His hand resembled a claw, the hard fingers feeling like sandpaper turning the foot this way and that, as if it were a pound of old beef, carefully examining it, twisting it from side to side in his hard palms. When that was finished, he dropped the foot as if it were yesterday's paper and turned to his worktable, pulling leather and supplies off racks above him.

He didn't say a word, so after a few moments, Doc's mother, standing nearby and blinking in embarrassment, said, "Aren't you going to measure it?"

The old man simply waved his hand at her over his shoulder. "Come back in a week," he said.

"What about the price?"

"We'll talk about it then."

A week later they returned and the shoe was magical. It was an extraordinary work of art, gleaming black leather, beautifully stitched, perfectly matched to the arch of Doc's foot, with an insole that was carefully crafted to give him comfort and support while the outer appearance was close to that of his existing shoe. The old bugger even added an inch to the sole and sloped it carefully, which made Doc's limp less noticeable and brought almost instant relief to his aching foot and even his back. All this for a surprisingly low price. Doc's mother was ecstatic.

While Doc was grateful, he was also humiliated. The old man never said a word to him. Not even hello. But he made a wonderful shoe, and each year Doc was obliged to return to have the shoe replaced. Doc dreaded the visits to Norman's basement, for despite Norman's gifts, he found the shoemaker's arrogance unacceptable. Didn't he know who he was dealing with? Didn't he know respect?

The resentment stayed with Doc for years, and after Norman died and his sons Irv and Marvin took over the business, Doc avoided them, paying three times what they charged to have his special shoe made in Philadelphia. Who cared that the Skrupskelis twins were as talented as their father and made some of the finest shoes in the state and were recommended by doctors all around? He knew them back when! They were just like their father: arrogant. How dare they! Doc bought his shoes from an American shoe store in Philadelphia, not from immigrant Chicken Hill Jews who didn't know their place.

After his disastrous date with Della, Doc quit his dating adventures. Still, it was not lost on him during those high school years that there was one other student at Pottstown High who shared his fate with shoes and old man Skrup: the Jewess Chona. She was a year behind him in school, but when she limped past him that first day of class, he noticed her immediately, for the limp was familiar. He looked down at her feet and saw it right away: the Skrup Shoe. She vanished down the hallway and he was glad. He avoided her at first, which was not hard, as most of those Chicken Hill Jews stayed together and avoided glee club, class trips, and after-school activities. But he noticed the Jewess was often shadowed by a willowy black girl from the Hill.

She morphed out of his sight that year and the next, but in his senior year, the two were assigned lockers on the same corridor, and on the first day of school, he spotted her from behind, fumbling with something inside her locker. When she closed the locker door and turned to face the hallway, he took one look and suddenly saw a haze of stars and heard the sound of a thousand jazz trumpets blowing on New Year's Eve. The gimpy, mousy girl had morphed into a gorgeous, matter-of-fact, nonchalant, straight-up-and-down beauty. A proud straight-backed teenager with black curly hair, bouncing boobs, beautiful hips, lovely ankles, the legs hidden by a simple woolen dress, and a light shining in her dark eyes that seemed to illuminate the entire hallway. Staring at her from his locker, Doc forgot all about Della Burnheimer. Chona was gorgeous. How come he hadn't noticed that before?

He eyed her in awed silence as she vanished down the hallway. He watched her clandestinely that first week. He imagined working up the nerve to take her out. What would other students say? What would his mother say? His father? So what if she was Jewish? She was beautiful. He imagined the two of them walking along Manatawny Creek talking about big things, maybe him becoming a doctor one day; telling her about his family, their great history, the great Blessingtons of Pottstown who arrived on the *Mayflower*, and how the Manatawny was so beautiful before the factories came, the Sundays going to church and getting ice cream after. Maybe she could convert. She could be flexible, couldn't she? He was sure she could. She knew what it was like to be on the outside, with her foot. They had that in common at least. She could convert, of course she could!

The feelings built up in him week after week then receded, then returned month after month and receded again; then one afternoon in the spring, nearing graduation, he finally drummed up the nerve to invite her to join the debate team, of which he was president.

He was clumsy and nervous—he was not accustomed to talking to Jews—and the moment went badly, for he had seen a Dana Andrews film recently and had taken to talking boldly the way he'd seen the actor do. Chona was standing at her locker when he approached, and when she turned around to see him standing close, she seemed startled. He managed to mumble his invitation and then watched her beautiful eyes dance over his shoulder down the hall, then back to him, his heart pounding.

She chuckled nervously and said, "Oh no, I can't do that," and slipped off down the hallway, followed by the tall, slim Negro girl who shadowed her everywhere.

He watched her back, feeling destroyed. A day later, his desolation gave way to indignation and finally to outrage. He had done the Christian thing. He'd reached out to haul her up to his level and she was too blind to see it. She lived on Chicken Hill, for God's sake! Her father ran a grocery store that served niggers, whereas his father was a city councilman and a Presbyterian associate pastor. He was a man of importance. He had reached down to pull her to his level and she had shunned him. Imagine. She was just like the old Jew shoemaker Norman, with his mean, arrogant self. The whole business disgusted him. Jews. She and old Norman probably made fun of him when he wasn't around.

The sting of it disappeared when he left for college and medical school at Penn State, falling into a whirr of biology, cadavers, and clinical studies, standing shoulder to shoulder with students from well-to-do families in Philadelphia, Pittsburgh, and even New York. And while his fellow medical students had big plans to move back to their big cities after medical school, he couldn't imagine being anywhere other than his hometown. He'd dreamed of moving to the big city at one time, working at a large hospital, living in an apartment in a high-rise with a Negro maid and a glamorous blonde wife. But who would look out for him in those places? There were too many strange people—Italians and coloreds, big markets and fancy cars and families whose money went back generations. The idea frightened him. It was safer to stay home, to return to his hometown to heal the sick. Even his snide medical school professors, two of them German and one of them Jewish, respected him for his commitment.

But the hometown he returned to after medical school, where decent white people knew each other by name and attended the same Presbyterian church and ate ice cream at Bristol Ice House after service, had become a town of immigrants. Greeks who drove trucks, Jews who owned buildings, Negroes who walked Main Street like they owned it, Russians, Mennonites, Hungarians, Italians, and Irish. The quaint horses and buggies of his childhood were replaced by tractor trailers hauling steel, the dairy farms replaced by oily, grim factories that belched smoke. Main Street was now filled with cars on Saturdays, and not one but two traffic lights and a trolley. His lovely Pottstown had become a city where no one seemed to know anyone else. Still, when he chose for his wife someone his father approved of, a simple farm girl from nearby Fagleysville, the wedding made the front page of the Pottstown *Mercury*. That was a big deal and a good thing.

But the years of tending broken legs and sewing fingers back onto the broken hands of factory workers chipped away at him, and his disappointments grew. More factories belched more smoke and more foreigners came. And when the simple farm girl he married turned out to be a lazy, dull soul who lived for bingo nights, cheap novels, and blueberry pie, which added to her burgeoning waistline as she proudly drove around town with their four children in the brand-new Chevrolet she insisted he buy every two years, he lost interest in her. He'd seen his youth vanish, his town crumble, the blood of its proud white fathers diluted by invaders: Jews, Italians, even niggers who wandered Chicken Hill selling ice cream and shoes to one another while decent white people fought off the Jewish merchants and Italian immigrants who seemed to be buying everything. Not to mention the Mennonites in town with their horses and buggies. And the Irish at the fire company. And Greeks mumbling their business at diners. And Italians kicking ass at the dairy. And niggers from the Hill wanting factory jobs instead of being maids and janitors like they were supposed to. Now Jews were buying homes on Beech Street, making plans to build a bigger Jewish synagogue, and what's more, they were polluting the town's good white Christian teenagers with Negro music—jazz—brought to town by none other than Chona's husband, yet another Jew who owned not one but *two* theaters. Where was America in all this? Pottstown was for Americans. God had predestined it. The Constitution guaranteed it. The Bible had said it. Jesus! Where was Jesus in all this? Doc felt his world was falling apart.

So a few years after medical school when friends approached him about attending a meeting of the Knights of Pottstown to spread good Christian values, he agreed. And when that Knights of Pottstown meeting actually turned out to be the White Knights of the Ku Klux Klan instead, he saw no difference. The men were like him. They wanted to preserve America. This country was woods before the white man came. It needed to be saved. The town, the children, the women, they needed to be rescued from those who wanted to pollute the pure white race with ignorance and dirt, fouling things up by mixing the pure WASP heritage with the Greeks, the Italians, the Jews who had murdered their precious Jesus Christ, and the niggers who dreamed of raping white women and whose lustful black women were a danger to every decent, God-fearing white man. Not all of them were bad, of course. The White Knights would decide who were the good ones. There were a few good ones. Doc knew several.

The meetings were more like hobby-club gatherings than actual fire-and-brimstone events. The men talked of farming and lost property, the challenges of growing and seeding crops in bad weather, the cost of cattle and transport, and rising prices. Many were former farmers, others were factory workers and bankers. Good people. Pottstown people. People Doc had known all his life. So when Carl approached him one afternoon after a White Knights meeting about the problem of the Jewess holding the deaf Negro child illegally, forcing him to work in her store, and keeping him out of school when a good school was ready to take him, Doc had an interest. He told Carl to come by his office the following week.

He knew Chona, of course. She had come once to see him about her fainting when he first set up practice. At that visit, neither acknowledged he'd actually tried to befriend her in high school years before. He suspected, even hoped, that she'd forgotten it. *He'd* not forgotten it, and when she walked into his office, he still felt the pounding of a thousand drums in his heart, for she had aged well. The beautiful breasts, the slim hips, the bright, shining eyes were still there, along with the Skrup Shoe on her foot. The Skrup Shoe styling, he noted, had evolved into a lean and handsome number, head and shoulders better than the expensive bricklike box that adorned his foot and hurt at that moment, and for which he'd paid top dollar. But that was the cost of principle, which he was happy to pay.

He kept matters professional at that visit, prescribed a few pain pills, and told her to call again if the spells continued, hoping she would. But she never did, and again he was offended. Did she think that just because he was a small-town doctor, he didn't understand her case? He had friends in the medical field in Reading and Philadelphia. He read all the latest medical journals. In fact, two doctors called him from Philadelphia not two weeks after she left, asking his opinion about her puzzling fainting spells. What had he found? they asked. They respected him more than she did.

He followed her case when she nearly died, felt strangely relieved when she recovered, then was outraged when she had the nerve to write to the newspaper complaining about him marching as a White Knight in the annual parade. How dare she! Their parades weren't hurting anybody. They were a celebration of the real America.

The whole business riled him. But when Carl appeared at his office to discuss her hiding a twelve-year-old Negro boy, Doc was careful to maintain his professional distance, for he wasn't fond of his cousin. Carl had been a bit of a rooster back in high school, but now his firm football player stomach hung over his belt. His sculpted shoulders sagged. His once-clear face bore the trace of whiskers from a bad shave. His fedora was worn, his cheap tie spotted. Still, Carl delivered a hanging curveball that Doc found impossible to resist.

"The state will pay you to examine the Negro kid," Carl said. He sat on the edge of Doc's desk as he delivered this news, pulling out a pack of cigarettes. Doc was behind his desk as they spoke.

"Why do they need an exam in the first place?" Doc asked. "Is he sick?"

"Deaf and maybe dumb," Carl said, extracting a cigarette and firing it. "The state wants to send him to a special school. They need a doctor to sign off on it. Simple as that."

"Which school?"

"Pennhurst. They got a school in there."

Doc had seen Pennhurst State School and Hospital. Just down the road in Spring City. It was a horrible, overcrowded nightmare, but he checked his tongue. "They take Negroes?" he asked.

"They take anyone who's insane."

"Deaf and maybe dumb's not insane, Carl."

"Do I look like a Ouija board, Earl?" Carl said, using Doc's real name, a sign of familiarity and, Doc thought grimly, disrespect. "The boy's twelve. Hasn't been to school in a long time. They have special things for kids like him there. It's better than what he's got now, living on the Hill and running around for them Jews up there. The state wants him. They're burning precious dollars having me run up and down there looking for him. Every time I go up there, nobody knows nothing. I even sent a colored up there who couldn't shake him loose. The niggers are hiding him up there. And she's in cahoots with 'em."

"Is it her child?" Doc asked.

Carl looked at Doc blankly a moment, then sputtered, "Her what? She's married, Doc."

"So?"

"Whatever you're thinking, Doc, I don't wanna know it." Carl sucked his cigarette thoughtfully, then said, "Now that you mention it, there's a lot of tipping going on in this town. Especially on the Hill. Could be."

Doc's face reddened. These kinds of conversations made him uncomfortable. He felt like a fool. He didn't know why he'd even brought it up.

"I've never seen the kid, to be honest," Carl said. "But from what I heard, he's a pure colored nigger. No father. His mother died not too long ago."

"From what?"

"You're the doc," Carl said. "All's I know is the kid's hiding at the store someplace behind the Jewess and her husband, the All-American Dance Hall and Theater guy. The husband finances the whole racket. I can have the cops go up there with you if you want."

"Let them do it and keep me out of it."

Carl frowned. "It's not smart to rile up those Chicken Hill niggers. She got a lot of sway with 'em. She was nearly dead this time last year, sick from something or other, and the coloreds got stirred up about it. She's the one who wrote the letter about our parade, remember?"

Doc shrugged. "Who reads the stupid paper around here? What about the Negro you sent up there? The state has Negro investigators now?"

"No. He's just a driver. He drives the superintendent around. We got a tip the Jewish lady was hiding the kid in the next-door neighbor's yard, so we paid him a couple of extra bucks and let him drive a car up there and ask around. Nobody would talk to him. He snuck around to the back to look in the yard and said there must've been twenty kids back there. He couldn't tell one from the other and had to leave quick. He said the coloreds smelled him out. They're all related on the Hill, y'know, cousins and whatnot. C'mon, Doc, my supervisor's all hot and bothered. Can you see about it? You examine him, sign off on it, they put him in Pennhurst. They pay you to write a little report. Case closed. It's easy."

"Okay. I'll write the report."

"Don't you need to see him first?"

Doc thought about it a moment. He hadn't seen Chona in years. He never forgot the Jewish goddess standing at her locker in high school, her shining eyes, the full breasts, both of them young and innocent, the years ahead of them looking so promising. Those years were gone now. They were both middle-aged. They still had something in common now. *Skrup Shoes.* That was one thing. Maybe she was like him after all. *Maybe her husband is like my wife*, he thought. *A loser. A mess. Why not? What was left?*

He nodded. "All right, Carl. I'll go see about the kid. Leave the police out of it for now."

11

Gone

It was close to 2 p.m. when the overhead bulb flickered in the middle of the Heaven & Earth Grocery Store, signaling to Dodo that someone was entering. The light bulb was a little tricky. Sometimes it flickered on its own, or the shaking of the floor set it off. So when it flickered the first time, he ignored it, because it was early afternoon—the usual slow time in the store. Aunt Addie had gone to the icehouse for ice. Mr. Moshe had gone to the theater. Few customers entered at that hour.

He was standing on the trapdoor ladder leading to the basement, his head nearly at floor level, hidden behind the butcher's case from anyone who entered the store. It was a good thing, too, for when the light flickered a second time, he saw Miss Chona, seated on a high chair behind the counter, reach for her walking stick and move around to the front of the counter. She had her back to him when she walked a few steps to reach the far end of the counter, but when she looped around the end and moved to the center of the room to greet the visitor, he saw her face for the first time. The alarmed look in her eyes caused him to freeze where he was.

Miss Chona was not a woman who lost her cool easily. Despite the odd tremors and occasional frightening seizures brought on by her disability, she rambled around the store freely, doing all manner of tasks. If there was a carton to be lifted, she would attempt to lift it herself. If there were groceries to be stacked or vegetables to sort, she went at those things. She did not like to be helped, and he'd learned to not help her unless asked. The only time she let him do work that kept him free and rambling, because he hated sitting still, was if she was reading. Dodo never saw someone who loved to read so much. She read all day. She reminded him of his mother. But his mother mostly read the Bible. Miss Chona read everything—books, magazines, newspapers—and urged him to do the same. He had grown to like reading in the past five months with her encouragement but not as much as he pretended to. He faked it, mostly, just for her. He reckoned he would one day, when he was all grown, sit and read one of the many books she gave him instead of pretending that he did. But not any day soon. He preferred working in the store, and playing in the yard next door with Miss Bernice's children. It was the only place he was allowed to roam freely. He had come to slightly resent that imprisonment. It wasn't fair. He should be free to roam around the Hill like before. But Miss Chona and Aunt Addie had drilled it into his head. *Stay close. Watch out for the man from the state. He's coming to take you to a special school. You don't want to go there.*

Dodo had no idea what the man from the state looked like, but a flash of fear in Miss Chona's eyes as the customer approached the other side of the butcher's counter gave him pause, and he instinctively lowered his head a few inches into the basement.

He couldn't be seen from where he was unless someone leaned over the counter and looked directly down into the trapdoor opening. Nor could he see clearly who was on the other side of the counter. But he could feel, and that was enough. Feel and smell. Vibrations, nearly as good as sight and sound. And the feel of matters he could sense right away was wrong.

Still standing on the ladder, he pressed the back of his hand to the floorboards on his left. He recognized the uneven bounce of Miss Chona's clumping footsteps as they approached the middle of the floor. This was followed by an unfamiliar sound, an eerie *clump-clump* of a similar gait coming from the store entrance. The two thumps stopped in front of the butcher's case not five feet from his head.

He could see Miss Chona's face just over the butcher's counter. The look of alarm in her eyes as she talked to the visitor, a man wearing a fedora and a black coat, was unsettling.

Then the man turned his head slightly for a moment, and Dodo saw the face from the side. Panic rose in his throat when he saw who it was.

Doc Roberts.

To the white folks of Pottstown, Doc Roberts was the kind of man whose bespeckled countenance belonged on breakfast cereal boxes. The kind, gentle country doc. Friend to all, deliverer of babies, a wonderful man, a Presbyterian. But for the black folks of the Hill, Doc was a running joke: "Why go see Doc Roberts and pay to die?" He was a special fright for black children of the Hill, center of a thousand nightmares shepherded by the exhausted mothers who needed sleep. Mothers whose children tumbled about restlessly past their bedtimes would burst into darkened bedrooms and warn, "If you don't shut your eyes right now, I'm taking you to Doc Roberts," which cut off the giggles and cackling immediately. Youngsters who refused to swallow the awful-tasting cod-liver oil and ghastly country remedies used to cure colds, fever, and unknown maladies were met with "Suck this medicine down right now or I'll fetch Doc Roberts. Old Doc'll give it to you—in jail," and down the hatch the awful concoction would go. Dodo was frightened of doctors. After the stove exploded in his face, his mother waited three long, painful days gathering money to take him by train to a colored doctor in Reading. The colored doctor firmly and without ceremony covered his swollen face with goop and wrapped bandages around his eyes and ears, which left him helpless. After the bandages were removed, the trouble in his eyes had slowly cleared up, and Dodo watched his mother weep bitterly, mouthing the words "infection" and "doc" to Uncle Nate and Aunt Addie. But neither she nor Uncle Nate nor Aunt Addie made any mention of taking him to Doc Roberts for better results. Doc Roberts was trouble.

And now he was four feet off, talking with Miss Chona.

Miss Chona was leaning on the counter with her left hand, tapping it nervously. Doc's back was to him, so he could not read the doctor's lips. But Dodo could see Miss Chona's mouth, and from his vantage point, he saw the conversation deteriorate quickly from carefully polite to stormy.

"*Wonderful weather . . . rain last week . . . has it been that long? . . . high school . . . graduation . . . feeling well*," she said.

But she looked anything but well. Her face was pale, and he noticed her left hand was trembling slightly. Seeing this, he grew panicked, for this was a sign she was about to faint or, worse, have one of her seizures. He'd seen those and they terrified him. She'd been shaky and weak in her movements the last week or so, and that, Aunt Addie had told him, was a sign. In fact, just before Aunt Addie left for the icehouse not twenty minutes before, she'd made it a point to tell him to keep a careful eye on Miss Chona, don't let her pick up anything, and to watch her so she doesn't fall. *Stay close* had been her words.

He'd gone to fetch the cartons of cans from the basement only because Miss Chona had insisted. He tried to do it quickly, but obviously not quickly enough, for now he was stuck in the trapdoor opening behind the counter and unsure whether to show himself, for he didn't want Miss Chona to fall while he was down there. The wrath of Aunt Addie if that happened would not be pleasant.

Just as he was about to poke his head out of the trapdoor opening, Miss Chona lifted her left hand off the counter and pointed toward the front of the store, which caused Doc to turn around and look toward the front door. In that instant, with Doc's face turned away, she shot a quick glance down at him in the trapdoor opening and stretched her left hand out, palm flat, fingers spread, like a traffic cop's, as if to say "Stay there!" so he stayed where he was.

He felt the urge to scamper down the ladder to the relative safety of the basement, but Doc had turned to her again, and the boy stared with alarm as the conversation heated up quickly, seeing only Miss Chona's lips and face from his perch below as she talked, her face reddening in anger: "*Marching in your parade . . . your problem . . . shameful . . . taxes . . . I'm American, too,*" the last she indicated angrily, pointing at Doc with a shaky hand. He saw the back of the doctor's neck redden and his shoulders hunch up as he responded. They were arguing full-out now, no question, and Miss Chona's face, which had been surprised when the door opened, was now tightened in rage, her eyebrows arched as she went on. "*Colored people . . . Negroes . . . don't know what you're talking about . . . police.*" He watched Doc respond, his head moving as he yammered something, cutting her off.

She was about to respond, but just as she opened her mouth to speak, Miss Chona whitened, gasped, and her eyes rolled upward; she shook violently for a second and suddenly dropped out of sight, her face disappearing on the other side of the butcher's case. It was as if someone had snatched her from a hole in the floor.

Dodo didn't need to hear to know what happened. The thump of the shaking floor told him she'd dropped like a sack of potatoes.

He slapped a hand to his mouth instinctively, knowing from experience that even his smallest utterances caused noises—he learned that from Uncle Nate when they went hunting. *No noise. Cover your mouth or you'll scare off the game.* But this was no hunting trip with Uncle Nate's old rifle that knocked you off your feet when it spit fire out of its eye toward a deer or squirrel. This explosion came from inside, as the fear exploded through his body with the shuddering of the floor, and for a moment, he could not remember where he was. Many months later, he would recall the ominous, life-changing *thump* that ran through his left hand held beneath the floorboard, and how that same left hand had smacked over his mouth so hard he bit his own lip, hanging on to the trapdoor ladder with his right arm wrapped around the rungs, for had that arm not been there, he would have fallen off altogether, as his legs gave way at that moment and he became overwhelmed with the same feeling he'd had when he was kneeling before the stove in his mother's house three years before and the stove exploded, sending shards of hot iron into his chest, arms, and head that felt like a thousand knives with a heat so intense that he felt cold for weeks afterward. The pain in his head then was so great that it had grown into a living thing; the burning in his eyes so unbearable that his ears, he reasoned, had shut down to defend themselves, so that by the time the bandages were removed, he was forced to stagger about wearing sunglasses for months, which he hated; the business of sound having been removed from the world felt almost secondary to the real problem: his mother's sudden illness, her life ebbing away as his own ears gradually closed. Then Uncle Nate, Aunt Addie, then what?

Nothing but Miss Chona and his ears. He could faintly hear a few things sometimes. A car backfiring. The vegetable man's horse as the cart clomped past. But sight and sound were replaced by sight and vibration—noises coming from inside. Inside his heart. Thus, as Miss Chona fell, he thought he heard the sound of his own heart cracking, as if there were a sound to it at all, breaking off, deep inside, for part of him knew he would never see her the same again, if ever. Going . . . going . . . gone. Just like his mother. Just like everything.

That thought pushed power back into his quaking legs and he surged upward, braced himself quickly, and pulled himself out of the trapdoor opening, leaping catlike onto the floor, where he crouched behind the butcher's counter. The counter's face was glass. Dodo peered through the glass case silently, breathing heavily. What he saw over the neatly assembled pigs' feet, sliced meats, ham hocks, cow parts, and ground beef in the case would change the rest of his life: Doc Roberts, his back to him, crouching over the prone figure of Miss Chona.

Every single road Dodo had taken up to that point, every turn, every crevice, every movement, had been divided into the rules of adults from his world that he trusted—his late mother, his uncle Nate and aunt Addie, his cousin Rusty, Miss Paper, even the grim Miss Bernice next door. To the outside world, he was a colored boy who was "slow" or "feebleminded" by those who knew no better. Only careful drilling in the months before by those same people, including Miss Chona, kept him in place at that moment: *Stay close. Play dumb. Do not leave the store. Do not venture past Miss Bernice's yard next door. Do not run about. Pretend you don't understand.* To do otherwise, he understood, would be a disaster for him. Even Miss Chona had repeated those same instructions just now, before she'd fallen, with her outstretched hand. "Stay there," she'd said. *Stay there. Just keep quiet. The trouble will pass.*

But now...

It was the thought of Aunt Addie, her fury—even worse, her disappointment—that caused him to place his foot on top of the counter and leap over it.

He was only twelve, so sex had more to do with odd pictures in his mind and an occasional curiosity about one of Miss Bernice's daughters he favored for reasons he wasn't quite sure of. His understanding of girls was that they were necessary, would one day be women, would be required in his life somehow and vice versa; but in the meantime, they were impediments in his daily quest to gather marbles, rocks, and stones, and send them skipping across the creek that ran behind both the yards of the Heaven & Earth Grocery Store and Miss Bernice's house. Girls were not important. Apparently, Doc did not agree, because he was running his hands through Miss Chona's hair and inside her clothes in a way that made the boy suck wind and lose his breath.

Miss Chona had fainted completely. She'd obviously had one of her seizures—they lasted only a few seconds—but afterward she was normally placed on her side by Aunt Addie, who wiped her face, and after a few minutes, she got better and usually sat up. But Doc didn't wait for her to sit up. He'd turned her over, and when the seizure quit, he pushed her so that she lay flat on her back. He quickly ran his right hand across her chest and squeezed. Then he held her there with his left hand and squeezed her chest with the other, the hand working into her blouse, holding her in place while he ran his other hand across her stomach, then down to her groin, pulling up her dress, her legs exposed to the thigh, the boot she wore lying awkwardly exposed, her blouse rumpled where Doc had run his hands so freely. It was a memory that would last much longer than the boy would have liked.

Dodo didn't remember yelling. And later, when asked about it, insisted he did not yell, saying if he had, he would have known it. "I know how to keep quiet," he told his Aunt Addie. But that was later, long afterward. Now, without thinking, he jumped off the counter and leaped across the room, knocking Doc into the shelves of cans and crackers behind him.

He'd never touched a white man before, not in his whole life, and was surprised at how soft and fat Doc felt, and how easily Doc flew backward when he piled into him, knocking him off Miss Chona and driving him into the shelves that cascaded groceries down on all three of them.

Doc recovered and shoved him off, but before he could rise, Dodo was on his feet and piled into him again like a football player; Dodo was thin but strong, and his weight and strength kept Doc in place. Whether he beat Doc with his fists like they said, the boy was uncertain, for Miss Chona had a second seizure at that moment, and while they usually lasted seconds, this one was worse than the first and lasted much longer.

The sight of her struggle seemed to awaken a strength in Doc, and the boy could feel him vibrating and knew he was shouting. Dodo ignored the shouts, pinning him against the shelf with his head and shoulders, glancing behind him as Miss Chona shook vigorously now, her body spasming wildly. He felt hands on his neck. Doc was strangling him and Dodo's struggle for life became real now. He could feel Doc's fury and wiggled free of Doc's hands and pushed him against the shelf harder, but Doc had his wind, and the boy raised his head just in time to feel Doc striking him. He instinctively struck back twice, hard in the face, and Doc's mouth ceased moving for a moment and blood burst from his lips, and at that moment, the boy realized he was in deep trouble.

Out of the corner of his eye, Dodo saw the light overhead blink, indicating that the front door had opened, and then Aunt Addie was rushing toward Miss Chona. His glance at her caused him to lighten his press on Doc, who flung him off onto the floor and crawled toward Miss Chona, who was shaking violently, her head pounding the floor. Aunt Addie placed her hand under Miss Chona's head. Miss Chona's mouth was wide open. He saw Aunt Addie glance at the countertop, and without being told, Dodo leaped over the counter, grabbed a spoon, and handed it to Aunt Addie. "I tried to help," he cried.

Aunt Addie ignored him, cramming the spoon into Miss Chona's mouth as Doc moved in. Both crouched over Miss Chona now, trying to keep her from shaking so violently, Doc placing his hands underneath her back. She seemed to shake forever.

Aunt Addie, still holding Miss Chona on her side, turned to Dodo and he saw her lips move, saying calmly, "Get some water. Hurry." He complied.

Several long seconds later, Miss Chona quit struggling and lay quiet, her eyes closed, seemingly dead, surrounded by Addie and several neighbors who had now entered and were swathing her face with towels. Dodo glanced anxiously at the door. Doc was gone. He noticed the neighbors there cleaning up, eyeing him nervously, righting the shelves and restacking the fallen items. Several Hill residents were peering through the front window of the store as well.

Aunt Addie wiped Miss Chona's face and stroked her hair and straightened her clothing, and a quick glance at him from her told Dodo she was furious. He stepped to her and tapped her shoulder. He wanted to explain, but she ignored him, speaking to a neighbor. He could see her lips moving. What was she saying?

Then someone tapped him on the shoulder and pointed toward the front door.

He looked up.

Doc was back, two policemen behind him. Over their shoulders, he could see several neighbors staring at all of it grimly.

Doc pointed to him. Dodo read his lips clearly. "There he is," he said.

There was nothing to do but run. He leaped up and tore into the back room of the store, bursting out the back door, a police officer hot on his tail. He sprinted through the yard, dodging the solitary cow that Miss Chona kept to sell kosher milk, but when he reached the creek embankment at the end of the yard, there was nowhere left to run. But he was a fast boy, quick and lithe, and when he spun about, he quickly ducked and dodged under the officer's grasp, then dodged the second officer behind him and sprinted back toward the building.

He knew he couldn't run back inside. Instead, he made for the fire escape ladder that hung from the second-floor window. It was six feet off the ground, above his reach, but there was a crate he kept beneath it just for that purpose. With one smooth leap, he swung himself on it, grabbed a rung with one hand, then the other, pulled himself up, and scurried up the rungs toward the roof.

The roof was flat. He thought maybe he would run to the front of the building, somehow climb down it—which he'd thought about occasionally but never tried—and make it to the railroad tracks. He knew every crook and crevice of the rail yard. He knew most of the trains that ran there. The policemen would never catch him.

But when he got to the roof, a third policeman burst out the door that led from the store's attic and ran toward him about ten yards off. Dodo stopped in his tracks and sprinted back toward the ladder he'd mounted and peered down. Both policemen were making their way up and they were not moving slowly. He was terrified now. He had to get away.

He looked down at the policemen writhing up the ladder, glanced behind him at the policeman who was approaching, and looked into the yard. From three stories up, it didn't seem far, not too far anyway. He could make the jump, then splash across the creek to safety. He'd jumped off trains before, and they were pretty high.

He jumped—just as the outstretched arm of the rooftop cop grabbed at his collar. But the policeman didn't grab enough. He grabbed just enough to spoil his takeoff. Dodo felt himself spinning upside down, then around and around. Then sweet blackness came as the silence that lived inside his head exploded into a crunching bang and became silent again. And this silence was real.

PART II
Gotten

12

Monkey Pants

Monkey Pants was the first person Dodo met on Ward C-1. He lay in the only other crib in the room. A boy around his age, just six inches away. Inside a steel crib adjacent to where Dodo lay in traction in his own steel-caged crib in a hot, overcrowded ward of ninety beds. It was the first stroke of luck Dodo had had in a while.

His neighbor was a small, painfully thin white child with dark hair—about eleven or twelve, Dodo guessed. He wore no hospital gown but rather a diaper and an undershirt, and was contorted in a way that seemed impossible. He lay on his side in a ball, his neck and shoulders hunched, curled in an odd tangle of twisted hands and feet, one leg impossibly reaching toward his face—the ankle nearly at his chin—the other leg lost in a cacophony of twisted arms, elbows, knees, and fingers, with one hand thrust out of the twisted cacophony of limbs gathered near his chest to cover his eyes. The boy looked as if he had tied himself up in knots and was hiding from himself.

Dodo had never seen anything like it. But because the child was twisted impossibly and curled like a primate, Dodo called him Monkey Pants, for he looked like a monkey with no pants. In reality, Dodo never learned his real name.

It was the impossible sight of Monkey Pants that brought Dodo back to consciousness and reality, as the explosion of suffering and shock that had descended on him during the first few days at Pennhurst State Hospital for the Insane and Feeble-Minded was compounded by the injuries sustained in his fall off Miss Chona's roof. The fall had reduced him to a state of absolute immobility. He broke both ankles, shattered his hip, and snapped his right fibula. He lay in the Pottstown hospital handcuffed to a bed, in traction, for a week. The handcuffs never left him after he regained consciousness even though he was in traction. The cops were obviously mad.

But the handcuffs were removed when he arrived by stretcher at the Pennhurst admissions office, where another doctor examined him.

He arrived there confused, for he was taken to the institution's hospital wing, not back home to face the music for the disaster at Miss Chona's. The fact that Aunt Addie and Uncle Nate were not at the hospital was not a tip-off, because he had never been in a hospital, even after he lost his hearing. He simply assumed that the white hospital people were prepping him for the arrival of his aunt and uncle, who would take him home.

But after several minutes of lying on the stretcher and not seeing his aunt and uncle anywhere, he became impatient, and he began to struggle to get out of bed. Two attendants held him down while the doctor produced a needle full of something that made him woozy, and after a few moments, he was in a fog.

The doctor measured his height, estimated his weight, moved his arms, checked his eyes, spoke to Dodo briefly, which Dodo could not understand for the doctor was a mumbler with a foreign accent, and even if he weren't a mumbler, the fog made it impossible for Dodo to decipher what the doc said to him. It took all of a half hour for the doctor to declare him an imbecile.

The attendants placed a hospital gown on him and gathered his effects, which someone, probably Aunt Addie, had carefully packed, including a shirt, a tie, some smaller items, shoes, socks, and several marbles he always carried around for good luck that Miss Chona had given him, and put them in a bag. He never saw them again.

He was wheeled out past two sets of doors and down several long corridors, and then something terrible began to seep into the dense fog that had lowered onto his brain. His sense of smell, always keen, had heightened since he'd lost his hearing, and while he had caught a slight sense of a new terrible scent, a tinge, a kind of warning, just a slight one, like a tiny thread coming loose on a shirt, when he first awoke, it rose quickly and disappeared, like a goblin that suddenly pokes his head out of the floor for a moment, then vanishes. Just a brief flicker of something awful.

But now, as the stretcher wheeled out of the cheery, polished, gleaming floors of the admissions office and spun through several sets of doors and corridors, through an underground tunnel and up a ramp, the cheery atmosphere gave way to a dim corridor, and the odor grew and morphed and developed its own life. It seemed to sprout from the granite walls as the stretcher moved, like moss or vines rising from the floor and covering the walls, the smell becoming a living, breathing thing, gorging on the walls, the windows, and finally him, evolving from strong to horrible to overpowering. He felt as if he were drowning. As the stretcher spun through the corridors, turning one corner and the next, he nearly passed out, but the motion kept him conscious, and the smell poured on him, coming again and again, stronger and stronger, morphing into new life the way his sunflowers grew in back of Miss Chona's yard. He loved watching them grow, smelling them as they did. They smelled so wonderful he often imagined that it was the fragrance that made the flowers, not the other way around. Their fragrance gave wonderful messages. Pretty. Happy. Joyful. But the smells here bore a different message. Cruelty. Anger. Powerful loneliness. And death. And as the stretcher rolled deeper into the corridors, his throat finally surged, and the contents of his stomach ran up his throat.

He raised his head and vomited over the side of the stretcher. The vomit landed on the pants of one of the attendants accompanying him, whereupon the two men stopped, departed for a moment, and returned with a straitjacket. They sat him up—his legs still in traction—and placed it around his chest and arms, tightened it, then proceeded. He was rolled to an end corner of a long room tightly packed with beds—Ward C-1—and left.

He tried to sit up, but he could not move, so he lay on his back, exhausted. He sobbed for a bit, then slept.

When he awoke and turned his head to look about, Monkey Pants was the first thing he saw.

They were only six inches apart, and at the first sight of Monkey Pants twisted into horrible knots, Dodo burst into tears again.

Monkey Pants seemed nonplussed by it all. Seemingly unmoved, one eye peered through the tangle of arms and legs nonchalantly as Dodo wept. Dodo noted the boy's nonchalance and felt the boy was being cruel, and he decided to tell someone about Monkey Pants and, at the very least, not look at old Monkey Pants any longer.

Dodo was in traction and couldn't shift onto his side, but he could turn his head, so he looked in the other direction.

There was no one on his other side, but the sight was not reassuring. There were rows of beds in the crowded ward, all of them mercifully empty, for it was daytime and apparently the people had gone elsewhere.

So he turned back to Monkey Pants, who peered at him with one eye through tangled arms and legs.

The two boys stared at each other a long time, and in that moment, Dodo had his second stroke of luck that day, the first being that he'd been dropped on the ward in the middle of the day when the ward attendants had already paraded the unlucky patients to the day room. For Monkey Pants, whose condition in thirty years would fall into the yawing labyrinth of spinning medical terminology known as "cerebral palsy," a clumsy, useless term, nearly as useless as the idea of confining a child with his physical challenges to an insane asylum where he was normally sedated every morning, had somehow been forgotten by the nurse who doled out the daily knockout drops that day. As Dodo stared into the eye of Monkey Pants, he could see, clear as day, that there was a boy in there.

"Monkey Pants," he said.

The boy could only see him with one eye, the other eye covered by his hand. But the eye peering at Dodo moved slightly. The eyebrow raised just a bit. Then Monkey Pants shifted his fingers and revealed a second eye.

Then Dodo saw, or thought he saw, Monkey Pants chuckle.

He could not hear it, but the tangle of limbs he was staring at shifted slightly. He knew what a pleasant chuckle looked like.

The fact that Monkey Pants laughed at him irritated him, so he said it again. "Monkey Pants."

And he saw it this time. For certain. Monkey Pants lowered his hand and his mouth moved into a twisted grin. Then he spoke.

His face twisted with the effort, and Dodo couldn't understand him at all because he could only lip-read. Moreover, Monkey Pants's lips moved about in an odd manner. But Dodo felt so grateful to talk to a living person. It was as if someone had opened a window and cranked in a blast of fresh air. They hadn't let anyone come to see him at the hospital. He caught the lips of one of the policemen guarding his room telling a nurse something about his attacking people. And while he had no chance to explain to anyone, even Aunt Addie, what had happened, he knew whatever trouble he was in involved white folks, and that was a problem. If only Miss Chona was here, she would straighten it all out. She would help him explain. Aunt Addie and Uncle Nate would be cross, but they, too, would help. Where were they? Then the thought of Miss Chona lying on the floor with her dress pulled up, shaking so crazily, and the ensuing struggle with Doc Roberts, and the memory of Aunt Addie's furious face as he ran off from the police overwhelmed him and the tears came again.

The casts on his legs itched. He had a headache. He needed to go to the bathroom and was afraid he would soil himself. He felt insanely thirsty. He raised his head and looked about the room again. Not a soul. There were empty beds everywhere, and in the middle of the far wall, a glass enclosure in which attendants sat to watch the patients. The attendants' room was empty.

He turned back to Monkey Pants and sobbed. "I want to go home."

Monkey Pants shifted. The spasm of bundled arms and legs seemed to twist even more as he painfully, slowly extracted an arm from around his head, showing a dark head of hair and an angular, handsome face. His mouth moved again, but his face and mouth puckered and Dodo could not read his lips. He shook his head, not understanding.

Monkey Pants paused for a moment, seeming to reconsider, then moved his eyes.

His eyes looked left. They looked right. They looked up. They looked down.

Dodo, staring at him, cried impatiently, "What you doing, Monkey Pants?"

Much later, he realized his good fortune. The two of them had been alone in the ward on that first day, and what an incredible stroke of good fortune it had been, for his injury and a misdiagnosis of his mental abilities had placed him in a ward of so-called lower functions. The attendants had led the entire ward, a pitiful drugged group of humanity, ninety men in all, on a daily parade from the ward to the day room, an empty room bare of furniture save two benches, to stare out the window for hours, toss feces at one another, and bang their heads against the walls if they so pleased. The two patients assigned to clean the ward of urine and feces, burnishing the floor with a polisher before turning their attention to the two "babies," Dodo and Monkey Pants, two boys among men, to clean their beds and their bodily waste, moving them from one side to the other like pieces of beef, had not arrived. They were alone. And for the first four hours, Monkey Pants gave Dodo a spellbinding, extraordinary performance lecture on the art of survival in one of the oldest and worst mental institutions in the history of the United States.

But this did not come easily. Watching Monkey Pants give a lecture was like watching an octopus trying to shake hands with a flamethrower. Nothing worked right. The boy fought to communicate. His chest constricted. His lips contorted. His limbs flapped around wildly in spasmic bursts. They seemed to have their own mind about which direction they wanted to go in. He worked like a madman, his limbs flailing, mouth moving in unintelligible bursts, then stopping as he exhausted himself, only to continue after catching his breath, only to exhaust himself again. This happened several times before

Dodo deduced that Monkey Pants was trying to say something important.

"What do you want?"

Monkey Pants went at it again, but the flailing limbs and spastic shaking head didn't make sense, and after some effort and squinting, Dodo burst into tears of frustration and despair.

"What's wrong with you?"

The outburst and tears did not bring sympathy. Instead, Monkey Pants's frustration and impatience began to show. His chest constricted and his limbs thrust about in squirming impatience with even greater agitation, which caused Dodo to stare in amazement, for there was clear irritation in the movement.

Then just as suddenly, Monkey Pants quit. His thrashing arms and legs, which pounded against the iron bars of the crib, stopped. He lay on his back and his legs and arms slowly came together and rose like spider's legs, wrapping around each other in an impossible fashion near his head. And from there, with his legs and arms twisted like pretzels and crammed near his chest and head, he stared at Dodo, his gaze as steady as headlights.

Dodo watched as Monkey Pants's eyes went up. Then down. Then up. Then down. Then left. Then right. Then the same business again. Up. Down. Left. Right. He was trying to say something. What?

Unable to make neither heads nor tails of the business, Dodo grew tired of it, and a song suddenly flew into his head. Why this happened, he was not sure. But the loss of hearing had not decreased his love of music. Indeed, it had intensified it. He often dragged his uncle Nate to a dressing room backstage at Mr. Moshe's dance hall where Uncle Nate listened to records on an old turntable kept back there. He liked to place his hands on the phonograph speaker to hear the music as the record played. It didn't matter that he could hear just a tiny bit of it. Just the act of listening fired the music inside him. And when Uncle Nate sometimes led a group of workers cleaning up Mr. Moshe's theater in singing his favorite old gospel hymn, "I'll Go Where You Want Me to Go," Dodo sang along out of tune, much to the amusement of the men.

"I know a song, Monkey Pants," he said. "Wanna hear it?"

Without waiting for an answer, he sang.

I'll go where You want me to go.
I'll say what You want me to say.
Lord, I'll be what You want me to be.

Monkey Pants stared, unblinking, wide-eyed, his eyebrows lifted. His face eased into something like a smile, and in that moment, Dodo felt comforted and a little less lonely.

Monkey Pants suddenly became agitated again. Lying on his back, he began to rock, twisting to the left and right, his thin gawky arms and legs moving crazily as he attempted to further unravel his face from his arms and legs. It seemed impossible. His arms and legs awkwardly twisted themselves together like spaghetti then pulled apart, then wrapped themselves around each other again; but with great effort, his limbs began to unbend themselves and his arms arced toward the ceiling. His right arm, which seemed to move on its own more than any other part of him, seemed to free itself first. It swung wide into the air over his face toward the ceiling, then pinned itself to the right side of the crib, as if a pressure hose had burst loose and sprayed water everywhere. The left arm followed, grasping an ankle that seemed to want to move on its own, slowly pushing a crimped-up leg off his chest and away from him, so now his upper body was once again clear of his ankles, legs, and feet. Then the left arm swung out wide through the bar of the steel crib toward Dodo.

Dodo could see the boy's face fully now as he lay on his back, his head turned toward him.

The two boys stared at each other, and in that moment, a remarkable thing happened.

It was as if the magic of the hymn Dodo offered up had marched into the room. Both boys became fully aware of the plight of the other. A knowledge, a wisdom, passed between them that no one outside of them could possess—a knowledge that they were boys among men, with remarkable minds trapped inside bodies that would not allow one-thousandth of any of the thoughts and feelings they possessed to emerge. Monkey Pants let it be known that if Dodo was to survive as a boy among these men, he must be wise and that he must listen to what he had to say.

Dodo found himself staring directly at Monkey Pants, who then did something amazing.

He raised a shaking hand to his face and put a finger to his lips. As if to say "Shh."

And in that moment, Dodo understood: Play dumb. Be stupid. Don't say a word. It's the only way.

Dodo sensed movement and turned his head to see what was behind him. He watched in terror as the doorway of the ward filled with a dark shape, then another, as several men wandered in—hulking figures, in all manner of disability, pawing at themselves, some half naked, shaking, nodding, not a single boy among them. He turned back to Monkey Pants in panic, but Monkey Pants had curled back into what Dodo would later understand was his usual protected Monkey Pants position, with his left knee near his chest and his arms twisted over his head and the other leg flung high over his chest so that his ankle nearly reached his face. Dodo smelled the odor of fresh feces coming from the direction of Monkey Pants's bed and guessed that Monkey Pants had filled his diaper. As patients approached him to gather around the new arrival, to poke and paw and touch, Dodo understood, even then, that his new friend was soiling himself to draw the danger away from him, to take their attention away from Dodo, to give Dodo new light in a land of darkness. Despite the smell of shit and piss, Dodo understood the act for what it was: an act of love and solidarity. And for that he was grateful.

13

Cowboy

Moshe leaned on the railing of the outdoor pavilion that stood high above the Ringing Rocks skating rink and stared absently at the skaters below, one hand thrust in his pocket against the freezing cold. Behind him, several teenage skaters sipping hot chocolate laughed, ducking and tossing light snowballs that whizzed past the short, squat man in a felt fedora hat and coat holding an unlit, half-smoked cigar. Moshe ignored them.

He loved coming to Ringing Rocks Rink, just outside of town. The rocks were a tourist attraction, a geographical curiosity left over from the Stone Age. When struck by a hammer, they rang in various tones. The rink and tower with its pavilion were built beside the clump of rocks to accommodate visitors. Climbing to the top of the pavilion and viewing the mountains surrounding Berks County forest was a release for him. He'd offer a Birkhot Hashachar, a morning prayer that helped to free his mind and clear his head and enjoy a temporary respite from the chaos of his theater. It was on the advice of his old friend Malachi that he'd begun these kinds of outings. His friend who had wowed his theater with his wild dancing to the glorious music of the great Mickey Katz, who had written him several times from a small Jewish settlement in Janów Lubelski, Poland, where he'd finally opened, of all things, a chicken farm, selling eggs and kosher chickens. Malachi's letters were full of his usual boundless enthusiasm, extolling the virtues of country life and the humorous lives of the customers he'd encountered. Moshe admired Malachi's ability to adapt after every failure despite his adherence to the old ways. Malachi's letters were always packed with jokes and light humor, and Moshe always tried to return the favor.

He'd come to write to his old friend this morning, and he'd planned to keep his news light and airy as much as he could, for that was the unacknowledged rule between the two, to keep the news bright and cheerful. Except now there was nothing to be cheerful about. His wife lay in a Reading hospital in a coma. Doctors were unsure what was next. The boy was in the hands of the state. He didn't want to think about it. It was a horrible spiral. How had this all happened?

He gazed down at the skaters and sighed. Chona had insisted on escaping with him to the skating rink after the boy came. They were an odd family, the Jewish merchant, his disabled wife, and their twelve-year-old Negro charge puttering up the hill into the parking lot in his old Packard, coming to a stop not more than ten yards from the rink entrance where a sign had been posted not many years before stating "No Jews, no dogs, no niggers." That sign had since been removed, but Chona never skated on her visits. Not once. Nor did she allow the boy to skate. She complained that her foot prevented her from skating, but Moshe knew better. Chona could do whatever she set her mind to. She could have a special skate made. Marv Skrupskelis would do anything for her—he would have made her one in a hot second. And the boy—he didn't need a skate. He could fly across the rink in his shoes, he was so athletic. Moshe tried to convince Chona to let the boy skate, but she refused. Instead, she commanded, "Go to the tower and smoke your cigar," and he happily obliged, climbing to the top, where he'd puff his cigar in peace and watch from above as the two clambered among the clump of ringing rocks below. He'd watch as she struck the rocks with a hammer while the child placed his hands on them to feel the vibrations. He thought the whole business foolish and at one point said so, but Chona disagreed. "The rocks are as old as the earth. He can hear them a little. They're helpful to him," she said.

Helpful, Moshe thought bitterly. *That's how she thought. Helpful here, helpful there. Now look. Who was helping them now?* "All that is past now," he said aloud, ignoring the teenagers who giggled behind him and playfully romped about the odd man at the railing chomping on the unlit cigar and acting as if they weren't there. An errant snowball landed near him, so Moshe moved to a bench. He dusted the light snow off it, seated himself, produced a pen and paper, and began his letter to Malachi.

He scribbled fast, the unlit cigar clenched between his teeth, ignoring the cold in his hands. It wasn't just Chona being in the hospital, he wrote. Nor the Negro child placed in the nuthouse, that was bad, too. It's the theater business, he explained. Times are changing. *You were right*, he wrote. *Jews here don't want Yiddish theater and Yiddish music and good old frolic and fun anymore. They want American things. They want to be cowboys. Even the Negro jazz musicians have grown difficult. Last night was the last straw.*

He paused, intent on telling Malachi in detail the events of the previous night. He tried three times, crossed out what he had written, then stopped writing and pondered how to explain it. He sat a moment, thinking back over it, unsure how to proceed, the cold beginning to work its way into his neck, for he'd forgotten to wear a scarf.

He reached into his pocket for a match to light his cigar, found none, thought a bit more, then simply scribbled, *Just so you know, I'm thinking of getting out.*

It was last night's incident that bore that out. After leaving Chona in the hospital, he'd rushed to the theater and arrived at 7:30—horribly late for an 8 p.m. start—to find himself in a hot mess.

Lionel Hampton's band and Machito and his Afro-Cubans were booked to play a dual date. The Afro-Cubans were a last-minute replacement for the original headliner, Louis Armstrong, who was hung up in Denver because of bad weather. It was not a good situation to start. Armstrong's manager was the powerful Joe Glaser out of New York. Glaser had offered a sub, but Moshe, distracted by Chona's illness and tired of paying Glaser's huge percentage, declined and decided to book the replacement himself. He called his old friend Chick Webb. But alas, his old pal, the first Negro he'd ever booked, the wonderful hunchbacked musical genius, was very ill. "Get Mario Bauzá and his Afro-Cubans," Webb croaked over the phone. "They're fantastic."

It was in tribute to the ailing Webb that he'd booked the Afro-Cubans, because he was certain that his Chicken Hill audience had no idea who Mario Bauzá, Machito, and the Afro-Cubans were. Mario was a wonderful musician, and Moshe was sure the Afro-Cubans were fantastic. But he'd assumed the Afro-Cubans would be the warm-up act and Hampton's band would close as headliners. He should have worked that out before the two acts arrived. Instead, when he walked backstage last night, both bands were milling around while Lionel Hampton's wife, Gladys, who ran her husband's band, and Mario Bauzá, who ran the Afro-Cubans, were at each other's throats about who would play last.

"We play last," Gladys said. "We're the headliners."

"You can go first," Mario said.

"Act your age, not your color, Mario. G'wan out there."

"Ladies first, Gladys."

As Moshe stepped in the door, both turned to him. "Moshe," Gladys snapped. "You better tell us something."

Moshe stood at the stage door entrance afraid to speak—he hated confrontations—while both bands, clad in suits and ties, milled about anxiously, clasping horns and smoking nervously, pretending they weren't listening.

He looked at his watch. "It's nearly eight," he said meekly. "Can't you two work it out?"

He spoke to both, but he was really addressing Mario, the cooler of the two. Mario was calm and professorial. Gladys, on the other hand, was a hurricane. She was a handsome Negro woman, always dressed to the nines, and would fight with any man in the business.

Instead of answering, Mario, a genteel Latino clad in a blue suit, bow tie, and wire-rim glasses, stepped to a billboard poster hanging on the wall, a few of which Moshe had managed to get printed up at the last minute to advertise the event. He dropped his finger on the words "Featuring Mario Bauzá and Machito and the Afro-Cubans." He did it calmly, like an economics professor pointing out an equation to a class, then said, "Gladys, what's this mean?"

"It means you can read English."

"It means we're the headliners."

"No, it doesn't. Pops was the headliner," Gladys said, using the name musicians affectionately called Louis Armstrong.

"That's right," Mario said, "and we're replacing him."

"Mario, you can look in the mirror ten times and comb your face ten times, and you still won't see Pops looking back at you."

Mario's professorial calm dissipated and he muttered in Spanish, "Tienes razón. Te pareces mucho más a Pops que a mí. Y eso es un hecho." (You're right. You look a hell of a lot more like Pops than I do. And that's a fact.)

Several Afro-Cubans standing nearby chortled.

Gladys turned to a member of her band. "Pedro, what'd he just say?"

The man looked away mumbling. "I don't know, Gladys."

Gladys turned back to Mario and pointed to the stage. "All right, ya cow-walking turd! Get to work!"

"I am at work!"

"On the stage!"

"The contract says we're the headliners!"

"What contract?" she said.

"Did you read the contract, Gladys?"

"We played DC last month with Pops and *we* went last, Mario!"

"That was DC!" Mario sputtered. "This is Potthead . . . Pottsville—"

"Potts*town*," Moshe interjected politely.

Mario was seething. He glanced at Moshe and mumbled in Spanish. "Todo el mundo alrededor de este maldito lugar está en la niebla!" (Everyone around this goddamned place is in a fog!)

Gladys broke in. "Stop jabbering, ya bush-league greaser! The crowd's waiting! G'wan out there so we can make our money and get down the road!"

The insult struck the demure Mario like a lightning bolt and rage climbed into his face. Before he could respond, Moshe stepped in.

"Please!" he said.

They both glared at him now. He was petrified, staring down at the floorboards, wishing he could disappear beneath them. He hated moments like this. He had no idea what to do. If only Chona was here. How many times had she helped him work these things out beforehand, talked through problems, made him put his foot down, and pointed him in the right direction? He glanced at Gladys's husband, Lionel Hampton, hoping for some help, but the great bandleader stood in a far corner with his vibes, which were on wheels, ready to be rolled onstage. Hampton seemed to be focused on his mallets, which suddenly needed all sorts of tampering and adjusting.

"Maybe Mario can go last . . . tonight," Moshe said weakly. "And you guys can go last tomorr—"

Gladys spun on her heel and stomped off toward the backstage pay phone before he even finished. "I'm calling Joe Glaser," she said.

That did it for Moshe. If Joe Glaser found out he'd booked another band behind his back, he was sunk. Glaser was a booking powerhouse. Cross Joe Glaser and the lucrative stopover dates that small theaters like his depended on—the Louis Armstrongs, the Duke Ellingtons, the Lionel Hamptons—would vanish.

He called out. "Wait, Gladys, please! Just gimme a minute!"

She paused and looked back, nodding satisfactorily as Moshe gently touched Mario's elbow and led the great musician through a side door as far away from the others as he could. The door led to a hallway that separated the stage from the dance hall.

Moshe stood with his back to the dance floor, the bustling of the crowded dance hall buzzing behind him, and looked at Mario, whose face was tight with fury.

"I'll never play this batshit town again," Mario said.

"I made a mistake, Mario. I'm sorry."

"You should'a worked this out before. You know how Gladys is."

"I couldn't reach her."

"That nut lives on the phone."

"She was on the road, Mario. I was . . . my wife is sick."

Mario nodded tersely, cooling slightly. "So I heard. What's she got?"

Moshe sighed. "Got" didn't seem the appropriate word. People "got" the flu. "It's a brain tumor . . . or something. The doctors . . . there was a fight in her store . . . she had a bad seizure. She hasn't come around yet."

The great musician, holding his trumpet at his chest with both hands, peered at Moshe for a long moment, the color returning to his face. Then the usual patient kindness for which the great trumpeter was so well-known worked its way back into his face. He glanced down at his instrument, fingering its valves nervously. "That's bad news, mijo. It's going around. Chick's sick, too."

"I know. You seen him?"

Mario nodded, frowning, at the floor. "Not good, mijo. He's not doing too good."

The two men were silent a moment. Moshe, thinking of the great Chick Webb, so heartful and talented, banging his drums, laughing with joy, shouting to his thundering band as the customers danced, his music roaring through the great All-American Dance Hall and Theater, bringing light to Moshe's life, his theater, the town, and his wife. It was too much, and Moshe found himself wiping tears from his eyes.

"I'm losing everything," he said.

Mario sighed, then said, "We'll open the show."

Moshe recovered and cleared his throat. "My cousin Isaac runs the Seymour Theaters down in Philly. I'll get him to book you down there. We'll do it next year, when you're going west. Then you can come here after."

"You gonna book it through Joe Glaser or me?" Mario asked.

"However you want."

"I don't wanna do nothing with Glaser. I want to go through my people," Mario said. "Lemme show you something."

Moshe was leaning on the door. Mario gently pushed him aside and cracked open the door behind him. The sound of excited Spanish chatter flowed into the hallway. Then Mario closed the door again.

"Hear that?"

"Hear what?"

"That's Spanish, mijo. That's the sound of the future. These people don't want swing music. They want the descarga, ponchando, tanga, piano guajeos, mamba, Africano-Cubano. Swing's not enough."

Moshe couldn't help himself. The promoter in him came through, and he thought, *Where do these people come from? Reading? Phoenixville? Where did Nate put up those posters?* He felt ashamed at that moment, thinking of business when his wife was in the hospital fighting for her life. But it was, after all, an opportunity. "I didn't know there were so many Spanish people around here," he mumbled.

Mario smiled. "To you, they're Spanish. To me, they're Puerto Rican, Dominican, Panamanian, Cuban, Ecuadorian, Mexican, Africano, Afro-Cubano. A lot of different things. A lot of different sounds mixed together. That's America, mijo. You got to know your people, Moshe."

Mario opened the backstage doorway, summoned his band, and moments later, Moshe watched in awe as the Afro-Cubans proceeded to burn the wallpaper off the walls of the All-American Dance Hall and Theater with the wildest, hottest Latin beats Moshe had ever heard. The audience went mad, dancing like demons. And when Mario's band was done, the hard-charging Lionel Hampton band took the stage demoralized, their swing music falling on ambivalent ears, leaving even the usual black customers in their seats, reaching for drinks, talking, chortling, and laughing, using the time to drink and joke and as a chance to rest their tired feet, which had carried them all week as they swept floors and poured coffee and emptied garbage bins and slung ice. It was a lesson. And Moshe received it in full.

Seated on the platform above the Ringing Rocks ice-skating rink as fresh snow began to fall, Moshe took his letter out again. *You are right*, he wrote. *The old ways will not survive here. There are too many different types of people. Too many different ways. Maybe I should be a cowboy.*

He sealed the letter and sent it.

THREE WEEKS LATER, Moshe received a package in the mail that was carefully wrapped in a series of three boxes, with newspaper in each, each carefully bundled with string with a label marked "Fragile." It took him a good twenty minutes to open it, and when he finally did, he burst out laughing, for inside was a tiny pair of cowboy pants made of what appeared to be some kind of moleskin, too small to be worn, infant-sized, with frills on the side and with a tiny Star of David sewn onto the back. Attached to them was a note from Malachi in Yiddish saying, *Try these, cowboy.*

Moshe responded by sending the awful pants back in a package that was even harder to open. He rolled them into a tight ball, stuffed them in a metal tobacco can, filled the top of the can with newspaper and corn husks, then inserted the can into yet another larger coffee can that he sealed with wax. He inserted that into a larger empty pretzel can stuffed with paper wrappings and cellophane, then walked into the theater and told Nate, who was atop a ladder fixing the curtain pulley, that he wanted it soldered shut.

Nate, high on the ladder, stared down in silence a moment, then said, "You want it what?"

"Soldered shut. I'm sending it overseas to my friend Malachi. It's a joke."

"I don't know how to solder."

"You know anyone who can?"

"Fatty learned to solder over at the Flagg factory. He can do it. He solders stuff all day."

"Can you ask him?"

There was a long silence. From the floor, Moshe watched Nate lift his head to stare into the dark shadows of the walkway above, the network of pulleys, ropes, and skeletal metal rods that lived atop the stage.

"I'll get it done."

Moshe placed the can on the floor. The delight in this silly exchange lightened his heart, and he began to think things through more clearly—about his wife, and their circumstance, and that of Dodo, of whom his wife was so fond. A clarity arrived in his head for the first time, and he called up, "Nate, can you ask Addie to come by the theater? I want to talk about Dodo."

"Why?"

"You know where they sent him, don't you?"

There was silence. From his vantage point, Moshe could only see the bottoms of Nate's worn shoes, for his face was upturned as he worked the pulley high above him in the stage rafters.

Nate spoke slowly without emotion. There was something about his deadpan voice that didn't sound right. "I reckon you can speak with Addie on it when you go over to see Miss Chona today," he said.

"Okay. I'll bring her back here. I want to talk about it. With you. And her. And my cousin Isaac."

"It's all right, Mr. Moshe. You done enough," Nate said. "It's in God's hands."

"Pennhurst is no place for a child."

There was a momentary silence from atop the ladder, then: "Like I said, Mr. Moshe, it's in God's hands."

Moshe turned and left for his office, puzzled. *There is still so much about America, and the Negroes,* he thought, *that I do not understand.*

But had he climbed the scaffolding and stood atop the stage walkway and seen Nate's face clearly, even from a few feet off, he would have turned and leaped off the scaffolding and run off the stage and out of the theater, for Nate, atop the ladder and holding a hammer in one hand and a wrench in the other, stared at the wall absently, his eyes burning with dark, murderous rage.

14

Differing Weights and Measures

At the end of Pigs Alley in Chicken Hill, outside a beaten-up old shack with a door sign that read "Fatty's Jook. Caution. Fun Inside," the proprietor stood on the front porch, his face a reflection of anything but fun. His gaze fell on a pile of firewood near the porch stairs. The pile, nearly three feet high, was a tangle of broken chairs, discarded wood, and tree branches used to heat the joint's woodstove. Fatty, clad in a flannel shirt, a gray vest, worn trousers, and a porkpie hat, walked down to the pile and sat on it, his arms crossed, lost in thought.

It was 2 a.m. and the joint was still jumping inside. Normally, the scratchy jukebox squawking the howls of Erskine Hawkins that floated above the chortling and laughing of the customers inside was good news. But right now, for Fatty, that was not good news. Not at all. There was a problem inside. A big one.

Nate Timblin was in there, sitting alone at one of the rickety tables, drinking.

Fatty leaned forward on the woodpile, silently cursing his luck.

The jook door opened. Rusty, holding an open bottle of beer, emerged and sat down on the woodpile next to Fatty and sipped.

"He still at it?" Fatty asked.

Rusty nodded.

"What's he drinking?"

"Sipping that shine, Fatty. One glass after another, the devil keeping score."

Fatty sighed and stared down Pigs Alley, considering the problem.

"What you so worried about?" Rusty asked.

"Nate Timblin running booster down his little red lane in my joint. That's what I'm worried about."

"You should'a thought it out before you rolled that gulp sauce up here."

Fatty silently agreed. Leaning back, he gazed out into Pigs Alley and mulled the issue calmly, like a lawyer. This was a complicated problem.

"You want me to ask him to stop?" Rusty asked.

"Do a donkey fly?" Fatty said.

"Nate wouldn't hurt nobody," Rusty said. "I never seen him mad. Ever."

"And you don't wanna."

"You seen him like that?"

Fatty, normally enthusiastic, suddenly grew irritated. "Who said I did?"

Rusty shrugged, rose, climbed the porch stairs, and went back inside.

Fatty watched him go, then licked his swollen top lip, from which twelve stitches had recently been removed. It was because of that busted lip and missing tooth—care of his buddy Big Soap—that he'd blundered into that goddamned rotgut in the first place. If Big Soap had cleaned that fire hose like he'd told him to, the inspector wouldn't have shaken that peanut out of it. If he hadn't shaken the peanut out of the hose, the two of them wouldn't have gotten fired. If they hadn't gotten fired, he wouldn't have let Big Soap have a go at his mouth. And if Big Soap wasn't such a moron and took his invitation seriously and busted his lip in two places and knocked out his tooth, he wouldn't have gone to Philly and blundered into the moonshine and this whole mess in the first place.

"Goddamnit," he said. "I need some new friends."

He rubbed his jaw, trying to clear his thoughts. His lip had been sheared and his tooth was gone and he needed some kind of fix for both. There was no safe place in Pottstown to get that done. No colored in his right mind went to Doc Roberts even before that living witch got Nate's nephew Dodo locked up. The emergency room at the Pottstown hospital drew the cops, so that was out. That left the colored Doc Hinson in Reading. But Doc Hinson was one of those Booker T. Washington–type proper Negroes. He wasn't fond of coloreds who ran good-time jook joints. Philly was safer. So he'd jumped into his car and headed to his cousin Gene's house, where he'd walked into more catastrophe.

Gene, four years older and the guy from whom Fatty took all his cues when they were boys, was one of Pottstown's greatest Negro success stories—if you didn't count Chulo Davis, the fantastic drummer who got shot over a bowl of butter beans while playing with the Harlem Hamfats in Chicago. Gene, unlike Chulo, set his sights on Philly, where he'd stumbled into a high-society Negro girl whose father owned a thriving dry-cleaning business in the city's Nicetown section. The father dropped dead of a heart attack soon after the two met, and Gene, a bright, enterprising soul, suddenly found himself full of lovelorn desire, his heart full of yearning, overwhelmed with profound, ravenous longing for a girl who was, he told Fatty, "quite the dish." Fatty thought her face was sour enough to curdle a cow, but then again, Gene was ugly enough to shake the scare out of a thicket, so they were quite the pair. After the two married, Gene took over the cleaner's. He always enjoyed Fatty's visits. They were a respite from his wife's constant insistence that he prepare their daughter for her upcoming Jack and Jill cotillion, where high-siddity Negroes gathered to tut-tut, tisk-tisk, and hold cheery glasses of cheap champagne in hands gnarled by years of yanking and knuckling tobacco and slapping pigs in the mouth down South where most of them came from, something they forgot as they were now enjoying life in Philadelphia trying hard to be white. It drove Gene mad, and several times he'd asked Fatty, who wasn't married, to move in with him, declaring there were women aplenty in Philadelphia.

Fatty ignored those entreaties, but after he got his lip busted, Gene was the perfect answer. His plan was to go to Gene's house, find someone to fix his mouth, hole up at Gene's for a day or two, then get back to Pottstown as soon as possible. Instead, he arrived two days after his dear cousin had fallen into a disaster.

Gene had purchased a horse-pulled water pumper from a local Philadelphia fire company just down the street from his house. The pumper was a relic, a leftover piece of junk that the fire company wanted to part with, having moved to gas-powered vehicles years before. Gene paid for the old contraption, pulled it into his backyard with his old truck, filled the tank with forty gallons of water, then ventured up to a tony Chestnut Hill horse-riding outfit where, in a burst of good Pottstown friendliness and Southern partiality toward white folks that the Pottstown colored had plenty of practice with, many having spent most of their working years as janitors and maids, he talked the white proprietor into letting him rent one of his riding horses. The steeds of the Chestnut Hill Riding Company were magnificent creatures: retired racers; gorgeous, well-bred animals spared from the bullet by the horse lovers of the city's well-to-do. The proud creatures enjoyed the remainder of their lives on easy street, trained to trot on a twelve-mile riding path through Fairmount Park, one of the largest city parks in America. The Chestnut Hill Riding Company was an exclusive club—closed to Negroes and Jews, of course, and the idea of a Negro even meandering into the entrance to request to join the club and ride one of its pride mounts was preposterous. But it just so happened that on the Sunday afternoon Gene arrived, the proud owner of the institution, an old Quaker named Thomas Sturgis, fully aware of his group's abolitionist history and affiliation with the Negro, had just received a letter from a dying fellow Quaker reminding him of a glorious sermon about Negro self-sufficiency the two enjoyed in care of Booker T. Washington, one of the Negro's greatest leaders, who had spoken at their Quaker meeting house some years before. The reminder of that great Negro leader's words, and the thought of his now dying friend encouraging him to attend that stirring lecture, moved Sturgis, and the old Quaker decided that here in the year 1936, seventy-one years after the end of the Civil War, which ended chattel slavery, it was high time a good Negro joined the ranks of the Chestnut Hill Riding Company.

Sturgis had just come to this conclusion that morning when Gene, nattily dressed in a suit, tie, bowler, and riding boots (having made a habit of nicking various "lost" clothing from his dry-cleaning customers), arrived, announced himself as the owner of his very own business, and declared he'd like to rent a horse. To Sturgis's eyes, the polite young black man with an infectious smile who owned his very own dry cleaner's was a perfect example of the kind of Negro needed to break the ice, and Sturgis happily acquiesced, believing that the Lord had sent him a sign. He led Gene to the stable and pointed to a large white horse. "Will he do?" he asked. "He's a palomino."

"Any pal of Mino is a pal of mine," Gene tooted, though the sight of the mighty stallion, which stood nearly six feet tall at the shoulders, made him nervous. So he said, "I don't need such a young horse. I'll take an older one. Or even a mule. You got a mule?"

The old Quaker chuckled, thinking the finely dressed Negro was joking. "Thy four-legged creatures of God are better judges of thy inner soul than thy man creatures," Sturgis said. "Size makes no difference."

"Indeed you is right, sir," Gene said.

"Thy horse is often a better judge of thine character than thy women, or even thine children, who are much more adept at it than one might imagine," Sturgis said. "Though not as keen as a horse. A horse instantly senses thine nature."

The fact that Gene, a clever snout who never finished sixth grade, was neither offended nor thrown by Sturgis's use of "thee" and "thy," for which the Quakers were known, and even used the words himself as he responded, helped the matter, for he had no notion of what the man was talking about. But he sensed victory and responded, "And I sense thee's kindness in the privy," not realizing until he uttered the words that they were probably an insult but guessing correctly that the old man probably either didn't hear well or know what "privy" meant; but just to be safe, Gene quickly upended the whole business by further chatting up his background, offering luminous praise about his upbringing in lovely Pottstown, Montgomery County, which he described as a "land aplenty with horses and cows and mermaids," leaving out the part that he was born in Chicken Hill and that the only horse he'd ever actually touched was a nag named Stacy he'd led around for a half-blind Jewish rag peddler named Adolph whom he'd fleeced out of a week's earnings before bolting for Philly four years before.

The deal was done, the fee was paid, and Gene mounted the horse and took off on the riding trail, enjoying the view atop the proud animal. The beast knew the trail by heart and they proceeded without incident. When the trail meandered toward the park entrance near Nicetown, just two blocks from Gene's home, Gene, in a burst of enthusiasm, veered the creature off the trail, out of the park, onto the cobblestone street, and into his yard. He hitched the horse to his newly purchased 1865 fire company water pumper, still filled with forty gallons of water, and attempted to take a quick rock-around-the-block to show off the new toy to his North Philadelphia neighbors. The poor horse, unused to the harness and traces of a wagon, bolted, careering wildly down the cobbled street, flinging the pumper onto its side and tossing Gene, who cracked three ribs and punctured a lung. The horse dragged the overturned pumper half a block before bystanders could corral it. By the time Fatty arrived two days later, Gene lay in a hospital bed, the furious Chestnut Hill Quaker had pressed charges, and there was no one left to run Gene's dry-cleaning business save his wife, who was too distracted by cotillion chatter to man the counter of any business. She begged Fatty to stay for a couple of weeks and run the dry cleaner's until her brother could make his way up from North Carolina.

"I can't run no cleaner's," Fatty said. "Look at this." He pointed at his mouth and missing tooth. "I got to get my tooth fixed. Who's gonna leave their clothes to a man with no front tooth?"

Gene's wife waved her hand dismissively, and to Fatty's surprise, her oinky-boinky haughtiness vanished and she got down-home on him. "You ain't got to eat the clothes, Fatty. Just collect 'em and give 'em out. I'll get you a dentist. I know a good one."

"Can't you get somebody else to run things?" Fatty pleaded.

"Nobody can run a business better than you," Gene's wife countered. "Gene said you can run any kind of business."

She had a point. In addition to owning Chicken Hill's only jook joint, Fatty drove his 1928 Ford as a taxi, delivered ice with his own mule and cart twice a week, cut back trees from neighboring houses, collected the old junk in town from whoever wanted it taken away, operated a hamburger and soda pop stand from the front of his jook during the day, booked a colored photographer out of Reading to shoot colored folks' weddings, and worked the 3 to 11 p.m. shift at Flagg with his Italian buddy Big Soap until he got them both fired. Fatty was a busy man.

He explained to Gene's wife that he had several businesses to get back to. But a guarantee of a week's profits from Gene's thriving business moved him, that and the promise that her brother would bring up several gallons of homemade moonshine—"the good stuff," she said, "not that watery crap they make up here"—for him to take back home. That sealed the deal, not to mention her knowledge of moonshine that convinced him she wasn't so hoity-toity after all.

Thus Fatty found himself behind the counter of Gene's Dry Cleaner's and Laundry for two weeks before returning to Chicken Hill.

At the time, it seemed like a good deal. He got stitches in his lip. His cousin's wife made good on her promise, sort of. She found a dentist who replaced his missing gold tooth with a wooden one. And when it was all done, he headed back to Chicken Hill, his gasping 1928 Ford loaded with fourteen gallons of some of the best moonshine he'd ever tasted—enough to sell well into the spring.

It had worked out just fine until tonight, when Nate Timblin walked in and ordered a drink.

Still seated on the woodpile outside as Erskine Hawkins wailed from the jukebox, Fatty glanced at the door and weighed his options. He actually considered walking down the alley to Miss Chona's store, going in the back door, which was unlocked—she never locked it, why steal when she gave you what you wanted on credit anyway and never asked for payment—and using the pay phone to call the cops to bust his own joint. He worked it out in his head: make the call, sprint back to warn Nate and the others before the cops came, hide the booze in the woods behind the jook, and let the cops bust the place, where they'd find nothing and leave. But that plan had a big hole. He knew all four cops on the town's police force. Two were drunks, easily bought off with booze. The third, David Hynes, was a devout Christian with a kind heart who looked the other way unless you gave him lip. But the fourth, Billy O'Connell, was a rascal who was also a lieutenant at the Empire Fire Company. Fatty had done everything he could to get on O'Connell's good side: He got the fire company cheap beer at a discount—actually stolen, but the good-hearted firemen didn't care. He fed the firehouse fellas free chicken from Reverend Spriggs's annual dinner sell-off. He'd even dragged Big Soap there and handed him over, since Soap was strong enough to pull the wet hundred-foot leather fire hose to the top of the fire company tower to let it dry out after use. The guys at Empire were crazy about Big Soap. They all liked him.

Except for Billy O'Connell.

Billy O'Connell did not like Big Soap, or Fatty, or even his own firemen. Billy O'Connell liked no one. Fatty had never met an Irishman like him. That made O'Connell dangerous.

Fatty leaned on the woodpile, considering the idea. It was Thursday. O'Connell was off duty today—unless he wasn't. If one of the other three cops had called in sick, O'Connell would be summoned, since the town always kept three cops on duty.

He considered the plan. Who would know if O'Connell was on duty?

Paper would know, he thought. That woman knew everything. But she was asleep or maybe busy loving up some Pullman porter. He beat back his own jealous feelings. What a song she was. If only she knew his heart. He closed that feeling off quickly and considered the matter again. A raid would bring all three cops, since anything on Chicken Hill brought the entire force. Was O'Connell on duty or not? Was it worth it just to get Nate out before he did some damage? He thought it through. Yes! But then he remembered he'd been told that O'Connell was the cop who'd chased Dodo down and took him to Pennhurst. Suppose Nate knew that O'Connell was the cop who had helped Doc Roberts send Dodo off? That wouldn't work, Nate being drunk and O'Connell showing up.

This town, he thought grimly, *is too damn small.*

He discarded the idea, briefly considered a scheme to empty his joint by walking in and announcing that several Negroes from Hemlock Row, a tiny black neighborhood just outside Pottstown, were headed over mad as hell with guns and baseball bats—he'd heard some crazy fool over there named Son of Man was apparently scaring the pants off everyone—but then diced the idea. The Hill Negroes might cotton to a good fight with the Hemlock Row guys. That was no good.

Finally, he decided to take the direct route. He stood up, took a deep breath, climbed the porch steps, went back into the jook, strode to the wall, lowered the volume of the blasting jukebox, and announced, "Closing early, y'all. I got to work tomorrow."

"C'mon, Fatty," one of the men said. "Let Erskine Hawkins finish."

"Erskine'll be on the box tomorrow. G'wan home now."

There were seven souls in the place, and they stalled, nursing their drinks, until they saw Fatty move toward the back corner table where

Nate sat in silence, a gallon jug of North Carolina Blood of Christ and a half-empty glass on the table before him. That got them moving. They downed their drinks and lumbered toward the door, except for Rusty, who remained behind the bar, a makeshift piece of claptrap wood and pine slabs.

Fatty sat down and motioned at Rusty to join them. Rusty came over and sat as Fatty spoke. "Evening, Nate," he said.

Nate was staring at his glass. After a long moment, his glazed eyes slowly rolled up from the glass to lock in on Fatty, then slowly rolled back to the glass again.

It was just a moment, that look from Nate, but that was enough. Fatty found himself staring at the floor, the hairs on the back of his neck standing on end. *Goddamn*, he thought, *what have I done?* When Fatty was nineteen, he'd served two years at Graterford Prison for a mishap he preferred to forget, and after fighting his way to better food and treatment, he'd mistakenly insulted an old prisoner named Dirt, a leader in his block who was serving a life sentence for three murders. Dirt was, at first glance, a butterfly: a thin, frail-looking elderly man with thick glasses and small shoulders, whereas Fatty was a stout, spirited youth, wide around the shoulders. Fatty didn't think much of the insult until a couple of days later. He was sitting at a cafeteria table when Dirt, seated at another table, got up, stretched leisurely, strolled over to Fatty's table holding a fork, and calmly gouged out the eye of the man sitting directly across from Fatty. He did it with the serenity of a housewife nursing a baby.

Fatty was sitting close enough to hear the squish of the fork landing in the poor fella's eye, and he never forgot the calm in Dirt's eyes as Dirt put the fork to work, the poor fella's eyeball popping out and rolling across the floor like a marble. It was a clean, clear operation. The sense of purpose shook him. The minute Dirt emerged on the block from solitary—and Fatty noted that it was a short stay, another nod to the little man's pull and power—he nearly fell over himself getting to Dirt's cell to apologize for his slight transgression. The older man was surprisingly gracious.

He asked, "You come from Pottstown?"

"I do."

"Then you know Nate."

"Ain't but one Nate in Pottstown. Everybody knows Nate. He's married to one of my cousins. We're all related out there in some form or fashion."

"Nate was here some years back," Dirt said.

Fatty was surprised. "He never mentioned that to me," Fatty said. "He's a lot older. Listen, Dirt, I wanna say I'm sor—"

Dirt raised a hand and cut him off. "I took that fella's eye out because he took something that belonged to me. But if Nate were to take something that belonged to me, I wouldn't twitch a muscle. I wouldn't cross Nate Timblin for all the cheese and crackers in the world."

"Old Nate? We talking about the same Nate? Nate Timblin?"

"That ain't the name he had in here, son. Ask around."

And Fatty did. He learned from the other older prisoners that the Nate he knew—trusty, calm Nate, the old man who came to Pottstown from the South and worked for Mr. Moshe at the All-American Dance Hall and Theater, who followed his wife, Addie, around like a puppy, who took his deaf nephew Dodo hunting—was not the same Nate Timblin who served time in Graterford Prison. Rather, he was a story, a wisp, a legend, a force, a fright. Why he was in no one seemed to know, but there were rumblings and they were not good. No one seemed to care much about the where or why except for one matter: Nate's name was surely not Nate Timblin. The prisoners called him Love. "Nate Love," they said, "not Timblin. Love's his name. Nate Love. We don't know no Timblin. We seen it on his paperwork. Love. That's his family name, son. Nate Love, said to be from down South Carolina way. The Low Country they call it. As good a man as you'll ever meet; as kind a soul that has ever walked round these prison walls. But God help you if Nate Love calls his family name on you, son. If he starts in on you that way, you're flower of the week."

When Fatty learned this, he returned to Dirt's cell and asked, "Did you know Nate well?"

"I knew him very well," the old man said.

"What'd he do to get here?"

Dirt shrugged. "It ain't what he's done to get here, son. It's what's inside him. Call it a curse or a devilment. Whatever it is, it lives in some people. There's not many types like 'em in this world. But Nate's one of 'em. He got that *thing* in him, son, deep inside. It's too bad really, on account of he's a good man, my kind of man. But a man can't control what's in him once it's turned loose no more than you or I can hold on to a bag of groceries if we was to get hit by a bus. Some things is just there, waiting to get turned loose. That's the way it is. You wanna keep clear of that side of him, son. If you thick enough to turn that devil loose in him, you in deep water."

Fatty, seated at the rickety table across from Nate, felt his mouth go dry. He swallowed his spit as he watched Nate stare at his half-empty glass of moonshine. Nate's eyes glowed eerily. Fatty saw it then. Saw what the men saw. Nate Love, beaming in from another world, his eyes calm and intense, brimming with calcified white-hot rage. Fatty felt as if he were looking at a volcano covered by a clear lake. He resisted the urge to leap to his feet and run out into the night. He silently cursed himself, cursed Big Soap for screwing up back at the Flagg factory, cursed his cousin Gene and Gene's wife and Gene's wife's brother, too, who gave him the North Carolina Blood of Christ moonshine, and then lastly cursed himself.

"I should'a never brought that shine up here," he said aloud.

Nate ignored him and sat, not moving, his long fingers still cradling the glass. Fatty glanced at Rusty, who was shaken, too. Rusty was a big man, strong and wide and young, and Fatty was no small man himself. But at the moment, seeing the fear climb into young Rusty's face and feeling his own fright pawing at him, he knew that even if both of them pounced on Nate, it would be like trying to douse a house fire with a glass of water.

Fatty decided to say nothing else. It was Rusty who spoke. He pointed at Nate's half-empty glass. "How's that coming, Nate?"

Silence.

"You all right?"

Nate didn't respond, his eyes unwavering, staring at the glass.

Finally, Fatty found his voice. "Nate . . . I got to close soon."

Nate's eyes slowly moved from the glass to Fatty's face and Fatty looked away. *Christ*, he thought. *I done it.*

Fatty glanced at Rusty, who, thank God, broke the ice in the oddest way. Young Rusty was tired. He leaned on the table, placing his hands on his face and rubbing his eyes. There was an innocence to Rusty that seemed to pull fresh air into any room he walked into. Everyone on the Hill loved Rusty, who would do anything for anyone. The simple yawn, his weariness, seemed to yank a bit of tension from the room. It thinned it out just a little, and Fatty decided to keep quiet for a change. He was glad he did, for Rusty pulled his hands from his face and continued.

"I don't like what happened either, Nate. It's not right. Dodo didn't do nothing wrong. Doc Roberts . . . he's just no good."

Nate's eyes moved to Rusty. The calm rage in his eyes that burned so brightly that looking into them was like staring at the sun locked in on Rusty's innocent face and the raging glow dimmed a bit. Rusty started to say something else but clammed up, finally sputtering, "Maybe there's a way to get out of it."

"That's right," Fatty chirped. "I know a few people over there at Pennhurst."

Nate looked at him, and Fatty felt as if an electric buzzing in the room had lowered. The sharp edge of the man's rage dulled, the energy of hate in the force that sat before him eased as Nate fingered his glass, moving his hands for the first time. Then Fatty saw his lips move and heard, as if in a dream, Nate mumble something.

The room was quiet. Fatty had turned the jukebox down and only the creaking of the rickety chairs and the popping of the woodstove in its last throes were filling his ears, yet he couldn't hear.

"Say that again, Nate?"

Both he and Rusty leaned over the table, their ears turned close to Nate's lips as the tall man spoke again, quietly, in so soft a voice that both had to strain to hear. But after he spoke, Fatty nodded and said, "Okay, Nate. We gonna take you home now."

The two of them stood, one on each side of Nate, and grasped him gently under the arms, stood him up, and walked him toward the door. Ten minutes later, they put him to bed without incident, for he hadn't said another word. They laid him down with his clothes on and left the house quickly, thanking God that Addie wasn't around, as she was spending most nights at the Reading hospital looking after Miss Chona, who was dying, people said, this time for sure.

It was only after they turned away from the darkened house and were walking up the muddy slope to Pigs Alley to close up Fatty's jook that Rusty asked, "Did you hear what he said?"

"I did," Fatty said.

"What's it mean?"

"It means what he said it means."

"Which is what?"

"Differing weights mean differing measures. The Lord knows 'em both."

"Ain't that from the Bible? Should I ask Reverend Spriggs?"

"Shit no," Fatty snapped. "Leave him out of it."

"What's it mean then?"

"It means we got to bust that boy outta Pennhurst or there's gonna be trouble."

15

The Worm

Mrs. Fioria Carissimi, mother of the young Enzo Carissimi, whom everyone on the Hill affectionately called Big Soap, heard about the ruckus of the Jewish storekeeper and deaf Negro boy from two people. The first was from Vivana Agnello, president of the Volunteer Women's Association of St. Aloysius Catholic Church in downtown Pottstown, where Fioria attended mass every morning. The group met twice a month in the church basement to sip coffee, gossip, and decide who in town needed what in the way of clothing. Vivana announced that the Jews had hidden the deaf child from the state to ransom money from the Negroes who wanted the boy hidden, then kept the money and called the cops anyway. She knew that for a fact, she said, because her husband was a foreman at the Enlevra Stove plant that made the stove that started the whole thing three years ago. The company gave the boy's family $1,200 after one of their stoves blew up and killed the boy's mother, making that little woolhead rich. Since his mother was dead, Negroes on the Hill took advantage of him and stole most of his money, spending it on fishing supplies and whiskey till one of them gave what was left to the Jews at the store to protect the boy from the state, which wanted him—then they turned him over anyway.

That sounded so stupid that it might be true, but then Vivana's gossip had become useless after she condemned Eugenio Fabicelli for selling his bakery to a Jew named Malachi instead of to her cousin Guido, who wanted to buy it. "The Jew ran the business into the ground and skipped town," she said. "So stupid, that Eugenio."

That last remark, spoken in English, had caused some dissension among the normally staid St. Aloysius women partly because Eugenio's younger sister, Pia, happened to be in the room at the time. Pia spoke little English, and while the remark did not register with her at the time, a later translation proved effective, for Pia withdrew from the group immediately. And since she worked as a cleaning lady in the mayor's office, which doubled as the headquarters for the police, electric, and sanitation departments, as well as the hub of the usual skimming and scamming by the city fathers—one third of whom claimed to be direct descendants of the *Mayflower* passengers—there went half of the useful city news, including information about valuable real estate coming up for auction, land giveaways, parade permits, bank-auction sell-offs of useful farm tools, and other handy information, much of which was scrawled on crumpled notes that Pia filched from office garbage cans and crammed into her apron pocket to bring to the women's meeting and share with the group, not to mention her secret recipe for pumpkin pie, which, after much badgering, she had finally promised to share. Gone. All of it. Because of one stupid comment.

Fioria took this news in stride. She had no interest in city news or Pia's pumpkin pie recipe—in fact, she was the one person who knew that Pia's pumpkin pie was actually more squash than pumpkin. Nor was Fioria a fastidious member of Vivana's women's group, for everyone knew Vivana got the job as president because her husband, Enrico, claimed to be a foreman at the Enlevra plant and even wore a shirt and tie to work each morning when he left the house, only to slip overalls over his fancy clothing at the plant to toil at the boiler like the rest of the immigrants. Fioria found Vivana's insistence on speaking English and always trying to be so American slightly distasteful as she encouraged the other housewives to feed their children hamburgers and Cokes instead of arancini and ribollita. But then again, Vivana was from Genoa, where no one was happy, so what could you expect? By contrast, Pia was a fellow Sicilian who lived on the same Chicken Hill street as Fioria did. So while Fioria quietly continued going to the women's volunteer group, she kept up relations with her good friend, and one afternoon less than a week after Dodo was sent to Pennhurst, she found herself in Pia's kitchen watching the younger woman pound her secret ingredient—squash—into small bits to make her pumpkin pie.

It was after Pia popped one of her pies into the oven and the two women sat down to have coffee laced with canned milk, conversing in Italian about the incident at the Heaven & Earth Grocery Store, that Pia dropped the bomb about Doc Roberts.

"The woman did nothing wrong, hiding the boy," Pia said. "Is she still alive?"

Fioria shrugged. "She's in a hospital in Reading. In a coma, they say, God willing that she'll awaken," she said, crossing herself.

"Does she have children?" Pia asked.

Fioria decided to step lightly. It was a sore point, for Pia, nine years younger, had not yet had any and had taken to visiting American doctors for cures, which Fioria discouraged. "No," she said, "but that's just a way to live longer, if you ask me. Children can be a headache."

Pia seemed suddenly irritated, then blurted out, "Where can you hide a boy around here? There's nothing around here but chicken wire and horse crap."

Fioria shrugged. She didn't like to repeat rumors. "All I know is the police went to take him and the coloreds got mad and the poor woman somehow got in the middle of it. That's what Doc Roberts told Father at mass."

At the mention of Doc Roberts, Pia's face reddened and she rose from the table. With her back to Fioria, she snatched her wooden spoon from the counter, scooped up some squash, and angrily dumped the contents into her mixing bowl.

"What's bothering you?" Fioria asked.

"Nothing," Pia said, mixing the pie filling furiously.

"Did you know her?"

"Who?"

"Chona. The Jewish woman."

"I wouldn't know her if she walked in here dressed like a moose and threw salt and olive oil all over the kitchen," Pia said. She stared at the door even though the house was empty, then snapped hotly in Sicilian slang, "Mi farei controllare in manicomio prima di lasciare che il dottor Roberts mi mettesse le mani addosso. È un verme cattivo." (But I'd check myself into the nuthouse before I let Doc Roberts put his fast hands on me again. He's a nasty worm.)

Fioria received this information with shock and alarm. There was trouble in that. Pia's husband, Matteo, was a plasterer, a nice, outgoing fellow except when it came to his wife, for Pia was a slender, pretty young thing.

Fioria changed the subject. "I'm too old for American doctors," she said quickly. "Thank God I had my children in Italy. I never go to doctors here. It's a quick way to die."

Pia slammed the pie filling into the piecrust, placed the pie tin into the oven, and sat back down at the table again in a huff. Then she said softly to Fioria, "Keep quiet. If Matteo goes to prison, what happens to me?"

Fioria reached across the table and gently placed her hand on Pia's shoulder. This assured Pia, for a good woman's heart can hold secrets better than any vault, and Fioria was a good woman. But later that afternoon, while standing at her own stove preparing dinner for her husband and Enzo, Fioria had a sudden panic that rushed across her temples so fast that she had to sit down at the table and dip her fingers into the salt dish to nibble at the salt, which she did at times of extreme worry. *This town is too small*, she thought, *and the kind of trouble Pia mentioned is very wide.* She'd heard a rumor or two about Doc Roberts, but it was better to keep out of those things. Still, if Pia's husband found out about Doc . . . she felt the hairs on her skin pricking and crossed herself, thinking of her son. Enzo knew Matteo well. In fact, Enzo knew everyone well. He was too softhearted. He would do anything for anyone. That was his problem.

She debated the subject in her head. If Matteo caused trouble, Enzo would follow and so would his buddy Fatty and, she thought with sudden clarity, so would la polizia, for they were never far from Fatty. That her son was thick with Chicken Hill's most notorious Negro was something that gave her increasing worry. The boys had been best friends since childhood. When she and her husband arrived in Pottstown from Sicily twelve years ago, Enzo was twelve and spoke no English. But Fatty, who lived around the corner, spoke enough English for both. The Hill's Italian immigrants generally stayed to themselves, but the children played without boundaries, and while most floated back into their tribes as they grew older, Enzo and Fatty had remained as tight as thieves. They were teammates on the high school football team and even took jobs in the same plant after graduation. And while her husband disapproved of Fatty, Fioria found him charming and funny, his crazy schemes amusing, like the time he welded every piece of junk he could find to an old ice wagon—spoons, ladles, cans, steel rods—and drove it around the Hill pulled by a mule, operating the whole thing as a taxicab. Even her husband burst out laughing when he saw it. And Fatty was handy. He could repair cars and trucks, was a good carpenter and an excellent welder, and taught Enzo all those things. And while Enzo had recently knocked out Fatty's front tooth in some dispute, they rarely argued. Fatty had even gotten Enzo into the fire department—the first Italian ever. That was something.

But this was something else. Enzo had just procured a new job at the Dohler plant after some business with Fatty cost him his last one. He needed no trouble. She decided to speak to him about poking his nose in other people's business.

It was already past 4 p.m., and the Dohler factory had already finished its shift, which meant Enzo was off work. She knew just where to find him.

She removed her apron, shut off her stove, left the house by the front door, marched past the tight row houses on her street, turned west at the intersection, cut through an empty lot full of tall weeds, turned onto the muddy trail toward Fatty's jook joint, where her son stopped after work every day to drink beer and listen to jazz music and baseball games on the radio with the rest of the regulars, mostly young Negroes.

Several young men were seated on crates sipping beers near a makeshift table out front next to a grill marked with a sign that read "Hamburgas 10 cents," and they could see Fioria from two hundred yards as she approached, a tiny figure in a housedress marching toward them purposefully, her hands clasped behind her as she took the hill hard and fast, Italian-style, leaning forward. As Fioria approached, she saw from a hundred yards off the towering figure of her son. At twenty-four, Enzo was six feet six and built like a brick oven. He was one of the tallest men in Pottstown and hard to miss. He was seated on a crate hunched over a checkerboard on the jook's front porch. Something about seeing her son's hulking frame across from the much shorter, stockier Fatty made the blood rush to her face and she grew furious.

Neither Fatty nor Big Soap saw her coming, but the other young black men on the porch did, and they hastily spilled off their crates, shoving beers underneath the porch, extinguishing cigarettes, straightening their collars, and hissing, "Soap! Soap! Your ma's coming."

But too late. By the time Big Soap heard them and turned his head, he saw his mother's finger pointed directly at his nose. He was so tall that, even seated, he was taller than she was, so her finger was pointed up at his nostril.

Fioria hissed at him in Italian. "You are headed for trouble," she said.

"What?"

"What happened at the store?" she demanded.

"What store?"

"You stay out of it," she insisted.

"Stay out of what?"

"Out of what happened at the store."

Big Soap glanced at Fatty, who sat in silence, then rolled his eyes good-naturedly. Big Soap was embarrassed. But since he and his mother were the only ones who spoke Italian, he decided to play it off, speaking calmly in Italian, "What did I do, Mama?"

"Don't get smart! The police were up there! Were you up there?"
"Up where?"
"Do I look stupid? What happened?"
"What are you talking about?"
"The nuthouse! You wanna go there?"
"What nuthouse? I just came from work!"

From there, Fioria lost her temper and would not remember the following day, nor the next, what was said. But for the young men watching, the torrent of Italian from the mother, followed by Big Soap's stumbling response, was pure entertainment, and they filled the air with snorts and muffled chuckles, all save Fatty, who carefully stepped off the porch and stood next to Rusty, the two of them watching, spellbound, as mother and son went at it.

"You keep away from the police or you'll be in the nuthouse, too!" Fioria said.

"They can't take me to the nuthouse if I'm at work," Big Soap said.

"Who said you were at work? Did the police know you were at work? Who wants to talk about their work to the police? You just lost one job and now you're gonna lose another. Why? Because of talking to the police! Don't talk to the police. Ever!"

"Who said I was talking to the police?"

"Don't mock me!" She pointed to Fatty, then turned back to Big Soap and rattled off in Italian: "Fatty's got fifteen jobs. You got one. You think jobs grow on trees? Keep outta trouble or you won't have a job! The police sent the colored child to the nuthouse! You're next, the way you're talking! And keep off that doctor. Medici americani! Ciarlatani con mani veloci. Una pillola per tutti. (American doctors! Quacks with fast hands. A pill for everything.) You can't trust them. I should tell your father." And on it went.

Rusty leaned over to Fatty. "Fatty, what'd Soap do?"

"Whatever he did," Fatty said frowning, "he ain't gonna do it no more."

Watching Miss Fioria rant, Fatty grew worried. Miss Fioria lived at the bottom of the Hill close to Main, just one street above Paper. Paper, who did her washing from a sink that faced the main road, was a megaphone. She basically lived in her outdoor flower garden when she wasn't washing clothes or breaking some poor railroad porter's heart. Her house was like the guardhouse to Chicken Hill. She saw every person or item that came up the Hill. That meant Paper saw Miss Fioria headed for his joint, because there was nothing past the weedy lot *but* his jook, which meant this news would spread in minutes. *In fact*, he thought, *it had already spread by now.*

He sighed, watching Miss Fioria rail at Big Soap. Fatty liked Miss Fioria. She was good people—a second mother even. She'd whacked him a few times with her belt when he was a kid while serving punishment on Big Soap—and both of them had deserved it. But she was white. And white folks moving around his jook on Pigs Alley brought the cops. And cops wrecked the economy. They could come right this moment and bust him for selling hamburgers and Coca-Cola during the day if they felt like it. And if it was Billy O'Connell, what's to stop O'Connell from digging around and finding his moonshine buried in the woods, not to mention a few other tangible goods that he'd hidden back there, including an eight-hundred-horse-power table grinder he'd procured from the Dohler plant the year before and a couple of other items he'd "found" in some of the nearby manufacturing plants, to be sold later.

He wanted to intervene, but he knew better. Instead, his mind clicked through solutions. How to get back to normal? Nate was recovering from his drunk, probably back to normal in a day or two. Check.

Nate's wife, Addie, was incommunicado, staying at the hospital in Reading where Miss Chona was. Check. Poor Dodo was gone. In the nuthouse at Pennhurst. He'd been there two weeks. Maybe Nate and Addie will give up on him and let their precious all-solution Good Lord take care of him. Check. Doc Roberts would want to keep things quiet with the white folks anyway. Check. No problem. This will all blow over. Let Miss Fioria yell and then let this settle. Wasn't it reasonable to expect this stuff would just blow over?

To Fatty's relief, Miss Fioria finished her rant, turned, and began her march down Pigs Alley. Then to his dismay, she turned suddenly and marched up to him, pointing a tiny finger and speaking in a thick Italian accent. "You should be ashamed, Fatty."

Fatty offered a "who me?" smile and spread his arms. "Miss Fioria, we wasn't arou—"

"Trouble trouble trouble!" Fioria said. "The poor lady is sick because-a . . ." Then she stopped and peered at him quizzically, and said, "What's a-wrong with your mouth?"

"My mouth?"

"Your tooth-a. What's the matter?"

"Oh, I got a new one."

"Show me."

Fatty opened his mouth. The tiny woman stepped closer and peered inside, examining the wooden tooth, grabbing his chin, and moving his head from side to side before dropping her hands and saying, "You oughta get your money back."

Behind him, Fatty heard several men laugh, but Miss Fioria saw nothing funny. She was staring at him with her hands on her hips.

"What happened at the store?" she demanded.

"I don't know. I heard Miss Chona fell dow—"

And she was off again, ranting in a spurt of Italian: "Ti porterò a casa e ti laverò la bocca con sapone di liscivia se hai intenzione di darmi un sacchetto di gomiti, okay? Cucinavo il cibo e vivevo prima che i tuoi primi denti crescessero." (I will take you home and wash your mouth with lye soap if you're gonna hand me a bag of elbows, okay? I was cooking food and living before your first teeth grew in.) Then she went back to English, ending with "Don't talk this-a-way and that-a-way to me! Miss-a-Chona this and Miss-a-Chona that . . . what happened there?"

For the first time, Fatty realized that he didn't really know quite what had happened at the store. He hadn't been there. He was in Philadelphia getting his tooth replaced and running his cousin's stupid dry cleaner's. But with Miss Fioria staring at him, he realized that he had to put it together anyway. Miss Fioria knew Bernice, who lived next door to the Heaven & Earth Grocery Store. If she marched up to his sister's house and asked her what happened, that would be trouble, because Bernice was sanctified, saved to the Lord, which meant she was unpredictable. Bernice hated his jook joint. What's more, Bernice had helped Miss Chona hide Dodo from the state, letting him play in the yard with her children when they sent that Negro looking for him. That would make Bernice an accomplice. And the state man was a Negro, too. He'd been told that. Who had blabbed? Either way, Miss Fioria going to Bernice would add gas to the fire. It had all started with Nate's dragging the Jews into it.

With Miss Fioria staring at him, Fatty offered up what he knew. "Dodo's mother died."

"Who's Dodo?"

"That's the boy. Dodo's his name—"

"Wait a minute," Fioria said. She nodded to her son, and Big Soap sighed and stepped over. She needed a translator.

She nodded at Fatty. "Go," she said. Fatty spoke while Big Soap translated.

"Dodo's Thelma's boy . . ."

And thus, Fatty Davis, the last person to care about anyone but himself, found himself recounting what he knew. That three years ago a colored lady named Thelma Herring, Addie's sister, who lived on the Hill, had an Enlevra stove, made in one of Pottstown's factories. And the stove blew up. Why it blew up, nobody knows. But the day it blew up was a day every colored on the Hill remembered. Thelma's boy Dodo—whose real name was Holly Herring—was standing near the stove when it blew up. And somehow it affected his eyes and his ears. "He got blind and deaf for a while," Fatty said. "His eyes came back. But his ears did not."

"And the stove did not kill his mother?"

"I already said it, Miss Fioria. No."

"Did the stove company pay her for the accident?"

Fatty looked incredulous. "Do a dog know it's Christmas?"

Big Soap translated and Miss Fioria chuckled. "So she did not die?"

"No," Fatty said. "But she wasn't the same after. She got sick this year and died, that's all. Nobody got paid nothing. Dodo's aunt and uncle took him in. He didn't want to go to school 'cause he couldn't hear nothing. The state wanted to send him to a special school, so his aunt and uncle asked Miss Chona to hold him till they could get the money to send him down South. They got family down there that'll look out for him."

"You sure?"

"Miss Fioria, would I lie to you?"

"You better not," she said, shaking a fist, palm up.

Fatty chuckled, for he could see Miss Fioria was cooling.

"Why'd the doctor come?" she asked. "Was the boy sick?"

"I don't know. Doc Roberts mostly don't treat the colored."

"How'd the doctor know the boy was up here? I live here and *I* didn't know he was up here."

"They was keeping it quiet."

"How'd the doctor find out?"

"Somebody told it, I reckon."

"Is that how the fight started in the store?" she asked.

For the first time, Fatty looked puzzled. "There wasn't no fight in there."

Fioria was firm. "There was a fight. That's how the Jewish lady got hurt."

"She didn't get hurt in no fight. Honest to God."

"What happened to her then?"

"Well . . . she fell out . . . kind'a . . . I don't know. They found her with her clothes . . . kind'a tore off her."

"She fell out and got her clothes tore up on her own?"

"I don't rightly know, Miss Fioria."

Fioria peered around at the young men standing about. She had known most of them since childhood, some for more than a decade. Some of them had been in her living room doing odd jobs, others had eaten her pasta, for after she served her husband and son, if she saw a hungry child pass by, she couldn't help herself. There was something about a starving child that pulled every string in Fioria Carissimi, who grew up in a small Sicilian village near Palermo where a dinner of rice with olive oil and real meat was something that happened once a year at Christmas. She just couldn't stand it. Her dark gaze fell on Rusty, who was nervously smoking a cigarette. She pointed at him.

"Were you there?"

"I . . . seen some of it, Miss Fioria."

"And?"

"Well, Miss Addie got there before I did."

Fioria fired off a string of Italian and Big Soap rolled his eyes. "Rusty, would you talk straight before she kills somebody here."

Rusty spread his arms to explain. "What I seen, when I come in, was Miss Chona lying on the floor with her dress . . . well, Addie was fixing up her dress and clothes. Like they was rumpled up. You know, like somebody had tried to pull 'em off her."

"Was the doctor there?"

Rusty swallowed and was silent a moment. "You mean Doc Roberts?"

"Was he there or not?"

"He was running out when I come in. He come back five minutes later with the cops."

"What about the boy?"

"Dodo was there," Rusty said. "Surely was. He was upset. He yelled some things about Doc Roberts as the cops was chasing him." And here, Rusty paled and said, "Miss Fioria, I ain't really see nothing. Honest to God. The only person who really seen something was Addie. She's up in Reading at the hospital with Miss Chona. You can ask her what she seen. I reckon the only person who seen what went on between Doc and Miss Chona was Doc and Miss Chona."

"The boy was there," Fioria said. "Did anybody ask him?"

"He's deaf and dumb," Fatty said.

Fioria frowned when the translation came, and then spoke to Fatty in English, directly. "Deaf," she said in English, pointing to her own ears. "Pero dumb . . . ?" She pointed at Rusty, Big Soap, and Fatty, counting as she pointed, saying in English, "One, two, three." Then to the rest of the young men standing about, she waved a finger as if to say "Careful. I'm watching you." She then turned to Fatty, said a few more words in Italian, then marched down the hill.

They watched her leave. Fatty asked Big Soap, "What's that last thing she said?"

"Nothing. She said we're in trouble."

"Don't jive me, Soap. I know how to say trouble in Italian. *Guaio.* I remember that word from when she was warming our asses with a switch in the old days. I didn't hear that in none of her words. Was she doggin' me some other way?"

"No."

"So what'd she say then?"

"She said God is watching what we do."

Fatty sighed. "I'd rather have Him holding me to charge than her."

16

The Visit

Chona lay in a private room on the top floor of the Reading hospital on a wing normally reserved for the critically ill or the dying. That was what the gentleman from Philadelphia, a rich theater owner of some kind, had insisted—and paid for—in cash. "I want it quiet," he told the nurses at the station on the floor. He was apparently used to giving orders, which caused some resentment among the nurses. There was a rumor that the Jewess in 401 was from nearby Pottstown and involved in some kind of lawless fracas. They had not seen many Jews on that floor, nor did they see many Negroes like the nursemaid who sat next to the woman's bed all day, her face often buried in a Bible. The Negro rarely smiled. She talked to staff directly in a terse voice. She was arrogant and disrespectful, the nurses decided. To make it worse, the Jew husband came and went at odd hours, not to mention there seemed to be Negroes shuffling in and out of that room all day. It was a bit much—rich Jews paying for private rooms, flooding the floor with Negroes. This country, they murmured among themselves, is going to hell in a handbasket.

Addie was unaware of these comments, as was Chona, who for four days lay comatose and presumed to be in a second coma from which, the doctors said, she was not expected to awaken. Addie was not so sure. Each morning Chona would stir, mumble, then fall back to unconsciousness. The first day, Addie thought nothing of it. But after three days of it, she suspected that the woman inside that body was alive.

Addie revealed this to Moshe when he arrived on the third day with Nate, with whom she hadn't spoken since the incident. The two men walked in looking exhausted, explaining that a three-day set with a Yiddish theater troupe out of Pittsburgh doing *Hamlet* had taken a lot of setup and break-down time.

"So long as the people liked it," Addie said. She tried to sound reassuring.

Moshe ignored her and sat without a word at his wife's bedside. He was a mess. His shirt was soiled, his jacket worn. The bags beneath his eyes looked nearly big enough to hold eggs. He stared at Chona several moments, then said, "Anything new?"

"She's trying to get it out."

"Get what out?"

"That thing she does in the morning. She does it every time."

There was a Jewish word for it, Addie knew, but she couldn't remember it. "It's a ditty. A prayer thing. She's trying to do that. Every morning. For three days now."

Moshe stared at his comatose wife, glanced at Addie, and waved his hand. "Leave us for a while," he said.

Addie and Nate retreated to the hallway. Noting the baleful stares of the nurses, they moved to the stairwell, walked down the stairs, and stepped inside the foyer that faced the grassy hospital entrance, away from white ears and eyes. It was their first moment alone since the incident four days before.

"Ain't no need to give him false hope," Nate said.

"I ain't joshing," Addie said. "She's yet living."

"Leave that to the doctors."

"I wouldn't go to a doctor in these parts for a hundred Christmas turkeys," Addie said. "Especially Doc Roberts."

"You can't right every wrong in the world," Nate said.

"What's that got to do with anything?"

Nate nodded at the hospital grounds, the white doctors, the neatly clad nurses patrolling past. "If someone ask you about what happened at the store, that's how you play it. Say you wasn't there."

"But I *was* there. And I did see something. I come in the back door and seen what I seen."

"Which was?"

"Doc Roberts ripping at her clothes, running his hands all over her like she was a piece of meat."

Nate shot a glance at the hospital personnel gliding past, the doctors and nurses glancing at them as they made their way across the lobby and into the busy area out front by the lawn and the long arcing driveway where cars awaited. Two black visitors, clad as the help, standing in the shiny foyer of the Reading hospital was not a welcome sight.

"Don't cite his name round here," Nate said. "They might know him."

"They oughta know him, foul rascal that he is."

"This is white folks' business. Keep out of it."

"If it weren't for him, Doc would'a had his way."

"Doc's having his way now," Nate said. "It's his word against a deaf and dumb colored child. That's just sugar in his bowl."

"Is that what Doc said?"

"To hear him tell it, he went to fetch Dodo and the boy jumped bad and attacked him. Miss Chona fell out on account of it. She got overcome and fainted away."

"With her dress pulled over her head?" Addie said.

Nate shot a hot glance around them and hissed, "Goddamnit, you'll sport real trouble fooling with these white folks' lies. Stay out of it. Can't nothing be done!" He spoke with intensity, but he kept his face impassive as a large group of doctors clad in white swept past them, laughing at some private joke.

"Is that why you was at Fatty's two nights ago getting sloppy?"

Nate frowned. "It won't happen no more."

"What's Dodo say?" Addie asked.

Nate was silent. Addie stared at him, her features hardening. Now it was her turn to be angry. "You ain't seen him?"

"No."

"Why not?"

"I don't know that they'll let me in there," he said.

"They'll let a knock-kneed cow in there. It's a nuthouse, not a prison. They ain't gonna make you into a bellhop. They got visiting times."

"I'm shy about going to them kind of places," Nate said.

Addie frowned. So that was it. A man with a history he won't share doesn't want to go to a locked place. Not even for a visit. Not if he's been in a locked place before himself.

"South Carolina's far away," she said, then added, "Whatever's back there don't matter. It's what's ahead of you that counts. Don't nobody know you here."

"They ought not to," Nate said, "for I changed my name, too."

Addie took that one in silence. That one was new.

She watched him sag and lean against the wall. His tall frame stooped, his eyes cast down in shame. She loved the gentle slope of his nose, the curve of his jaw, the way his head moved when he looked down, the arc of his shoulders. She placed a hand on the side of his face and rubbed it gently.

"You can forever remember the wrongs done to you as long as you live," she said. "But if you forget 'em and go on living, it's almost as good as forgiving. I don't care who you was, or what you done, or even what you calls yourself. I know your heart. You look so tired."

She snatched his hand fiercely and held it to her chest over her heart. Nate felt a surge of that old feeling, that shine, the light that she lit in him, and the anvil that sat atop his heart lifted.

"I planned to go. Took off work and everything. But I couldn't make myself," he confessed. "So I went to Fatty's and made a fool of myself instead."

"You ain't the first in this world to put liquor to work."

"Worse. I was rolling with that home brew. From down home."

Addie chuckled. "No wonder you look so bad."

Nate smiled bitterly. "I woke up the next morning feeling like the South Carolina State marching band was banging in my head. I seen them once, y'know. I was working a road crew, blacktopping a highway. You could hear 'em hammering them drums a mile off. Lord, when they turned the corner, must've been two hundred of 'em from the colored school there, pounding drums and tooting horns, dressed pretty as peacocks. That was something."

He sighed, then rubbed his forehead and looked through the glass doors at the calm hospital grounds. "I expected Dodo might go to a college like that someday, make something of hisself. He's smart, y'know. He can talk, can still hear things, y'know, little things. He had a chance."

"What you mean *had*?"

"He ain't getting outta where they sent him."

"Who says he ain't? We got to go see somebody about it."

"We might as well be singing to a dead hog," Nate said.

"What about asking Mr. Moshe?" she asked. "He's got some sway."

Nate shook his head. "Mr. Moshe ain't hisself. Can barely run his theaters." Nate thought a moment, then said, "Maybe Reverend Spriggs. He knows lots of the white folks."

"He wouldn't know nobody," Addie said quickly.

"It won't hurt to ask," Nate said. "I can ask him."

"Leave him be," Addie said. "He's too busy booming and Bible shaking and church yelling."

"What's Reverend done to you?"

Addie looked away, not trusting herself to speak, for if she did, she was afraid the truth would reveal a history that might send Nate, as a relative newcomer to Pottstown, having been there only nine years, trotting at Earl Spriggs with a knife, for she'd known Ed Spriggs from childhood to now. Ed Spriggs was a combination lowlife and nervous Nellie. Easily frightened, easily bought, easily deterred, especially when it came to the white man. *His calling to God*, she thought, *was either a miracle or an excuse, but it didn't matter.* It was Ed Spriggs, she was sure, who had given Dodo away to the colored man from the state. Ed Spriggs was one of the few from Chicken Hill who knew Miss Chona hid Dodo over in Bernice's yard, because Bernice went to his church. Bernice was a hard, difficult woman, moved neither by threats nor by nonsense. She would not tell the white man anything. But Bernice's children went to Ed Spriggs's church, too, and Ed Spriggs, lizard that he was, wouldn't have to ask Bernice a thing about who played in her yard. He had only to ask one of her kids. Surely one would spill it.

"Ed Spriggs ain't done nothing to me," Addie said.

"Him and Bernice had some hot words in church yesterday."

"'Bout what?"

Nate shrugged, then asked, "Bernice been here?"

"She come yesterday. She come in her church clothes. Must'a been right after church."

"What she say?"

"I ain't heard Bernice talk more than ten words since her daddy died and that was years ago. She set with Miss Chona awhile, then left."

"Seems to me . . . ," Nate said, then paused and asked, "How'd Doc Roberts know Dodo was on the Hill?"

"The colored man from the state must've told him."

"And who told the man from the state Dodo was up there?"

"Nobody I know. Miss Chona hid him in Bernice's yard with Bernice's children when the man come. I was there most times when he come. He didn't even look over at her yard."

"Maybe Bernice told it."

Addie frowned at him. "Bernice would not tell it."

Nate spoke slowly. "Paper told me yesterday that Bernice was ranting in her house and whupping on one of her young'uns with a larded limb. One of the younger ones."

"It ain't nobody's business how she raises her children," Addie said, but she watched nervously as Nate began to put it together on his own. She watched the idea work its way into him, his tall figure looking thoughtful. He'd been bent and tired when he'd arrived, keeping his eyes averted as the doctors and nurses swept past, casting puzzled glares at the two Negroes in the lobby. But now, as the idea that Reverend Spriggs may have revealed Dodo to the state, given away the one good secret that Nate had for the price of a coffee cake or a down payment on a car or some small amount of acknowledgment from white folks, it was as if a caterpillar had cracked loose from its cocoon and an evil butterfly was emerging.

He leaned against a window and placed his arm against it, a slow, mellow movement that usually gave the impression of an easygoing fellow moving leisurely, with kind purpose. But the grim glow in his eyes held a kind of coiled fury, and it gave the slow movement an air of a tiger preparing to spring.

He asked softly, "Has Reverend Spriggs been by to see Miss Chona?" Before she could speak, he answered his own question. "Of course not."

He stared straight ahead as he spoke, unaware now of the white folks passing by. There was some small wild thing in him trying to tear itself loose, kicking around just past his eyes, waiting to bust out. Watching it grow, Addie grew frightened. *The devil*, she thought. Watching him leaning his long, muscled arm against the windowpane, she briefly thought she was losing her mind, for she was exhausted from lack of sleep. Nate had never lifted a finger to anyone in their years together, not even to Dodo when the boy deserved it. She could not imagine it. Except she'd been warned. Paper had come to visit the hospital the day before, and Paper had delivered an explicit warning from Fatty.

"Fatty said watch Nate close."

Addie had pegged the nervousness in Paper's voice. And now, watching her husband standing in the hospital foyer, his face showing a suppressed, coiled fury, made her afraid. So she said, "Reverend Spriggs got no cause to come round here to see Miss Chona."

"He's a reverend, ain't he? Don't they visit the sick?"

"She got her own Jewish reverend. She don't need Reverend Spriggs."

"He went to see the baker Mr. Eugenio when Mr. Eugenio was sick, didn't he? I believe Mr. Eugenio was Catholic."

"A reverend don't have time to see everybody," Addie said, trying to ward him off. "They mostly see people from their own church."

Nate was silent a moment, then said, "Spriggs is close to that Doc Roberts. Even I know that."

"Let's do what you said," Addie said quickly. "Let's keep out of white folks' business, honey."

Nate was silent. He was unreachable.

Addie tried once more. "Would you do me one favor, sweetie?" she said.

Nate looked at her out of the corner of his eye. "What is it, woman?"

"Don't call me woman! I'm your wife!"

She saw the rage in his eyes give way to sulk and hurt, and in that moment, Addie knew she still had his heart. So she made her pitch.

"Go see how Dodo's getting along. I got a few things together for him at the house. Some things to wear, some sweet things to eat. Go fetch them things, then g'wan down to the store—Paper's running it—and put her on the phone to them people over at Pennhurst. She's good at talking to white folks. Let her set it up so you can go see him. It'll do you good."

Nate peered into his wife's searching, pleading brown eyes, then down at her hand on his chest, the long fingers that wiped the sweat off his face after work, that knitted his pants and stroked his ear and cared for him in ways that he'd never been cared for as a child. And the rage that overcame him eased.

"I ain't good in them kind of places," he said. "But I will think on it."

17

The Bullfrog

The news of Chona's hospitalization and the circumstances surrounding it couldn't have come at a worse time for the Ahavat Achim congregation of Pottstown. The tiny temple, built atop Chicken Hill by Chona's father fifteen years before, had been upended by the arrival of several new Hungarian members—and one four-legged one—a giant bullfrog. The enormous creature was discovered by one of the new wives in the mikvah, or women's bathing pool. Her husband, a successful Budapest hatmaker named Junow Farnok, recently arrived from Buffalo, New York—who insisted he be referred to by his adopted American name, Mr. Hudson—was outraged. He offered to toss $145 at the shul toward the construction of a brand-new mikvah, along with the demand that the new one be double the size and constructed of the finest marble from Carrara, Italy.

This was an unusual request for the tiny shul, whose coffers contained all of $59.14, not including nineteen pairs of brand-new John Keasler shoes and a pile of scrap iron, horseshoes, and rags, all of which were donated by a former congregant, a peddler who vamoosed the previous year with a Mennonite farmer's wife from nearby Pennsburg. The two met while the peddler was traversing his normal route. They had done quite a bit of haggling and negotiating through the years over morning milk and freshly baked bread, and apparently one thing led to another. She was a big woman, nearly six feet tall and built like a truck, whereas he was so skinny he looked like a mop with hair. Neither spoke English—she spoke German and he spoke Yiddish. But love is the language of all mankind, and before departing, he left behind his entire life savings, $27, including his peddler's cart and all its contents to his beloved temple, along with a letter to his best friend that said, in part, "Be careful in America. One good fuck can break you." And off he went, last seen heading to Indiana.

It didn't hurt the shul much, as its membership had exploded from seventeen families to forty-five by 1936, including the services of the still-nervous but ever-enthusiastic Rabbi Karl Feldman, a kind soul still affectionately called Fertzel behind his back by the congregants who preferred Yiddish—or Frabbi by the members who preferred English. Feldman was grateful to have a job. It was upon his slim shoulders that the question of what to do about the new mikvah fell, for while he was salivating at the prospect of a huge cash donation by the rich new Hungarian congregant, who favored crisp white shirts bearing a newly monogrammed family crest embroidered on their breast pockets, he'd neglected to mention to the gentleman that there was a question of where the water for the new mikvah was going to come from.

This came up at the monthly meeting of the chevry, the men's group that decided important matters at the temple, which was attended by Rabbi Feldman; Irv Skrupskelis, the better half of the evil Lithuanian Skrupskelis twins; five members called meat slabs because they kept silent and voted however needed; the new donor, Mr. Hudson, who was clad in a fine leather coat, gloves, suspenders, bow tie, top hat, knee-high boots, and starched white shirt; and the usual minyan kidnapping victims, since there needed to be ten people for a minyan and they often only had eight. In this case, the victims were two fresh young immigrants from Austria, brothers Hirshel and Yigel Koffler, snatched off the street on the way home from work, having been recently employed as brakemen for the Pennsylvania Railroad. The exhausted Koffler brothers slumped into the meeting covered with soot and grime. They gulped down coffee and wolfed down giant portions of Hungarian coffee cake and promptly fell asleep when the usual small talk about card games and American baseball ensued in English, which neither spoke. Rabbi Feldman, who disliked card games and baseball, quickly pinwheeled the discussion to Yiddish, whereupon the discourse turned to the growing political turmoil in Germany, where president Paul Von Hindenburg had chosen a young Austrian named Adolf Hitler to serve as chancellor to keep the Nazi party "in check," at which point both Koffler brothers woke up instantly and offered a round of cursing and swearing, after which the group settled down to the matter of the mikvah donation from Mr. Hudson.

Mr. Hudson was a man of detail, and he grilled Rabbi Feldman.

"Can we double the mikvah in size without a problem?" Mr. Hudson asked.

"Of course," Rabbi Feldman said.

"You seemed hesitant about it when I asked before," Mr. Hudson said.

"Oh no," Feldman said. "We can handle it."

"And what about the frog?"

"What about it? It's gone, isn't it?"

"There is the question of where the frog came from. How did it get in the mikvah?"

"Probably one of the boys dropped it in there," Rabbi Feldman said.

"My wife said it came from beneath," Hudson said. "A drainpipe underneath."

Here Rabbi Feldman glanced at Irv Skrupskelis and blanched. "We'll look into that," he said.

"She also mentioned something about the water," Mr. Hudson said. "One of the women said something."

"The water?"

"Yes. Something about there not being enough of it, or some question as to where it comes from. Where does the water come from?"

"Where does *all* water come from?" Feldman said, chuckling nervously. His eyes rolled up toward the ceiling in a happy way, but Mr. Hudson was not amused.

"Well, what about it?" Hudson asked.

"What about what?"

"The water? Where does it come from?"

"Well, this side of town has had problems getting enough running water," Feldman said. "But the city just built a reservoir on the hill above us a year ago. We had to make adjustments in the past."

"What kind of adjustments?"

Feldman shrugged. "Nothing major. It's an occasional problem," he said, "getting water to the mikvah from time to time. There's simply not a lot of water around here."

Mr. Hudson, a thin man with glasses, fingered his waxed handlebar mustache and frowned. "This isn't Nevada. How can you have a mikvah with not enough water?"

"We have water, but not *quite enough*."

"How is that?"

"At times... occasionally, we have a water supply problem," Rabbi Feldman said.

This was news even to Irv Skrupskelis, who was an original congregant and was there when the original mikvah was built. "Karl, how can we not have enough water? Either we have enough water or we don't."

"We do have enough... except when we don't," Rabbi Feldman said.

"Is the tap broke?"

"No."

"What's that supposed to mean? We get water from the town, right?" Irv asked.

Rabbi Feldman shook his head. "Actually," he said, "there's been a hiccup in that way."

Irv's face reddened. "There're fourteen churches in this town and you're telling me our shul is the only house of worship that doesn't get water from the town? You call that a hiccup?"

Feldman sighed. "When the shul was built, the town wouldn't run water up to Chicken Hill. The water came from the public water faucet and was hauled up here in barrels."

"Don't we have a well?"

"No," Feldman said. "There's a farm near the top of the Hill, the Plitzka farm, that had a well. We offered to pay the Plitzkas for use of their well water, but they refused. So the previous administration"—he didn't mention Chona's father by name, but he didn't need to. Everybody knew the temple only had one rabbi before Feldman—"made an arrangement."

"That's news to me," Irv said.

"It worked fine for years," Feldman said. "Except now there's a problem with the arrangement. Why? Because the er . . . previous administrator, er . . . the one who made the arrangement, he died four years ago."

"You mean Yakov, Chona's father, didn't make a contract?"

"Nothing."

"Where's the water coming from?"

"Well . . . ," and here Feldman blanched. "It's, um, not really clear. I have some ideas, though," he said.

"Don't worry about it," Irv said. "We'll fix it. We'll go to the city and make arrangements to tap into city water. They're running pipes in this direction now, aren't they? That's what the new reservoir at the top of the Hill is for."

"It's not that simple," Rabbi Feldman said.

"Why not?"

"We're still tied up in the first arrangement."

"What the hell does that mean?"

Feldman sighed. "You recall, Irv," he said, "that the original builder of our temple, er . . . absconded with the funds, and our founder was forced to make arrangements with another man, a local builder, who did a wonderful job. Unfortunately, the builder who took off with our money did not test the water table below the shul to see if water ran there. So when the shul was built, there was no water nearby."

"And?"

"Since the town did not supply water to that area, our water problems worsened during long dry spells. We made several offers to old Mr. Plitzka to buy his well water, but he refused us, and one year during a long dry spell, a certain fine young member of our shul—may she be blessed with a miracle for she is now ill—called the police on him, which only made matters worse. She ended up hauling water in barrels from the public spigot for a while, or so I was told."

This caused a pained smile from the usually grim Irv, for he and his brother adored Chona. "Have you gone to see Chona in the hospital yet?" he asked Feldman.

"Not yet."

"What are you waiting for?"

"I . . . she's only been there four days. She's down in Reading."

"I know where she is."

"Well, my car—"

And here Mr. Hudson broke in. "Can we deal with one matter at a time? What happened with the water?"

Irv cut a hot glance at Hudson, then nodded at Feldman, who looked blitzed. "Tell us what's going on with the water now, Karl."

"As I explained," Feldman said, "after Chona upset old Mr. Plitzka, she hauled water for the mikvah by hand. That made for some difficulties."

"So let's just arrange to have our water piped from the city now," Mr. Hudson said.

"That's the problem," Feldman said. He explained that the eldest Plitzka son never forgot the insult to his father's memory, as Chona wrote a detailed letter of complaint to the Pottstown *Mercury* about old man Plitzka, the police, and the city's water department. The son saved Chona's letter to the editor for years and waved it about in his campaign for city council, chirping about Pottstown's Jews "taking over." He had gotten elected on that premise three times.

"Every time we ask, the city says they don't have the money to run a water line toward our part of Chicken Hill. They say they're getting to it. Or it's coming soon. Or the reservoir has problems. It's one delay after another."

"That's ridiculous," Mr. Hudson snorted. "We can get a lawyer and force them to pipe us water. They run pipes around here all the time."

Rabbi Feldman looked doubtful. "Old Plitzka was popular."

"What was his first name?" Irv asked.

"Gustowskis."

"The head of the city council?"

"No," Feldman said. "That's his son. Gus Plitzka is a junior."

Irv rolled his eyes. "I remember the father. A mean old ferd (horse) with three front teeth. His face looked like he had a hobby of stepping on rakes. He used to sell trefah sausage and buckwheat at the old farmer's market. We're losing our water because of him?"

"Not him. His *son*. The city council president. Gus Plitzka is a junior, I said."

"How long ago did Chona write that letter again?" Irv asked.

"Years ago. She was a kid. Before she married Moshe."

"Just so we're clear, how is this tied to the bullfrog in the mikvah?" Mr. Hudson asked.

Irv turned to Hudson and said, "Can we table the bullfrog for a minute?" Then back to Feldman: "The mikvah's working fine. Either that or my wife's been drowning in spit for these past six months. We have water now and then. So where's it coming from?"

Rabbi Feldman sighed. "The shul didn't want to raise a fuss, so my understanding is that we just tapped into the well that brings water to the public water spigot near the Clover Dairy. We actually don't pay the city for the small bit of water that we use."

"Well, let's pay them now," Mr. Hudson said. "We can fix that right away. We'll make an arrangement."

Feldman sighed. "That arrangement is going to be difficult to roll out."

"Money moves the world," Mr. Hudson said.

"Not this world," Feldman said. He cleared his throat. "Um . . . since the original arrangement happened before I came, permission to tap into the water spigot's well was never gotten. It was just done."

"Who did it?" Mr. Hudson asked.

Feldman glanced at him nervously. "You're kidding, right?"

"I am not."

"Well, I understand that the previous rabbi paid a man to get a crew, dig down, put a Y connection on the well's pipe, and cover it back up. The connection is buried four feet down, just across the road from the dairy building at Hayes and Franklin. That's where we get our water."

"Well, we're obviously not getting enough of it," Mr. Hudson said.

"This town is growing, Mr. Hudson. The dairy, which draws from the same well, has increased capacity. And the water table is dropping. So the well occasionally runs dry. That's why it sometimes takes a long time to fill the mikvah. That's why they built the new reservoir."

"Is that why the bullfrog turned up?" Mr. Hudson said.

Irv was the milder of the Skrupskelis twins but not that mild. He turned to Hudson and barked, "Could you stop working your mouth about the frog for a minute till we figure this out?"

Mr. Hudson's face reddened. "This would've never happened in Buffalo!"

"I'm sure they all walk around holding hands up there," Irv said. He turned to Feldman. "Karl, we'll approach the Clover Dairy. We'll get them to let us go into the well and take the Y off, and attach our own water pipe to the same line that services their diary, the line from the city's main to us. We'll get a lawyer and get it done."

Feldman cleared his throat. "It's not that simple."

"Why the hell not?"

"The dairy was sold a month ago. Guess who the new owner is."

"Plitzka?"

Feldman nodded.

Irv thought a moment. "This town is run by thieves. Between him and Doc Roberts . . ." He shook his head. "Is it true about Doc going in Chona's store? What the Negroes are saying?"

Feldman pursed his lips. "I don't know many of the Negroes."

"Did you talk to Moshe?"

"Not yet."

"What are you waiting for?"

Hudson broke in. "What are you talking about?"

Feldman turned to him. "There was an incident . . . one of our congregants, the daughter of our founder, she's very ill. She's been sickly for years. The doc here in town went to see her. There's some question about his behavior."

Mr. Hudson rolled his eyes. "How did we go from a bullfrog in the mikvah to this?"

Irv turned to Mr. Hudson again, and this time the beast known as the Skrupskelis was loose. "Listen pisher (squirt), if you mention that bullfrog one more time, I'll hang a zets (punch) on your head."

"Get a hold of yourself," Hudson snapped. "My wife uses that mikvah!"

"Well, the alt mekhasheyfe (old witch) can scrub her dimples at home!"

"Take it easy, Irv," Rabbi Feldman said.

"Take it easy? Chona's in the hospital and you haven't even gone to see her. Have you thought about how she got there? I'm hearing a lot about it."

"She's always been sick."

"Not that sick. You should ask."

"Ask who?"

"Anybody. The police maybe. How's that?"

"What is there to ask?"

Mr. Hudson grew irritated. "You two work that out. Meantime, I'll go to the town myself and pay them to run a new pipe."

"Bring a printing press with you to punch out twenties and fifties," Irv said. "Plitzka and Doc run everything around here. The police. The water department. They all go back years. You think goyes like that will let a bunch of Jews dig up around Plitzka's business? They'll fine us first, then charge us through the nose—if they let us dig at all." That brought silence to the room. Even the Austrians, who did not understand much of the English being spoken, seemed cowed.

Mr. Hudson stood up and paced back and forth, his hands behind his back. "This is a serious legal problem," he said. "We are stealing water from a town run by a goy who hates Jews. We could be prosecuted."

"*We* didn't attach that pipe to the city's well," Feldman said. "The person who arranged it passed away. Not a soul from our shul was involved. Of that I'm sure. Chona's late father told me that himself."

"Who did it?"

Feldman's face reddened and here he looked at Irv. "There's a local Negro involved."

Mr. Hudson stopped pacing. "A nigger?" he asked.

The Koffler brothers were now awake. "What's a nigger?" one of them asked in Yiddish.

"A Negro," Feldman said in English. "We say Negro here."

"Which one?" Irv Skrupskelis asked.

"I don't know him," Feldman said. "But he . . . uh . . . Chona's husband works with a lot of Negroes. He might know him."

"Do you know his name?" Irv asked.

"Chona's husband? Of course."

"Not Moshe, Karl. I mean the colored who dug up the ground and did the connection to the city's well," Irv said tersely. "Who is he?"

"A local fellow. He's dead now. He did a lot of odd jobs years ago. He was a builder of sorts. Talented, as you can see by our shul. His name was Shad, I believe. Shad Davis. He has a son. He's a scrap collector, does odd jobs and such for the colored on the Hill. I believe they call him Fatty," Rabbi Feldman said.

Here again the two Austrian brothers looked at each other. Hirshel said in English, "Fatty?"

"Your first English word," Yigel muttered dourly. "It's about time. What's it mean?"

"We need to move this shul off the Hill," Mr. Hudson announced. "The days of doing bad deals with trefah and niggers and swimming with bullfrogs is over. It's nineteen thirty-six. Come into the modern age, gentlemen." He turned to Feldman. "I will leave it to you to unravel this." To Irv, he said, "I will pretend that you did not insult me." He moved toward the door and then stopped. "The congregant in the hospital? Is she dying?"

Here the poor rabbi blanched, for Irv Skrupskelis's face grew dark with rage. "I will find out," Feldman said.

Mr. Hudson nodded and left.

Irv turned to Feldman. "You brought us here to listen to this schmuck complain?"

"I should have thrown him a welcome dinner instead?" Feldman said.

"Throw it so I can plant it in his face," Irv said. He stared at the door where Hudson had exited. "Moron. Him and his fucking frog."

18

The Hot Dog

A week after she'd been assaulted, Chona, lying in her hospital bed, found herself awake with the words of the song-prayer Barukh She'amar swirling about her head like butterflies. She felt the prayer more than heard it; it started from somewhere deep down and fluttered toward her head like tiny flecks of light, tiny beacons moving like a school of fish, continually swimming away from a darkness that threatened to swallow them. She was witnessing a dance, she realized, one that originated in a place far out of her view, someplace she had never been before. Her lips felt suddenly dry. She was overcome by a sudden massive thirst and must have announced it, for water came from somewhere. She felt it touch her throat and heard the words of the prayer, "Blessed be the One who spoke the world into being." She was grateful. She loved that prayer as a child. She sang it with her father as she held his hand on Sabbath mornings as the two walked to shul. It always drew the same response. He'd chuckle and say, "You can never go wrong when you express your love to the master of the world," then slip a marble or a coin or a small gift into her hand.

Wonderful. How come she hadn't remembered this before? Then she sensed, more than felt, a hand slipping into hers, and she knew then that she was alive and that he was near, somewhere, her Moshe; and in the recesses of her mind, far from the conscious place where it should have been, and forever from where it might ever be again, she heard once again the sweet trumpet, the lovely cornet, that beautiful longing, the message that everlasting love, forever impressed, forever stamped, forever noted, the one great piece of sensibility stamped into the life of those lucky enough to receive it, remained. She also knew at that moment that she was not long for this world, that she was dying, and that she must tell him and release him.

With that knowledge came the smell of something strange. Something trefah, forbidden. Unmistakable in its odor. And delicious.

A hot dog.

There was a hot dog in there somewhere, in her dream. In the room. Somewhere close. The aroma was unmistakable. It was so strong and present, she felt embarrassed and unclean, for the two things did not belong together—the precocious call of the universe and the sloppy, happy piece of trefah that her friend Bernice considered life's greatest treat when they were in school. She had tasted one once. It was delicious. She and Bernice had ventured to Fatty's dilapidated hamburger stand up on Pigs Alley when—*Was she fifteen then? Was it after Mrs. Patterson's cooking class?* Then, as her mind pushed into the memory, she felt pain slice in and smash the memory to bits, rendering it cold— pain, real pain, in her middle section, inside, somewhere deep—and the faint cloud of memory and the aroma vanished; and slowly, gradually, she opened her eyes and peered around the room.

She found her hand in Moshe's, who was asleep on a chair next to her. He sat parallel to where she was lying, facing outward so that his head could be near hers, just inches away, but in full slumber, his chin at his chest, his hand cradling hers. He looked ghastly, pale and exhausted, and her guilt was so extreme she wanted to call out, "What have I done?" But she could not. The young man who wandered into her father's basement that November afternoon twelve years ago, so funny and innocent, with a pocket full of flyers and not a dime to his name, so charming, always so positive, was gone. In his place was a frightened, downtrodden, middle-aged man. She wanted to beat herself over the head for the times she'd chastised him for being so naïve, for eating losses from musicians who flayed him with their drinking and borrowing and constant quarreling, and for yammering in his ear, saying, "Why would you do something so stupid?" She felt rent in two by guilt, for not once in all their years together had he muttered a word of grievance or protest about her store, which never made a dime, and her unwillingness to move off the Hill or that she'd been unable to give him a son or daughter. He was a true Jew, a man of ideas and wit who understood the meaning of celebration and music and that the blend of those things meant life itself. And how she regretted, watching his face locked in grief even as he slept, his lip trembling, that she'd frittered hours away reading about socialists and unions and progressives and politics and corporations, fighting about a meaningless flag that said "I'm proud to be an American," when it should have said "I'm happy to be alive," and what the difference was, and how one's tribe cannot be better than another tribe because they were all one tribe. An extraordinary wisdom came upon her, one she had not imagined possible, and she wanted to share it with him in those first—or perhaps last—moments of her consciousness. But after seeing his lovely face, she felt yet again an enormous burst of pain from her stomach and her head. It was so great that it felt as if her arteries were ripping out the back of her skull, and the little white flecks of magic that zipped about ahead of the chasing darkness as the Barukh She'amar danced in her dream went zip, poof, then fluttered away and was gulped by the dark and the wonderfully horrible odor of the hot dog that seemed to press against her nose. She waved a hand in the air and said, "Throw that thing out."

Out of the corner of her eye, she saw figures in the room move. There was a quick shuffle of feet and Moshe was awake.

He saw her gazing at him and his face brightened. "Throw out what?" he asked.

"The hot dog," she said.

Moshe looked around the room. Her gaze followed his. Surrounding her bed stood Moshe's cousin Isaac, Rabbi Feldman, the twins Irv and Marv Skrupskelis, and behind them Addie, Nate, and Bernice. There was someone missing.

"Where's Dodo?" she asked.

"We'll get him back," Moshe said.

But she did not hear the rest, for the suffering at the moment was too great to dwell on what had happened in the store. Dodo had tried to defend her, poor thing, and he'd been denied. She saw Moshe spin out of his chair, still clasping her hand, and place his other hand on her face, kneeling beside her bed. He said a few words to her, but she could not hear or speak. She felt movement on the other side of her bed and glanced over to see Addie, who grabbed a towel and wiped her face. Bernice was behind her and looked ashen, which touched Chona, for Bernice was very shy, and she had not seen Bernice away from her house in Chicken Hill since they were children.

"Are you eating a hot dog, Bernice? That's cheating."

It was a joke, and Chona was immediately sorry she said it, not because both knew Bernice wasn't kosher but because the act of speaking sent a thousand daggers of pain through her insides. Bernice appeared confused, and it was only after Moshe turned to her and translated did Chona realize she had spoken in Yiddish. Bernice, her gorgeous dark face always so grim, the smooth black skin of an unmelting armor draped over the gorgeous nose and full lips, smiled sadly. That was a rare thing to see. It was as if a sweet drizzle of desert rain had come into the room and washed them all.

Bernice, a torrent of sadness dripping off her long, beautiful face, said softly, "No, Chona. I haven't had a hot dog."

That was the last Chona saw of Bernice, for the pain was too great for her to keep her eyes open so she closed them. She heard another shuffling of feet and Rabbi Feldman singing, intoning the prayer of Mi Shebeirach for healing, mangling it with his horrible cantoring, and she wanted to thank him and say, "Well, you're improving," even though he was not, but she appreciated his presence. And then she heard Moshe's voice speaking firmly, almost angrily, to the room, saying, "Get out. Please. Everyone." She heard more shuffling of feet and sensed bodies leaving. They were alone. As always, Moshe knew what to do.

IN THE HALLWAY of the Reading hospital unit, the odd group of wellwishers gathered in front of the nurses' station. Three white nurses glanced at them, then turned back to their charts. No one bothered to mention if there was a place for the group to go, so they stood there. There was nowhere to sit, no coffee to drink, no kind Presbyterian minister to offer words of solace. They just stood uncomfortably as the odd clump of Americans they were: Jews and blacks, standing together—Marv Skrupskelis leaning on the wall in workman's clothing, his large fists balled in his pocket; Irv, fresh from work at the shoe store, in salesman's garb, suspenders and white shirt; Isaac, tall, proud, imposing, and impeccable, clad in a wool suit and black homburg, his stern face etched in stressed sorrow; Rabbi Feldman, his nervous hands fingering a worn siddur (prayer book). A few feet from them stood Nate and Bernice, worlds apart from each other, staring at Addie down the hall, who stood nervously outside the doorway to Chona's room, her hands clasped before her chest, peering inside.

There was nothing to do but talk, which at times like these is all that's left.

Rabbi Feldman gently touched Isaac's arm and spoke in English. "How was your travel from Philly?" he asked.

Isaac shrugged.

"I take it you received my letter?"

"What letter?" Isaac said.

"The one I sent telling you about the shul and the rumors about what happened at the store. We wanted to contact the pol—"

Isaac thrust a quick finger in the air to silence Feldman, who was intimidated by the barrel-chested well-dressed stranger with the stone face. He had never met Moshe's cousin. He had only heard rumors. A hard man. Not to be fooled with.

Isaac turned to the Skrupskelis twins. He spoke Yiddish. "Which of you were here when Chona's father built the shul?"

Marv was silent and looked away. He was the grimmer of the two Skrupskelises, and no rich Romanian theater owner from Philadelphia would speak to him like he was chopped liver. It was Irv who answered. "We were here."

"And?"

"And what?"

"Did he build it?"

"Of course he did."

"Alone?"

Irv shrugged. He was in no mood to answer demanding Romanian theater owners who gave him the third degree.

It was Marv who spoke out. The gruff Lithuanian answered with the kind of gravity and directness that Isaac appreciated. "He built it with a colored named Shad."

"So the colored would know where the water pipe is connected to the public faucet's well?" Isaac asked.

"He'd tell us but he's dead."

"Who worked with him?"

Marv nodded at Bernice. "That's his daughter. Her brother might know."

Isaac glanced at Bernice, then at Nate, who stood next to her. He started to say something, then stopped. Instead, he said, "I'll see it repaired."

Marv shrugged. "Go ahead if you want. Doc Roberts, though, that's another matter."

"I don't know that name," Isaac said.

Rabbi Feldman said, "I wrote about him in the letter to you."

Isaac didn't respond. He didn't even look at Feldman. The man was weak. Weak Jews were a waste of time. Weak Jews would never survive in America. Or anyplace. He kept his eyes trained on Marv. The two men eyed each other for a moment. Then he turned to Feldman and said, "I told you I don't know that name."

"It was in my letter."

"I never received any letter. And I never heard that name."

Rabbi Feldman started to interject that he had clearly spelled out the whole business in his letter and that the letter was probably misplaced or lost, but he was interrupted by Moshe's long, piercing howl, which rang down the hallway. The group turned and saw Addie at the doorway of the room, her hand clasped to her mouth now, her shoulders hunched as she stepped into the room.

The odd group of well-wishers slowly moved down the hallway as Moshe's sobs cascaded up and down the walls, bouncing from one side to the other. The discourse on Doc Roberts was forgotten now as the group tromped forward, a ragtag assortment of travelers moving fifteen feet as if it were fifteen thousand miles, slow travelers all, arrivals from different lands, making a low trek through a country that claimed to be so high, a country that gave them so much yet demanded so much more. They moved slowly, like fusgeyers, wanderers seeking a home in Europe, or erú West African tribesmen herded off a ship on a Virginia shore to peer back across the Atlantic in the direction of their homeland one last time, moving toward a common destiny, all of them—Isaac, Nate, and the rest—into a future of American nothing. It was a future they couldn't quite see, where the richness of all they had brought to the great land of promise would one day be zapped into nothing, the glorious tapestry of their history boiled down to a series of ten-second TV commercials, empty holidays, and sports games filled with the patriotic fluff of red, white, and blue, the celebrants cheering the accompanying dazzle without any idea of the horrible struggles and proud pasts of their forebears who had made their lives so easy. The collective history of this sad troupe moving down the hospital corridor would become tiny blots in an American future that would one day scramble their proud histories like eggs, scattering them among the population while feeding mental junk to the populace on devices that would become as common and small as the hot dog that the dying woman thought she smelled; for in death, Chona had smelled not a hot dog but the future, a future in which devices that fit in one's pocket and went zip, zap, and zilch delivered a danger far more seductive and powerful than any hot dog, a device that children of the future would clamor for and become addicted to, a device that fed them their oppression disguised as free thought.

Had the group of stragglers moping down the hallway seen *that* future, they would have all turned en masse and rushed from the hospital out into the open air and collapsed onto the lawn and sobbed like children. As it was, they moved like turtles toward Chona's room as Moshe's howl rang out. They were in no hurry. The journey ahead was long. There was no promise ahead. There was no need to rush now.

PART III
The Last Love

19

The Lowgods

It was nearly 9 p.m. and raining heavily when the ancient Packard rounded the corner of the muddy road and ground to a halt on Hemlock Row, a claptrap group of shacks located three miles west of Pottstown, Pa. Fatty peered through the muddy windshield at the exhausted-looking homes, some of them made of nothing more than two-by-fours nailed together with plywood and tin, then frowned at Paper, who was seated next to him. She was clad in a heavy coat and slacks, her hair tied in a wrap with a worn oilskin cloche atop her head. She sat patiently with her hands in her lap, looking out the rain-streaked window. In the back seat, the hulking frame of Big Soap, fast asleep, his head crammed into the rear corner, blocked a good portion of Fatty's back window.

"I should'a brought my pistol," Fatty muttered.

"Gun won't do you no good here," Paper said.

"How do I know one of these cowboys out here won't come and kick in my windshield?" he said.

"If you can show me a pair of cowboy boots in these parts, I'll give you a hundred dollars right now," Paper said. "They ain't the type out here."

"What type are they?"

Paper sighed. "I'll go inside. Just wait for me, Fatty. I know what I'm doing."

Fatty frowned and tapped the steering wheel. He was nervous. He'd never been to Hemlock Row, a tiny hamlet of black life that most Chicken Hill blacks avoided. Chicken Hill's Negroes were, by their own definition, "on-the-move," "moving-on-up," "climb-the-tree," "NAACP-type" Negroes, wanting to be American. But the blacks who lived in this clump of nine tiny shacks spread over two acres just off the road heading west toward Berks County had no desire to be in the white man's world. They were Lowgods, said to be from South Carolina someplace, all related in some form or fashion. Who the first Lowgod was that came to Hemlock Row and why they settled there instead of Chicken Hill, or Pittsburgh, or Reading, or Philly, no one knew. Fatty heard rumors that the Lowgods were actually Nate's people, though he'd never had the nerve to ask Nate about it. And why would he? The Lowgods were private, suspicious, unpredictable, and kept to themselves. They grew their own vegetables, tended their own animals, and kept their own counsel. They walked different. They talked different. Their language was odd, full of lilting phrases that pelted the ground like raindrops. Gullah-speak, they called it—half English and half African—full of hoodoo sayings and things that only the Lowgods understood. They were also not to be fooled with. A few years back in Fatty's jook joint, a big, hulking Chicken Hill resident named Bunny Hales picked a fight with a tiny, skinny little stranger who claimed to be a Lowgod from Hemlock Row. Fatty had never seen somebody move so fast. The Hemlock Row man fought with his hands and feet, using some kind of kicking art that sent Bunny's teeth flying out his mouth like Chiclets.

"If your girl wanted to be civilized, she'd live on the Hill," Fatty said.

"Her people's here," Paper said simply.

"Does she like living like a monkey?"

"Will you quit? You wanna get Dodo outta the nuthouse or not?"

"I want to keep something in my pocket other than a handkerchief. That's why I'm here."

"For a guy who dreams big, you think awful small," Paper said. "That kind of thinking'll keep you in Pottstown the rest of your life."

"Who said I want to leave?"

Paper grabbed the door handle, pushed the door open, and stepped into the rain. She turned and leaned in, speaking through the open door, the rain dripping off the narrow brim of her hat past her glowing dark eyes. "I'll call out if I need you to come in."

Fatty thought he saw a glint of fear in those beautiful spirals and couldn't help himself. "Oh hell," he said, reaching for the door handle. "I'll go in with you. These rusty, hoodoo niggers don't bother me."

"Just set tight," Paper commanded. She nodded at Big Soap in the back seat, fast asleep. "And keep him in his cage. Y'all come inside *if* I call. And if you do come in, step in with your hat in your hand and a smile on your lips. Don't say nothing. That sassing mouth of yours'll earn you a lesson out here that'll last."

She slammed the car door, pulling the hat tightly over her head and splashing through muddy puddles over to one of the houses. She knocked on the front door. The door was pulled opened by an unseen hand. She vanished inside and the door closed.

Fatty eyed the door anxiously. A mist laid itself on the windshield. He turned on the wiper blade and watched it make one exhausted swipe across then quit. Then another. Then quit. It didn't help.

He drummed the steering wheel again, impatient, biting his swollen lower lip while having an argument with himself. Between the near disaster of Nate two nights ago and Big Soap's mother marching up to his jook yesterday, he'd about had his fill of Dodo. How could a man get ahead if he had crap dropping on him all the time? Paper's arrival at his jook yesterday made it a trifecta—three disasters in a row. He wished she hadn't come, because he could tell by the mourning clothing she wore when she arrived—a crisp black dress and black hat—that she'd come from Chona's funeral, which everybody on Chicken Hill had attended but him.

She sat on the porch in that pretty black dress and said simply, "Where was you?"

Fatty shrugged. He didn't want to hear it. Chona's death was a tragedy, but he'd walled off that sort of grief when he was a boy, long ago after his father died. That was the last funeral he'd ever gone to. No more death extravaganzas for him.

"You know I don't go to them kind'a things."

"You look low, Fatty."

"Actually, I'm feeling jiffy."

"Stop fending and proving," Paper said. "I know you and Miss Chona go back." She was right, but who was she to say that? How did she know Chona's father had been one of the few who helped his family after his father died? Paper was four years younger than he was. She was a kid then, living six blocks away, farther down the Hill, which might as well have been a hundred miles. Boys had been lining up outside her house doing back flips to get her attention even then. What difference did it make now?

"She got her people to take care of her," Fatty said. He was silent a moment, then asked, "Did Bernice go?"

Paper nodded. "You know how Bernice is. She came. She didn't speak. She didn't sing—which she should'a. But it was a nice service. A lot of it was in Jewish so I don't know what was said. But *I* enjoyed it. Jews bury their dead quick. They don't set 'em on the cooling board for days and fool around like we do."

Fatty nodded, frowning. "What about Nate and Addie?"

"What about 'em?"

"You know what I mean."

"They taking it hard. Specially Addie."

Fatty was silent, watching the smooth lines of Paper's face etched in concern. Even when she was worried, Paper was fine. There was something in her manner so truthful and light, the way she covered her pain with mirth, that always shifted his heart a little, except at the moment, for she wasn't laughing or smiling. He started to offer a word of comfort. The next thing she uttered, however, made him realize he was a fruitcake for being soft on her.

"Addie and Nate are planning to free that boy. And you gonna help."

"Who am I, Abraham Lincoln?"

"Stop playing dumb. They plan on breakin' Dodo out the nuthouse."

"Sure. And I quit selling oil wells last year."

"Nate got it set up to send him down to South Carolina after we get him out."

"We?"

"That's right. I need you to run me over to Hemlock Row tonight. I'll pay for the gas."

"Hemlock Row? I know bums living in packing houses who wouldn't go over there."

"Why not?"

"Them rusty-skinned niggers is setting over there doing hoodoo and eating butter beans and white livers as we speak. No thanks."

"I said I'll pay your gas."

"You can save your chips."

"Fatty, you don't like money?"

"Keep your little quarters. Whoever sold Nate and Addie a story about getting Dodo out of Pennhurst is trading hog slops for piss. That place is run by the state, Paper. If Nate and Addie had any sense, they'da sent that Dodo down South *before* Miss Chona got herself eaten alive by Doc Roberts."

"So you know what he did?"

"I don't give a hoot about that witch!"

"If you don't care, why you so hot and bothered?"

"I ain't like the way the vote came in, if that's what you asking, them taking Doc's word and blaming Dodo for nothing."

"That's why you're coming."

Fatty chuckled. "Just 'cause a train can toot don't mean it's gonna roll down the track."

"You going anyway."

"Sorry, Paper."

"You're going 'cause I need a man to take me."

"There's plenty fellers round here happy to do that," Fatty said. "Great big fancy fellers with elephant-sized pockets full of dollars. They'll carry you wherever you wanna go."

"But they ain't you," Paper said. And here Fatty expected Paper—whose glorious beauty broke some boneheaded man's heart at least twice a month—to laugh off her own remark. But she didn't laugh. Instead, she looked directly at him with big dark eyes that seemed to contain every blue sky and country mountainside he'd ever seen and said, "I need somebody I can trust."

That threw him.

Sitting behind the steering wheel, Fatty cursed himself. He had to confess he was no different than most men. There was something about Paper that made him want to kneel down. She had a way about her, a power. Even as a child she had it, and when he came home from prison four years ago and saw her for the first time after two years away, he'd harbored a faint hope that maybe she'd see that he'd grown, that prison had changed him for the good. But she was gone then. She'd grown herself—from a cute, sassy child to a woman of laughter and easy gossip, playing life easy, making light of the darkest news, the most wonderful walking newspaper in the world—all without a man. He would've done anything to win her attention when he came out, which, of course, he could not. She didn't seem to see him—and why would she? Why would someone so special fool with an ex-con whose reputation bore the stamp of prison stink, selling hamburgers and booze and scrap metal when she had royalty tripping by her house every week—railroad porters and teachers and such, even rich numbers runners from Philly, fellas who traveled and wore clean shirts and smooth ties every day, not workman's clothing like he did. He knew of one Pullman porter from Baltimore who came every month and asked Paper to marry him, promising to spirit her down to a land of marble steps and swinging jazz and more soft-boiled crab than a soul could toss down their throat. The fella even showed up at Fatty's jook one night, laughing and joking, a handsome, slim, light-skinned chap with smooth skin and shiny shoes. Fatty had to stifle an urge to march up to him and punch him out. But the fella drank and danced to the blues and spent money and proved to be an easygoing, fun fella. By the end of the night, Fatty felt ashamed. He realized then that he was dangerously soft on Paper. He'd seen the results of that softness in his own jook and back in Graterford, too: the fights, the scratching, the hollering, the knifings, the cells full of stories about some poor lovelorn sucker who got his feelings hurt, then reached for whiskey with one hand and his pistol with the other only to wake up to find himself doing an eighteen-year bid. He wanted no part of that.

And yet he was staring out the windshield at the doorway waiting for the source of the problem while feeling sorry for himself, running his tongue over his wooden tooth and his lower lip, still swollen from the giant gash he got from Big Soap. He could have let Big Soap slug him anywhere in the world after he'd gotten them fired. He chose the front of Paper's house. *Who am I fooling?* he thought.

He glanced in the mirror at Big Soap still sleeping in the back seat. "Soap!" he yelled.

Soap woke up groggy, rubbing his face. "Yeah?"

"Set up and pay attention. Less'n things get thick out here."

"Why we here again?"

"'Cause of Paper. She's trying to figure a way to spring Dodo."

"From where?"

"Pennhurst."

"That's a shame. How's old Dodo doing?"

"If he was eating biscuits and gravy, would we be here?"

"What's he done again?"

"Nothing, Soap. He didn't do nothing wrong."

"Why'd they send him to the nuthouse then?"

"He got in a mess."

"Is that why my ma's so mad?"

"I don't know why she's mad, Soap. She's your ma."

"Rusty said Doc Roberts was pulling Miss Chona's clothes off and Dodo saw it."

"I don't know what he saw."

"She died some kind of way."

"Soap, do I look like a doctor? She was sick a long time."

"That's not what Rusty said."

"What's Rusty know? She fell down in her store and just died. That's it." But in his heart, Fatty felt sorrow, and behind it, a burst of simmering rage. He'd known Chona all his life. "Of all the white people in town, why her?" he said.

"What's that mean?"

Fatty didn't bother to reply. Chona wasn't one of *them*. She was the one among them who ruined his hate for them, and for that he resented her. *Miss Chona*. She wasn't Miss Chona when they were kids. She was just Chona, his sister's best friend, the odd girl with the limp who walked to school with Bernice, the two walking behind him, ignoring him, which was fine with him in those days. But then life happened. He'd gone to jail after high school, and when he returned home, the die was cast. Chona got married and went back to being white and Bernice had all those kids and got saved to the Lord and inherited his daddy's house—which he should've gotten, being his father's only son. Bernice had opened up that very house to hide Dodo—and that's something no one else in Chicken Hill did. The two had shown loyalty to each other in the end. Whom had he showed loyalty to? It frustrated him, thinking of their friendship. He wanted no part of either of them. They were lame. Stumblers. Losers. He had to make his own way in the world. Where was the money to be made fooling around in that complicated mess? He had to survive. That's just the way it was.

Big Soap lit a cigarette and Fatty glanced at him through the rearview mirror. In the sudden light, Big Soap's face was a silhouette. "All 'cause of a stupid stove," Fatty said.

"A what?"

"Way back when, Dodo lived with his mama in a little house off Lincoln Avenue. She had a stove that blew up some kind'a way. He lost his sight on account of that. His ears went bad. After a while, his eyes come back, but his ears didn't. After his ma got sick and died, he stopped going to school on account of he couldn't hear nothing."

"That's why everyone calls him Dodo?"

"A name don't mean nothing."

"If it don't mean nothing, why don't they call him horse? Or car? Or spaghetti?"

Fatty stared out the windshield, disgusted. "I don't know who's dumber, Soap. Dodo or us. You wouldn't see him out here setting in the rain waiting for these bone-in-the-nose niggers to cook him for breakfast." He stared at the doorway where Paper had disappeared.

"What's keeping her?"

INSIDE THE LITTLE clapboard house, Paper found herself in a room of folding chairs that faced a table at the front of the room. A typewriter and a set of blank white cards sat atop the table. Nine people, four men and five women, sat in silence facing the front of the room. They glanced at her when she came in, nodded silent greetings as she took a seat in the back row, then looked ahead again in silence.

Moments later, a side door opened and a stately black woman with large black eyes and smooth dark chocolate skin entered. She was so well-dressed that even in a city like Philadelphia, just thirty-five miles distant, where fashionably dressed Negro businesswomen walked up and down Broad Street regularly, she would have stood out. She wore a drop-waist dress, with a sash around the hip and a skirt that went to her ankles. A cloche hat adorned her neatly pressed hair, a simple amulet hung around her neck, and double-strap Mary Jane shoes decorated her feet. She moved with the air of a queen, striding to the front of the room, standing behind the table that bore the typewriter, and gazing about.

The sight of this regally dressed figure standing behind a meager table facing an audience seated on folding chairs in a dilapidated two-room clapboard house four steps from Pennsylvania Route 23 with the tin roof clattering with the sound of rain and the wind howling into the cracks of the walls seemed so ridiculous that Paper had to stifle the impulse to laugh. But she knew better. For this was Miggy Fludd standing before her. And Miggy Fludd—Fludd being her married name—was a Lowgod. And if there was any colored soul on earth, any soul below Jesus Christ himself, who could get Dodo out of Pennhurst without the white man's help, it was a Lowgod.

Miggy peered about the room.

"Are y'all ready?" she said.

A soft-looking cherubic woman who sat in the front said softly, "We been ready, honey. We been ready."

THE BLACK WOMEN of Chicken Hill were a tight community. Most worked as maids for the white man, walking down the Hill to town each morning to wash the clothing, cook the food, raise the children, care for elderly parents, and allow the white women their privilege. But the colored women of Hemlock Row sang a different song. They were Lowgods. Unlike the black women of Chicken Hill, who were, for the most part, subservient, willing to toil as day workers for the white man, the Lowgod women were not good servants. They were distant and aloof, splendidly beautiful, with long necks and rangy arms. They did not smile or scrape or offer small talk. Their baleful stares, careless shrugs, and strange accents made them terrible hires as maids, for their dark beauty intimidated the white housewives and aroused the sexual slumber of their husbands. Their smooth skin glowed with an ebony arrogance that made the blistering pink of their white bosses seem weak by comparison. Neither were they especially keen on outdoor work and gardening, which a few, when pressed, did to some effectiveness. Instead, the Lowgod women, by and large, laundered. They fetched their laundry each morning on foot. It was not unusual on any given morning to see five or six Lowgod women lugging huge bags of clothing up dusty Route 23 from Pottstown to Hemlock Row, a good three miles, bearing the laundry of the town's prominent families, for they cleaned and pressed skirts with such care and precision that even the most intolerant white housewives put up with their frightening long silences and odd accents. The Lowgod women were known for their laundering skills. They stood head and shoulders above those of most other laundresses in the area, save Paper's. That's how Paper met Miggy.

Miggy was a former coworker. The two washed, tag team, for the same customer, an insanely scrupulous housewife whose husband was a vice president of the National Bank of Pottstown. When one wasn't available, the other was used. Eventually, the two formed a friendship, for Paper's easy presence, wonderful laugh, and disdain for the quivering, testosterone-driven weaklings known as men won over the most hardened, suspicious females, and Miggy was a curious soul indeed. They were nearly the same age, and Miggy's thirst for learning to read and a curiosity about Paper's seemingly glamorous life as hostess for several handsome Pullman porters resulted in Miggy's marriage to a railroad porter, a short affair that ended badly, for the man had a temper and no experience with a Lowgod, whose women took backwater off no man. Paper's intervention saved the man's life and likely saved Miggy a turn in the penitentiary. Thus, the friendship between the two women solidified.

Paper had not seen Miggy in some time, as Miggy had retired from the laundering business three years before for reasons she never explained. But when Paper wrote saying she had a problem with something at Pennhurst, Miggy had written back saying, "I got an answer for you," and described in exact detail the time and place where Paper should come, ending her letter with a strict message: "Don't come out here judging." Paper, feeling suspicious that perhaps Miggy had fallen into prostitution, dragged along Fatty and Big Soap as a safety measure because she was aware that if a Negro on the Hill took an occasional misunderstanding too far, Big Soap and Fatty could be depended on to handle matters discreetly and, if necessary, with force.

Seated in the back row, Paper watched, fascinated, as Miggy stood before the small assembly. Her eyes scanned the room. They fell on Paper and moved past with no acknowledgment at all. Instead, she took a seat at the table, pulled the typewriter and cards closer to her, and said, "Who's first?"

A man raised his hand.

Miggy nodded at him. "Go ahead."

"My daughter is sick. Will she get well?"

Miggy rose from the table, removed her hat, raised her regal head toward the ceiling, spread her arms out, and, to Paper's utter surprise, gave a long mournful cry, her mouth wide, her white teeth visible, as if she were crying to the gods. She closed her eyes, then slowly, methodically swerved, dancing in place, hips swinging around easily, sensuously, arms moving about in a cool, curved manner over her head, then down at the waist, then pulled back and forth as if she were rowing a boat; then faster, her body moving in tandem, the wide hips swaying in place, eyes closed, then faster, the bracelets and bones-and-teeth jewelry she wore clattering together over the sound of the rain banging against the tin roof—a kind of feverish African shake, faster, faster, super-fast; then the assemblage of bracelets, necklace, curves, and breasts slowed, like a train coming to a halt, slowing, slower, then stopped, and standing before them again, regal like a queen, breathing deeply, was Miggy of old, her eyes closed, head bowed, humming softly to herself. Then she opened her eyes, her dance-call to God complete, seated herself at the table, all business again, pulled the typewriter close, inserted a card, and started to type.

When she was done typing, she held the card up. The man rose and proceeded to the front of the room. She handed him the card and he sat down. Miggy peered around the room and said, "Next."

On it went, as Paper watched, astounded. Old Miggy Fludd, who could barely read when they met—a typing fortune teller. Who would'a thunk it?

The questions came from each of those assembled, and they ranged in scope and manner. *Is mama sick back home and not telling me? Is my husband coming back? Is my wife dating my best friend? Why has my cousin been so mean to me?* After each question, Miggy rose, retreated into the zone, danced a marvelous short dance, reemerged from her zone, typed the answer on a card, and handed the card to the questioner.

When she covered all nine people in the room, she stood behind the table with her hands touching the top of her desk like a schoolteacher and said, "Are we all done here?" She glanced at Paper.

Nobody turned around to look, but Paper felt as if the room were looking at her anyway. She found herself staring holes in the floor. *No Lord*, she said to herself, *I don't want to know nothing about tomorrow.*

"Nobody? All right. Goodbye then," Miggy said. She sat behind her desk as the room rose, each person placing a few coins in a donation jar on her desk as they filed out.

But she called out to one as he reached the door, a slim gray-haired man bearing a beaten fedora in his hands with flecks of black in his ragged gray mustache and beard. "Bullis, can you stay a minute?"

He stopped and turned, standing by the door as the rest filed out of the room into the rain. "What I done now?" he said pleasantly.

Miggy took the jar full of coins, emptied the coins onto her desk, and separated them slowly. "How you doing out there, Bullis?"

"Out where?"

"At work."

"I'm doing good."

Miggy slid all of the coins over to him. "I needs a favor," she said.

The man eyed the coins. Then pushed them back toward Miggy. "All right."

Miggy nodded at Paper. "See that pretty thing setting back there? She'll tell it when she's ready."

"Who's she?"

"One of them from Nate's side of town."

The old man paused for a moment, blinking thoughtfully. "Nate's still living?"

"Can she call on you or not?"

"Course."

"I'll fix it up."

"All right then. I'll be round."

Paper found herself struggling for words as the man departed, then said, "Miggy, you got all them fancy clothes doing this kind of job?"

"Oh no, honey. This is my work. Not my job."

"Telling fortunes?"

Miggy frowned. "I'm an oracle. I'm a messenger. God's word comes to me when I dance, and I give His answers to people who asks."

"I ain't seen nar one of them reading what you put on them cards," Paper said.

"Most of 'em can't read," Miggy said.

"Then why write their answers?"

"They'll find somebody who can read. Or I'll read to them myself later. I see most of 'em every day."

Paper wanted to ask, "What if they don't like what you wrote?" But she reminded herself where she was, so instead she asked, "What you giving 'em, Miggy?"

"Hope, honey."

"Ain't that what church is for?"

Miggy smiled. "Last year some gangsters from Reading come out here looking for a fella named Sanko. Hear tell they had a four-hundred-dollar ransom on Sanko's head. Sanko was what you would call in our language a twi, someone who says nice things about people, sells air castles about 'em, makes 'em feel good about what they doing even if it ain't always on the dot. He can talk the horns off the devil's head. He makes a few dollars that way. He don't do nobody no harm. What he done against them gangsters, the who-shot-John part, I don't know, but them two come out here to the Row dressed in suits calling theyself preachers. Said they come to give Sanko the Gospel."

She paused, finished up counting her coins, and placed them in her pocket.

"That is why the earth is troubled, Paper. You will not find one parent in ten thousand who would raise their child to be a murderer acting like they got God's understanding. God's Holy Hand has been laid on most folks out here on the Row long before they come to this country. We got our own church and our own way of doing things going back to how we was raised in the South. We keeps our reckonings against unjust sorrows in the family. We know when someone is giving God's milk and not the devil's water. So them two fellas looking for Sanko left outta here on a cooling board. And don't nobody round here know nothing about it. Sanko is walking round the Row building air castles and telling lies to this day. And I'm oracling on as I please."

She paused, straightening out the cards on her desk and the typewriter. "You a good woman, Paper. I owes you for your kindness when that Pullman porter put a beating on my heart. I ain't the same person I was the first twenty-seven years of my life."

"I didn't tell you why I was here," Paper said.

"I already know. There must be three hundred folks working out there at Pennhurst. And most of your colored workers out there is from the Row. You know why? Your basic Chicken Hill colored wants to eat their food off the high fryer. They aiming to be high siddity like white folks. But pretending to know everything and acting like you're better than you know you are puts a terrible strain on a body. It makes you a stumbling stone to your own justice. Your basic Lowgod don't care about that. Us Lowgods understand that when them patients at Pennhurst throw their poop at us, or pisses on the floor, or spits at us, they ain't got no peace. They understand what most people in this land don't: that you can't restore what you ain't never had. Living on a land that ain't yours, pretending to know everything when you don't, making up rules for this or that to make yourself seem big, that puts a terrible strain on a body. This land don't belong to the people that rules it, see. And it's made some of 'em, the best of 'em, the most honest of 'em, it's made 'em crazy. We is in the same place, you and I, being colored. We are visitors here. Thing is, us Lowgods, wherever we is from, the old Africaland, I suppose, we were *keepers* of our fellow man. That was our purpose. We're still that way. That's all we know of our history, the one that was moved from us before we was brung here. You know what Lowgod means in our language? Little parent. We know most folks are weak and wisdom is hard to know. So the poor souls at Pennhurst is not hard for us to handle. I work up there myself. The patients ain't hard to deal with. It's the workers. The doctors and medical people and so forth. Those are the hard ones."

"I ain't studying them," Paper said. "I'm just looking for—"

"I already know who you want," Miggy said. "And I know how to get him out."

She pulled her chair close to her typewriter, reached for an index card, then looked at Paper, holding the blank card in her long, slender fingers.

"They put your boy in Ward C-1. That's not an easy place. It's for what they call the lower functions. The ones they reckon can't feed themselves and such. We got a Lowgod in there. Well, he's *from* the Row, let me put it that way. He used to be one of us, but he's gone astray. He got hisself into a tight round here, so he don't come round no more, for we don't want him. He's unjust. And twisted. That's why he lives up there at Pennhurst. Stays up there one hundred percent of the time now. Handles the worst patients. I heard about . . . well, there's a few like him in this world. They finds room for folks like him up at Pennhurst, for so long as his evil is fed every now and then, he keeps order. He ain't never gonna leave there, for if he ever comes back here, we'll send him home to his milk. You got to deal with him to get your boy out free and clear."

"Will he help?"

"Maybe. Maybe not. He's twisted. But I can get your people to him."

"If he's twisted, how we gonna deal with him?"

"I ain't said *how* you deal with him. I just said you got to."

"We don't know nothing about that kind of thing, Miggy."

"You got a Low Country colored living right there on the Hill. Ask him."

"Who?"

"I am not so big a fool as to think you don't know," she said. "Bullis, who you just seen, he'll get your people inside. After that, it's up to you what to do."

With that, she pulled the typewriter close, placed the card in the carriage, typed a few letters, handed Paper the card, and gathered the rest of her index cards in a neat pile. "Come back and see me sometime. And bring that street-ways fella you thinking of marrying with you. The one waiting outside. He'll do, by the way, for a husband. He got a good heart."

With that, she turned from the table, strode to the side door, stepped out into the dark rain, and vanished, the door closing behind her.

She was gone so fast that Paper forgot to ask her for the name of the Lowgod man inside the ward. She looked down at the card in her hand. It bore three words: "Son of Man."

20

The Antes House

Gus Plitzka, chairman of the Pottstown city council, hated Memorial Day. Every year for as long as anyone could remember, the annual meeting of the John Antes Historical Society's Cornet Marching Band was held in conjunction with the meeting of Pottstown's city council. The meetings were held five minutes apart—one after the other. First the city council met. Then the entire historical society assembled out front. Declarations were made, proclamations exclaimed. Then the John Antes Historical Society's Cornet Marching Band played. Next, everyone put down their instruments and breakfast was served with German beer and sausages because the Germans had to be thrown in there somewhere, since they owned practically everything in town. Then the band played again. Then the fire engines from the Empire Fire Company showed up ringing their bells, and finally, by afternoon, with lots of harumphs and yahoos and boops and bangs and fits and starts and proclamations, the Memorial Day march began, with the city council members clad in Revolutionary-era costumes serving as parade marshals.

It was a nod to history, a sentimental bid to the great John Antes, Pottstown's greatest composer. Nobody outside Pottstown had ever heard of Antes, of course, in part because he wrote trumpet sonatas that nobody played, and in part because the John Antes Historical Society's Cornet Marching Band, which was composed of forty-five souls—numbskulls, pig farmers, heavy smokers, bums, drunks, cheerleaders, tomboys, bored college students, and any other white American in Montgomery County who could purse their lips tight enough to blast a noise through a trumpet—sounded like a cross between a crank engine trying to start on a cold October morning and a dying African silverback gorilla howling out its last. It was all a nod to Antes, the great composer, husband, father, revolutionary, statesman, plunderer, iron maker, wife beater, cornetist, Indian grave robber, and all-around great American who served as president of Pottstown borough *and* as a colonel under the great George Washington himself—and still found time to write marching band sonatas for trumpet, imagine that. After the daylong party and parade celebrating his life wound its way back to the Antes House, more speeches were delivered, followed by a giant outdoor pig roast party, followed by fireworks blasted into the night, at which time everyone got drunk and forgot all about old John.

The entire celebration began and ended every year at the great composer's Revolutionary-era home, an exhausted, crumbling, stone-and-stucco structure hunched at the corner of High Street and Union guarding Chicken Hill like an old witch, the tattered neighborhood that rose up behind it like a drunk male cousin hovering over little cousin Mary at Christmas, who just turned eighteen and suddenly evolved from a gap-toothed tomboy into a flamethrower. The beloved Antes House was a cherished treasure, admired and saluted, the center of the universe for Pottstown's white citizens on Memorial Day. It also faithfully honored the town's Negro citizens the other 364 days a year, serving as a wonderful shithouse, beer-guzzling headquarters, hideout from the cops, playpen for runaways, tiedown spot for errant mules, and last-resort sex spot for Chicken Hill teenagers in lust and love, all of whom graciously vanished a week before Memorial Day when a truck bearing the words "Pottstown. History in IRONG" with the G crossed out—a painter's mistake—clunked to the curb. A crew of men tumbled out and the annual transformation began. American flags were hoisted. Plywood coverings were removed from the windows, sashes painted and repaired, the sidewalk swept clean, the brick walkway hosed down, the house scrubbed from top to bottom, and when they finished, the exhausted workmen did the same thing they did every year: they stood back and gazed at the old house with their hands on their hips, shaking their heads like a mother who had just washed her son's face ten times only to realize that he was just plain ugly in the first place. But American history is not meant to be pretty. It is plain. It is simple. It is strong and truthful. Full of blood. And guts. And war. "Iron," the mayor announced with his usual cheery bluster at the end of the 1936 annual city council and Antes society's meetings, "is what made this town great. We are the cannon makers. The gun makers. The steelmakers. The blood! The guts! The glory! God is on our side! Remember: George Washington's victory here at Pottstown was the precursor to the great battle of Valley Forge! Never forget!"

Plitzka, seated at a table inside the Antes House among the council members, received this speech with a grumble and a wince. His big toe was killing him. It was swollen to the size of a meatball. Plus, he had a headache—two of them. The first was in his head. The second no aspirin could solve.

Plitzka was the new owner of the Clover Dairy, employer of twenty-nine people—the first in his family to do such a thing, which, if that wasn't the American dream, he told friends, what is? Imagine that. Of course, the friends who knew him well liked to imagine him drowning, but that wasn't the point. He was the boss! The top dog. Owner of the deck.

Problem was, the deck dealt him from a bottom card. Not a month before, just as the deal closed, he discovered he hadn't lined up his nickels properly and was $1,400 short. In desperation, he called on his cousin Ferdie, who had a wonderful head on his shoulders for swindling suckers and banking horses at the nearby Sanatoga Racetrack. Ferdie declared himself short as well but recommended Plitzka to a "good friend" in Philadelphia who happily loaned him the money. The friend turned out to be a frightening mobster named Nig Rosen.

Every time Plitzka thought of Rosen, his insides felt like liquefying Jell-O. He was $1,400 plus interest in the red to a bona fide gangster and had nowhere to find the money. Now, instead of spending the day scheming up ways to burn himself out of that hole, he had to waste a precious day limping around as a parade marshal while hoping Rosen's palookas wouldn't make a public appearance. They had already shown up at his office twice. It was a mess. Sitting at the table, with his toe throbbing, he wanted to burst into tears.

When the meeting ended, he sat drumming his fingers on the table as the other council members headed for the door and band members clambered into the room bearing all manner of cornets. Plitzka lingered, scanning the newcomers for Doc Roberts. He was hoping that Doc, who was a member of just about every historical society in town and marched in every parade, was a member of the John Antes Historical Society as well. He sighed in relief when he spotted Doc's recognizable hobble at the far end of the room. Doc was holding, of all things, a tuba.

Plitzka rose from the table, his toe aching, and made his way past the band members to Doc, who was busy fumbling with the instrument. "Hey, Doc, my toe is killing me," he said.

Doc glanced at Plitzka and turned back to his instrument, fumbling with its valves. "Come by my office tomorrow," he said.

"It's bad. Can you take a look now?"

Doc turned and took a quick glance around the crowded anteroom. "Here?"

"Outside."

"I gotta play."

"It can't wait," Plitzka said.

Doc turned back to fiddling with his tuba as Plitzka stood behind him, helpless. He couldn't stand Doc. Old-money clubfoot snob. One of the *Mayflower* children. Parade co-marshal because his family had been here since the Indians and all that. Got to blow a tuba in an all-trumpet marching band. The two had tangled years before on the city council back when Doc had served. Plitzka wanted to spend seventy dollars on a bronze plaque to celebrate the establishment of the town's first Polish business. Doc had objected, saying, "We can't give a plaque to every family that baked bread here. The Polish have only been here since 1885—that's *after* the Civil War." Plitzka never forgot the insult and was happy to engineer Doc's exit from the council by moving a few political odds and ends around and getting him to resign.

Doc, for his part, bore equal distaste for Plitzka, whom he regarded as a climber, a two-fisted political-club fighter, and the "new" kind of Pottstown resident: i.e., a man without honor. Plitzka supplied cases of bourbon to locals for their votes. He bullied local bankers into submission by threatening to ban coal deliveries on streets where their businesses were. Even the big boys at McClinton Iron and Bethlehem Steel answered his calls. His house on the west side had a living room the size of a rugby field and a welcome mat written in Old English. How did a Pole, whose family's pisshole of a farm atop Chicken Hill couldn't sprout fleas, get that kind of money? But given what happened up at the Jewish store on the Hill, Doc didn't need any new enemies, especially now. Especially Plitzka, who was dangerous.

"All right, Gus," he grumbled.

The two men moved toward the door. Neither noticed the two Italian women picking up papers and sweeping, moving around like ghosts. Pia Fabicelli, the city council's official janitor, was also reluctantly in attendance, having been summoned away from her usual duties at city hall to clean up behind the masters at the Antes House. She'd brought Fioria to help.

As the two swept through the room removing coffee cups, cake crumbs, and leftover papers that were the city council's usual fare, they noticed Doc and Plitzka hobbling for the door, both limping, with Plitzka leading the way.

Pia nudged Fioria and quipped in Italian, "Look. Twins."

Fioria chuckled. "If you stick your finger in the mouth of one, the other will bite."

They laughed and went back to work as Doc followed Plitzka outside.

Plitzka took a seat on the cracked brick front steps of the Antes House, removed his shoe, peeled off his sock, and revealed the toe. It was ghastly: bulging, red, and wrinkled. "What do you think?" he asked.

Doc stared at the wrinkled toe. "Whatever it is," he said, "it needs pressing."

"Ain't you gonna check it out? It's killing me."

"I need my instruments. How did it get that way?"

"That's what you're here for."

"I'm not a mind reader, Gus. Did you hit it on something? A desk? A chair? Did something fall on it?"

"No."

"What have you done lately?"

"What's that supposed to mean?"

"Maybe you went for a walk somewhere and stepped on something. Or maybe something fell on it, maybe in the plant, on the job?"

"This *is* my job," Plitzka said dryly. "I don't work in a plant, Doc. I'm city council president."

"Gus, give me a break. I'm trying to figure it out."

"I'm in pain!"

Doc sat on the stoop one step below Plitzka, gingerly picking up the foot by the heel but avoiding touching the disgusting toe, hoping it didn't smell like mustard gas. He placed the foot down gently. "When did it start? The pain."

"I'm not sure," Gus said. "Last month me and the missus went to John Wanamaker's department store in Philly. She wanted to ride the elevator. The thing got stuck on the fifth floor for twenty minutes. I think it started then."

That was partly true. He had done those things. But his foot had actually started aching later that afternoon when he had left his wife in Wanamaker's to shop and walked four blocks to the gangster Nig Rosen's tavern on Broad Street. It was all so innocent. His cousin Ferdie said Rosen was a straight shooter. Clean. A good guy. And at first, Plitzka found him just as his cousin described: down-to-earth, reassuring, as Plitzka explained the situation to him. "I'm a farmer's boy," Plitzka said. "Worked my way up. Street sweeper. Clerk. City council. Now I'm at the door. *This close* to buying the dairy that owns half the milk in town. I just need to get over this last hump." Rosen had been reassuring. "I'm a tavern owner," he said. "I know a little about supply and demand. Thank goodness Prohibition didn't kill us off." He gave Plitzka the $1,400 with a smile and a 5 percent monthly interest rate on a handshake. Then, the next week, he arrived at Plitzka's office with two large goons, demanding 35 percent interest starting that day, with that interest bringing the loan payoff to $2,900. Plitzka refused. "Do I look stupid? That's more than double the amount," he said. "I won't pay." Rosen's kindly features vanished and he coolly pulled back his jacket to reveal a pistol and said, "How about I show up at your house and jam this in your face?"

And just like that, the deal that was supposed to boost him into the echelons of Pottstown royalty had closed up tightly around his neck, strangling him. An extra $420 a month over his normal expenses, including payroll, that were figured to the penny. Where would he get that from?

Sitting on the steps, his toe bristling with pain, thinking of Rosen and those gorillas standing at the front door of his house, with his wife and kids just inside, made Plitzka's skin prickle.

"So it's from nerves?" Doc Roberts said.

"If it's nerves, it's working overtime, Doc. This feels like a mousetrap."

"Soon as the rehearsal's done, before we march, I'll run by the office and pick up a little something," Doc said.

Plitzka seemed relieved. He reached for his sock and gingerly placed it on his foot. "Thanks, Doc. You might want to take something, too. You look a little peaked yourself."

"I'm okay." Doc shrugged, trying to seem nonchalant. The truth was, since Chona died a week ago, his nerves were frayed to pieces. No one questioned his version of events. No one suspected. The matter died away quietly. But in the confusion of the moment, he'd somehow—he never did figure out how—snatched a pendant off Chona's neck, a mezuzah bearing an inscription in a foreign language. He had no idea what it said or how it landed in his fist. It couldn't have been intentional, grabbing the darn thing, but the truth was he simply couldn't remember. It was just a moment of passion, that's all. He'd gotten carried away. Women do that to men sometimes. Happens every day. He wanted to return the cursed thing, but to whom? He could have thrown it out, but that made it feel like murder, which it was not. He was a decent man. He decided to mail it but was afraid someone might track it to him. Instead, he carried it in his pocket to the parade. His intent was to leave it somewhere near Chicken Hill, where it might be found, knowing that the Antes House was close to the Hill. Just set it on the ground and walk away. But now Plitzka had shown up; plus his stomach was bothering him. It was tension. Things simply had not gone well since the . . . accident. There were rumors. He had heard plenty. Did Plitzka know? Plitzka, of all people, a shady carpetbagger, a one-generation-removed immigrant who would sell his grandma for a quarter. Had someone said something? And now the parade, right at the foot of Chicken Hill, basically in the Negroes' backyard. *I shouldn't have come here today*, he thought.

Even as he said it to himself, Doc noticed a Negro woman walking briskly past on the road glance at him, then move on, turning up the dirt road to Chicken Hill. Two more Negroes followed, men in work clothes, cutting suspicious glances, then hurrying on.

"A lot of new darkies in town," Plitzka said.

"Yeah." Doc shrugged. *Had someone said something?*

"There's more niggers coming every year," Gus said. "They're like roaches."

Doc sat up painfully and said, "I'll be over after we rehearse a few songs. Then we'll run over to the office."

He was about to push himself to his feet when he heard Plitzka say, "Too bad about the Jewess."

Doc felt his heart racing with panic, and suddenly felt too weak to stand. Still seated facing the road, he managed to murmur, "Shame," and rose to his feet, anxious to leave.

Just then a Negro couple walked past, and Doc, now standing, froze with his back to Plitzka. The Negro man didn't look at him, but the woman slowed to a halt, glaring straight at Doc. She wouldn't stop staring. Doc's head felt light. He suddenly felt thirsty. He needed a drink of water.

"You know her?" Plitzka asked.

"Huh?"

"I asked did you know her."

"Who? Her?" Doc said, pointing at the Negro woman who suddenly turned and moved up toward the Hill.

"Not her. The lady who died."

Doc nodded, still facing the road, his back to Plitzka. He placed his hands in his pockets, trying to be nonchalant. "She was sick a long time."

He heard Plitzka say something else, but a blast of a trumpeter warming up inside the Antes House drowned out Plitzka's utterance. Something about "letters."

"What?" Doc asked.

"The letters. She was the one who used to write letters to the *Mercury* complaining about our White Knights march. Not to speak evil of the dead and all, but this is America, Doc. Everybody gotta play by the rules."

Doc, his insides feeling like jelly, merely nodded.

"Whatever happened to the boy?" Plitzka asked.

Doc wasn't sure whether to leave. He wanted to. *But do . . . guilty people run?* he thought to himself. *No. I did nothing wrong.*

He decided to sit back down on the steps just to show indifference. He lowered himself to the step just beneath Plitzka and cleared his throat. "The kid?" He tried to sound nonchalant. "Oh, we got him some help. He's up at Pennhurst."

"That's good. He'll get a good education at least."

Doc found his eyes searching the road again. Another Negro walked by, this one a man. The Negro slowed, staring perceptively, then stopped, openly staring now, facing them, twenty feet off. He looked as if he were about to shout something. Then, to Doc's relief, he waved. Doc did something he rarely did. He waved back.

Plitzka frowned. "Some of 'em are all right," he said. "If they'd just clean themselves. Have you been up on the Hill lately? The filth up there, the open sewers, gosh . . ."

Doc felt his throat tightening; he was afraid to move and afraid to stay. How did he get in this fix? Sitting here, gabbing with Plitzka, a low-life cheating farmer turned political thug. He had given his whole life to the town. His family had been in Pottstown more than one hundred years. And now he had to sit here and listen to this moron quip. He felt anger working its way into his throat. He couldn't help himself.

"Speaking of clean," he said. "You know the basement bathroom in the Antes House? The one you guys voted to put in three years ago for the public? I turned on the faucet today and muddy water came out."

"It did?"

"Came right out the tap. I ran it a couple of minutes, but it didn't clear up. Is the city running water from the reservoir into Chicken Hill?"

Now it was Plitzka's turn to be nervous. "I don't know where the water comes from."

"Doesn't the new reservoir near your old farm supply water to the Hill?"

"I don't read every city contract, Doc."

"You guys gotta look into that. Muddy water coming out of a tap on the Hill will keep my office full of people from around here, Gus. And they don't pay."

"We can't keep track of every colored on the Hill, Doc. We got big numbers up there. How many, who knows? We got open sewers up there running down to Main Street. We close 'em up, they dig new ones. We gotta straighten that out before we dig new water lines. Otherwise, they're crapping and throwing slop in the open sewers all over."

"Water and sewers are two different things, Gus."

"The Hill's a zoo, Doc. Believe me. My old farm is up there."

Doc nodded. He'd heard the stories about the Plitzka farm. How they had made a deal with the city in years past to supply water to the town before the new reservoir was built. And how the city was still paying the farm for its well water. Now Plitzka, as head of the dairy company and owner of his family's farm, was collecting on both ends—from the city for supplying water *and* getting free water from the city for his business to boot. A real winner. Typical immigrant gangster. No honor. No sense of history.

Doc couldn't help himself. "You been up to the new reservoir?" he asked.

"Many times," Plitzka said. "It was a pond when I was a kid."

"Has someone from the city ever gone up to look at those old pipes around it? Maybe one of 'em's cracked and mud's getting in there."

"If those pipes are cracked, I would have heard complaints from the Hill," Plitzka said.

"Why would the Negroes complain?" Doc said. "They still got wells, a lot of 'em, don't they?"

"If you want to draw a map of every house that has a well up there, go ahead. It's a maze up there."

Doc's anger boiled over. Why did Plitzka have to be such a jerk about everything? He heard himself say, "You could ask the Negroes, Gus. You're their city councilman. You ought to talk to your constituents."

Plitzka's face reddened. "If I did, maybe they'd tell me what they heard about you."

"What about me?"

"You and that Jewess. I heard the rumors."

"What rumors? The boy attacked me."

"Not the rumors I heard."

"Rumors don't prove much."

"They prove people can talk is all," Gus said coolly. "You ever think of talking to Chief Markus about it?"

"I already talked to him. She had a seizure. I tried to help her. The boy got antsy and attacked. He's deaf and probably dumb. I ran out and got the cops. They wrote a report."

"That they did," Plitzka said slyly.

"She died of a stroke, Gus. That's what the hospital in Reading said, too, by the way."

"Too bad there wasn't a white man in the store when it started. That would put an end to it."

"To what?"

"The rumors."

Doc rose, furious now. "Look after your own foot," he said.

"Don't lose your shirt, Doc," Gus said. "I didn't mean nothing. We cleared the air. Got to the truth of the matter and all. C'mon, Doc. Let's bury the hatchet right now, okay? The past is the past. We gotta march in the parade today. We're co-marshals, remember?" He held out his hand.

Doc sighed, then shook, feeling his temper ease somewhat. It was not smart to make an enemy of Plitzka. "Come by my office in a half hour and we'll get it done before the march. Then I'll send you to a guy who can fix your shoe so your toe won't bother you for a while. That toe's not gonna heal in a week."

"Who's the guy?"

"An old shoemaker on the Hill. Skrup, they call him. He can do anything with shoes. He can even make you a special shoe if you want. He does good work."

"You're all right, Doc."

Doc headed back inside. He decided not to tell Plitzka that Marv Skrupskelis was a Jew. And not just any old Jew. Marv Skrupskelis was a rough shuffle. Let Plitzka find out on his own.

21

The Marble

Ward C-1 had three shifts of attendants, and they seemed to change constantly, so it was a full five weeks before Dodo first saw Son of Man. He never saw him till he saw him, as they say, for the first days at Pennhurst were a blitz of shock from sorrow and suffering. His mind was drunk on hazy medicine for long stretches, which made focusing impossible. The overwhelming smell, the fear, the silhouettes of bodies that hovered over his crib to stare, munch at his food tray, pluck at his ears, occasionally wheel him out for this or that, change his bedding while grunting and cursing, all blended together in a kind of fuzz. Some of the activity came from curious patients. Others were attendants. In his drugged state, Dodo could not tell who was who.

Moreover, the transformation from living in his own room in the back of Miss Chona's grocery store with his own bed, lamp, comic books, and cardboard airplane that dangled on a string from the light bulb overhead to a ward of two hundred men in an institution that housed three thousand souls was such a shock that Dodo might have died in those first days were he not in traction. His immobility actually saved him, for he was an active, athletic child by nature, with arms and legs that lived in constant motion. But now he was in pain, drugged, and immobile, all of which kept him still and allowed his body to heal. While it did, he learned how to talk to Monkey Pants.

Their communication was helped by his near deafness. He could hear very little, thus his attention was not disrupted by the spine-curdling noises of the ward, which made sleep for normal-hearing newcomers just about impossible. The moanings, groanings, coos, burps, sighs, growls, yells, chirps, yelps, chortles, cacklings, farts, chatterings, and howlings of his fellow residents went over his head. They plundered his food tray when it was left by his bed until he learned to gobble it down immediately, and after that, most ignored him, wandering about the ward like ghosts, men in "johnnies," or hospital gowns, a few in their underwear, and one or two who tore their clothes off and marched about naked. Those first few days were the hardest, for civility from the overworked attendants was not wasted on the so-called lunatics. His linen changers were gruff, coarse men, shoving his tractioned and bandaged limbs aside impatiently, ignoring his howls of pain, mouthing what appeared to be oaths as they did so. Only after a few days did he realize that some of those changing his bedding and tossing him about as he sobbed pathetically were not attendants at all but rather fellow patients. His inability to execute even the most basic functions, such as turning on his side and scratching his back while lying in traction in a steel crib in a room that stank horribly left him in a kind of horrified trance a good part of the time. But his body was only twelve. It wanted to live. It wanted to heal. And Monkey Pants turned out to be a curious soul, in possession of something that drew Dodo's mind out of its fog and depression, yanking him out of the dread that soaked him every second.

A marble. A blue one.

Monkey Pants produced it from beneath his pillow shortly after Dodo arrived, holding it in his left hand, over which he had some control and strength, as opposed to his right, which seemed nearly useless.

"Where did you get that?" Dodo asked.

Monkey Pants replied with a curling of the lip.

"Where?"

And so it began.

At first, it seemed impossible, for neither boy knew sign language. But Dodo could speak and Monkey Pants could hear, and just the act of trying to communicate with someone, anyone, brought Dodo a bit of light. Before Pennhurst, other than occasional forays into Miss Bernice's yard next to the store, he'd lived mostly in a world of adults, ignored by most of them save Uncle Nate, Aunt Addie, and Miss Chona. With Monkey Pants, he found himself the center of attention with someone close to his age. And while their communication was crude at first, their unwritten understanding that a thousand thoughts lay in the head of the other forged their common ground.

In the beginning, Monkey Pants did most of the talking, for he was curious with many questions, whereas Dodo was depressed and withdrawn. But eventually curiosity took over, and after a few days of Monkey Pants's squirming and grunting efforts to communicate, Dodo took over, interrupting him with many questions. Monkey Pants's responses, gestures, and facial expressions at first seemed meaningless, and several times the two were halted in the middle of their discourse by Dodo suddenly bursting into tears, at which point Monkey Pants would patiently wait till the bawling stopped and begin again with a series of gestures and wiggles. The gestures were earnest and insistent and forced Dodo to answer, even though he was often unsure of what his new friend meant. But they had hours to while away in those first days, and by the end of the first week, the two established a few crude modes of talking.

Raised eyebrows from Monkey Pants meant "yes," furrowed eyebrows meant "no." "Maybe" was a slight raising of the left forearm. A balled left fist and forearm across the chest meant "watch out," "bad," or an expletive. A more pronounced lip with the same meant "really watch out," "pain," or "trouble." Crossed forearms, with the left hand pinning the right hand down on the chest meant "danger." The showing of teeth meant "good" or "tastes good" or "okay." Monkey Pants could not control his spasms, which kept his head and every limb of his body in some sort of shake. His right hand was hopelessly curled into a useless fist, and his legs would occasionally spasm uncontrollably. But he could, with effort, control his left hand, left wrist, and left forearm all the way up to his shoulder, which gave him the use of all five fingers—a valuable tool, for it was that hand that poked out of his crib and gestured through the bars to Dodo and shook his crib to awaken him when Monkey Pants felt the need.

It was from that left hand that the miracle of communication occurred.

It began with the marble. After producing the marble and allowing Dodo to hold it several times and demanding it back by gesture, Monkey Pants sought to communicate something about it. He was unsuccessful each time. Dodo, for his part, countered with questions of his own that brought on further frustrated communicative gestures from Monkey Pants until the two gave up. Were it any other subject, Dodo would have let the matter drop. But he loved marbles. They reminded him of Miss Chona—who'd provided him with so many marbles he had to store them in a jar—and his aunt and uncle, whom he missed so dearly. He presumed all three were angry at him for what had happened at the store, for not one of them had come to fetch him or even see him. He deluded himself that perhaps the three were busy gathering all kinds of marbles to bring him as a special gift so he might heal faster and get out. But that delusion faded more and more each day, and most nights he fell asleep with tears in his eyes.

Only the marble kept him hopeful, for despite his guilt, a tiny part of him believed that the kind woman who doled out so many of those precious marbles to him would forgive him. So each day Dodo asked Monkey Pants to produce the marble from beneath his pillow, and inquired as to where he got it. After several hundred gestures and facial expressions from his friend, Dodo surmised that Monkey Pants had gotten the marble as a kind of gift from someone. Who that person was, he was unable to determine. That frustrated him, and one afternoon while Dodo was poking for answers, Monkey Pants became frustrated and turned his head away in bored irritation.

Dodo, though he could not hear his own voice, knew how to raise it, for the vibrations in his head told him so, so he spoke loudly. "Stop being stupid!" he said.

Monkey Pants turned back to him, facing him through the bars of the crib, his spastic head shaking back and forth, his expression saying, "What do you want me to do? I can't make you understand."

"We're not finished," Dodo said.

So they went at it again, driven only by the aching loneliness of their existence, two boys with intelligent minds trapped in bodies that would not cooperate, caged in cribs like toddlers, living in an insane asylum, the insanity of it seeming to live on itself and charge them, for despite the horribleness of their situation, they were cheered by the tiniest of things, the crinkle of an eyelid, an errant cough, an occasional satisfied grunt or burst of laughter as one or the other bumbled about in confused impatience at the other, trying to figure out how to communicate the origins of Monkey Pants's precious marble. It was outrageous.

Fortunately, time was something they had a great deal of, and they made good use of it. They had nothing to do all day during those first weeks, for the deadening routine was the same. The patients were awakened at seven. Linen, diapers, and hospital gowns were removed and changed—or sometimes not. Those who could be washed were washed. Others who could be washed sometimes weren't. Those who were mobile were paraded to the toilet by an attendant. After the toilet, the parade of so-called lunatics was led to the cafeteria by two day-shift attendants, then directly to the day room down the hall, where they stayed till just before lunch. They were then marched back to the ward briefly, then to the cafeteria for lunch, then to the day room again until dinner. After dinner, there was a rare activity that usually was nothing but going to the day room again, then all were put to bed by 8 p.m. The two boys in cribs were fed where they lay, along with a third patient, a young man who lay totally unmoving and moaning in a crib at the far end of the ward near the day attendants' desk. Usually, the two attendants on duty switched off, one manning the desk in the morning while the other led the patients to the cafeteria and the day room, then they switched in the afternoon, leaving the desk manned with one attendant who normally slept or read while the other did the heavy lifting of leading the ward around. The desk was always staffed by one attendant, and whoever was there seemed satisfied that the boys spent the day amusing each other. They were not a bother. They were one less thing to do.

But the boys were solving a puzzle. And after the third week, the breakthrough came when Monkey Pants pointed with his finger to Dodo's cast and made several gestures. Dodo deduced, incorrectly, that Monkey Pants wanted to ask him what happened and why he was wearing the cast, which brought back the whole business of what happened at Miss Chona's store, and he burst into tears.

"I want to go home," he cried.

Monkey Pants stared at him, his eyes immobile, seemingly unmoved. Seeing this made Dodo angry. "Forget your dumb marble, Monkey Pants." He closed his eyes, shutting him out.

Monkey Pants reached over and shook Dodo's crib.

Dodo opened his eyes. "What!"

Monkey Pants tapped the bars of his crib five times.

"So what. You can count to five."

Monkey Pants shook his head, insistent. He tapped again on the crib bars. Five times. Then held up the marble. Then held up his thumb.

This piqued Dodo's interest. "Do it six times if you're so smart."

Monkey Pants frowned a "no," and tapped five times again.

"What you want, Monkey Pants?"

Monkey Pants tapped again and again, pointed to the marble, to his mouth, then reached across into Dodo's crib and pinged Dodo with his first finger and thumb.

Dodo, irritated, snapped, "Hey!"

Monkey Pants went wild with enthusiasm, his head bouncing on his pillow.

"Hey what?"

Several shakes of "no."

"What?"

Monkey Pants's head shook a "no." He moved his mouth, and Dodo, seeing his mouth move, took a wild guess, knowing vowel sounds looked alike, thinking he'd said, "Hey," so he retorted. "Hey yourself."

More enthusiastic wild gestures by Monkey Pants.

"Hey?" Dodo said.

Yes. Monkey Pants nodded.

"Hey what?"

No. Monkey Pants shook his head.

"Just hey?"

Yes. A nod.

It took all day, with Monkey Pants pantomiming, grunting, grinding, and pointing, for Dodo to figure out that Monkey Pants was not nodding "yes" to "hey" but rather to "A," the first letter of the alphabet, which he finally made clear by pointing to one of the attendants seated at his station eating an apple.

"Your thumb means 'A'?"

Monkey Pants pointed to the man and raised his eyes, which meant "yes!" and shook his head wildly. It was a breakthrough. The first letter of the alphabet!

It took two more days for Dodo to figure out that the letter B was the first thumb also. So were the letters C, D, and E.

From there, the rest of Monkey Pants's one-handed formula rolled out quickly.

His thumb represented letters A through E.

The next finger represented F to J.

The middle finger, K to O.

The fourth finger, P to T.

The pinkie covered the last six letters, U to Z.

Twenty-six letters of the alphabet. Five fingers. Five per finger. Six for the pinkie. Dodo was exhausted from figuring it out, for it had taken them several days of two steps forward and one step back, using the word "apple" as a start. But within days, he became sure of the code. They checked it and rechecked it using various words, "man," "food," "cake," "ice cream," and, of course, "marble," a word of the greatest interest to Dodo. When he deciphered that word correctly three times, and it was clear to them that they were both solid on their new language, Dodo declared, "Monkey Pants, you're so smart!"

Monkey Pants waved his hand impatiently, for he was starving to talk. He began waving his palm and fingers one through five again, motioning for Dodo to hurry up and decode the letters he'd spelled. He began by asking Dodo his name in their sign language, but Dodo ignored that, for while he, too, was excited, there was the question that had fired their friendship from the very first. So he ignored Monkey Pants's extended fingers and asked impatiently, "Where did you get the marble?"

Monkey Pants rolled his eyes and patiently spelled out as Dodo spoke the letters. He held up his middle finger.

"K? . . . L? . . . M?"

Raising of the eyes. Yes. Then he held up his fifth finger.

"U? V? W? X? Y? Z? . . . Y?"

Raising of the eyes. Yes.

"Y."

Then closing of the eyes.

"New word?"

Raising of the eyes. Yes.

Monkey Pants began spelling the rest. Dodo's eyes carefully scanned the fingers and his lips moved as Monkey Pants spelled M.Y. M.O.T.H.E.R.

It was taxing, but the riddle was solved. Dodo sighed happily, then asked, "Where is she?"

But Monkey Pants did not answer. Instead, his eyes shifted to something past Dodo, then widened in fright. He balled his fist and crossed both his forearms over his chest, the sign for "danger."

Dodo looked behind him as a shadow crossed the window and

blocked the barren light for a moment, then moved past the edge of his crib to the foot. Dodo glanced at Monkey Pants, but he'd turned away and his knees drove up toward his face and his body took a curled stance, which Dodo had learned was Monkey Pants's position of fear.

Dodo looked down at the foot of his crib to see a slim, dark figure standing there, staring.

He was a tall black man, handsome, with deep brown skin and a long mark on his forehead from an old wound of some type. His skin was smooth, his hands long and bony. Thick arms and shoulders filled his white attendant's uniform and his broad chest roared out from beneath it. He was a man of strength, clearly, with a face that bore a gentle sardonic grin, as if to say "I'm here now and everything will be fine." His deep-set eyes were calm, but there was something behind them, a muted wildness and thirst that awakened a terrible fright in Dodo, for he was a child who lived by sight and vibration.

"You the new boy?" the man asked.

Dodo stayed mute, feigning misunderstanding.

"You lip-read? That's what they say. They say you read lips."

Dodo stayed still.

The man reached out a huge hand and stroked Dodo's forehead. It was the first kind gesture he'd felt in weeks. And Dodo would have normally wept with joy at the first kind hand that didn't flip him over, turn him this way and that, and grunt with displeasure after cleaning his rancid sheets, for while one leg had been moved out of traction and was healing, the second still remained in a cast. The white attendants appeared afraid to touch him, and that hurt, for he was a child of touch and feel. He was starving for a loving touch. But there was something about the gentle stroke of the man's hand that ran across his face, down his cheek, across his chest, down his navel, and toward his pelvis before slowly lifting away that terrified him.

"What's your name?"

Dodo shrugged.

The man smiled.

"Don't matter," he said, running his large finger across Dodo's head. "We'll get to it." Then with a quick glance over his shoulder at the nurses' station, which was empty, he suddenly grabbed Dodo's good leg at the thigh, lifted him off the mattress with one hand, snatched the hospital johnnie up high with the other, and peered at his soft, smooth bottom. "You pretty as a peacock, boy." Then he gently lowered him.

"Pretty as a peacock."

Then he left.

No sooner had the man turned away than Monkey Pants was rattling his crib with his strong hand, his left, his fingers gesturing wildly, his eyes wide with fright.

"Who is he?" Dodo asked.

Monkey Pants spelled it out slowly.

S.O.N. . . . O.F. . . . M.A.N.

B.A.D. B.A.D.

V.E.R.Y.

22

Without a Song

The closing of the Heaven & Earth Grocery Store was not something that Moshe ever imagined doing. It was harder than going through Chona's things in their bedroom, for closing the store involved working in the basement, and in the basement, he found a tiny wooden barrel and wooden spoon that he recognized. She was spinning yellow into butter in that barrel when he first wandered into that basement twelve years before with a head full of problems and a world full of debt. She was the only one in the world who would remember that first moment. When he peeked inside the barrel and found it full of tiny toys, marbles, and knickknacks that she had collected to dole out as gifts to Dodo and the neighborhood children, he sat on a nearby crate and burst into tears.

Nate and Addie were there helping him clean out matters, working the far side of the room, for his plan was to rent the first floor of the building and continue to live in the apartment above. The two worked silently as he sobbed but they said nothing, for they had their share of suffering, too. Neither had mentioned the matter of Dodo in

Pennhurst. Moshe suspected they felt guilt about Chona's death because it was Nate's idea that he and Chona take Dodo in the first place. Moshe felt no anger toward them, for the boy had brought his wife joy, and he would have told them that at that moment had his heart had the strength to allow him to speak of such matters, but it did not. Still, he felt relief that they were with him at this moment, for they were the only ones he wanted near. The new faces at shul were strangers. The world had shifted.

As for what happened at the store, Addie had given him the details of what she saw that afternoon. Doc's contrasting version of the event, that Chona had been attacked by the Negro boy and collapsed, made the whole matter troublesome, for Moshe was certain the boy had done no such thing. Yet to question Doc's version of the events was to swim against the tide, as that would call attention to Chona's protestations about Doc's involvement with the Klan. Neither the town fathers nor the police would want to discuss those things. Neither were overly fond of Moshe and his business. To protest was to bring too much unwanted attention, and perhaps more police. His only allies were the shul, which was small and powerless, and the coloreds, who were terrified of the police, especially Nate. He'd noted in years past that when the police were occasionally called to quell the odd disturbance at the theater, Nate seemed to disappear. He suspected Nate had had some trouble in the past. It did not bother him, for underneath Nate's quiet nature, Moshe sensed an iron-fired solidity not unlike that of his cousin Isaac. That kind of bearing was a window into a troubled heart, he knew, one forged by past troubles and unjust treatment. It bothered Moshe that Nate, who was his best friend in town, likely had such troubles. He thought he might be the cause of it, somehow, and that thought caused him even more worry.

Seated on a crate, Moshe let his short burst of sobbing work through, then felt a sudden pain in his chest, which caused him to lean over and cough a moment, gasping for breath; then it passed. He looked up to see Addie standing on the other side of the basement looking at him, concerned. Nate, taking down shelving in the far corner, also stopped his work. Neither moved to console him. It occurred to him in that moment that he had rarely touched either one of them physically. His wife had done those things. His wife had not been afraid to hug Addie or grab a reluctant Nate by the hand to show him something or hug Dodo or cuff a female customer playfully on the face or arm or place an arm around a woman's shoulder or pick up a Negro child who was wailing. Those things were almost forbidden in this country, he realized. Chona had never been one to play by the rules of American society. She did not experience the world as most people did. To her, the world was not a china closet where you admire this and don't touch that. Rather, she saw it as a place where every act of living was a chance for tikkun olam, to improve the world. The tiny woman with the bad foot was all soul. Big. Moshe was a foot taller, yet she was the big one. He was just a man who put music shows together. A promoter. A man without a song of his own. His chest hurt.

He heard Addie say, "You all right, Mr. Moshe?"

"Fit as a fiddle," he said, wiping his face. He put aside the barrel full of toys and gifts, and continued sorting out crates, boxes, decorative items, and old tins. After a few moments, he turned to Nate, who was emptying some old papers into a garbage bin, and said, "There's nothing here we need to keep. But maybe there are some items you'd like."

Nate nodded, silent, dumping the papers and grabbing a broom.

"Have you been to see Dodo?" Moshe asked.

Nate shook his head and began sweeping. Addie, working near the far wall, spoke. "We gonna see him in a week or so," she said.

"Has it been arranged?"

She glanced at Nate. "We're working on it."

"I'll set it up for you."

Nate, as if to answer, moved back to a far corner of the basement with his broom, leaving Moshe and Addie standing alone.

"Leave it to him at his own time," she said.

Moshe nodded. Nate had not spoken much to him in the past few days, even during shiva. It occurred to him that the last thing Nate had spoken of was his suggestion that Moshe invite a few of the fabulous musicians who had played at the All-American Dance Hall and Theater to perform at Chona's funeral. Moshe's grief at the time was too great to consider such a suggestion. He thought he'd later ask one of the great musicians who came through his hall to write a song for Chona or perhaps he would give a dinner in her honor and invite a few of her Chicken Hill customers, but that was too much trouble, for it meant just about every black person on the Hill. He could not handle even the shiva. It was Feldman who made the hasty arrangements. The burial and the seven days of shiva were a blur. He largely spent them sleeping in his living room chair as a few souls from the shul came and chatted and ate with Isaac while Nate and Addie managed things. It was over in no time and she was gone. Just like that. And the absence of her meant a thousand tomorrows empty of whatever promise they had once held.

After a few more moments of shoving crates around and packing boxes, he sat down and said, "I've had enough." He was winded and felt a tightness in his chest.

"We'll finish here," Addie said.

He picked up Chona's barrel and was about to head upstairs with it when he heard the sound of a car outside rumbling up to the store. From the tiny basement window, Moshe saw the polished steel of a black sedan and shiny whitewall tires. He heard heavy shoes clumping into the store, moving toward the back room and the basement stairs. From the top of the stairwell, he heard the familiar voice of his cousin Isaac calling out.

"Moshe?"

"What are you doing back here, Isaac?"

"Come look at this."

Moshe peered up the staircase. He was in no mood to see anything. He could see Isaac's familiar bowler hat blocking out the light above. He spied a face behind Isaac, but he could not make out the features.

"What is it?" he asked impatiently in Yiddish.

He heard a chuckle. Then from the top of the stairs, an item was flung down, a towel or rag of some kind. It landed on his face. He yanked it off, irritated.

It was leather or some kind of moleskin . . . a pair of pants. Tiny leather moleskin pants. Infant-sized. With a Star of David on the backside. Then he heard laughing, and a voice from the top of the dark stairwell—a familiar, gay voice—spoke out, in Yiddish.

"I did not have time to wrap them," Malachi said. "So I brought them myself."

AFTER THEIR FIRST exultation and cries of delight, followed by a short burst of tears on Moshe's part, the three of them—Isaac, Moshe, and Malachi—gathered in the back room of the store to sip hot tea in glasses while Nate and Addie worked in the basement. Moshe could barely believe his old friend was there, seated before him.

"How did you get here so quickly?" he asked.

Malachi seemed nonplussed. "The SS *Normandie*. Five days. Very fast boat."

"How did you hear about my wife?"

Malachi glanced at Isaac, who shrugged. Moshe wiped his eyes. "Dear cousin," he said, "that was not necessary. I do not have the money to pay for such a gift."

"He did not buy my ticket," Malachi said. "I bought it myself."

Moshe sat up straight. "What trade have you that you can float back and forth across the Atlantic so easily? Are you a pickpocket?"

"All the pickpockets are here in America now. Not in Europe."

"How will you get home?"

"I am home," Malachi said.

"But you don't like it here. You said that many times."

Malachi was silent a moment, then replied: "I like to live. There is trouble back home, friend. Do you not read the Jewish papers?"

Moshe felt his chest tighten again as he said, "My mother . . ." And once again felt a squeeze in his chest and so much sadness that he didn't know if the pain was coming from his heart or his sagging spirit. He coughed and swallowed, taking a moment to catch his breath. He glanced at Isaac, whose stern face, so lightened by the joyous reunion he had witnessed moments ago, once again darkened with sorrow, for Isaac had no mother. Moshe's mother had raised them both. "She won't come. She feels the same way about America as you. She thinks this land is dirty."

"I would not disagree," Malachi said.

Isaac was now frowning, as the conversation had taken a dark turn. The three were speaking in Yiddish, but Isaac spoke now in English. "I need to speak to your help," he said.

"About what?"

"About what happened here."

"Isaac, let's not sweep out the corners. It's done."

"Of course. I'd like to speak to them anyway."

"There'll be trouble for me after you leave."

"There'll be no trouble, cousin. I just want to chat with them. To thank them. Are they about?"

"They'll be around later," Moshe lied, but Isaac knew him too well, for he simply stood up and made for the basement stairs.

Moshe spoke to his back. "There's nothing to be done, Isaac. We are not in Europe anymore. We are free here."

But Isaac's bowler was already heading downstairs.

Nate saw the brilliant shiny shoes first, then the creased suit pants, moving with the sprightliness and power of a man who was sure of himself. He leaned the broom against the wall as the rest of the man, clad in a fine gray suit, appeared.

Isaac stopped at the bottom of the stairs, his shiny shoes on the dirt floor, one hand on the railing, and he peered at Nate, who came to the staircase to meet him. Addie never stopped work. She continued to move crates and box up items as the two men, the powerful theater owner in the crisp suit and the tall Negro in the Irish cap, his shirt blanched with sweat, faced each other.

"I never got a chance to speak to you at the hospital," Isaac said. "You avoided me at shiva."

Nate shrugged.

"Were you here at the store when it happened?"

Nate looked at Addie, then back at Isaac. "No."

Isaac looked over Nate's shoulder at Addie.

"I wonder if whoever was there might speak on what they saw," Isaac said. He looked at Nate as he spoke, though they both knew it was Addie he was addressing.

"There's trouble in that," Nate said.

"I'll look out for whoever might speak on it," Isaac said.

"If it's all the same to you, we'll stay outta that territory. We doin' fine on our own."

Isaac reached in his pocket, withdrew a thick roll of money, and held it out. He realized his mistake instantly, for Nate smiled bitterly.

"I reckon it's hard to live in a world where a man's word ain't worth a pinch of snuff when there's money about," Nate said. "You can keep your chips, mister. We ain't telling what we seen. You got my word."

"This is to thank you," Isaac said. "For looking out for my family."

"We been thanked."

"Everybody needs money."

"The last time I took money from a stranger it cost me eleven years. So if it's all the same to you, you can keep that."

"But I am not a stranger."

"I didn't say you was. You're a boss man."

"No bossier than you."

Nate smiled grimly. "You and I are strangers in this land, mister. Mr. Moshe told me a little about your raising, the two of y'all coming up as you did, all the troubles you had getting to this country. I reckon that struggle's made you strong in some ways and weak in others. And I figure it's made Mr. Moshe strong in ways that you ain't, and weak in ways that you is not. It all evens out. Me, I'm just a poor colored man who knows the ways of his own self. But if I could choose it, if God allowed it, I'd choose Mr. Moshe's ways over yours and mine, for his ways is the right ways. There ain't many people about these parts like him, or his wife, God bless her soul. They been good to our Dodo. So you can put your money up."

"Not *all of* it," Addie said, staring at the money from across the room.

Nate turned to her and wagged his first finger slowly back and forth at her, then turned again to Isaac. "Like I said, we're all right."

"I'll leave it here on the banister."

"That's where you'll find it in the morning. And the morning after. Till you come fetch it," Nate said.

Isaac bristled. "Don't be a fool."

"Whatever names you call me can't hurt me. And all your money can't get our boy out from where he is now."

"It could. Over time. I can make a few calls. I know some people. I can get you a lawyer."

"If it's all the same to you, we got one or two ideas 'bout how to fetch him out."

"Don't be ridiculous. A lawyer will get it done. This is a land of laws."

"White folks' laws," Nate said softly. "The minute you leave the room, the next white fella comes along and the law is how *he* says it is. And the next one comes along and the law is how *he* says it is. So whatever money you burns up to get Dodo, come time Doc Roberts and his kind gets ahold of whatever rulin's your man fixed up, they'll put other rulin's together and make sure Dodo goes back in that place again and never gets out. Or worse, send him to the penitentiary. Then we got to come to you again with our hand out, and round and round we go. The law in this land is what the white man says it is, mister. Plain and simple. So you'd be wasting your dollars on us. We already in debt to Mr. Moshe. We got to pay him back for what he and his missus already gived us."

"And what is that?"

"If you can name another man in this town who would do what him and his missus done for us, I'll find a roll big as the one you holding and give it to you outright. You know somebody?"

Isaac frowned. He was unaccustomed to talking to anyone so arrogant, especially a Negro. On the other hand, Moshe trusted this man more than any other. He had seen with his own eyes the tall, lanky Negro standing at the hospital window as Moshe and the others gathered, sobbing around Chona's hospital bed. He'd watched Nate as he stood with his back to them, wiping the tears from his face. *He's like me*, Isaac thought bitterly. *He suffers his sorrows in private.*

He glanced upstairs, where Moshe and Malachi could be heard chatting, and spoke softly so that his words wouldn't carry up through the wood-paneled floor, for if he could hear their words, they could hear his.

"I'm a patriot," he said. "I love this country. It's been good to me."

"Good for you then."

"Moshe's an honest man. Chona, she was a . . . she had opinions. Writing letters to the papers about things she had no business talking about. She was a good person. A kind woman. She shouldn't be dead."

"We agrees there, too," Nate said.

"I wonder, then, about Doc Roberts."

Nate glanced at Addie, who turned away and began sweeping.

"What about him?"

"What he might do now."

"Better part of nothing is my guess. So long as he don't come round here, he ain't a bother to us. Ain't but one person other than Dodo seen what he done. And that person ain't told a soul other than Mr. Moshe what they saw. I don't know that Doc even knowed he was being seen. There was others round who come to the store quick right after the mess was over. I got there pretty quick myself—someone come and fetched me. The cops was chasing Dodo off the roof when I come. Everybody cleared out pretty fast then. Folks pawned it off as the usual trouble and forgot about it already. They ain't got no more Heaven and Earth Grocery Store to shop in is all. And they lost a friend. But they'll pray for Miss Chona as they should. And that's it."

"Was she alive when you got there?"

"Yes, she was. She had passed out but was yet living. She smiled a little bit before they took her off. She asked after her husband. And Dodo." Nate stared at the floor. And though he was several feet off, Isaac sensed something he hadn't sensed before from the tall, rangy man. Something he had felt in his own heart. Silent, burning, utter rage.

"Can I ask you, then, about Bernice?"

Nate was silent a moment. "What about her?"

"Is she still next door?"

"She been there all her life. Her and them children."

"She and Chona were close?"

"Very close. Went to school together as children."

"Will she talk to me?"

Nate shrugged. "She don't talk to nobody. But she did help Miss Chona out by keeping Dodo over there when the man from the state came to try to collect him."

"That means you owe her, too, then. Because by helping Chona, she helped you."

Nate nodded. "I don't need you to figure out my debts for me. That's why I'm sending you over to her, since you standing there waving them chips around. She got a whole heap of children. More'n likely she could use a little help. Tell her Nate sent you. That might go a little distance. I done a few favors for her from time to time, fixing things and so forth. Her father was a builder. He built that temple up the hill yonder."

"I'll call on her now."

"Just so you know, Bernice don't like a whole lotta talk."

"I'm not going to talk," Isaac said. "I'm going to listen."

23

Bernice's Bible

Fatty and Big Soap were in the thick woods behind the jook joint. Fatty's head was stuck inside the hood of an ancient-looking convertible when Rusty emerged from the back door of the jook and yelled out, "Fatty, your sister's here to see you."

"What's she doing here?"

"Don't ask me," Rusty said, strolling up to take a closer look.

"Tell her I'm busy. I got to see if this thing runs. I think it's a Great Chadwick Six."

"Any relation to a Great Big Dimwit?" Rusty said, nodding at Big Soap, who was underneath the car scrubbing the frame with a wire brush. Only Big Soap's feet could be seen.

"If it's a Chadwick Six, it's worth some big chips. Those cars were made right here in Pottstown," Fatty said.

"This piece of junk?" Rusty said, stepping back to look at the torn seat, dead tires, and an old gas lamp where the horn should be. "Where'd you get it?"

"They tore down an old house over on Bartelow Street where one of the big shots who ran the Neapco company lived. I found this behind it."

"You *found* it? Don't it belong to the house?"

"I *freed* it, Rusty. From the woods. Me and Soap here. I plan to sell it. Who knows what something like this can bring? What's Bernice want?"

"She's your sister, Fatty," Rusty said. He headed back inside to the bar.

Fatty unfurled himself from the chassis and left the tools where they were in the dirt. He wasn't exactly sure the car was a Great Chadwick Six. He'd never seen one, nor a photo of one. But he'd read someplace that there were only a few thousand made, back in the early 1900s. The company had gone belly-up two decades before, and while the car had no insignia that he could make out, if by chance the car *was* a Great Chadwick, well . . . what luck! That would be fly-the-coop money. Get-out-of-town money.

He found Bernice sitting on the porch bench, her hands folded neatly in her lap, wearing one of her church hats. She was, to his surprise, alone, for she was usually trailed by one or two of her brood of kids when she made her occasional outdoor forays, which were mostly to church.

"You going to a fish fry?" he asked, stepping onto the porch and seating himself on a crate.

Bernice frowned. The two were not close. They had not had a conversation that lasted more than five minutes in years. Their dispute over ownership of their father's house had morphed into a general dissatisfaction that had lasted for years. It bothered him that his once beautiful sister had let her life fall to pieces and had kids with every Tom, Dick, and Harry who came along. Three fathers. Eight children at last count, or so he'd heard. They lived blocks apart. It might as well have been miles.

"I didn't see you at Chona's funeral," she said.

"She was Miss Chona to me."

"Stop talking foolish," Bernice said. She glanced about at the jook joint's yard, the junk, the high weeds, the piled wood, the car carcasses, the tattered stand where he made hamburgers and sold them every afternoon, the sign on the battered front door that read "Fatty's Jook. Caution. Fun Inside."

She pointed at the sign. "You having fun?"

"Bernice, get the show on the road."

"What?"

"Get to your point."

"You need to get saved."

"I'll see you later," Fatty said, disgusted. He rose off the crate and moved toward the porch steps.

"I got something for you," she said. "You'll like it."

That stopped him. He paused at the top of the stairs, his hand on the banister. "You making your own money without a printing press now?"

"That's all you think about."

"Did Daddy leave me some money?" he asked.

She frowned. That was a sore point. Their father, Shad Davis, had been saving for them to go to college, but had died early, leaving only the house they lived in. "You need to let go of that one," she said.

"I ain't hanging on to it," Fatty said. "That was fifteen years ago."

"It would'a worked out, you going to college. There was a little money in there, to start."

"Well now, I got a better plan. I'm moving to Hollywood to make movies."

"Better than working your way down past the label on every bottle of booze you come across?"

"I don't drink booze. I sell it."

"That's worse."

"When you open a riding academy for Bible thumpers, call me, okay?"

"You can't judge me for walking God's road."

"Glad you walking some kind'a road. 'Cause you and Jesus wasn't wearing out the road between here and Graterford when I was in there picking my teeth off the floor."

"Momma was dying."

"Did they stop making pen and paper in those years, too?"

"You put yourself in there. And I sent you a Bible."

"Whyn't you make something of yourself, Bernice? What you come here bothering me with all this nonsense for? All that stuff is past. It's gone now. What you want?"

"I said I got something for you," she said.

"If it ain't money, I ain't interested."

"It's valuable," she said.

"Where'd you get it, finishing school?"

Bernice, her calm nearing its edges, pursed her lips. "You just like the white man," she said. "It must be a terrible burden to pretend you know everything."

"Hurry on home, Bernice. And don't stop for bread."

He stepped down off the porch and walked a few steps, and as he did, he heard—or thought he heard—her mumble a number. That stopped him. He turned back and put his foot on the bottom step.

"Did I hear right?" he said.

"You heard right."

"If you said four hundred dollars, it's a parlor trick."

"I ain't here to show no tricks. Jesus is my salvation."

"If you wasn't my sister, I'd throw you off the porch right now."

"I ain't here for myself. Just so you know. I'm doing missionary work."

"Do it somewhere else then. You ain't got four hundred dollars anyway. If you had that kind of money, you'd be packing the kids up and catching the first thing smoking outta here."

"I ain't got to go no place to know my Savior."

"Listen to yourself, Bernice!"

Bernice sighed. "I got one question. And after you answer it, I'll leave what I brung you and go on about my business. And I don't want to see you no more and have nothing to do with you because I have lived too long and you are too nasty. I know I'm a hard woman. I've made a few mistakes in life. But I'm no worse than these other mothers out here who pray 'Lord, let my child be wise and good' when they really mean 'Let this child have more power and money than I have.' I don't do that with my children. That's what our father did to us. He built things. The Jewish church, a lot of houses and buildings and things. He tried to build us, too. But he never finished. Maybe he wasn't building us the right way before he left this life. Maybe that's why we're like we are now."

"What's that got to do with the price of tea in China?"

"Who helped us through when Daddy passed?"

"Just 'cause somebody brings around groceries and helps you cart water and walks you to school from time to time don't make 'em a friend."

"Where'd you get such an evil heart?"

"Look who's talking. You ain't said two words to nobody out here in years. I ain't against Chona's people, Bernice. They was good people."

"But you ain't had the decency to show your face at her service."

Fatty rolled his eyes. "If you want a wailing wall, use the woodpile over there. I don't know nothing about Jews servicing their dead."

"Neither do I. But I went."

"If you want to knucker yourself to the Jews around here for tossing us a few nickels in the old days, go ahead. You paid 'em back by hiding Dodo from the state. That's aiding and abetting, by the way. Somebody was telling the man from the state everything. You could'a got caught 'cause of that blabbermouth, whoever it is."

"My own preacher!"

"Snooks? You lyin'!"

"I'm telling you what God's pleased with."

"Snooks ain't that stupid."

"Reverend Spriggs. Stop calling him Snooks," Bernice said.

"I'll call that peanut head whatever name I want. I don't believe it."

"He told me hisself. He confessed to me last Sunday after church. Said he told the colored man from the state about Dodo. He didn't mean to, but turns out the colored man didn't want no part of catching up to Dodo anyway. His job was to drive around the big bosses from the state. So when they sent him to fetch Dodo, it was just extra butter beans and soup for him. He ain't had no intentions of catching nobody. He got to drive the big state car by hisself and burn up a whole day and get paid. He didn't no more care for catching Dodo than you and I would care to snatch a flea out the air and swallow it. Every time they sent him to fetch Dodo, he'd call on Reverend Spriggs first. Then Reverend Spriggs would call on me. And I'd step over to Chona's and hide Dodo where they couldn't find him. He stayed free playing in my yard for a long time, and the state never did pick him up. Doc found him by accident. He didn't bring nobody from the state with him when he came by the store. Doc coming that day by hisself, that was a surprise."

Fatty felt his face growing hot. The mention of Doc Roberts made him furious. He sucked his teeth. "You come all the way up here to tell me about them rascals? I couldn't give a sh—" And here he shifted, because Bernice was sanctified and still his sister, so he deferred. "I'm glad the colored man from the state tipped his mitt to Reverend Spriggs. But we don't owe him or Reverend Spriggs nothing. What do we owe each other on this Hill, Bernice? We got nothing. Ain't never gonna have nothing. Everything good in this town is *off* this Hill. Miss Cho—Chona, I looked in on her from time to time. But she had her own people to look after her. We don't owe them. They don't owe us."

"It wasn't no them and us. It was we. We was *together* on this Hill," Bernice said.

"Stop tricking yourself, sis. Them days is gone. The Jews round here now, they wanna be in the big room with the white folks. All they gotta do is walk in the room and hang their hat on the rack. Let me and you try that. See what happens."

"Chona wasn't like them."

"If she wasn't a cripple, she'd a been just like them."

"Something's wrong with you, Fatty, to let that kind'a evil thinking in your heart."

Fatty frowned. He hated these kinds of talks. "I said Miss Chona was . . . she was all right. We ain't never gonna meet nobody like her again, that's for sure."

Bernice was silent a long moment. She seemed to be trying to make a decision. Then she nodded.

"You ain't really got nothing to give me, do you?" Fatty said.

Bernice, for the first time, smiled. And for a moment, the years dropped away, and beneath the church hat, the prissy posture, and the fortress of silence that she barricaded herself behind, she was the Bernice of old, the tall, gorgeous girl who sang like a bird.

"I do got something to give you. But I got a question to ask you first. You worked a lot with Daddy back when we was little. When you worked with him, did y'all lay any water pipes?"

"Dug a bunch of everything. Wells. Graves. Laid pipes. Daddy did everything."

"A water pipe?"

"We worked on two or three at least."

"On the Hill?"

"Yeah, I reckon."

"Any around Hayes and Franklin?"

"Don't remind me. There's a well there 'bout fifteen feet deep."

"Is it near the public fountain in the lot where everybody gets water?"

"Yep. Daddy did that for the Jewish church, I believe. I don't know why that well is so deep. I think the water table runs under the bottom of that well. There's a well pump at the bottom there. It was a nasty job, setting that up. That was a long time ago. I was young."

"Can you find it?"

"Course I can. It's in the lot near the Clover Dairy, not far from the public faucet. The well's capped. The city put a concrete manhole cover on top of it and it might be covered by grass and junk. But it's there. The pipes are down under that cap, maybe eight or nine feet, or maybe even fifteen feet. I believe it's fifteen, though I can't remember exactly."

She stood. "All right then."

She opened her purse, withdrew a large brown envelope that appeared to contain a book, and gently placed it on the bench where she had been sitting. "This is for you."

"What is it?"

"It's a gift."

"If it's a Bible, take it to the store and get your money back. I still got the last one you gave me."

"Nothing wrong with a Bible," she said. "Bible's got a good message."

"Does that package got four hundred dollars in it?"

"Look at what you've become, you cheatin' low-life swine. No. It does *not* have four hundred dollars in it."

"So it is a Bible!"

But she was gone, off the porch and down the muddy road, moving in a hurry.

Watching her leave, Fatty was so mad that he had to stifle the urge to toss the package at her head as she took the shortcut that sloped down onto the Hill, her hat bobbing up and down in the weeds and going out of sight.

The brown envelope sat unopened on the porch all afternoon and was still there when he opened the jook joint that night. Only because customers began rolling in with the usual cursing and shouting and staggering around the porch as the jukebox blasted Erskine Hawkins records did he take it behind the building to the back staircase where, in the low light of the bare light bulb and out of sight of customers, he ripped open the brown paper packaging.

He was right. It was a Bible. And there was not four hundred dollars in it. There was five hundred. And an envelope bearing a two-page note.

He read the first page quickly, glanced at the second page, and found an extra four hundred dollars taped to it. He ripped the four hundred dollars off the second page so fast that he didn't realize he'd torn off part of the page.

"Praise God," he said.

He ran off to the front of the jook joint, laughing as the rest of the second page, bearing the rest of the note, fluttered to the ground. Later on, he was sorry he had been in such a hurry.

24

Duck Boy

Sweet potato pie was the bait. Everybody on the Hill knew Paper cooked it like no tomorrow. So assembling Nate, Addie, Rusty, and Fatty at the table in her kitchen two days after visiting Miggy on Hemlock Row was easy. But getting Miggy, who worked at Pennhurst seven miles away, was more difficult.

She was the last to arrive. She came by bus, and when she walked in, the oracle of Hemlock Row that Paper had seen dressed to the nines the previous week was gone. In her place was a neatly clad health care attendant dressed all in white—white dress, shoes, and stockings. She moved with the air of a professional, with quiet confidence, until her gaze hit Nate seated at the table sipping coffee.

She froze in the doorway.

"You didn't tell me who was coming, Paper," she said.

"Miggy, we're family here."

Miggy hesitated a moment longer, then took a seat next to Fatty at the far end of the table. "This pie better be worth it," she said.

"It is," Paper said, quickly pulling the warming pie out of the stove and chatting to smooth matters out. "Miggy here works at Pennhurst," she told the others. "She tells futures, too."

"Can you tell mine?" Fatty piped up.

"No, but I could blind you," Miggy said.

It was as if a barrel of sardines had suddenly fallen from the ceiling, for Fatty's smile vanished. Paper thought she saw a faint, thin smile work its way across Nate's lips as Fatty sat back, cowed. "I'd rather you didn't do that, miss," he said.

Miggy chuckled. "Not with a spell, honey. I drink with my pinkie out. Every time I sip, I blind the person setting to my right. You serving coffee with that pie, Paper?"

Paper chuckled as she turned to grab cups from the cupboard while Miggy took a deep breath, held her hands out to admire her nails, cleared her throat, and finally said coolly, "I'll try not to be so big a fool as to imagine that you remembers me, Mr. Nate."

"You was but a knee-high child back in them years, but yes, I remembers you. And your daddy, too. I heard he passed," Nate said.

"He always liked you. You done us a service over at the Row is how he felt about matters," Miggy said.

"Ain't no profit in going into that now," Nate said. "That's all done and over with. Paid in full."

Fatty felt a slight icicle slice through his gut and found himself spinning back to Graterford, remembering Dirt, his old cellmate, telling him, "I wouldn't cross old Nate for all the money in the world." What had Nate done over in Hemlock Row? What was all paid for?

He would've drifted further in that thought had not Paper laid slices of pie in front of everyone and said, "Miggy, we ask you to come on account of—"

Miggy cut her off. "The who-shot-John part of your mess ain't my business," she said. "I don't want to know. 'Cause when the white man lays down his lying laws, he dines on the lie part of that fat meat while you and I get turned this way and that munching on the truth part. Howsoever that meal ends, when the table is cleared, one or more of us will likely leave hungry. I just come to talk about my life.

"I'm speaking about what happens to me from the time the sun goes up to when it goes back to rest. It all goes together, my life. And if there's anything you can learn from my life that might help you in whatever that cause may be, well, that's all the better, for I live in a land that don't want me. My job is to try to live right, which to me means coming over here after work to get a piece of sweet potato pie, which I favors, with an old friend and some of her people."

She dug into her pie, cutting a bite. "Now, while I'm eating this pie, should I happen to talk about my job can't nobody tell me later that I planned up some backdoor, unjust nonsense to hurt this or that part of the good state of Pennsylvania. And if I was to tell someone what they might do or do not do in a place that happens to toss me a few coins every week for my services, there ain't no law against that to my knowing. That's the truth, which is how I try to live. It's how all God-fearing people should try to live."

"All right then," Paper said. "What's your job?"

"I'm a cleaner," Miggy said. "I cleans things. I cleans my house. I cleans outside my house and inside. I cleans the yard and the kitchen and all manner of things. On the job, I cleans beds, and bed pans, and people. Mostly people. Mostly men. I don't like working with the women on my job. Some of 'em are nastier than the men. They throw things at you—their waste and all. The men ain't no bother, really."

She carefully lifted the bite of her pie, raised it to her face, and peered at it.

Fatty couldn't stand it. "Are you gonna write a sermon on that thing 'fore you eat it?" he asked.

Paper shot Fatty an icy look. "Don't mind him, Miggy. Sometimes real thoughts work their way up to his mouth."

"It's all right." She turned to Fatty. "It's my pie, honey. You against me eating it like I want?"

"Not at all. But I'll be in the cacklehouse if I have to set here waiting for you to tell us a way to do uh . . . what Paper wants done."

"Is it just Paper that wants it to be done?"

Fatty fell silent. He felt Nate's eyes boring into him. He cleared his throat. "I'm here 'cause Paper asked me to come," he said.

"And I'm here to eat pie," Miggy said. "And I will do it in the manner I please." She placed the forkful of sweet potato pie in her mouth, chewed slowly, swallowed, then continued.

"Now there's man's understanding and there's women's understanding. There is white folks' understanding and Negroes' understanding. And then there is just plain wisdom. Every child that breathes their first on this earth will drive their fist through the air and strike nothing. But all children are born with will. I was not a particularly willful child nor a particularly smart one. I was raised on the Row. I'm a Lowgod. We is raised to believe that for any child to be righteous, it must have a love for those things which brings knowledge. Before I come to Pennhurst, I laundered, which is how I come to know Paper here. After I got tired of laundering, I did days work for a white family over in Pennsbury. The father was a judge. His wife was lazy and weak-willed. They were both trained to ease and unjust. An unjust parent will raise an unjust child who is a snare to righteousness. The truth is, I raised their child more than they did, but I did not raise him long. For if I was to raise a child, I would teach that child to love what

I love and hate what I hate. That is why your colored from Hemlock Row are not good day workers. We are too close to the earth. We bang the drum of the old country too much. Even our church is different. We don't sing with a piano. We chant the old songs and dance in circles, and we don't cross our feet when we dance, for that is worldly dancing. Why we do these things, I do not know. It's one of the many things passed down to us from the old people. But it makes us odd and strange, even to some of our own people, like y'all on this Hill.

"Your basic Lowgod from the Row is all from the same bloodline. Same father and mother from many years past when we was first brung to this land. How that worked out, why the Lowgods come to the Row from the Low Country, and who married one another and so forth, I do not know, for the old people don't favor talking about yesterday. But there ain't but two families on the Row. The Lowgods and the Loves. Mostly Lowgods. The Loves"—and here she cast a quick glance at Nate—"there ain't many Loves left."

And once again Fatty felt his memory spinning back to Graterford. "Nate *Love*," Dirt had said. Nate was a *Love*, from the Love family. He couldn't resist. "What happened to the Loves?" he asked. He was afraid to even look at Nate.

Miggy shook her head. "That's a story that I do not know the whole of. The Lowgods and Loves are not that different. They are close in nature. They travel straight on. They cannot drive a side road or a curve. If a Lowgod is with you, they with you. If they not, they not. They can't do otherwise. They move to truth, for they fear God more than you then. It's been banged into 'em. So if you on the other side of that, shame on you then. It won't be good then, in your dealings with 'em."

Here she cut off another bite of pie, raised it, eyed it, cut a slow glance at Fatty to see if he had any further questions, and once she was satisfied he had none, she continued.

"I come to Pennhurst like this: A lady on the Row named Laverne got hired to sweep out the baggage and cheer up the tide out there. She gived word on the Row they was looking for people to do what she did, so I went over and got hired. There was already a bunch of Lowgods working there. The white folks out there ain't allergic to colored, not for what they want us to do. Did I say I cleaned? I cleaned from that day to this. But *what* I clean. That is the question."

She glanced around the room and continued.

"Pennhurst is a city. Thirty-four buildings spread over two hundred acres. It's got its own power plant. Its own farm. Its own police. Got its own railroad, houses, stockyards, clothing factory, farm animals, tractors, trucks, wagons, wards, everything. It's bigger than all of Hemlock Row and Chicken Hill together. It looks right clean and pretty on the outside. But on the inside, well . . . that's where the devil does his work."

She put down her fork and took a sip of coffee.

"I can't say that in these past years I've walked out of Pennhurst on any given day not wishing that the Good Lord would press His finger upon the place and crumble it to dust and take the poor souls in there home to His heart, for many of 'em's the finest people you'd ever want to meet. Their illness is not in their minds, or in the color of their skin, or in the despair in their heart, or even in the money that they may or may not have. Their illness is honesty, for they live in a world of lies, ruled by those who surrendered all the good things that God gived them for money, living on stolen land, taken from people whose spirits dance all around us like ghosts. I hear the red man hollering and chanting in my dreams sometimes. This is my punishment for being an oracle. For those locked up at Pennhurst, it's too much. The truth has driven them mad. And for that, they are punished.

"What I seen is not fit for any person to see. It's not the filth, or the buck-naked folks running about banging their heads on the wall, or even the smell, which stays in your nose for the rest of your life. A yard dog living on a chain is better off than any poor soul living in Pennhurst. You ain't seen suffering till you seen forty grown people setting around a day room all day long for years, clawing to get a glimpse out the window. Or seen a full-grown educated man peeing on a radiator while pretending to be a radio announcer because he's afraid to ask an attendant to go to the bathroom, or a teenager girl wheedling a grown man attendant for a cigarette by showing him her private parts. I seen women locked in solitary in straitjackets for days at a time out there, locked in so tight that when you pulls the jacket off, the marks left behind last the rest of their lives, which sometimes ain't that long.

"On the wards, the attendants run everything. They can restrain a patient long as they want, for hours or days or even weeks, so long as they write in the logbook exactly how long they done it. They restrained this poor woman for six hundred fifty-one hours and twenty minutes. I happens to know the woman, and if I was in charge, I would put those that done that to her in the straitjacket and give *her* the key. And were I not a God-fearing woman, I'd give that woman a little bit of my own body dirt to toss at them that done that to her, along with whatever she could come up with, for some of them attendants are evil somethings. They got to watch their points, some of them. Because a lot of them patients, they do not forget."

With that, Miggy paused and looked about the room. "Have I given you something to chew on?"

Paper nodded. "You have. But . . . we . . ."

"You need to hear more about my life?"

"Yes. Tell us more about your . . . can you tell us about the *children* in your life?"

"I got none."

"Other children you might have seen? Or know."

"It ain't the children, honey. It's the doctors. They're mostly foreigners. You can't make heads or tails of what they say. They come round the wards from time to time, recommend this or that medicine, scratch a few things down on a pad, and go away. A month later they're gone and a different doctor comes back and he don't know what the first has done. Nobody gets punished for nothing. There's mules on Hemlock Row that live better than folks out there at Pennhurst."

And here she sighed, then said, "But you wanna know about the children."

"Yes," Paper said.

Miggy nodded. "All right then. I'll tell you about a child I knowed. But first, gimme another slice of that pie."

AFTER RECEIVING HER second slice of pie, Miggy slid it toward herself, but instead of eating it, she sat back, folded her fingers together, and continued. "There was a little boy once, nice little fella, a white boy, 'bout eleven or twelve. He quacked like a duck. Couldn't speak a lick. I don't know what his problem was on the inside, but he was a smart child other than he quacked like a duck. He didn't do nothing wrong on God's green earth that I could see other than he quivered and shook a lot when he walked and didn't know how to speak proper. His parents seed there wasn't nothing they could do for him, I reckon, and dropped him off there and didn't come back. Never came to visit him once in all the time he was there.

"Well, he didn't like that, and after a while, he made a fuss about staying there, and before you know it, they dropped him down from the higher wards to what they call the low wards. V-1, 2, and 3. And finally C-1. Them V wards is bad. But C-1 is the worst. He went from bad to worse down there. Went from the worst to the very worst when he got to C-1.

"He was a smart little thing, quick—a funny child. Liked to smile. Well, I took to him and looked in on him when I was down there on C-1 working and cleaning. At first, he was all right. But after a few weeks, I seen something gone wrong with him. Somebody had been at him. I don't work the night shift, and they only sent me down to C-1 once a week in the mornings, but I'd always look in on him and I could see it when I come to him. This is in the morning now, for I don't work at night—but I seen he was afraid of this one attendant. Every time that man come close to him, he'd shrivel up. He took to running behind me.

"Now I knew this fella, this attendant. Knowed him well. And he's rough work. So I tried to stay clear of it. But the boy was doing so bad, I couldn't stand it no more after a while. So I told the feller, 'You watch yourself. I'm watching you. Remember, I tell futures. And your future ain't bright.'

"What I done that for? This feller made it hell for me down there. He was a Lowgod, see. One of us. I knowed him from the time he was a boy. He's a grown man now. A big, strong young fella. Calls hisself Son of Man. I won't bother to call out his real name, for it's a blight to his parents and a shame to them. He's a good-looking man, a pretty feller. He could have his way with all the girls he wanted. But his mind is twisted.

"He made it hell for me down there. He got the white folks drummed up against me, telling them lies this way and that, for he's a smooth talker. And one day when I got on him about going after that youngster, he buggied up to me, sneaked up on me one day when I was in a broom closet, pushed in close, got tight on me, saying, 'If you open your mouth wrong again, I'll jam a knife down your throat. I'll send the wind whistling through your neck.'

"Well, I let off him then. There was an evil to him when he touched me. It was strong in him, and it made me afraid. Weren't no use complaining or telling the white folks. He got the run of things down there. The white bosses love him on account of his size and his tongue, for he is a smooth-talking devil. But when they ain't looking, he runs them patients and the other attendants like a gang. He works the evening and overnight shifts, sometimes both, for he's a king down there. He got the run of that ward. Every patient there will do whatever he says, white and colored. They will turn on each other for him. They'll steal for him. They're terrified of him—and they oughta be, for he'll send his knife rambling or, even worse, turn 'em around so they hurt their own selves, hang themselves and so forth. He's a walking witch. Got nerve enough to call hisself Son of Man. Son of the devil is what he is."

At that point, she turned to Nate. "I'm wondering if it's God's purpose that you might be bothered with all this. Maybe that's the reason behind it, to make you come back. Is you coming home?"

Nate looked at Addie.

"I am home," he said.

AFTER SHE PAUSED and took a drink of water, Miggy's pie lay untouched, but she continued.

"The patients at Pennhurst love me when they see me, for I understands 'em. They're like everybody else. They want to live. They want to be happy. They want friends. And when it come to following nature's ways, loving and all, they're sick but they're not that sick. This evil, rotten man gived it to the duck boy in the worst way. They had to put that child in the hospital behind what that twisted rascal done. He ripped that boy up inside, and when the boy was done healing, he turned a few screws so them white folks got the excuse to send the child right back to the same ward, so he could tear up that little sprout some more.

"Well, I couldn't stand it. But me talking to doctors and nurses about things, I'd have better luck talking to that wall over there than to get them to listen to me. So I prayed on it, and don't you know, a few weeks later that little duck boy went missing."

And here she looked at Nate and began cutting into the second piece of pie. She cut it carefully into pieces, then said, "If you was a mouse and there was a cat about and you wanted to get out this way, would you take this route here?"

And she pointed to a tiny alley in one piece of pie she had cut.

"Or this route here?" And she pointed to an opening near a second piece on the other side of her plate.

"I think you'd *want* to go that way," she said carefully, pointing with her fork to her original piece. "But being that way is blocked, you might want to go here."

She hovered her fork over the pieces and shifted them around a bit, drawing a map. "Now, to get out this way," she said, pointing, "you'd have to pass this, this, and this. So that's no good. So where would the mouse go? Knowing that the cat is nearby and he ain't got but so much time 'fore that cat hunts him down, and knowing there ain't but one way out, which is here"—she pointed at the top of her plate—"that's the way out. What's he gonna do? He got to move."

She considered this. "Well, that mouse *could* . . . eat his way through this big piece of pie, and that piece, and that piece, but by the time he got here, here, and here, all the other mice, they'd be on him, following behind him, making noise and all, because it's crowded in pie country, with lots of other mice that wants out, plus there's cats and all. Your mouse can't fly. He can't go over the top . . . *but* . . ."

And here she laid her fork in a direct line from her large piece of pie to the crust's edge over several of the pie pieces cut to represent buildings, where she indicated an exit.

"If the mouse could tunnel from the large piece of pie here, he could make a straight line to the get-out door. Then he'd be home free in no time."

She placed the fork down, glanced at Nate, folded her hands, and rested her elbows on the table. With her hands folded before her face, she spoke slowly.

"There's tunnels all about Pennhurst. Miles of 'em. They used 'em in the old days to carry food and supplies and even coal from the old powerhouse during wintertime. Most of 'em ain't been used in years. Big empty tunnels. Lots of 'em. Going every whichaway."

She slid the plate with the pie pieces away from her and continued.

"They moved heaven and earth trying to find that little duck boy when he went missing. Looked all over. Couldn't find him. Somebody said they heard quacking from what might be a tunnel beneath Ward C-1 where the boy had maybe escaped from. But nobody knows for sure if there really *is* a tunnel below C-1, for it's one of the older buildings, far from the main buildings. They say the boy *mighta* got out that way, for the rumor is that *if* there's a tunnel below C-1, it leads out to the railroad yard that was used in the old days to bring coal to the old furnace house. The old furnace house is right next to C-1. They don't use it no more. They built a new furnace building on the west side of the campus. So he might'a gone that way, if there was a tunnel there. But who knows? Nobody at that hospital knows.

Whoever built them tunnels is long gone. You'd have to be a brave soul, you'd need God on your shoulder, to even *think* of walking through one of them old tunnels anyway."

She sighed and sipped her coffee.

"They never did find that boy. They looked for him awhile, then said, 'Well, he's probably dead, wandered off, or murdered maybe, who knows.' Or . . ."

She paused and a sly smile crossed her face.

"I gived this a lot of thought," she said. "I got to thinking. I said, 'Now how could a little ol' boy who don't even know how to speak for hisself, who quacks like a duck, how could he figure out how to get out them tunnels?' Somebody said, 'He probably got a map.' But nobody's ever mapped them tunnels. They made them tunnels a hundred years ago when Pennhurst was new. Then they added new buildings piecemeal, one at a time, one tunnel here, another there, closing 'em off, opening 'em up here and there, the tunnels going every whichaway. Most of 'em are closed off, I'm told, except the ones near the administration building. So how could a lil ol' boy know them tunnels? Impossible.

"But if he *did* know them tunnels"—she pointed at the pie plate—"he'd know that the tunnel under *this* building here"—she pointed to the biggest piece of the pie—"was the north section of Pennhurst where the administration building and hospital are. And the tunnel under *this* one"—she pointed again—"would let you out to a manhole on the west where there's nothing but woods and nobody can escape there because it's been tried many times. And *this*"—she pointed to the far corner where her fork was—"is Ward C-1, where he was, which if there *was* a tunnel, it would take him to *this*"—she pointed to the edge of her plate, connoting an exit—"the railroad yard.

"He *could* have made it out that way. To the railroad track. And then walked two miles on the track to the road and got picked up by a buggy, or a car, or a horse and cart. Or maybe even hopped on one of the train cars that hauls goods in and outta the hospital once a week."

She shrugged. "But how could he? He was but a child. And you'd have to really know those tunnels."

"Who would know those tunnels?" Fatty asked.

Miggy shrugged.

"Then why you wasting air talking on 'em?" Fatty said.

"Because of eggs."

"What?"

"Eggs."

"What's eggs got to do with the tunnels?"

She looked at Fatty for a long moment and smiled serenely. "That's the difference between the coloreds on the Hill and us on the Row. We believe in God like ya'll do. We pins our hope on Jesus just like you. But on the Row, we is connected by a past that we has been trained to believe in whether we likes it or not. When we go to church, we prays not just to God, but to the ones who come before us, from a land far distant, who speak to us in ways that we don't understand but still believe in. For us, everything in life—all God's creatures and things—is connected. Here on the Hill, y'all just scream and shout."

She turned to Fatty. "Eggs got everything to do with tunnels. Everything got everything to do with everything."

It was several more minutes before Miggy continued, for she had decided that some more warm coffee was needed, which Paper quickly provided. After a few sips in silence, with her head thrown back and her eyes closed, she took a deep breath and continued.

"Pennhurst makes its own food," Miggy said. "They got a farm.

The patients work it. They grow vegetables of every type out there. Corn, okra, potatoes. But the one thing they can't grow is eggs. Eggs means chickens. For three thousand people, that's too many chickens to look after for a state hospital. You can't have people that's looking after the chickens when you got to watch the people, too. For eggs they got to have them brung in from outside.

"There's an egg farm about two miles north of Pennhurst. Every day that farm sends a wagon full of eggs to the hospital. Four thousand eggs. That's a lot of eggs. The man who moves 'em uses a mule and cart. He drop off eggs and hot coffee to every ward in the hospital. It's a great distance between the wards," she said, pointing at the pieces of pie on her plate with her fork. "The main buildings here"—she pointed—"where security and all is, that's a good two miles of trailing roads from where the lower wards are. The newer buildings, the administration and the hospital, they got full kitchens and cold iceboxes and all the things they need to warm food and cook big. But them lower wards ain't got hot kitchens in the morning. Only lunch and dinner. Well, in the morning, the staff there want the same thing the folks in bigger new buildings get: hot eggs *and* hot coffee. They don't want cold eggs and cold coffee or the cold porridge they serve the patients. They want to have their own good, hot eggs *and* coffee for breakfast."

She raised her fork, then stabbed it down into the crusted piece of pie at the far edge of her plate. "Ward C-1," she said. "That's Son of Man's little kingdom." Then she continued.

"The feller who runs them eggs from the farm to Pennhurst is a Negro. A Lowgod. He gets hot eggs and coffee to every building on the lower ward side of Pennhurst by 6 a.m. every morning. That's fourteen buildings. Imagine that. Must be four miles of running up and down hills, taking stairs, upstairs to this kitchen, down to that one. How does he get them hot scrambled eggs and hot coffee to fourteen buildings when they're so far apart, him having all them eggs and coffee in place by 6 a.m.? A car couldn't move that fast up and down them roads, going around corners, taking stairs to the second floor in this ward and out the next. Not even on the sunniest day with the clearest road could a car do it. And in winter when there's snow? All them buildings? All that distance? Been doing it for thirty-six years, too. How's he do it so fast? You'd need God to move that fast. Or tunnels. That's my thinking."

Nate spoke. "Do you know him?"

Miggy shrugged and said coolly, "I told you I'd talk about my life, not go to the penitentiary for you. But I reckon someone here might have met him a day or two past."

And here she glanced at Paper and let that sink in, then continued.

"Now I heard—it's been *said*—that my little quacking friend got abused by Son of Man so bad that somebody felt sorry for him and put him onto the man who runs them eggs in his egg cart, who took him through one of them tunnels right under Ward C-1 where Son of Man lurks, and got him to that railroad yard. And from there, some of them railroad fellas, them union Jews who likes to raise hell, put him on one of them freight trains to New York with a paper sack full of food and twenty dollars, and they say that boy's been in New York City quacking like a duck ever since."

"What about that fella you spoke of?" Nate asked. "Is he still there?"

"Son of Man is yet there, I am sorry to say. And while I keeps off his ward these days, I heard a new boy has come to his ward three weeks ago. A Negro child. Deaf and maybe dumb. Don't know if he can talk or not. But I heard the boy was hurt some kind of way. They had him in traction. He's better now, I'm told. Healed up. His casts is off, from what I hear. Which cannot be good for him."

A cone of silence worked its way into the room. Finally, Nate spoke. "Is you done with that pie?" he asked Miggy.

"I am," she said.

Nate slid the plate over and stared at it. It was a diagram. Of buildings, roads, and walkways. He studied it closely, then closed his eyes, as if memorizing it.

"Eat that pie or give it to me," Paper said. "Don't waste it."

"It ain't wasting," Nate said, his eyes still shut. When he opened them, he spoke to Miggy. "You said the Egg Man brings eggs to every ward?"

"Every one."

"Does the Egg Man bring Son of Man his eggs?"

"He yet brings him his eggs."

"How does he like his eggs?"

"Who?"

"Son of Man. How do he like his eggs?"

"I don't know. You'd have to ask him."

"I don't know him," Nate said.

"It doesn't matter," Miggy said. "He knows you."

25

The Deal

The blonde secretary with the red-hot lipstick who sat at the front desk of Philadelphia's Blitz Theater on Broad Street thought he was a union man. Otherwise, she would have tossed the middle-aged Jew in the overalls out the moment he walked in. He sat erect in the plush lounge chair of the office waiting room, fingering his hat with thick, calloused fingers. He had to be a union organizer of some kind, she thought, for he was not pleasant. Nonunion workmen were usually smiling and obsequious, happy for the work, impressed by the handsome waiting room, the leather couch, the polished coffee tables. Union organizers, on the other hand, were arrogant men in workmen's clothing who sat on couch arms, smoking and chatting, rabble-rousers all, too smart for their britches. This man was more that type. He announced his name as Marvin Skrupskelis, then spelled it—as if she couldn't spell, which was actually true, since she wrote it down as Scoopskalek, until he glanced at her scribbling and corrected her. He said he had no appointment with Mr. Isaac Moskovitz but needed to see him. Only because she assumed he *might* be a union rep did she buzz Mr. Moskovitz at all. And even then, Isaac didn't respond but rather clicked off immediately, which meant he was irritated and that she should tell whoever it was to get lost. She took her hand off the buzzer and was about to do just that when Mr. Moskovitz opened the door of his office, walked up to the man, shook his hand, and said, "This way," motioning him toward the door leading to the elevator.

As he opened the door, he said to his secretary, "I'll be back in a while."

Five minutes into the car ride, cruising down Broad Street in Isaac's heavy black Packard, Marv cast a long glance at Moshe's cousin, the tall, strident fellow who occasionally showed up in Pottstown to steer his meek cousin through disaster or disorder. He watched Isaac steer his heavy black car through Broad Street with ease. He looked like an older, firmer version of Moshe, without the grin; but unlike Moshe, he was not hospitable, for he wasted no time. "How'd you find my office?" he asked.

"It's listed. You want I should come to your house?"

"That would have been better."

"I didn't know I was welcome there."

"I didn't say you were. I said you should have come to the house, not my business."

"Just to be difficult," Marv said, "are you one of those crazy Romanian theater owners who knows a lot of useless crap, like butterflies taste with their feet?"

"Just to be difficult, are you?"

"I'm Lithuanian." Marv snorted, then grew silent, peering out the window as Isaac drove slowly, carefully.

Isaac snatched a glance at Marv. He'd seen Marv at Chona's shiva. Or was it his twin? He couldn't tell them apart. Whoever it was, he stayed long and said little. Isaac got to the point. "What did Moshe do wrong this time?"

"He did nothing. He lives right. Which is more than I can say about some of us in this country."

"So you wanna go back to the old country?"

"I like it here. The politicians try to cut your throat with one hand while saluting the flag with the other. Then they tax you. Saves 'em the trouble of calling you a dirty Jew."

Isaac chuckled. "You hungry? You wanna eat? You need something? You've come a long way."

Marv looked out the window, his brown eyes peering at the row houses as the sedan spun past. "He's soft, your cousin."

"Tell me what I don't know."

"I make shoes," Marvin said.

"I'll remember that the next time my bunions rise up like yeast to shake my hand."

"I make 'em for all types," Marv said. "They come to me from far off. Reading. Baltimore. Even New York."

"You got a twin, don't you?"

"I do."

"Were you the one I saw at the shiva? Or was it the other?"

"Probably the other."

"Where were you?"

Marv bristled. "I don't remember seeing you the day I came. And I was there all day. Me or my brother. One of us was there every day. You check attendance at shivas, do you?" He rode in silence for a moment as Isaac took the reprimand, then continued.

"A fellow come to me last week. He had a problem with his toe. He needed a shoe made. Doc Roberts sent him over. You remember him?" Marv asked.

"Why should I care about that kucker (defecator)?"

"Because this guy could squeeze Doc."

"How do you know?"

"Just because a man doesn't wear shiny shoes and know how to tell fairy tales in pictures doesn't mean he lacks a ready wit. The guy's name is Plitzka. Gus Plitzka. He runs things in Pottstown."

"Like what?"

"Everything. City council, the waterworks, the cops. He's dealing cards from two decks. He tried to buy a dairy and fell short. He borrowed money from a guy named Nig Rosen. A businessman from here. Maybe you know Rosen?"

Isaac nodded, spinning the big sedan through traffic. "You could call him that, but who are you fooling? He lives on bail bonds and Benzedrine. No one to play with. How do you know about him?"

"Pinochle."

"What?"

"Not every Jew in Pottstown sits around sucking their thumb waiting for handouts from the German Jewish Society. Pinochle. I play every week in Reading. Heavy-money games. A couple of players from Reading, they work for Rosen."

"So?"

"They're in Pottstown every week squeezing Plitzka. He owes Rosen a pile. He borrowed from Rosen to close the deal on his dairy. The dairy gets its water from his old farm, but the farm has no water."

"So?"

"Our temple on the Hill tapped into a well that pumps water for a public faucet. That well is dry, and I know that for a fact Plitzka's water is coming from the new reservoir. So he's not paying for his water. If the state knew he was getting his water for free and was running the town's water department at the same time, they'd come in and take over. They need water in that town. The factories need it. So he's vulnerable. Since he runs the town, maybe somebody can put the squeeze on him, so he can put the squeeze on Doc Roberts."

"That goy won't ever confess to raping a Jew."

"He didn't rape her. He tried to."

"Doesn't matter. He ripped her clothes off. That's close enough. What's the end run here?"

Marv spoke in Yiddish. "Yoysher." (Justice.)

"Got any other jokes?"

"I liked Chona."

Isaac thought it through carefully, then took a deep breath. "Religion and politics. Not good for business."

"So you'll do nothing. What's the life of a Jew worth?"

"Save the lecture, friend."

"What are you gonna do?"

"If you need Irene Dunne to show up and sing songs for a week, cut-rate, I can do that. If you need Cab Calloway to sing hi de hi de ho at Moshe's theater, I can arrange that. But cutting deals with dummkopfs who pinch politicians for marshmallows and cigarettes in a town I don't know, that's out of my range."

"So you'll do nothing."

Isaac said carefully, "I didn't say that. Let Rosen have Plitzka. Maybe he'll be so busy bothering Plitzka he'll stop leaning on me about putting his ding-dong floozies in my shows. Nobody wants the cops involved. Nobody wants the state or the feds. Nobody wants taxes. Nobody wants problems. Nobody wants to pay. Forget the cowboy nonsense. To make things work in this country, you don't throw water on a man's face. You keep it quiet. You cut deals. Leave Rosen and Plitzka alone. Maybe they'll stumble over a manhole and fall in together. I need help with something else."

"What kind of help?"

Isaac sighed. He took one more long glance at Marv, spun the wheel, and guided the sedan off the crowded boulevard and pulled into a side street of row houses. He eased the sedan to the curb, pulled the emergency brake, then turned to Marv.

"What Chona wanted," he said, "was for the shul to survive. Pull back the covers on the water problem with Plitzka and you pull the covers off the shul. No sense squeezing Plitzka about that."

"So what do we do?"

"Let Plitzka fix his own water problem at the dairy. I'll get the water problem fixed for the shul. It's in the works, so the temple won't be responsible. I just need your help with one thing to make that fix happen. Nothing else."

"What?"

"I need two men, Jews, to run a train for me. Union men."

"A union man can't run a train. The Pennsylvania Railroad runs the trains."

"I'm not talking about *run* it. They just need to be on it. Two of them. Working on it."

"Which train?"

Isaac glanced in his rearview mirror, then out of his window at a car that swooped past, followed by a horse and cart. "The colored boy of Chona's, the one who saw it all, he's in Pennhurst. There's a freight train that delivers coal and flour to Pennhurst every week. I need two men on that train to snatch the kid when he comes out of the nuthouse. I'll handle the rest."

"Snatch him from where?"

"Wherever the train drops its load. He'll be there when it comes."

"Who's gonna put him in place?"

"Don't worry about it. He'll be there."

"And where will they take him?"

"Just get him on the train. Everything else I'll take care of. Can you find two Jews you can trust?"

"Course. There's probably forty Jews out there in the Reading area working for the railroad."

"How much you think it'll cost?"

"For you? Nothing."

"You kidding?"

Marv shook his head. "The railroad Jews are all union men. They read the papers, they sing the songs, they're nuts. They're all swelled up with the whole bit about American justice for one and all. They know about Chona, the letters she wrote, the crazy things she did. The coloreds weren't the only ones she fed for free. Half her store was railroad workers, especially on weekends. Chona's was the only store open in Pottstown on Sundays. I can get you ten union Jews from the railroad."

"Two is all I need. How much will it cost you to get them for me?"

"I said it's free."

"Nothing is free."

"I'll take care of it."

"How?"

"Everybody needs shoes."

"You're kidding, right?"

"Do I ask you how you run your business? You offer a union man a bribe and he'll spit in your face. They know I don't have money like you to throw around. But you offer your trade, your work, they'll honor that. They honor principle."

Isaac reddened as a flush of shame washed over him. Principle. In all the years of being a fusgeyer, when he and Moshe were children, running for their lives from the soldiers and starving, that was the one thing that Moshe never gave away. He never hated anyone. He was always kind. He'd give away his last crumb. And here in America, he'd married a woman who was the same way. Kindness. Love. Principle. It runs the world. "No is not a no. It's just the beginning of a negotiation," Moshe would say. What a wonderful negotiator Moshe was. He could've been rich here in America with all his talents. Instead, he was in a shitbox town with a dead wife care of a . . . Isaac swallowed and bit his lip.

He heard Marv asking something.

"What?"

"The water," Marv said. "What about the water? Who's gonna fix the water problem? Are you sure?"

"The water fix is already in the works," Isaac said. "Just have those men there when the kid comes out of the nuthouse. That's my end of the deal."

"What about Plitzka?"

"Maybe he and Nig Rosen will end up in an urn someplace. Who cares?"

"When do you want the men there? Which train?"

"There's only one Pennhurst train a day, I'm told," Isaac said. "I'll send word on the day. Just have your guys ready. And would you do me a favor?"

"Maybe."

"Next time, come to my house. My secretary's a goy with a large mouth."

Marv smirked. "Where you dip your wicker is your business."

Isaac frowned. "We can't all be like Moshe," he said.

26

The Job

The next afternoon Fatty was working on the engine of the Great Chadwick Six as Big Soap watched over his shoulder. Fatty tightened the last spark plug in place, then clipped the distributer cap on. "This ain't a Great Chadwick," he announced.

"How do you know?"

"These are Ford parts," he said. "A Ford distributor won't fit on a Chadwick Six. The Ford cap is smaller. Get in. I'll drive."

Big Soap leaped into the back seat while Fatty hopped into the driver's seat. He turned the key and the old engine fired, belching forth a cloud of black smoke.

"Put it in gear," Big Soap wailed. He clapped his hands twice, *clap clap*, and said gaily, "Home, Charles!"

"Very funny. It won't go in gear." Fatty cut the motor, then glanced in the mirror as Big Soap relaxed in the back, stretching a long muscled arm across the seat. "Soap, you wanna make some dough?"

"No, Fatty. I wanna wander the earth spreading joy and love. Of *course* I wanna make some dough."

"I got a job for us."

"Doing what?"

"Connecting a water pipe on the Hill."

"Is it illegal?"

"Not really. We're just pulling an old pipe off another and connecting it to city water. Everybody pays for city water. So it's not technically illegal. But we gotta do it at night."

"If it's just connecting to the city line, why not get the city to do it?"

"On the Hill? You kidding?"

"How deep do we gotta dig?" Big Soap asked.

"Not much. Just pull off a cover, go down, and disconnect one pipe and connect it to another. Then put the cover back."

"Connecting live water lines is wet work."

"You wanna make money or not?"

"Just so you know, Fatty, I'm making good dough at the Dohler plant."

"How much?"

"Three dollars and fifty cents a week."

"What you doing over there, stuffing ballot boxes?"

"Firing furnaces."

"They gonna bump up your dough soon?"

"When they're ready."

Fatty nodded, tapping the ancient dashboard of the old car. *There it is*, he thought bitterly. Big Soap gets fired from one job, gets hired elsewhere, his mother cusses him out in front of his friends, the Irish over at the Empire Fire Company make him yank one hundred feet of wet hose to the top of their tower while they sit around drinking beer, and he's still happy to work for nothing. The moron.

"You'll make ten times that in three hours. And I'll add Rusty to the job."

"If Rusty's coming, it must not be easy."

"You want the job or not?"

"You ain't said how much."

"Thirty-five dollars for you."

Big Soap whistled. "That sounds like robbery. Is it a bank?"

"What do I look like, a thief? It's a simple plumbing job, Soap. Pull off the manhole cover. Go down a well. Move a Y valve to the six-inch feed from the reservoir. Connect another line to it. Climb out. Close the manhole cover. That's it. I done it a hundred times."

"Whose house is it for?"

"It's not a house. It's on the lot over at Hayes and Franklin. Where the public faucet is."

Big Soap frowned. "Ain't that where the Clover Dairy is?"

"It's across the street from the Clover Dairy."

"It's for them?"

"No."

"Who's it for then?"

"I can't say. But they're paying long dollars. You want the job or not?"

Big Soap thought a moment. "Thirty fish is a lot of fish. How long will it take?"

"A couple hours."

"That doesn't sound too hard. What you need Rusty for?"

"Backup. The manhole cover on the well is old cement. If we break it, Rusty can fix it up, make it look like the original. He's good with mortar and cement stuff."

"You need water to mix cement, Fatty."

"We'll use water from the pipe we're working with."

"What we gonna mix the cement with?"

"I got that old gas-powered cement mixer behind the jook."

"That hunk of junk? You can't run that thing at night. It sounds like a bullhorn. It'll wake up the whole Hill."

"It's got a hand crank, too."

"Which works fine if you're Tarzan."

"Rusty will oil it up. He knows how to work that stuff. Or we'll use a wheelbarrow. Rusty can color the cement just right to make it look like the kind the city uses."

"We can't roll that mixer down the Hill if it's full of cement, Fatty. It's too heavy."

"Rusty will mix the cement while you and I fix the pipes—if the cover breaks when we pull it off, which it probably won't because we'll be careful, okay? It'll be a snap."

"You sure Rusty's in?"

"Why would I say he was in if he wasn't?"

Big Soap, sitting in the back seat, nodded, peered up at the blue sky overhead, absently lost in thought, then said, "Fatty, the front door of the dairy is right at Franklin Street."

"There's two more doors on the Hayes Street side."

"They get going at four in the morning at the dairy."

"It's Memorial Day weekend, Soap. The Antes parade. Speeches, barbecue, beer, fireworks. Every business in town's closed."

"All the same. They probably got a watchman at the dairy, and he'll be looking out."

"The watchman'll be at Antes House having fun with the parade and fireworks like everybody else. I know him. He's colored," Fatty said.

"Then he *won't* be at the parade," Big Soap said. "I don't know one colored that goes to that parade."

"It's Reverend Spriggs."

Big Soap paused a moment, thinking, then said, "Ain't Snooks your pastor?"

"He ain't *my* pastor," Fatty said. "He's *the* pastor."

"I didn't know Snooks worked as a watchman," Big Soap said. "Father Vicelli runs our church full-time."

Fatty dismissed that with a wave of his hand. "Anytime this town needs a Negro to stand around at celebrations and eat and look happy, they call Snooks. That's his real job."

"That don't sound like a bad job," Big Soap said. He looked up over Fatty's shoulder. "Uh-oh."

Fatty spun around to follow Big Soap's gaze to see Paper at the front grill of the car, hands on her hips.

Seeing her standing amid the junk in his yard, her yellow dress swishing about in the breeze, the sunlight bouncing off her smooth brown face, made him feel as if he were in a room full of warm marshmallows. His heart felt as light as that of a four-year-old.

"C'mere," she said, waving him over with an impatient swipe in the air.

He climbed out of his convertible by standing on the seat, stepping over the windshield onto the hood, and jumping off, landing next to her, whereupon she grabbed his elbow and spun him around so their backs were to Big Soap.

"Haven't you ever heard of the early bird?" she said.

"No. But I heard of the wriggling worm."

"You was supposed to go by to see Nate this afternoon to figure out what time to run him out to Hemlock Row. He wants to move. Tonight."

Fatty felt a sudden urge to confess, to tell Paper he'd accepted another job, one that involved a huge payoff with little risk, that would provide him—maybe even them, if there *was* a them, which he hoped there was—with some real money.

"Tonight?" he sputtered. "I got things to do tonight."

"What kind of things?"

"A job come up."

"You can sell icebreakers at your jook tomorrow. It's all set. Just get down to the theater. Nate needs you to help him move some drums and parade stuff to Antes House before he leaves out."

"I thought I was supposed to drive him over to Hemlock Row. Nobody said nothing about volunteering me to haul cotton for Doc Roberts's parade. And nobody said nothing about me doing all that today."

"Just play along, would you? It's a lot of drums and parade stuff."

"There's plenty folks around to help Nate. Why's he want me?"

"Because you're the only one on the Hill who can come up with something big enough to bring all them instruments in one big swoop on short notice. Otherwise he'll be hauling that stuff back and forth all day. He ain't got all day. He's got to get moving tonight."

"Why?"

"Miggy set him up with the Egg Man. *Tonight*."

"Why can't the white folks haul their own stuff for their parade? They allergic to work?"

"Get down there and ask Nate yourself."

"Can you tell him I can't make it, Paper?"

Paper leaned on the hood coolly and reached out to touch his face gently. "Be good, Fatty. I know you can."

As a nod to the Jewish community, the John Antes Historical Society every year allowed Moshe's All-American Dance Hall and Theater the privilege of storing in its vast basement their assorted drums and parade supplies used for the annual Memorial Day parade and fireworks display. Seventeen snare drums, eight tom-toms, four huge bass drums, eighteen drum harnesses, banners, floats, two miniature fire trucks, platform materials, and other assorted paraphernalia for the parade dignitaries, which included Doc Roberts and several city council members.

Normally, the city sent a truck around to pick up the gear. But this year, no truck arrived. Instead, the request for the drums arrived via a high school kid who bore a note to Moshe, asking that the gear be brought over.

Moshe was not at the theater when the note came. He was home not feeling well. Thus, the note was handed to Nate, who could not read, who handed it to Addie, who could, who walked it over to Moshe's house to deliver the request to Moshe, then returned to the theater, where Nate was backstage preparing for the weekend appearance of the great blues singer Sister Rosetta Tharpe.

"What'd he say?" Nate asked.

"He was fast sleep. He's not feeling well. So I didn't bother him," Addie said.

"He used to run himself to death to please the white folks round here," Nate said. "Anyway, we'll hold him up. We'll get the drums and stuff there. I'll still have time to get to Hemlock Row tonight."

"Hang the parade," Addie said. "We got our own business to tend to. Let them get their own parade junk."

"I'll have time."

"Who's gonna fetch that stuff back here after the parade and fireworks is finished?"

Nate waved her off. "It'll take 'em all night to close up Antes House. I'll fetch the drums and things in the morning."

"Not if the police are hunting you."

"They ain't gonna be hunting me. 'Cause I'll be back here."

Addie was silent. She'd hidden her dread about the whole business at last night's meeting with Miggy, but as the hours to Nate's departure drew closer, she'd grown more nervous. "Maybe it's best to leave Dodo in God's hands," she said.

'He *is* in God's hands," Nate said. "That's why I'm meeting the Egg Man at Hemlock Row. I'll tell him what I want. Pay him a few shekels, then let him do the rest. I'll be back by midnight. So if they find out the boy's gone and the police come looking for him here, they won't find him. They'll find me in bed instead. I ain't going out there to fetch him, honey. I'm just going to meet the Egg Man. The rest I'll leave to him and Miggy. You got nothing to worry about."

At that moment, Addie realized that there was no actual plan laid out that she knew about. Fatty had agreed to drive Nate to Hemlock Row to meet Bullis, the Egg Man, care of Miggy. She couldn't remember what else she'd actually heard at last night's meeting beyond that, for Miggy talked in parables and the notion of Dodo at the mercy of that . . . *heathen* Son of Man drove her ill, not to mention the discovery that Nate, her Nate, was . . . she always knew he had a secret. He said he was from the South. South Carolina was his home, he'd said. But Hemlock Row? She decided she'd take it up later, for there was trouble ahead now. Nate, her Nate, was not going inside that hospital, Dodo or no Dodo.

"My mind's troubled by some things that was spoken about yesterday," she said.

"We'll get to it when we're done with what's ahead."

"Just to be sure. You ain't going inside that place yourself, is you?"

"I don't want to go in there," Nate said dismissively.

She wanted to scream at him that he'd better not go in there, but the sound of horseshoes clopping along Main Street toward the theater interrupted her thoughts. She turned around to look and murmured, "Oh my . . ."

Fatty, the only Negro on the Hill who could on short notice create—or think of—a contraption big enough to carry the assorted paraphernalia for a parade of 350 people, clomped up to the curb in a cart pulled by a mule. Next to him sat Big Soap, grinning.

"Taxi?" Fatty called gaily.

Addie rolled her eyes.

"It's just a few blocks," Fatty said.

Nate wasn't amused, but he led Fatty and Big Soap around to the theater's stage door, where the three of them hastily piled the gear into the cart, strapped it down with ropes, and set off. Fatty and Nate rode up front. Big Soap rode on the equipment stacked high in the cart's rear, facing backward, his legs dangling off the back.

As they clunked forward, with Big Soap out of earshot, Fatty got to the problem quickly. "Nate, do you have to meet the Egg Man in Hemlock Row tonight?"

"Got to. Heading out around seven o'clock."

"Can it be another night?"

"What's wrong?"

Fatty looked to see if he could be overheard, though they were atop the cart and out of earshot of everyone. "I got another job," he said.

"So?"

"It's for tonight. Just a little job. Can I get you to Hemlock Row a little early? Maybe take you at four. Is that all right?"

"What time would you fetch me after?"

"It'll be late. About midnight or so."

Nate frowned. "All right. So long as I'm back by morning."

"You got someplace to sit tight over at the Row while you wait for me later?"

Nate smirked. "Don't worry 'bout me out there."

"I'm sorry, Nate. I'm in a tight spot. I need the dough from this job. It's a lot of money. But you can count on me."

It sounded phony even as he said it, and as the cart approached the Antes House at the bottom of Chicken Hill, Fatty glanced beyond the old building, three blocks up the slope, to the Clover Dairy. He decided to fess up.

"Nate, I got a note from my sister yesterday."

"Glad y'all is speaking again."

"Somebody passed some money to me through her. They want me to dig up the water pipe across from the Clover Dairy. There's a Y under there that connects the Jewish church to the faucet well. I'm gonna take it and connect it to the city's water from the reservoir. The public spigot's well must be drying up."

Nate nodded. "All these springs under the Hill are drying out. Too many wells. Water comes out the tap muddy and wrong nowadays. How do you know about pipes under the Hill?"

"I helped my daddy put in a lot of the pipes when I was little. It wasn't legal back then, but that's how they did it. Just ran pipes where they could. I guess they don't wanna go through the town to get it fixed."

"They don't wanna pay off crooks, is what it is. Who wrote the note?"

"I don't know and Bernice didn't say. But there was a lot of money in that note. And something else was in that note, but I . . . lost part of it."

"You lost it?"

"There was a second page. I tore it by accident. I found some of it, but the rest . . . it fell behind my jook, and by the time I went back and found it, it was all wet. I couldn't make it out."

"None of it?"

"Just something about the railroad men. Union workers . . . Jews . . . and the Pennhurst train. But what all, I don't know."

Nate pondered this for a moment, then smiled before he finally spoke. "Mr. Isaac's running this thing from the back."

"Who?"

"Mr. Moshe's got a cousin by the name of Isaac. He's a deep-pocketed fella from Philly. Theater man. Same business as Mr. Moshe but bigger, three times over. He's all right then. Was there any money in that note for the railroad people?"

"There was four hundred dollars extra in there taped to that note on that page about the railroad men. I don't know what it was for."

"Was that all the money in there?"

"Heck no. There was five hundred dollars for the water main besides the four hundred dollars for the railroad men."

Nate was silent for a long moment as the *clop clop* of the mule making his hard journey rung into the street. Finally he said, "You gonna have to surrender that part of it to me. I know it's a lot of money, but it ain't meant for you. That's for Dodo."

"My ass!" is what Fatty wanted to say. And would have said were it anyone else, were it not Nate Timblin.

When they arrived at the Antes House, Nate dismounted, stepped to the side of the cart, and spoke up to Fatty, who was still in the driver's seat. "Go home and fetch that four hundred dollars and bring it to Addie at the theater right now. You and Soap walk it over. I'll unload this stuff here."

"That's a lot of dough, Nate."

"Surrender it, son. It's gonna bounce back on you one way or the other if you don't. Somebody's paying for a service. Your job is to deliver it."

"What's the service?"

"I'll take care of that," Nate said. "After you give the money to Addie, go on and take care of your business here tonight. I'll get out to Hemlock Row on my own. I'll bring your mule and wagon back to your jook when I'm done here."

If any other man in Pottstown had demanded four hundred free dollars that had landed on his lap and told him to walk home and fetch it and bring it to his wife to boot, Fatty would've told them to get lost and cuffed them on the neck and kicked them in the rear as they ran out the door. But Nate Timblin was not any other man. Fatty did as he was told.

27

The Finger

Dodo was awakened by a shaking of the crib and looked up to see Monkey Pants staring at him. His left hand, which Monkey Pants could hold steady and which he used mostly to communicate, was pointing at Dodo, and his mouth was moving.

"Later," Dodo said.

The last cast had come off the day before. Dodo had been taken from the bed and been escorted to a room where he was issued hospital johnnies and slippers, and was shown his locker, which had nothing in it and to which only the attendants had the key. He was placed in the parade of men to the cafeteria, then the day room, back to the ward briefly, then the cafeteria for lunch, where he collapsed, for his legs were still weak from lack of use, so he was sent back to his crib on the ward, where he'd fallen asleep, to spend the afternoon and evening with Monkey Pants in the relatively empty ward. He was glad to be away from the men.

Monkey Pants wanted to know what the rest of the ward looked like. The bathroom, the day room, the cafeteria. But Dodo was in no mood to talk. The enormity of where he was had crashed on him a second time once he walked among the general population. The desperate loneliness of the place didn't just chafe him, it began to destroy him. He could feel it. The patients, some of whom were kind, spoke to him—he could read their lips—as men speak to children, yet they were powerless when the attendants showed up. Everything was up for grabs, and the kindest patients suffered the worst. At meals, when Dodo turned his face away from the gruel on his tray to lip-read a conversation, hands grabbed at his food. There was a pecking order. The most able patients ran everything, the less capable ones were left on their own. The constant movement—the talking, chattering, biting, shoving, making deals, and pilfering of newspapers and cigarettes—was maddening. He was forced to sit on the floor in the day room because to sit in a place that someone else regularly sat in drew wrath and curses. The constant flow of questions from his fellow patients, many of whom he could not understand, for they had speech disorders or disturbing mannerisms, made lip-reading difficult. Several spoke to him as if he were mentally incompetent. Others discussed matters of great complexity. All seemed to think they didn't belong there. One man said: "Everybody here is sick mentally except me. I have a bad nervous system. Do you have a bad nervous system?" Another confided: "I got here by mistake because I was at night school." Still another, a white man, declared: "You can't be sick, son. When I was a Negro, I never got sick." Their talk frightened him. When Son of Man appeared, the room snapped to attention. Several patients avoided him, but most, especially the more able ones, gathered around him. He towered over them in his all-white uniform, an ebony messiah exuding power, standing over the flock of society's tossaways, who drifted about him as he moved, an entourage following Moses. Even the second attendant, a white man, seemed to acquiesce to Son of Man. Dodo eased as far from him as possible, burying himself into a corner, but there was no running away in the day room. He noted Son of Man watching him, and when Dodo caught his eye, Son of Man winked. That attention, and the constant buffing of the floor with some kind of powerful-smelling disinfectant, left him with a tremendous headache.

But Dodo could not communicate those things to Monkey Pants. He was too exhausted and confused that day. Also, for the first time, now that the pain in his legs had receded, he began to feel something even more painful: guilt. He thought of the many things he'd done wrong. The occasional swiping of a piece of chocolate in Miss Chona's store. The snatching of a marble from one of Miss Bernice's daughters in her yard. Why had he done those things? Why had Miss Chona been hurt? Why had Uncle Nate and Aunt Addie not come to visit? *Because of me*, he thought. *I did wrong. I attacked a white man. I am in jail. I am here for life.* He ignored Monkey Pants's frantic hand waving and looked away until Monkey Pants finally gave up.

They lay there a long while, and when eventually he looked over, he saw Monkey Pants lying on his back, staring at the ceiling, his mouth open, his legs curled in a fetal position toward his chest. He looked odd, as if he were having trouble breathing. Dodo sat up.

"What's the matter, Monkey Pants?"

Monkey Pants was not listening. He stared at the ceiling, drawing his breath in fast huffs and puffs. Dodo thought he might be having a seizure, for he knew what they looked like, having seen Miss Chona have several. Monkey Pants had had several since Dodo arrived. They were short, more frequent than Miss Chona's but equally frightening bursts of gyrations, which sent Monkey Pants heaving and lifting, as if a hand were pushing his back into an arch, his body curved awkwardly, his stomach and pelvis thrusting high in the air, then coming down, several times, followed by the windmilling of his legs and arms as if they were operating on separate motors, his body twisted so horribly and the crib shaking so violently that the floor shook. Those events usually brought several attendants and a nurse bearing needles or pills, which seemed to calm him and brought long hours of fitful sleep afterward. Monkey Pants hated his medicine, and many times Dodo watched him pretend to swallow the litany of pills that were his daily dose only to spit them out the moment the attendant turned away.

As he watched, Monkey Pants's breathing seemed to slow as if he'd willed the spasm away. Then he turned to Dodo again and nodded, signaling that he was better. But Dodo had already retreated under his cloud of depression. "I made a mistake, Monkey Pants," he said. "That's why I'm here."

Monkey Pants's furrowed eyebrows frowned a "no."

"If it wasn't for me, Miss Chona wouldn't have gotten hurt."

Monkey Pants frowned a "no no no," but Dodo shook his head. "Yes yes yes. Don't tell me."

Monkey Pants held out his finger to sign something.

Dodo ignored it.

Then he produced the marble, which always drew Dodo's attention. "What?"

He watched as Monkey Pants signed a *T*.

"What else?"

O

"What else?"

And on it went until he spelled out:

T.O.U.C.H.

M.Y.

F.I.N.G.E.R.

"Why?" Dodo asked impatiently.

The disappointed smirk of his friend was too much. So Dodo reached out and the tips of their first fingers touched. Then Monkey Pants removed his finger.

"I bet you can't hold it like that," Dodo said.

Monkey Pants chuckled, and Dodo read that to mean "I bet I can."

"All right then," he said. "Let's see who can hold it the longest."

Monkey Pants thrust his finger out of the crib. A challenge.

Dodo accepted and the two boys held fingers together through the bars of their cribs. Five minutes. Ten minutes. But Dodo's arm became tired and he withdrew. "Not fair. You can rest your arm on the bed."

Monkey Pants shrugged.

Suddenly the gloom and the guilt and the pain fell away, for here was a challenge, and Dodo became a boy again. He shifted to his right side, propped his left fist under his head for support, and thrust his right hand through the crib bars, first finger outward, and said, "Again."

Monkey Pants obliged, and they battled again, fingers touching. Five minutes. Ten minutes, twenty. Thirty. As they held, Dodo began to talk, for Monkey Pants needed his left hand to talk, which meant Dodo was free to do the talking for both of them. He told Monkey Pants what the day room looked like, and the bathroom, and the weird attendant who had the hiccups all day, and the patient who said he was a Negro once. His arm was so tired that he wanted to quit, so he chatted more, hoping that his talk would cause Monkey Pants to tire. But Monkey Pants held on.

After an hour, Dodo quit and dropped his finger.

A glint of white teeth and laughter from Monkey Pants's crib drew a frown out of him.

"You're cheating. You're lying on your back."

Monkey Pants motioned that he should do the same.

So he did, turning on his back and offering his right finger to Monkey Pants's left finger. "Let's battle."

They held like that for twenty minutes. Forty minutes. An hour. Two hours. Dinner came. The attendant who came with their dinner trays, amused by the game he saw afoot, left the trays and returned to pick them up later, the food uneaten. The two boys ignored him, their contest of wills now full-out. Monkey Pants soiled his bed. Dodo did the same. The attendants noted it and moved on to the next bed. Nobody else came. Both boys held their fingers tightly together, neither willing to give up.

Then night came, and with it, change.

At first, they held on, like the men they imagined themselves to be, but as the patients filed in from the day room and stirred about, finally settling into bed, the new shift of attendants dimmed the overhead lights, then the room went to blackness, leaving only the lights from the attendants' work station reflecting into the room. Most of the men lay in their beds fitfully, trying to sleep.

Still the boys held on.

Dodo could not see Monkey Pants's finger now, but he could make out the shape of his arm from the light of the attendants' desk. The ward was U-shaped, with beds lining both sides and the attendants' desk in the middle, so that light from the attendants' station cast an eerie glow on both sides of the unit. But the light only stretched to the middle of the floor, just enough so that Dodo could make out the thin white arm of Monkey Pants but not much more.

Most of the men were asleep now, for they were an hour into bedtime, with several of the men snoring, Dodo guessed, as he recognized the familiar humps going up and down steadily. Drowsiness laid on him hard now, and he could not hold up his head but rather lay with his head back on the pillow, looking at the ceiling, with his arm out, touching Monkey Pants. He realized he could not hold out much longer. Sleep was winning. Monkey Pants, too, was weakening. Finally Monkey Pants's finger fell off his, then he recovered and offered his finger again, which Dodo took on, for he was up to the challenge. He was the better man! Then Monkey Pants's finger dropped off again.

"Come on, or I win," he hissed, holding out his finger.

But Monkey Pants's finger did not come.

Dodo lay on his back, fighting sleep, satisfied. Exhausted, he raised his head to look over at his friend in triumph just to make sure, but in the dim light, he could not see Monkey Pants or his arm. He had triumphed.

Then the light that came from the attendants' desk suddenly shifted and he saw movement at the foot of his crib, and Dodo forgot all about his victory. For there he stood, clad in his sparkling white attendant's uniform, smiling, his teeth visible in the dim light, his handsome face silhouetted against the light that reflected from the attendants' desk.

Son of Man.

"Hey, Peacock," he said.

The two cribs were five inches apart, and Dodo felt terror squeeze his throat as Son of Man lifted the edge of his crib away from Monkey Pants's crib, making no noise, then slipped into the space between them, blocking out the view of Monkey Pants. It was as if a wall had been set between him and the only safety he'd known in that place.

With one quick motion, Son of Man flicked the locks on each side of Dodo's crib and slid the bars down.

Dodo sat up quickly but his legs were weak, and an arm slammed him down. Dodo opened his mouth to scream but a hand clamped over his mouth and nose, and squeezed, crushing his face so hard that he felt his nose might break off. Son of Man placed a finger to his lips as if to say "Shh."

In one swift motion, he pushed Dodo's head to the side, grabbed him, flipped him onto his side, slammed a pillow on his head, and pressed it tightly against his face. With one hand holding the pillow, Son of Man yanked up Dodo's hospital johnnie, baring his backside.

Dodo squirmed and resisted, but Son of Man was strong and powerful. Dodo kicked his legs but the man pressed one knee on his bottom leg and held the other up easily.

Then Dodo felt cold salve being rammed between his butt cheeks and then an explosive hot burst of pain—but only for a second—for at that moment the floor began to shake and the knee that held down his legs drew away swiftly as Son of Man turned away and loosened his grip. Something had distracted him.

He tossed the pillow off Dodo's face, and Dodo felt the shaking of the ward floor at the same time—a heavy shake, heavier than he had ever felt—as if an earthquake had come. The lights were suddenly snapped on and there was a quick scrambling about the room as several patients sat up and began squawking, with several already out of bed and wandering about, confused. Son of Man stood among them, ignoring them, enraged, ripping off his white attendant's jacket, using it as a towel to wipe his face and head, which, to Dodo's surprise, were covered with human feces.

In the crib next to him, Monkey Pants was wriggling uncontrollably, having his biggest seizure yet, his legs and arms twisting wildly, his mouth open—obviously yelling, Dodo guessed, but with intent, for his good hand, his left, was holding what was left of the excrement he'd tossed at Son of Man, striking him in the head and smearing some on Son of Man's jacket and pants as well. His seizure and yelling had awakened the entire ward and summoned other attendants.

Dodo saw two attendants rush to Monkey Pants's bed and try to place a spoon in his mouth, but it was impossible, for his seizure was in full charge. After several long seconds, his seizure ended, and he lay back on the bed.

An attendant moved to change Monkey Pants's bedding. But Son of Man stopped them. Now that the lights were on, Dodo could read Son of Man's lips.

"Leave him be," he said. "I'll change him."

They stepped aside and were about to return to the attendants' station when a young white doctor appeared. Dodo could not understand everything he said, but he got the gist of it, for Son of Man and the other two attendants turned suddenly obsequious. The doctor noted that the cribs of Dodo and Monkey Pants had been moved apart and seemed to want to know why. He noted the side of Dodo's crib had been pulled down and asked about medication being delivered at that hour. Whatever explanation Son of Man offered did not seem to impress the doctor. He indicated that Monkey Pants should be cleaned up, and that the two cribs should be placed close together again, as Dodo's crib was against the poor patient whose bed was on the other side. The doctor examined Monkey Pants and quickly ordered something from one of the attendants, then examined Dodo briefly, declaring that since he was now healed, Dodo should be moved to a bed in the morning. He issued other instructions that Dodo did not understand. But by the time the doctor was finished talking, Son of Man had left the ward.

The doctor then turned to examine Monkey Pants again, this time more carefully. Monkey Pants had not spoken. He lay inert, breathing in and out in quick, shallow breaths. An attendant returned with a tray of medicine, the doctor administered a shot, and Monkey Pants seemed to recover. He moved normally, sleepily, before closing his eyes and settling into sleep. Order was restored. Then the lights were doused again.

But Dodo could not sleep. He lay in terror that Son of Man would return. He fought sleep. He was terrified that he'd awaken to Son of Man returning to visit that extreme pain on him again. He did not know what to do. He could not help himself, and once again, guilt assailed him. *I did wrong*, he thought. *I did wrong, wrong, wrong. I'll be here forever.*

Sleep began to push at him again, and as it did, his terror grew. He began to wonder whether he was sleeping or not, and since he could no longer tell, that increased his terror. He began to sob. He was doomed.

He knew that talking after lights out would bring an angry attendant, perhaps even Son of Man himself, but he could not help himself. He sobbed out, "Monkey Pants."

He felt a soft tap on the bars of his crib. He was so exhausted that he could not turn on his side. Instead, lying on his back, he flung an arm through the crib bars into the dark and swept his hand blindly through air. Once. Twice. Until he felt an arm. Then a wrist. Then a finger. One finger. One finger like before.

He placed his finger to it.

"Thank you, Monkey Pants."

He lay there like that, their fingers connected, till he fell asleep.

When he woke the next morning, his arm was still extended through the slit of the crib. Monkey Pants, too, had his finger still extended. He lay on his back, with his mouth open, his arm still poked through the slit of his crib, his finger still extended in friendship and solidarity.

But the rest of Monkey Pants was gone.

28

The Last Love

Anna Morse, owner of Morse's Funeral Home, had decided to move out of Linfield, Pa., many times since the passing of her husband three years ago. Running a funeral parlor was too much work, and good help was impossible to find. Just managing her building, a flamboyant brick structure at the edge of town that housed her apartment upstairs and what she called the "works"—the mortuary—on the first floor, was a headache. White workmen refused to work for a colored woman. Colored workmen had other ideas, hoping to fall in love and find themselves in a monied future. That's why when she needed repairs on her building, she always called on her old worker, Nate Timblin. Nate was a sweetheart. Dependable. Solid. No matter what hour, no matter the job, he always came. Knowing he was available was one reason she had decided to keep her business in Linfield.

Thus, she was happy to oblige when Nate called that Saturday afternoon of Memorial Day weekend asking for a ride out to Linfield, which was just north of Hemlock Row, to visit a friend. Hemlock Row was just a mile from Pennhurst, and Anna guessed his intent immediately. He wanted to visit that nephew of his. She'd read the papers. A twelve-year-old colored boy, deaf, attacking a white woman? She had her doubts. But then again . . . trouble fell on the Negro like raindrops. She was sorry it happened to Nate and Addie, two of the best folks on the Hill.

It was a quick twenty-minute ride to pick him up and she was in a good mood, for no one, so far, had decided to die that weekend, though four possibilities—two in Chicken Hill alone, one in Royersford, and another in Reading—were percolating. The one in Reading concerned her most, because that was a good twenty miles away, and the only other colored funeral home in the county was in Reading, and whoever reached the howling family first usually won. But Anna knew the pastor in Reading, and the colored doctor, plus she had a cousin there who had invited her to come over for the Memorial Day weekend, and she'd decided to take her up on it. It would be fortuitous if the customer died while she was in Reading, God's will. But a troublesome leak in her building gave her pause. Water was seeping through the second-floor bathroom wall, and the night before had stained the ceiling of the viewing room below. That was unacceptable. The idea of tiny water droplets plopping onto the head of the deceased during a viewing gave her the willies. She planned to have Nate take a look.

He seemed unusually quiet as he sat next to her in the gleaming Packard as it rolled down Pottstown's High Street and cruised south toward Linfield.

"You been busy?" she asked.

"A little," Nate said.

"Can I help in any way?" she said, careful to avoid the subject of his nephew.

"You helping me now."

Anna didn't press the point. Nate was never one to talk much anyway. Silences were part of who he was. So she said, "You need a ride back?"

Nate shook his head. "I'm staying overnight on the Row. I'll be all right getting back tomorrow."

She wanted to ask "Where are you staying on the Row?" for she knew just about every family on the Row. Instead, she saw an opening.

"Nate, I got a leak. I think it's coming from the roof down through the upstairs bathroom and into the viewing room below it. You got time to take a look?"

"Course. I'll look at it right off before I head out."

"You mind if I leave you? You know where everything is. I was thinking of running up to Reading. My cousin and her husband's frying up a turkey."

"Go 'head. I'll walk over to the Row when I'm done. It's just up the road."

"You ain't afraid of the dead, are you?"

"No."

"Well, there's a cot in the storage closet over the little vestibule in the viewing room. The closet where I keep things. You're welcome to sleep there if you want."

Nate shook his head. "I got a place to stay."

"You sure I can't help, Nate?"

"I'll look at the leak right off and be on my way."

She nodded, satisfied. "Nate, when you're ready to make some real money, come back and work for me. I'll pay you good enough to buy a car."

Nate nodded absently, gazing out the windshield at the passing farmland. "I don't need no car," he said.

He worked at Anna's house until close to seven, first climbing to the roof to clean leaves out of the overflowing gutters, then repairing the small stain in the bathroom and viewing-room ceiling. He knew where Anna stored everything and the job was easy. The work calmed him and gave him time to think. He was in no hurry. He was early, for Miggy said to meet her at eleven thirty after her shift, and Hemlock Row was only twenty minutes away by foot. He had nowhere to stay hidden at the Row for four hours if he got there early.

After he was finished, Nate returned the tools, then stepped into the empty viewing room. He moved to the vestibule in the back where Anna stored bodies waiting for funeral services. She always had one or two, as she liked to joke, "lying about." He found two open coffins, both men, lying in repose waiting for final viewings, their coffins lined up like railroad cars, one behind the other. The closest to him was a middle-aged man with his hands neatly folded on his chest. Atop his hands lay a brand-new neatly folded janitor's shirt with a specially printed label above the pocket that read "Herb's Diner, in honor of our Ted S. Culman." The second was a younger man, seventeen or eighteen. Nate stared at them both for a moment, stepped past them into a back closet, selected a few items, then set out for the Row.

Miggy would take him to the Egg Man and leave. That was the arrangement. He thought it through again as he made his way down the dark two-lane highway toward Hemlock Row. Miggy wanted him there at eleven thirty sharp. No sooner. No later. Then she planned to take him to the Egg Man named Bullis, who she said would leave for a nearby farm at 4 a.m. to get his eggs, which to Nate meant that the Egg Man had to get out of bed by three to get to work on time. But where? Was he a Hemlock Row man, a Lowgod? He hoped not. There were a few Lowgods on the Row who might be looking for him. If they discovered him, it would not be pleasant. Miggy assured him no one would see him coming or going from her place. But what if she got cold feet? What if she'd already spread the word about him? *Nate Love is alive. He ain't in jail. He ain't down South either. He's right over there on Chicken Hill.* He'd thought about it carefully. Why should she take a risk and help him?

He trudged forward, uncertain. He didn't like it.

It was two thirty when Miggy, still dressed in her hospital whites, finally rose from the front window of her home on the Row. She opened the front door, removed the lantern hanging from the hook on the front porch, and closed it. She peered out the window another ten minutes, then gave up. She went to her back door, left the house quietly, and moved down the row of houses to the fourth house, where the illumination of a bare light bulb could be seen through the window. She tapped on the back door and an old man in a white beard and somber face answered.

"He ain't coming, Bullis," she said.

"Just as well," Bullis said.

"You think he got stuck or waylaid along the way?"

"I hope somebody popped him with a pistol," Bullis said.

"You ain't gonna get far with them kind of thoughts."

"What kind'a thoughts am I supposed to have?"

"You made a deal."

"With that pretty young friend of yours, the one you call Paper. I ain't make no deal with him. I ain't losing my job over him—or that evil young 'un out at Pennhurst."

"Has any of my futures ever gone wrong on you, Bullis?"

Bullis frowned, then said, "I was hush-mouthed about Nate. I didn't tell a soul about him. Didn't throw out no giveaways to nobody, as God is my witness. But truth to tell it, I'm glad he ain't coming."

"I had some words with Son of Man yesterday," Miggy said. "He did not take it well."

"You ought to steer clear of him."

"Can you wait five more minutes?" Miggy asked.

"No, I can't. You said eleven thirty. It's almost three. I got to get moving to the farm. I'm late now."

He closed the door and Miggy turned to walk home.

Something, she thought, *is wrong*.

FOR BULLIS, the walk from Hemlock Row to the farmhouse where he picked up the cart and the eggs usually took thirty minutes, but he was late, so he cut through the farmer's cornfield, careful not to disturb the growing stalks, for his boss would notice and not be pleased. He arrived at 3:10 a.m. Not bad. It was a forty-five-minute ride to Pennhurst with the horse pulling a cart full of eggs and a coffee urn. The horse, named Titus, was an Appaloosa that, at fourteen, was nearly blind, but Titus was a dependable soul. He knew the work and the trail, and the two got along.

Bullis found the horse in his stall, tossed him some hay, let him eat, then led him from the barn to the chicken coop, a long rectangular building that stank of chicken shit. The door was locked with a hasp to keep out foxes and other critters, and the cart was parked in the middle of the building. Bullis pulled Titus in, fastened his trace and harnesses, then quickly moved to the eggs, which he'd carefully crated in stacks the day before. He stacked the crates into the cart on shelving rigged for that purpose, one atop the other.

He worked quickly, but after a few minutes, he realized that the chicken coop was oddly silent. The roosters, who normally began crowing at that hour, were silent. He heard several pigeons in the rafters fluttering, and the hogs in the nearby pen were gathering near the far corner closer to the pasture, all unusual. *Were those signs of rain*, he thought, *or had Miggy gotten mad and mojoed him? Would she do that?*

He dismissed those thoughts as he climbed onto the cart, grabbed the reins, and called out, "Har!"

Titus had turned toward the gate and moved forward several feet when Bullis suddenly pulled the reins and said, "Cuss it, Titus . . . I forgot something."

At the tip end of the wagon was a large silver urn that held hot water for coffee, which he drew from a hot-water heater at the coal furnace house every morning on the way to the lower wards. The trip to the furnace house was the first stop every morning. He put the coffee in place and poured steaming hot water from the giant hot-water heater, and the five minutes that it took him to hit the first wards allowed the coffee to brew so that it was just right by the time he reached them. He was careful to clean the filter every day, for the hot water from the heater sometimes held ash and grit. He wasn't supposed to use hot water from the water heater, but who at Pennhurst knew the difference?

The old man dumped the contents of the filter in the nearby hog pen, then made for the well pump at the far end of the chicken coop to wash it clean. As he reached the well pump, Bullis heard Titus offer a surprised whinny and snort, but he ignored it. He had to hurry. He washed out the filter, put it back on the urn, trotted to the warehouse where the farm owner kept the ground coffee beans, filled the filter with freshly ground coffee, then climbed up and sent Titus onward.

The horse seemed restless and unsettled. Bullis wanted to push him to move faster, but the old steed did not seem to like it.

"C'mon, Titus," he said. "I'm old, too." But Titus went at his own pace.

At Pennhurst's huge wrought-iron gates, Bullis waved at the gate guard and made a beeline for the lower wards, guiding the horse along the winding single-lane road. When he reached the lower wards, a good mile from the main entrance, he came to another gate and waved at a second guard before passing through, then he followed the road as it wound down a slope to the giant coal-fired furnace house. He stopped outside, ran a hose to the spigot on one of the giant water heaters inside, filled the coffee urn with steaming hot water, then drove Titus back up the pathway. But instead of turning toward the lower wards, he drove behind Ward V-1, where the path wound toward the railroad track, and from there, out of sight of both wards. He drove the horse and cart into a thicket that contained a rarely used path through the woods, which was overgrown with thistles and brush. They didn't have to go far. Ten feet in, the path arced toward a slight hill that sloped down toward the railroad yard below where the train depot was. Titus, despite being nearly blind, picked through the thickets easily, bumping the cart only slightly. When they reached the edge of the small ridge, out of sight of both the train below and the ward behind them, Bullis leaped off the wagon, stepped into the thickets, and removed two long planks and placed them by the cart's wheels. From there, he carefully drove the horse over a set of old unused railroad tracks, placed the wood planks aside out of sight, drove a few feet farther, dismounted from the cart, and pushed aside some bushes and thistles, revealing a thick, old wooden door with rusted strap hinges.

The tunnel.

An old railroad tunnel, used in the days when the Pennsylvania

Railroad train dropped coal directly from a freight car to the old furnace house near the lower wards, which was now a vacant weedy field between Wards V-1 and C-1. He slid back the door, lit his lantern, and drove the horse in. Titus picked his way across the buckling cement and potholes, the floor occasionally revealing the tracks beneath, which had been cemented over. Bullis again noted that Titus was laboring, and he became alarmed. Was the cart full of eggs and coffee that heavy?

"All right, Titus. We'll lighten this load soon enough."

Titus plowed on, but the horse was clearly laboring. Bullis eyed him, concerned. The horse was fine yesterday. *Could it be,* Bullis thought again, *that Miggy mojoed me?* He'd never seen Titus so tired—he seemed exhausted. Should Titus collapse and die in that tunnel, they were both ruined. He was out of a job and out of a friend.

Did Miggy mojo him? She wouldn't do that, would she? Not for a goddamned . . . He wouldn't even say the man's name. It was bad mojo. Instead, he said aloud, "Miggy didn't put a spell on you now, did she, Titus? C'mon . . . har up!"

Titus responded, pulling hard as he turned a tight corner in the dark tunnel, and finally they were at the first door. There were only three doors down there, each leading to the lower basements of Wards V-1, V-2, and C-1. He delivered to the first two wards without incident, for the attendants there seemed always eager to get away from their wards and sometimes tried to chat with him. He never did, so they quickly hauled their eggs and coffee inside, pouring coffee from his giant urn into the smaller urns they had hauled downstairs, and Bullis moved on to his next stop.

But at the last ward, when he leaped off the cart and moved to the door to knock, he paused a moment, slightly afraid.

Bullis knew Son of Man. He had heard rumors about him, many of them unsettling. But Bullis was not a man to speak out. He was an old man who lived in a world of wrong. He just delivered eggs. Still, when he delivered to C-1, he always made it quick. Son of Man never said much, and Bullis hoped today would be more of the same.

But when he knocked and the basement door opened and Son of Man's smooth, handsome face was silhouetted in the gleam of the lantern light as the door swung wide, Bullis saw that today was not going to be normal. Son of Man was smiling. He'd never seen the young man smile before.

"Morning," Son of Man said.

Bullis grunted a greeting, produced a wooden wedge from his pocket, and slid it under the door to keep it open. Then he moved to the cart to grab a crate.

Son of Man withdrew the prop and closed the door, sealing off the light from the basement, leaving the tunnel lit only by the lantern on Bullis's cart. His face was tilted oddly, his gleaming white teeth showing.

"That's a neat trick, old timer, bringing your cart to escape somebody."

"What you talking about?" Bullis demanded, trying to sound fierce.

"Miggy was on my ward last night, talking harsh and packing a bag for a boy."

"I don't know nothing about no boy, nor no bag."

"No horses is allowed in this tunnel. No people at all. You know that, right? You ain't supposed to be here."

"Don't tell me how to do my job, son. I been doing it long as you been living."

"I ain't your son, old man."

"Don't be a sass, boy."

Son of Man smiled. "You ought not talk to Son of Man that way."

Bullis sucked his teeth, irritated. "Someday when I learn to write, I'm gonna put some wee little old letters on cards and call myself Al Capone and pass 'em out to folks. Then I'll have a fancy name like you. Now could you step out of my way, please?"

Bullis stepped toward the door to push it open, but Son of Man blocked it. "You could go to jail for breaking somebody out a state hospital," he said. "For a lot of years."

"I ain't got years," Bullis said. He sighed. "Son, I'm just an old man trying to make a dollar change pockets."

"What about my pocket?"

"What about it?"

"My pocket's full of lint."

"I ain't here to clean your pocket."

"This is my ward."

"Do this building got your name on it?"

"Keep talking sideways, old man, and I'll send you outta this tunnel hooting and hollering."

Bullis's temper snapped and he felt the blood rush to his face. "You ain't sending me no place, ya ragged little skunk! You got no respect, talking to an elder like you is. Now move your skinny ass aside." He spun around, grabbed a crate of eggs, and shoved past the young man, kicking the door open wide with his foot and stepping inside.

As he did, he felt something hard crash into his skull and his knees gave out. He fell sideways against the doorjamb, the crate flying forward into the room as he fell. Eggs spattered everywhere on the basement floor.

"My eggs!"

He tried to stand up and felt something strike his head again and found himself on the floor. He spun on his back and then saw what hit him. A packed sock, which this time landed on his face. He raised his arms to cover himself, but the young man was strong, pinning Bullis's arms to the floor with his legs and sitting on his chest, raining blows with the sock and talking calmly as if he were a father spanking a child.

"Old!" *Whap!*

"Black!" *Whap!*

"Squirrely!" *Whap!*

"Bastard . . . comin' in *my* house!" *Whap, whap, whap.*

Bullis knew then that Miggy had put the mojo on him, for as the dazzling pain washed over him and through his nerve endings, he was seized with the humiliating knowledge that the young attendant was beating him as if he were a patient, using a sock because it left no mark; and in the blinding flashes of white pain, he saw over the young man's shoulder a pair of feet suddenly burst out of the built-in cabinet of the cart, still parked in the tunnel and visible through the open doorway. The cabinet, which sat beneath the shelves that held the eggs, was about two feet high and covered the length of the five-foot cart. It was handy but he rarely used it. It was big enough to hold scythes and shovels and big farming tools. Big enough for a man to squeeze in. Big enough, even, for a ghost.

The ghost that wriggled out of it was not a normal-looking ghost. It was a settled-aged black man with a face set in calm silence and eyes that bore a hurricane beneath them. It was a face that Bullis had not seen in thirty years, but even so, after all those years, the face, aged now but still carved in grim purpose, was instantly recognizable.

"I left you behind!" Bullis cried.

The ghost didn't answer. Instead, he moved like a swift gust of wind, stepping into the room with deft speed and grabbing Son of Man's wrist as it was raised high for another blow.

"I wish you had," Nate said.

Son of Man looked over his shoulder and found himself looking into Nate's eyes. What he saw made him freeze, and he remained there, like a statue, his right wrist held in the grip of a hand that felt like iron, the other hand out of his line of sight. He could not see what was in Nate's right hand, but he understood it. Still, he sat where he was, atop Bullis, his right hand holding the sock high like a torch, an odd Statue of Liberty, the torch held with the help of a Negro brother—*Give me your tired, your poor . . . yearning to be free*—and he felt all of those things, for the eyes gazing at him were not filled with hate or anger but rather with sympathy and hurt. Son of Man looked into Nate's eyes and saw beneath the swirling pools of iridescent calm both Nate's past and his own future and the future of the community that they both had left behind and even the reasons why. The sight stunned him and he felt for a moment as if he were blinded by a great light.

Nate, for his part, had endured the punishing cart ride with gritted teeth. He'd wanted the elders from his past to speak to him as he rode, for he was terrified. Not of being discovered, but of being in a position where someone would unleash the evil poison in him. He'd spent his entire adult life running, ever since he was thirteen—just past Dodo's age—for he was thirteen when he, too, experienced his own accident, his own explosion. Not from a stove, but from a father who had dragged his family from the perilous Low Country of South Carolina to the promised land of Pennsylvania only to discover that despite living on Hemlock Row among the peaceful Lowgods, justice and freedom had as little currency in the new land as it had in the old. The white man despised him in Pennsylvania as much as he did in the Low Country. The difference was that the white man in the South spoke his hatred in clear, clean, concise terms, whereas the white man in the new country hid his hatred behind stories of wisdom and bravado, with false smiles of sincerity and stories of Jesus Christ and other nonsense that he tossed about like confetti in the Pottstown parade. Living without means, surviving without hope, dependent on God to even matters. Son of Man indeed. Son of Man was better than Nate's own father, who had been destroyed by the move north, who in turn took a pipe to his mother, and who in turn was delivered to grace by his own son after he ordered the boy to bring along a crosscut saw and walk with him into the woods to cut down a tree. The child took matters into his own hands then and evened out matters. And it was all for naught, for there the reckless life of an abandoned child who lost to death both parents became the last legacy of the Loves, once one of the finest families in the Low Country, for Nate was the last Love on Hemlock Row who had come north to live among the Lowgods, who somehow forgot him and plunged him into a childhood of begging and stealing. And when the later years of earning a living as a grown man by laying suffering on any human for a price was stopped by a trip to the penitentiary that was visited upon him for the killing of a worthless rapist and thief who would have otherwise been laid low by some righteous man, it was as if that killing became Nate's only redemption, if there was such a thing, as he came to hope that perhaps God might forgive him and find a purpose for him. When he emerged from prison and met Addie, who dipped her hand into the pool of injury and hurt that was his heart and drained it of every evil and refilled it with love and purpose, he became sure of it. She cleansed him. And he'd lose it all now. He didn't want to lose it, but he knew it was gone.

"It ain't your fault," Nate said to Son of Man.

And with that, he plunged the kitchen knife he held behind him in his right hand deep into Son of Man's heart.

As the man fell off him, Bullis heard in the distance the whistle of the morning train bearing coal and supplies. And the ghost before him, bloody knife still in hand, spoke calmly.

"There's a boy upstairs I come to fetch," he said. "And you gonna carry me to him. We can't tarry."

"I ain't going up there."

"You serve coffee, don't you?"

"I drops it here. In the basement."

"Not today. Today you bringing it upstairs. And if anybody asks, I'm your helper."

29

Waiting for the Future

The parade start was delayed for two reasons. First, the Empire Fire Company's hook-and-ladder truck broke down inexplicably right in front of the Antes House, blocking the parade route. Second, the costumes were a mess, which drove Hal Leopold, the parade director, nearly mad. Leopold was a stickler for detail. He served as tea master for the ladies' auxiliary and was head dog for all things celebratory in Pottstown. He also baked the best coffee cake in town and ran his own catering outfit. The sorry state of the Revolutionary-era costumes drove him into fits. He stalked around inspecting the milling parade marchers and was outraged to find that four of his ten parade marshals, including Gus Plitzka and Doc Roberts, were wearing red British coats with red facings and white linings and white buttons on their uniforms instead of buff facings with white linings and blue buttons.

"You two are a mess," he scoffed, tapping Plitzka's coat with his finger. "Gus, you're in a British coat with red facings and white linings and white buttons. That means a British jacket with Pennsylvania trim. And Doc, why are you British? We're the Continental Army, people. We wear *blue* coats. Not red. The Continental Army wears blue tricornered hats, too, not red British private hats. Whose side are you on?"

"I put on what they gave me," Doc said. He was exhausted. He and Plitzka had rushed over to his office so he could administer a shot to Plitzka's toe to numb the pain, then rushed back to find that the uniforms had already been doled out. What's more, the uniforms, normally pressed, cleaned, and repaired, were a mess. The leather sashes and belts, normally pristine, were ragged and torn. Moths had eaten away at the edges of the coats. The musket rifles, always shiny and the wood polished, were rusted and the wood moldy. "Who takes care of this stuff?" Plitzka asked Leopold.

Leopold frowned. "The Jewish tailor, what's his name, Druker? He does the uniforms."

"Does he do our holsters and buckles and rifles?" Doc said. "Look at this," he said, noting the rough leather and the dull musket. "This is a mess."

Leopold shook his head. "No, that's . . . the crazy ones. The Skrup brothers, they do the leather, the sashes, the buttons, shoes, rifles, all that. They didn't do it this year."

It didn't occur to any of the three men that every stitch of the costumes and paraphernalia was cared for, stored, tailored, and repaired by the town's Jews for free. Nor did it occur to anyone that the small contingent of butt-kissing English-speaking German Jews who normally participated as members of the John Antes Historical Society's Cornet Marching Band were not present today, neither was Avram Gaisinsky, the Russian Jew who was actually an excellent cornet player and who always brought along his four sons, Todrish, Zusman, Zeke, and Elia, all of whom could play cornet as well. They were a remarkably musical family.

"At least the instruments are in good shape," Doc said.

"Moshe keeps them," Leopold said. "He's good about that."

"Who's he?" Plitzka asked.

"You know Moshe," Leopold said. "He's the theater guy. His wife passed a couple of months ago? She got attacked by the crazy colored boy they sent out to Pennhurst."

There was an uncomfortable pause as Doc looked away.

"You guys look like crap," Leopold said. "You gotta fix yourselves up. You're parade marshals. Get rid of the red jackets. And Doc"—he shook his head—"you can't wear a purple Continental Army major general's sash *and* a red British private's hat and coat. Ditch the coat. Get a new hat. Trade with one of the kids. You gotta be in blue, fellas. You're parade marshals. *No red.*"

"Can you round up a kid to switch?" Doc asked.

"Doc, if you wanna be famous or important, die at the right time. Otherwise, carry your own load. Find your own kid. I got a million things going on. We gotta get the fire truck started." And with that, he was off.

Gus watched Doc lean against a nearby telephone pole to take the weight off his bad foot. The ride in Doc's car to his office and Leopold's dressing down had unified them somewhat, along with Gus's bad toe, which, thanks to Doc, no longer throbbed but simply ached. Gus felt sorry for him.

"Sit tight, Doc," he said. "Gimme your coat. I'll find us blue ones."

Doc took off his red coat and sat down on the bench behind the Antes House, relieved. "Find me a hat, too, if you don't mind."

Plitzka limped off, heading toward the fire truck, where several men were gathered around the hood, frantically working. He noticed several high school kids standing in a knot wearing Continental Army blue uniforms, but their coats were at least two sizes too small for him or Doc.

He spotted another clump of bigger teenagers ten yards away and was about to head toward them when a man in a gray suit appeared out of nowhere and put his arm around his shoulder. "Hey, Gus, you're on the wrong team. Why you wearing red?"

The man was big, and the weight of the arm felt heavy, the bicep stiff and hard against Plitzka's neck. He spoke with a foreign accent. Plitzka guessed Russian. Probably Jewish. Damn Jews. Hoodlums. He felt rage and fear in his gut.

"Get your arm off me."

The man's arm felt like a block of wood. The heavy arm lifted slowly. "Mr. Rosen said to tell you he's lonely," he said.

"Tell him to get a dog."

"He's already got one. Me. Wanna see my teeth?"

Gus glanced around nervously. No one seemed to notice them. The flurry of men near the fire truck down the hill suddenly backed away as the engine roared to life and burped a cloud of black smoke from its tailpipe. This was followed by a cheer and a hasty scrambling to collect instruments, costumes, hats, and banners.

"I'll have his money next week," Gus said.

"You said that last week. And the week before."

"What do you want? I'm tapped out."

"Me, too. What a coincidence."

"You can't get water from a stone," Gus said.

The man nodded and clapped Plitzka good-naturedly on the shoulder. His hand was so big, it felt like an anvil striking him. "Speaking of water," the man said, "I'm thirsty." His gaze danced over to Chicken Hill above them. "Where does the drinking water around here come from anyway?"

Gus felt rage working its way into his chest. "You wouldn't dare."

The man shrugged. "You're out of time, Gus."

"The hell with you."

"You ain't gonna get many gold stars talking that way."

"I said I ain't got it!"

The man's expression, one of calm consideration, never changed. He nodded slowly, sadly. He was not an evil-looking fellow. He appeared, Gus thought, rather sorrowful. "We'll talk later, Gus. Maybe at home. Tonight. After the parade."

"I'll call the cops."

"How do you know I ain't the cops?" the man asked, and with that, he pushed down his hat brim and slipped past the Empire Fire Company's truck, turned down High Street, and melted into the crowd.

Plitzka felt bile rise in this throat. He heard Hal Leopold calling him. "Gus! Line up!"

He drifted toward the front of the parade, rubbing his forehead, flustered. *I have to find a way*, he thought. He was nearly at the front of the gathering marchers when he remembered that Doc was waiting for him behind the Antes House.

As he passed the side of the Antes House, he saw several high school kids moving into line wearing Continental Army uniforms. He made one last effort to finagle a blue coat out of one of the taller ones by offering him fifty cents and his red coat in exchange, and he finally succeeded.

He walked to the back of the Antes House, where Doc was standing impatiently, still holding his red coat.

"You couldn't find a blue coat for me?" Doc asked.

Gus was distracted. Who cared about the blue coat? What if the guy really did come to his house? His wife! His kids! "Here," Gus said, peeling off his blue coat. "Take mine. You can be American. I don't mind being British." He held out his blue coat.

Doc took the blue coat. Then in a decision that would alter forever his already fraught, twisted, small-town American life, he changed his mind and handed it back to Plitzka.

"Hell with it," he said. "I'll be British. Your coat is too small for me anyway."

"You sure, Doc? You don't wanna wear the blue coat?"

"Blue coat, red coat, who cares?" Doc said. "It's just a damn parade. What difference does it make?"

It turned out to make a big difference. All the difference in the world.

THE GOON WHO worked for Nig Rosen didn't wait for Gus to get a long look at him. He turned right on Washington Street and doubled back up into Chicken Hill as the front of the long flow of parade marchers passed on High Street behind him. He was distracted. It was nearly 5 p.m. and not yet dark. Now he had to wait for hours for the parade to finish and then find a safe place to plant brass knuckles in poor Gus Plitzka's face. It could be done. But he had to rest. He was tired. He'd taken the train from Reading, and there was a pinochle game tonight back in Reading with some big dollars in play, which he'd have to miss now.

He strolled up the street lost in thought. His name was Henry Lit. He was thirty-four, a Russian Jew from Kiev, a former boxer, and a hopeless gambler. Like many in that world, Lit was normally a gentle man who did not like violence, largely because he knew how much damage it could do and the cost, financial and otherwise, involved in getting whatever was broken fixed. He couldn't understand why anyone would be so stupid as to borrow money from Nig Rosen. But those were his marching orders, and when Nig delivered them, they were iron.

At the corner of Washington and Beech, Henry removed his jacket and placed it over his shoulder. He was, in fact, quite thirsty. He noticed a heavyset Negro followed by a huge, barrel-chested white man bearing a handful of tools and pipes. The man looked like a Sephardic Jew, with dark hair and brooding looks, so Lit called out in Yiddish as the man passed, "Is there a water fountain around?"

Big Soap stopped, puzzled, then answered in Italian. "I don't understand."

Lit quickly recovered and asked the same question in English. Big Soap never stopped moving. "Over there." He nodded to what looked like an empty lot full of weeds down the street. "In the middle, there's an outdoor faucet."

"Thanks. Does the parade come back this way?" Lit asked.

"There's a fireworks display and a pig roast after," Big Soap said over his shoulder, "and free beer. Stick around."

Lit nodded and moved on while Big Soap hustled to catch up to Fatty, who had turned up the hill and was moving toward the Clover Dairy. "What's he want?" Fatty asked.

"He thought I was Jewish."

Fatty was irritated. "I oughta collect from Mr. Moshe for letting Nate use my wagon and mule. This crap is heavy."

"How would you know? I'm carrying it."

"I'm looking out for you. Did you talk to Rusty?"

"He's coming by the jook at seven. You wanna carry something?" Big Soap said.

Fatty ignored that. "We might have to go back and help him haul that mortar down here—without my dang cart, which Nate took."

The two had come to take one more look in the daylight at the outdoor faucet and the manhole cover over the well, and hide some tools and supplies for the job. They chose for their hiding place a back corner of the empty lot, for no one ventured to the lot's edges, which were lined with junk. The two strolled past the dairy, noting that it was, as Fatty predicted, closed for the day, then moved on up the hill to the lot behind it, which was full of weeds and discarded crates and garbage. They walked past it as if they were moving to the next block; then at the last minute, they cut into the high weeds of the lot and hid the shovel, wrenches, drill, pipe threader, short pipes, and two valves under an old crate. They then reemerged onto the street, walked down the long block, and doubled back to the well-worn path that led to the center of the lot where the well and the outdoor faucet were located, joining five people who stood patiently in line waiting with barrels and pails to draw water.

"I hadn't counted on that," Fatty said, glancing at the line and at the sun above. "It's hot."

The two waited their turn, and when they reached the fountain, Fatty leaned over with his hands cupped while Big Soap turned on the spigot. While leaning over, his eyes probed the top of the well, and he saw what he needed to see.

A cement manhole cover. And along the edges, an old pry hole. Perfect.

The two reversed places, with Fatty pumping. He took a long look around again, this time at the base of the fountain and the cement manhole that covered the well, chatting and joking with folks in line as he did so, for Fatty knew just about everyone on the Hill. From there, they walked to the corner and turned up the Hill toward Fatty's jook.

"That's a lot of eyes," Big Soap said.

"Don't worry. Nobody hauls water at night," Fatty said. "By nine o'clock, this place will be deserted. There won't be a Negro fool in sight."

HE WAS RIGHT. By 9 p.m., there were no Negroes around. But there were plenty of white people. The John Antes Historical Society's Cornet Marching Band, having been two hours late to start, was delayed another hour when they got to the far end of town, for the Empire Fire Company's truck coughed a few times, backfired, and stalled again. This time there was room for the marchers to move around it, but the backfire frightened the horse of a nearby Mennonite family who had come to town by buggy to enjoy the parade. The poor creature was tied loosely to a parking meter, and the backfire caused him to bolt, snapping his line and allowing him to gallop off—with the family buggy in tow. The parade was halted by cries of "Wild horse!" while the farmer and several men corralled the terrified creature, which galloped from one crowded street to the next. That took forty minutes. When the parade finally got moving again and returned to the Antes House, it was eight o'clock. Most of the cheerful women volunteers who had been up since dawn preparing the pig roast had departed to watch the fireworks from home. It took another hour to cram the cornets, costumes, and drums back into the Antes House under the ever-watchful eye of Leopold, who was exhausted and went full-blown German on everyone, yelling that everything must be neatly lined up inside the Antes House hallway for morning pickup, ticking off the few good-natured souls who tried to show good faith by sticking around, so they departed as well. It was the beer that the paraders wanted most, and after the parade, it was beer they needed.

Plitzka quit the moment they arrived. "I gotta get home," he told

Doc. "The missus wants me there when the fireworks start." Actually, his wife was the last thing on his mind. He was in a state of panic, convinced that Rosen's man was headed to his home. For a moment, he considered calling the police as he departed, then decided against it. He decided to call his cousin Ferdie instead. If he was going to end up in an urn, at least Ferdie should know that it was his fault.

Gus left his coat inside the Antes House neatly folded in place in the exact manner that Leopold demanded and hastily withdrew.

Doc, on the other hand, decided to stay. He wanted a beer. He'd earned it. He worked hard to get on the good side of that creep Plitzka, and the parade had left him in a better mood. There was no need to rush home. His wife would only yammer at him about some financial problem or other. Plus, his mother-in-law had come to town to see the fireworks. No rush to see her. Still dressed in the red British army outfit, he grabbed a glass from a nearby picnic table, filled it, and took a seat on the bench behind the Antes House along with several other leftover volunteers, mostly firemen, who were already holding beers. "Here's to America's fire engines and wild horses," he said, raising his glass as several volunteers laughed. "God bless this damn town." He drank deeply. He was so happy. He loved Pottstown.

FATTY, STANDING IN the empty lot two blocks away, heard the sound of men laughing in the backyard of the Antes House and didn't like it. There was no more time to delay. He'd taken the man's money from his sister—whoever that man was. When you take a man's money, you do the job. It was time to move. He could see the shimmering lights from the lanterns of the Antes House and hear the laughter, but the lot was black, as was the dairy across the street, and the dairy watchman—Reverend Spriggs—was, as he'd suspected, not in sight.

He was probably down at the pig roast joking with the white folks and sopping up free beer.

Fatty and Big Soap made their way to the outdoor faucet, which stood about four feet high and was connected to a pipe protruding from below. Big Soap held the pry bar. In the dark, Fatty lay on the ground and blindly groped around the manhole's cement perimeter for the notch. He found it and guided the end of the pry bar into it.

"Go 'head, Soap," he said. "Pry it off. Easy now. The cover's old."

Big Soap moved slowly. The cement cover rose an inch, then two inches, then, as it came out of the hole, it snapped in two and clattered to the bottom of the well with a splash.

"Christ, Soap!"

"What do you want, magic? I did it slow like you said."

They stood at the top of the well, staring down into the blackness.

Fatty lit a lantern, lay down flat, and stuck the light in the hole. The well was circular, with sides of stone that were moss-covered and dripping water. It was, he guessed, maybe fifteen feet to the bottom. A crude ladder was attached to the side of the well. At the bottom, an old pump could be seen, as well as the pieces of concrete.

"Lucky that concrete didn't fall into the spring below," he said.

"What do we do?" Big Soap said.

"We gotta make another cover," Fatty said.

"Now?"

"One thing at a time. Let's do the job. We'll worry about covering it up after. Maybe Rusty'll show up."

The two climbed down, Fatty holding a lantern. Two pipes protruded from a connection at the bottom of the pump. Fatty could see where the original pipe that fed the faucet above ran down to the pump, came back up, and had been run to both the dairy and the shul pipes. He could see also where the outdoor faucet's and the dairy's pipes had been cut off and capped and run to a new six-inch pipe coming from the city's reservoir, leaving only the shul's pipe attached to the old well pump.

"Somebody at the dairy's been playing games," Fatty said. "Look at this connection. This ain't supposed to be here. The dairy's supposed to be getting their water from the old Plitzka well, not the city. They're getting free water from the city, Soap. A lot of it."

He knelt at the bottom of the well and reached his hand around the well pump to feel the aquifer below.

"I can't feel nothing, Soap. The aquifer's run out. This well's dry as a bone."

"Maybe when it rains the water comes up."

"Don't ask for the devil to show up. Let's get to it."

They got busy quickly, dragging their wrenches, drill, hand saws, and pipes into the hole. It was peaceful, and with the lantern, they could see fairly well. Shortly after they began, the booms and sudden lights from the fireworks overhead lit matters even more for seconds at a time. Because they were in the center of the lot, surrounded by high weeds, they were out of sight of passersby. The booming thunder from the fireworks pushed adrenaline into their systems and they worked fast.

First, they had to draw water from the big reservoir pipe. Shutting it off was impossible. They'd have to impale it. Fatty grabbed a short pipe with a closed shut valve on it and handed Big Soap a hand-cranked drill with a brazen bit.

"Once you start cranking on that pipe, water's gonna come busting out," he said. "I don't know how much pressure's behind it exactly, but it's a six-inch pipe. That's a lot of pipe, Soap, and a lot of pressure, so it's a lot of water. You keep cranking with that drill and don't stop. Crank till the bit goes in and threads through all the way. Once you're through, don't pull it out. *Back* it out. *Reverse* it, okay? Otherwise you'll strip the threads. Then I'll screw this pipe in with the valve and stop the water."

"Okay."

"You gotta do it fast. It's gonna be some water now."

"Okay."

Big Soap took the hand drill and tapped the pipe twice for good measure, like a baseball player prepping himself for a hit, bracing himself, leaning in to crank. But Fatty stopped him.

"Don't stop cranking, Soap, once you start. Or we'll drown in here."

Big Soap nodded. He cranked for fifteen seconds, twenty seconds, then they both heard an odd *thunk*, followed by a small trickle, then a powerful burst of water, which knocked Fatty off his feet.

The water surged out with the power of a fire-engine hose, pinging against the stone walls and flying in all directions, but only Fatty fell. Big Soap somehow managed to remain standing, his feet planted on solid earth, straddling the pump, albeit under two feet of water now and rising fast, for the water came hard, the water pouring in up to their waists.

"Hurry up, Soap!"

Big Soap, still straddling the hole in the floor where the well pump lay, leaned against the drill, grit his teeth, and turned the hand drill as the spray blasted his face. He drilled with his head down, his huge arms straining, the water goring into the top of his skull, burning his head and gushing into his nose and mouth.

"C'mon, Soap!"

Big Soap leaned in. The big man's hair splayed back in a straight line as the water blasted him. Fatty stood behind him, shielded somewhat, his head against the big man's shoulder blade, the force of the water so strong that he had to brace himself against the wall with his other hand to keep from falling. He had to protect the pipe holding the valve fitting and the wrench. The water was up to his armpits when he felt Big Soap's back relax and heard him yell above the hissing water, "Got it."

"Get out the way then!"

Fatty reached up to screw the fitting in, but the water pressure was so great that it took both of them to mash the fitting into the pipe and screw it in. But once they did, the closed valve on the pipe fitting held, and instantly the water stopped and once again the well was calm and quiet.

Fatty found himself standing in water up to his neck holding Big Soap by the shoulders. But they were both, gratefully, alive.

"You're a man, Soap. You're much of a man."

"Fatty, don't ask me to do that again. Not for a measly thirty dollars. Not for a hundred dollars."

"Okay, okay, let's finish."

They slopped in the high water to finish the job, but the rest was easy. In half an hour, they cut the shul pipe from the well pump and, using a three-quarter extension, fastened it to the reservoir pipe that fed both the outdoor faucet and the dairy—and just like that, they were done. The shul had fresh water. From the reservoir. Free.

They climbed back up the ladder and sat at the edge of the well, soaked through and exhausted. Only then did Big Soap utter the obvious.

"We got to get that thing covered. Where's Rusty?" Big Soap asked.

Fatty was thinking the same thing but afraid to say it.

"He must'a not found the mortar. I told him where it was."

"I recall he said yesterday he was thinking about stopping by the creek up near the reservoir to get sand," Big Soap said.

"What for?"

"He said it'd be good to use sand from the creek to color the concrete to match just in case we broke the well cover."

"Well, we broke it, goddamnit. Now where is he?"

Fatty thought a moment. He reached down into the mouth of the well where the lantern hung and killed the light. The well went dark.

"All right. We gotta hurry. I'll go to the jook and fetch some mortar mix and some planks. You go on down to the theater and fetch the wheelbarrow to mix it in. It's likely in the wagon where Nate left it. Don't go round Antes House. Take Hale Street or Washington. Better still, go by the old John Reichner mill. That's the fastest back way. If you see Rusty, tell him to get his ass up here quick, creek sand or no creek sand. We'll just mix the mortar we got. We ain't going to jail 'cause Rusty's stupid."

They took off in different directions as the last firecracker from the Antes House soared overhead and boomed its last glow.

AS THE LAST firecracker broke across the sky, Doc, fully drunk, howled out his joy. "It's all a dream!" he shouted. "This great America. This great land of opportunity. Give us your poor. Your tired. Your weak. And we will give them jobs. And homes. And businesses! We will make them men. And women. And they *will*"—he burped loudly—"*replace us!*"

The men of the Empire Fire Company, who along with a few stragglers were the only ones left, laughed. They were not used to seeing Doc Roberts drunk. This was good.

He was seated at a picnic table, and hearing the laughter, he looked around at the firemen winking at one another. He knew many of them, many of whom he had treated. Some he liked, a few he despised. They were largely Irish, uneducated—good for certain things, he thought, but mostly good-for-nothings. The new people in town. Immigrants. Sullying up matters. They didn't go to the opera or horse events. They didn't know history. They went to movies and boxing matches and drank all day. Peasants. No understanding of books or medicine or poetry or women. Wine stains on the white American tablecloth is what they were, foreign duds amid the bright glow of places like London and Paris that he should have, would have, could have known if he'd wanted. Europe. Land of artists and music and women. Beautiful women.

And then the visage of Chona, the beautiful teenager, the sight of her standing at her locker, her bare white wrist reaching inside it, her lovely eyes that nearly drove him mad. Chona, whose exceptional dark hair and gorgeous limp that made his horselike canter and grubby shoes seem clunky by comparison. Chona, who married a frumpy theater owner, a flowering beauty wrapped in the dimness of grubby store life. Who was she to turn him down all those years ago? And then to turn him down again, years later, when she was nothing but a clerk in a store serving niggers? A Jew!

"Didn't she know who I *was*?" he roared.

There was a short silence as the guffawing Irishmen stopped laughing and looked at one another.

"Go home, Doc," one of them said.

"Easy, Doc . . ."

Doc snapped out of his reverie long enough to realize it was time to leave.

"This country," he declared, "is going down." He downed his beer. "Good night, America."

And with that, he sauntered off up toward the Hill instead of down High Street.

His house was only nine blocks away, but he decided he'd cut through the Hill. There was an empty lot up there where the outdoor faucet stood across from the Clover Dairy where that Polish thief Plitzka made his pennies, and if he cut through that, he'd eliminate four blocks off his walk. He knew the Hill like the back of his hand.

"Ain't you going the wrong way, Doc?" he heard one of the firemen call out.

Doc kept walking, staggering a bit, waving away the question in disgust, not even looking back. "Son, I knew this town when you were a glint in your mother's eye."

He marched forward with their laughter ringing in his ears. As he did, he felt something small and hard in his pocket and reached in. The mezuzah pendant. The one that had somehow made it into his hand during the . . . the event . . . at the Heaven & Earth Grocery Store. He'd brought it to the Antes House to discard it on the Hill. Perfect. He'd toss it in the lot when he was out of sight of the Antes House. He withdrew the fist clasping the mezuzah and marched forward. Up the Hill he went. Up, up, up, to Chicken Hill.

NIG ROSEN'S GOON, Henry Lit, woke up at the last boom of the fireworks. He'd fallen asleep behind a tiny Baptist church a few blocks from the Antes House. At first, he thought he'd missed everything. But when he made his walk back down the Hill, stopping at the corner so he could see the plaza behind the Antes House from above, what he saw made him sigh in relief. In the dim light of the lanterns at the table, there was Plitzka, stone drunk, still wearing the red jacket, holding up a beer and yelling something. Perfect.

He watched in amazement as Plitzka made his way up into the Hill toward him. As the red coat neared, Lit turned and leaned against the wall of an old shed, ducking out of sight as Plitzka tromped past, made his way down the gravel road, and staggered into the empty lot where the outdoor faucet was that Lit had satisfied his thirst from earlier. He was sure it was Plitzka because Plitzka had the red coat, and he had some kind of limp, which he'd noted earlier. Lit waited until he saw the red jacket move into the lot, then removed his shoes and carried them as he walked softly on the path behind Plitzka, hoping not to step on broken glass.

There was no need to be quiet as he approached Plitzka, for the man was humming softly to himself. Lit took two or three steps and then decided not to wait. Tough jobs need to be done fast. No sense thinking it through. *Get it over with*, he told himself. *It's just part of the job. In America, everyone works.*

He was four steps into the lot and could see Plitzka's red coat clearly in the moonlight now, ten feet off. It was a beacon, a light.

Give me your tired, your poor, your huddled masses yearning to be free . . .

As Lit trotted, holding his shoes in his left hand, his right hand reached into his pocket and his fingers threaded through a pair of brass knuckles. He did it in one motion.

The man did not even hear him until Lit was two steps away. He turned his head just in time to meet Lit's fist—*wham!*—which smacked his jaw once.

Lit heard the crack and felt the bone break, and as an old boxer, he knew the jaw was broken. He'd done damage. He knew what it felt like. There was no need to do more. He saw the red coat fall back, but that was all, as he spun off.

It was time to leave.

Lit turned and trotted away quickly, and for the life of him, and for as long as he would live—which would not be that long—he always wondered why he heard a big splash after Plitzka fell. For there was a faucet back there. There was no pond. He had seen the faucet.

Later, when Nig Rosen said to him, "How did you get Plitzka to fork over the dough so fast?" Lit said, "I whacked him and broke his jaw, and he fell in some kind of pond."

Rosen said, "You got some kind of imagination, Henry. I saw him. He came here and he didn't have no wired jaw. He talked my ear off, begging. And he didn't say nothing about no pond."

Four inches.

If Fatty had bothered to shine his lantern down four inches lower, he would've seen the odd shoe that stuck up in the water at the bottom of the well and the glittering mezuzah pendant that shone next to it, still on its chain, hanging from a rock protruding from the stone sides, the mezuzah now clear of the fist that had clenched it and then released it as the body fell. He would have seen the pants and tail end of the red British coattails that floated in roughly five feet of water that stood over the now useless old pump and broken manhole cover at the bottom of the well. The pump was connected to nothing. And sadly, neither was the man. For his wife did not love him. His children did not miss him. The town did not erect a statue in his honor. All the myths he believed in would crystallize into even greater mythology in future years and become weapons of war used by politicians and evildoers to kill defenseless schoolchildren by the dozens so that a few rich men spouting the same mythology that Doc spouted could buy islands that held more riches than the town of Pottstown had or would ever have. Gigantic yachts that would sail the world and pollute the waters and skies, owned by men creating great companies that made weapons of great power in factories that employed the poor, weapons that were sold cheaply enough so that the poor could purchase them and kill one another. Any man could buy one and walk into schools and bring death to dozens of children and teachers and anyone else stupid enough to believe in all that American mythology of hope, freedom, equality, and justice. The problem was always, and would always be, the niggers and the poor—and the foolish white people who felt sorry for them.

So it was appropriate that a nigger and a foolish white man buried him.

Fatty had no idea of what was in the well when he and Big Soap convened back there that night to make a new manhole cover. That was the least of his worries anyway.

"How do we make a manhole cover?" Big Soap had asked.

"We just put the planks in across the top of the well. We wedge them between the stones and pour the mortar. Let the grass make it round. It's already there. The circle. It's a mold."

"It's like a hockey puck," Big Soap said.

"A what?"

"They play it in the Olympics. Hockey."

"You ever seen hockey?"

"No, but I'm gonna someday."

"Soap, can we just get the planks in place?"

Big Soap climbed down the ladder until his head was even with the well's opening, and they wedged in several planks, using the pry bar on the last one to make the flooring tight. Then they mixed the concrete using the wheelbarrow and water from the water fountain and poured it.

The cement manhole cover was perfect. Then they tossed a little dust and dirt on top of it to make it look not so new.

"Should we put a little pry-bar wedge in the cover?" Big Soap asked.

"Why not?"

They stuck a piece of wood in the freshly poured cement to create a wedge hole. Fatty decided to wait a few minutes for the cement to dry before extracting the wedge to keep that pry-bar hole solid. It was safe to be there now. It was after 1 a.m.

"Shouldn't we head out?" Big Soap asked.

"Why? We can wait till the wedge dries a little. If anyone comes by, we're just two guys sitting in a field in the middle of the night, waiting."

"What are we waiting for?"

"Waiting for the future, Soap, waiting for the future."

Epilogue

The Call Out

Hirshel Koffler, twenty-two, and his brother Yigel, twenty-four, had only been in America six weeks when they were hired on as brakemen for the Pennsylvania Railroad freight train known as the Tanker Toad, *which shuttled coal from Berwyn, Pa., to the Pennhurst hospital. For these two former Austrian railroad men, Jewish refugees, America was a land full of surprises. There was the language, of course—incomprehensible. Then there was the food, nonkosher and sometimes delicious. And finally, the grinding, churning smoke of the great factories as people moved about the towns and cities in large numbers. But nothing they'd experienced in those first weeks was as strange as the scenario they found themselves in that Memorial Day weekend in 1936: staring at a tall, lanky Negro seated in the corner of their empty box car cradling a weeping child in his arms as their freight train rolled out of Pennhurst toward Berwyn. In a land of surprises and mysteries, this one was a topper.*

They did not speak to the man, for their orders from the union boss, Uri Guzinski, had been clear. Uri was a fellow Yid, also a railman, from Poland, who'd been in America seventeen months, and while Uri was terse and his English was not great—though he spoke it better than the two brothers combined—Uri always showed them kindness. He even gave them his lunchbox that morning, since today was some kind of strange American holiday and the kosher store near their Berwyn flophouse was closed. "Memorial Day," Uri had called it. Memorial for what? *they wondered.* Still, they did not ask, for Uri's directions that morning as they stepped aboard their 5:20 a.m. train for their first run to Pennhurst had been explicit and in Yiddish: "Put the Negroes on the train and drop them at Berwyn and hand them over to a Pullman."

Neither Hirshel nor Yigel had any idea what a Pullman was and were afraid to ask. Nor were they sure what he meant by "lunchbox," for he'd uttered that word in English. Still, Uri was the boss. So as the Tanker Toad *slowly churned into the Berwyn yard at 6:05 on schedule, and as dawn crested over the glorious Pennsylvania sky, the two anxiously looked up at the signal tower window for Uri and spotted him nodding at two tall, impeccably dressed Negroes in white shirts, ties, shined shoes, and distinct Pullman porter hats who were standing at the far end of the freight yard.*

The two Negroes strode to the freight car, handed Hirshel and Yigel an envelope without a word, took one furtive glance about, then hustled the tall Negro and the youngster across the rails to the nearby passenger terminal, where the 6:14 Sandy Hill *was steaming up to make its run to Philadelphia's 30th Street Station.*

The two had no idea who those two passengers were, and they would never know, but when they opened the envelope, they found forty dollars for their "union job" and a note bearing the words "Come see me about your free new shoes." It was signed "M. Skrup," who had a Pottstown address.

As they watched the train pull away, Yigel, holding the lunchbox, said to his brother in Yiddish, "Remember that minyan?"

"Which one?"

"The one in Pottstown. At the shul. Where they fought about the frog in the mikvah?"

Hirshel chuckled and nodded.

"You think this gift comes from that?" Yigel asked.

Hirshel shrugged. "Why would it?"

"They spoke of Negroes there."

Hirshel waved his hand in dismissal. "Don't be stupid. There are thousands of Negroes in this country, Yigel. Why would this money come from that?"

But that, too, was one of the many wonders of America. For the gift did come indirectly from the minyan at that shul. The promise of shoes, of course, came from Marv Skrupskelis, whose twin brother, Irv, was at that meeting. The money came from Moshe's cousin Isaac, who placed it in the hands of Bernice, who placed it in the hands of Fatty, who placed it in the hands of Nate's wife, Addie, who passed it to her husband, who placed a bit of it in the hands of Paper, who took that bit to two of her Pullman porter friends, who arranged with Uri to meet the two and ferry them along, from one Pullman porter crew to the next, from Berwyn to Philadelphia first, then to the General Lee, a southbound express train inside a first-class Pullman sleeper car to ride back to Charleston, S.C. The Low Country. Nate's home.

Nate would never see Addie again. He felt sure of it. And as the train made its way south out of Philadelphia, Nate resolved himself to it. He did not deserve what she had to give. But fortitude and love's reason have many a season, and one day she would return to him. He did not believe it then. As far as he knew, he was the last of the Loves. There would be no more.

As for Dodo, the memory of Uncle Nate's arms cradling him, lifting him out of bed in the ward and carrying him through the basement, the bumpy cart ride to the open air of freedom, the feeling of being lifted into the arms of the two Jewish brakemen who handled him with the gentleness of an infant as Uncle Nate clambered aboard the freight car, that would be forgotten. As would the train ride all the way to Charleston—in a first-class sleeper with Pullman porters doting on him the whole way, feeding him rice, ham, chicken, cake, and ice cream, as much as he wanted. All that, too, would be forgotten. For the haze of drugs took weeks to fade, and the memories of Pennhurst and the sad events that put him there bore the boom of howitzers blowing off in his brain, which, given his disability, would not have bothered him so much. For the fact is, after Pennhurst, he was done with sound. He didn't need it. He had his own sound now. It was sound sung to him as the sight, smell, and feel of the beautiful Low Country. And as the years passed on his South Carolina farm—bought with three hundred dollars, care of a Philadelphia Jewish theater owner named Isaac, who would one day with his cousin Moshe and several other Jewish theater owners create a camp in the Pennsylvania mountains for disabled children like him called Camp Chona, a camp that lasted long after every one of those Jewish immigrants had died—the boy became a man who raised crops and milked cows and attended church three times a week; a man who learned how to "shout dance" without crossing his legs; a man who taught his children how to patch a roof, and cane a chair, and boil meat in iron pots, and wander through Spanish moss in summer; a man who watched his children learn from their great-uncle Nate how to build a horse-drawn mill to grind sugar cane, and from their great-aunt Addie how to thresh rice and grind meal, and from his beloved wife how to grow azaleas and his favorite, sunflowers—sunflowers of all colors and sizes. All life in Pennsylvania was erased in his mind and his heart and his memory.

Still . . .

As hard as he tried, he could not erase the memory of the woman with the shining black hair, sparkling eyes, easy laugh, and magic marbles; he could not forget the friend who thrust his finger out and held it in the dark like a beacon, all night till the sun came up. The memory of that finger, that one solitary white finger, reaching out in friendship and solidarity, shone in his memory like a bright, shining star. The memory lasted until the end of his full and very fruitful life, so that when he died, he was not Dodo of Pottstown but rather Nate Love II, the father of three boys and two girls. Nate was not the very last Love after all. There would be more. They surrounded him as he died, his children and their children. He died on June 22, 1972, the same day Hurricane Agnes wiped much of Pottstown off the face of the earth and a day after an old Jew named Malachi the Magician vanished forever from the hills of southeastern Pennsylvania.

And as he faded to eternal slumber, surrounded by loved ones, just feet from the sunflowers and summer moss that had helped wipe away the tumult of his first twelve years of life, he would offer four words in his final murmurings that were forever a puzzle to all that knew and loved him and surrounded him in his final moments of life, save for one who was not there, who was far beyond them all, now living in the land where the lame walked and the blind could see, who awaited him even at that moment as he drifted upward, eager to hear the news of the many adventures that had befallen him since they'd parted ways. It was to him that he spoke, not to them.

He called out . . .

"Thank you, Monkey Pants."

Acknowledgments

This book began as an ode to Sy Friend, the retired director of The Variety Club Camp for Handicapped Children in Worcester, Pa. Like many works of fiction, it morphed into something else. I worked at the camp for four summers when I was a student at Oberlin College. That was more than forty years ago, but Sy's lessons of inclusivity, love, and acceptance—delivered not with condescending kindness but with deeds that showed the recipients the path to true equality—remained with me for the rest of my life. In that spirit, I am thankful to the entire Variety Club family: the late Leo and Vera Posel, who donated the land for the camp in the thirties; the late camp trustee Bill Saltzman, who insisted I become a counselor when I applied for a job as a dishwasher at age nineteen; my friend and former co-counselor Vinny Carissimi, who later became a brilliant, two-fisted Philadelphia attorney who dug me and many former camp staffers out of several horrible legal scrapes, usually for free. And of course Sy and his husband, Bob Arch, now living in retirement in Lake Worth, Fla. Sy served that camp from age sixteen until his retirement three decades later (1950–1979). I've never met a more brilliant, compassionate person. He was a slender, handsome man, a fast-moving object who slipped around the campgrounds like a spirit, in clean white tennis shoes, shorts, and golf shirt, bearing an ever-present cigarette between his fingers and the melody of some spellbinding opera in his head, for he loved that genre. He knew the name of every camper and often the names of their parents as well. He was decades ahead of his time. His staff looked like the United Nations, long before the word "diversity" echoed around America. We were all poorly paid and overworked. But the lessons we learned from Sy left us rich. Many of the former staffers went on to excel in various fields.

The kids loved him with an extraordinary intensity. Each night at bedtime, he played a scratched recording of a bugle performing taps on the camp's ancient loudspeaker, followed by a gentle "Good night boys and girls." And if you stood outside facing the rows of cabins, which were not air-conditioned—he refused to let the trustees install air-conditioning, saying, "They need to feel the air. Let them live. They're inside all year"—you could almost hear the murmurs of all ninety-one campers, the children lying in their bunks, the words echoing up and down the row of dark cabins, *"Good night Uncle Sy."*

He served as a principal in the Philadelphia school district during the year, but was a summertime legend to the children of the camp. One of my campers, Lamont Garland, now fifty-five, a born-and-raised North Philly kid who never allowed a lifelong dependency on crutches brought on by what was then called cerebral palsy to stop him working for the Philadelphia Electric Company for twenty-five years before his retirement in 2014, told me a story about Sy years ago that I never forgot. Lamont, who today lives in Columbia, S.C., told me this story when he was seven or eight. He was attending the Widener Memorial School in Philadelphia at the time, which has admirably educated Philadelphia's children with disabilities for the last 116 years. We were sitting on the porch of one of the camp cabins on a summer afternoon and he said, out of the blue, "Uncle Sy came to Widener once."

"Why?"

"I don't know."

"Did he work there?"

"No. He just showed up. We were in assembly in the auditorium one morning, and he just walked in."

"What happened?"

"We gave him a standing ovation."

I leave it to you, dear reader, to picture that crowded auditorium more than forty-five years ago, the conglomerate of crutches, wheelchairs, and children with all types of disabilities bursting into roaring ovation. Those who could stand, I suppose, stood, the rest roiling into the usual roar of joy that I witnessed when Sy would turn the camp on its head via some special event he or some staffer had dreamed up to make it into the dazzling carnival of life that every one of us would remember for the rest of our lives: the hooting, the clapping, the yelling, the cheering, the howling, the crutches being waved in the air, the gorgeous cacophony of humanity in wheelchairs, some wearing special eyeglasses, others in hearing aids, signing and gesturing, the winks and chortles and grunts of pleasure, the grimaces and shaking of heads and excited howling of those without "normal" ability. It's impossible to describe.

But it all boils down to the same thing.

Love. Of a man. And the one principle he gave his life to: equality. Thus this tome.

The author
Lambertville, N.J.
December 2022

James McBride's books bring the American experience to life.

His classic memoir, *The Color of Water*, heralded a new voice in American literature. More than twenty-five years later, it is a beloved hallmark text.

McBride's fiction—including the National Book Award–winning *The Good Lord Bird*, the Oprah's Book Club selection *Deacon King Kong*, the transcendent *The Heaven & Earth Grocery Store*, *Miracle at St. Anna*, *Song Yet Sung*, and *Five-Carat Soul*—chronicles the intimate human stories of our shared history. From John Brown's Harpers Ferry antislavery raid to Italy during World War II to 1960s Brooklyn, McBride's stories captivate, surprise, and move us.

The rollicking story of a Brooklyn shooting and its unexpected aftermath

In 1969, an elderly church deacon shuffles into the courtyard of a Brooklyn housing project and shoots the neighborhood drug dealer. The reasons behind this act of violence and the consequences it triggers in the neighborhood and beyond lie at the heart of *Deacon King Kong*, the uproarious novel that was an Oprah's Book Club pick.

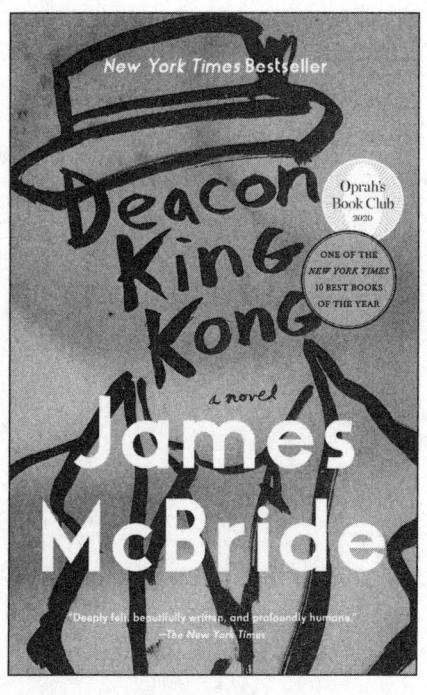

"McBride has a way of inflating reality to comical sizes, the better for us to see every tiny mechanism that holds unjust systems in place." —*Los Angeles Times*

"A raucous, poignant, humanity-embracing novel." —*O, The Oprah Magazine*

The National Book Award–winning story of a young boy born a slave who must pass as a girl to survive

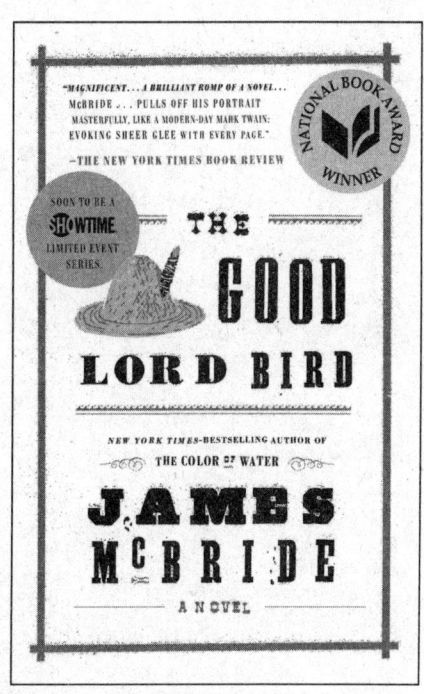

Henry Shackleford is an enslaved boy living in the Kansas Territory in 1856, when the region is a battleground between anti- and proslavery forces. When John Brown, the legendary abolitionist, arrives in the area, an argument quickly turns violent. Henry is forced to leave town with Brown, who believes he's a girl. In this gripping novel of identity and survival, by turns dramatic and uproarious, James McBride creates an unforgettable cast of characters against the background of the Civil War.

"Superbly written . . . [McBride] transcends history and makes it come alive." —*Chicago Tribune*

"Outrageously entertaining . . . never has mayhem been this much of a humdinger." —*USA Today*

Classic stories from a master storyteller

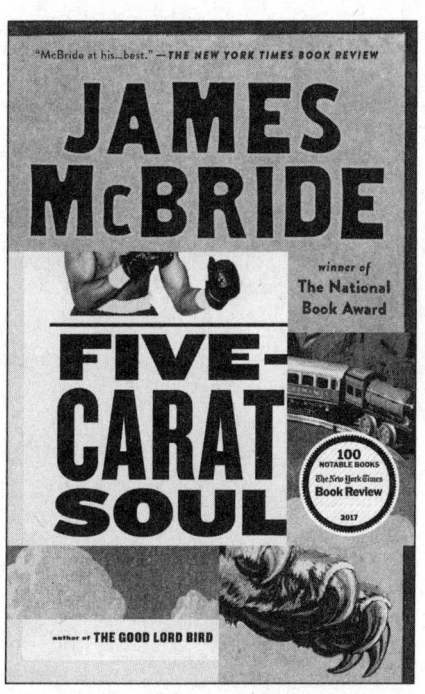

An antique-toy collector makes two astonishing discoveries. Five boys in a small town learn that secrets can hide in plain sight. A Ph.D. candidate uncovers a long-hidden promise. In *Five-Carat Soul*, James McBride brings to vivid life captivating characters with extraordinary tales to tell. Spanning centuries and defying categorization, these stories are full of the humor and humanity that are the hallmarks of McBride's work.

"A furious joy drives these glimpses of brave lives in perilous places."
—*San Francisco Chronicle*

"McBride is such an agile writer that each voice feels authentic and somehow familiar. . . . These are stories of and from the soul."
—*Minneapolis Star-Tribune*

A universal tale of courage and redemption, inspired by historical events

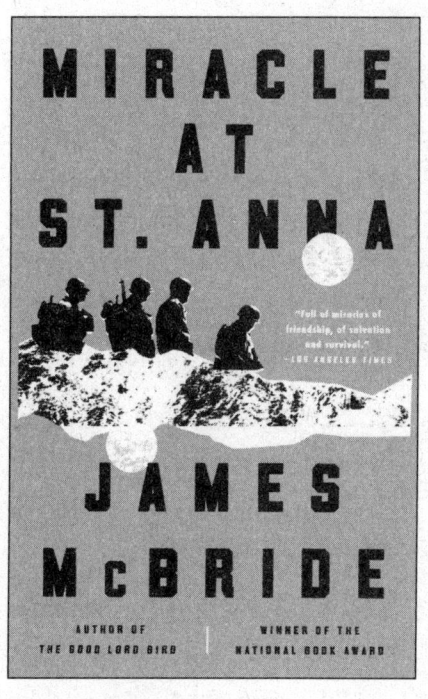

As World War II draws to a close, four Buffalo Soldiers from the United States Army's Negro 92nd Division are separated from their unit behind enemy lines in Italy. Risking their lives for a country in which they are treated with less respect than the enemy they are fighting, the soldiers discover humanity in the small village of St. Anna di Stazzema. Even in the face of unspeakable tragedy, they learn to see—and treasure—the small miracles of life.

"Full of miracles of friendship, of salvation and survival."
—*Los Angeles Times*

"Searingly, soaringly beautiful . . . the book's central theme, its essence, is a celebration of the human capacity for love."
—*The Baltimore Sun*

A riveting Civil War–era tale of haunting choices

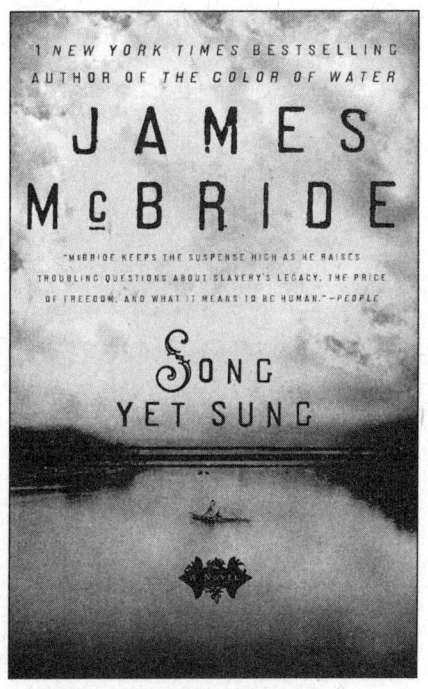

A group of enslaved people breaks free in the swamps of Maryland, setting loose a drama of violence and hope among slave catchers, plantation owners, watermen, and free Blacks. Among them is Liz Spocott, a runaway slave near death who is wracked by disturbing visions of the future and is armed with "the Code," a fiercely guarded means of communication for enslaved people on the run. As she makes her way through the swampy peninsula, Liz's extraordinary dreams of tomorrow create a freedom-seeking furor among the community.

"Gripping, affecting, and beautifully paced."
—*O, The Oprah Magazine*

"McBride keeps the suspense high as he raises troubling questions about slavery's legacy, the price of freedom, and what it means to be human." —*People*

The acclaimed memoir that has enthralled millions around the world

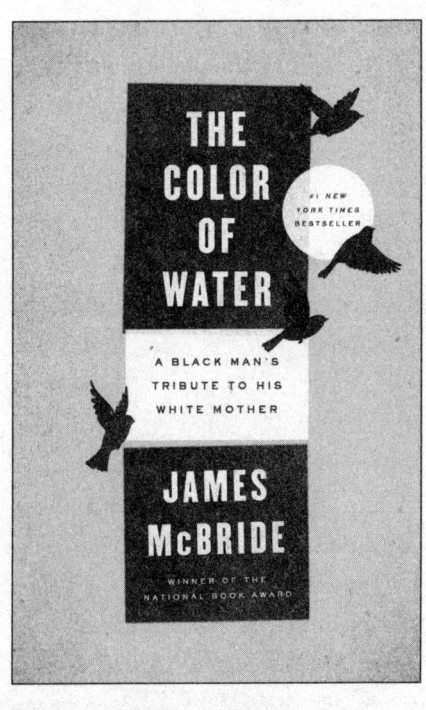

As a boy growing up in Brooklyn, James McBride knew his mother was different. But when he asked her about it, she'd say, "I'm light-skinned." And when he asked what color God was, she said, "God is the color of water." As an adult, McBride persuaded his mother to tell her remarkable story—of a rabbi's daughter, born in Poland and raised in the South, who fled to Harlem, married a Black man, founded a Baptist church, and put twelve children through college. *The Color of Water* is both an eloquent exploration of family and a groundbreaking memoir that transcends racial and religious boundaries.

"[A] triumph." —*The New York Times Book Review*

"As lively as a novel, a well-written, thoughtful contribution to the literature on race." —*The Washington Post*